ZOMBIE'S DOOM?
"Chronicles of Jack Doom"

A ZOMBIE NOVEL SEQUEL

By Will Lemen

DEDICATION

To my faithful dog
"Tecumseh"
May 6th 2004 ♥ May 28th 2015

TABLE OF CONTENTS

ALONE WITH ZOMBIES, NATURALLY

It has been well over a year since the zombie apocalypse began, and my family and I climbed out of that god-forsaken burnt-out Abram's battle tank that was our only sanctuary from the massive horde of the dead that had descended upon us.

Over a year after the Sarge, my so-called friend, left us behind to fend for ourselves against that monumental army of zombies; and the vicious prehistoric monsters that inadvertently saved our lives, or so I thought at the time.

After we did our stent inside the armor plated martial mechanism, we were on our own again, not giving too much thought to the Sarge.

Although the thought of him and what he had done continued to fester in the back of my mind, our main concern was to find some transportation and get on with the chore of surviving this inhuman holocaust.

It has also been over a year now since everyone in my family except for me were killed, not even two days after we left the confines of the tank that had given us a safe refuge from the vast zombie legion.

I'm alone now, and from the looks of things, most of the population of the planet has either been killed, or has turned into one of those undead cannibalistic devils; or both.

I don't know if the Sarge and the girl he was with, Beth was her name. I don't know if they made it out of the area alive after abandoning us, I had other things to worry about at the time.

All I know for sure is that we were all being attacked by a massive advancing zombie horde that had us surrounded, and the Sarge, hightailed it out of there in the only working vehicle that we had.

On the one hand, I hope the Sarge and Beth didn't get out alive. Because at the time of their untimely departure, I took the liberty of expending several of my precious rounds of ammunition into the back tires of their getaway vehicle as they drove off into the preverbal sunset.

After all, they had left us standing there with our dicks in our hands (except for my wife of course) in the midst of thousands of ravenous zombies, with only a few bullets and an old WWII flamethrower to fight off those stinking maggot infested undead resurrected cannibals.

On the other hand, part of me really hopes that they made it out alive and are still roaming around the countryside somewhere; so that there is still a possibility no matter how slim, of us meeting up again at some point in time.

A short time after we had left the National Guard Armory in what was to be in our minds our *third* epic journey into the unknown dominion of the hungry tribes of the undead. The first being our extraordinary yet hair-raising voyage down the Mississippi River as we traversed its grisly waters. Second being our transcontinental trek through the zombie wasteland into Texas after we had jumped ship at Vicksburg.

Not far from where the Sarge and the girl had abandoned us, my family and I had found what was left of the modified school bus that had driven us to the armory from the Sarge's strong hold.

It was definitely the Sarge's getaway vehicle. It was hard to erase the image of that huge bus that had been modified to be able to survive the combative forces of a zombie apocalypse going out of sight as we watched him and Beth drive away. The 40-foot black bus with two gun ports built into the roof, the inverted snowplow blade attached to the front, tinted windows, and the driver's seat enclosed within sheets of thick steel panels, there was no doubt that it was our bus.

However, we found no sign of either the Sarge's, or of Beth's body, just a few bloody footprints that pointed in a southwesterly direction, and told us that they had at least escaped the initial zombie incursion.

Giving little or no thought to the Sarge's whereabouts came to an abrupt end a couple of days after the death of my family. After my immense sorrow had morphed into a monstrously obsessive hunger for revenge, finding the man that had deserted me and my family, and left us stranded and nearly defenseless in the middle of an undead onslaught seemed to be the only thought that was allowed to enter my mind, and so I began my relentless search for my old Marine Corps buddy the Sarge, and my old acquaintance and his probable consort Beth.

Don't get me wrong, I've got nothing against Beth, she was a good fighter and seemed to be on the ball for the short time that I knew her. That's one reason that I hope they're still alive.

However, in these times of trouble sometimes sacrifices have to be made, and if I have to sacrifice Beth as a means to the end of the Sarge's miserable existence, then tuff shit for Beth.

Although, the main reason that in the back of my mind I hoped that they had survived, at least I hoped the Sarge had survived, is that I wanted to find him and ask why he left my family and me in such a dire situation.

That is, just before I make that no good son-of-a-bitch'in piece of shit wish that he'd never been born.

Okay, I'll stop sugar coating it now.

Let me be completely clear on this subject.

I want to be the one that is totally and completely responsible for his long and agonizingly painful death.

I want no living person, no dead person, no prehistoric lizards, or anything else to have the pleasure of causing his death and watching him die.

I want to be the one that gets to watch him expire. I want to be the one that croaks him and sees him die right before my eyes, just me and me alone.

After all, the Sarge sacrificed my family, at least that's the way I see it, and he would have sacrificed me too if not for a quirk of fate that separated me from my loved ones just moments before their untimely and ultimate demise.

Vengeance is the principal factor that motivates me, and now I spend most of each of my lonely days looking for any signs of Beth and the Sarge.

I have followed one dead-end lead after another searching all over hell's creation and most of southern Texas for the two of them.

For almost a year, my endeavor to find them has been met with no identifiable results.

Survival too is paramount to me now, second only to my unquenchable thirst for retribution. Not because I give shit about living, hell everything that I had to live for is gone now, thanks to that chicken-shit Sergeant I used to call my friend.

No; survival is pertinent to me *now* because I want to stay alive long enough to find the Sarge and make him pay dearly for what he did to me, what he took away from me.

I'm going to look for that man until I find him or find that he is dead, or until I get murdered by something this piss-hole of a world has to offer up.

Just before he drove off into the mass of undead humanity in the bus that had all of the guns and ammo we needed to fight off the converging monsters, the last thing I heard him say or saw him do, was lean out the door of the bus and yell to me that he was sorry, sorry for leaving us there.

When I find him, he *will* be sorry all right, he'll be sorry he met me in the Marine Corps; he'll be sorry he found me and my family months earlier and took us to his compound. He'll be sorry that he drove off and left us all right. In short, he'll be damn sorry he ever heard of me, *Jack Doom*!

******

Many years earlier...

The Sarge and Jack met in boot camp at M.C.R.D San Diego, *that's the Marine Corps Recruit Depot for all of you slimy civilians out there.*

7

That's where they suffered the rigors of becoming Marines together.

Then after graduating from boot camp, they were sent up the coast a few miles to the infantry training regiment at Camp Pendleton.

That's where they marched up and down the southern California hills until their legs were like steel trip-hammers and their minds had been molded into the perfect killing machines that the Marine Corps had intended for them to become.

When they had accomplished that part of their training, they received their M.O.S. (Military Occupational Specialty) and were attached to a unit that was sent to Afghanistan, and then later to Iraq.

The Sarge and Jack became what are known as *Assaulters* (Specialized Combat Troops). They stalked the enemy, staged ambushes, set booby traps, and generally harassed and killed as many of the enemy as possible.

They both showed a temperament for the job; however, Jack always seemed to be able to get into a certain mindset while doing the job at hand. A mindset that some of his fellow Marines said was scary even for a combat marine.

It was not that he was so efficient that it was scary, or that his operational plans were so brilliant that it was scary, but they said that he was so cold hearted, callous, and brutal toward the enemy, and that he seemed not to have a conscience. That's when his fellow marines began to call him Jack Doom, of course that wasn't his real name.

Due to the covert nature of some of the operations Jack took part in, his real name is still classified.

And as you might have already guessed, I could tell you his real name, but then I'd have to kill you.

Anyway, the name stuck because they said it matched his personality, and that the enemy was "*Doomed*" when he was on a mission.

That was the type of scary that Jack was back in those days.

However, he looked at it like this, he had a job to do, the job was to kill the enemy, and he did his job very well.

After Jack returned home from the war, he put those days behind him and became a model citizen and a pillar of his community.

He never talked about his time in either Iraq or Afghanistan, or what he had done during the war. He never would tell his wife or his sons anything about his tour of duty there, and after a while they stopped asking.

Whenever the war would come up from time to time in different venues, he would quickly change the subject. All people really knew about him was that he was an ex-marine and that he had served over seas.

However, now things were different, now he had over a year in country under his belt fighting this new war, this zombie war.

He had re-honed his former skills to a very sharp edge, and added a few more capabilities to his skill set that were suitable for fighting off the undead, and he couldn't help but to think that if his Marine Corps buddies thought that he was scary back then, they'd shit

down both legs if they could see him now. Hell, they'd
probably try to grow a third leg so they could shit down
it too!

******

Although my family is dead now, they are
constantly on my mind, I think about them every day. I
haven't forgotten them, and I will never forget them.

I see their faces every night when I close my eyes to
go to sleep, that is, when I can go to sleep.

I remember the day that they died as if it were
yesterday, and I am determined to use all of my skills old
and new to track down the Sarge and make him pay for
my loss.

I am resolute in my desire to take *everything* from
him, just as he took everything from me. And like they
always say. "Payback is a motherfucker!"

AS IF IT WERE YESTERDAY

Almost in tears, Gin announced to our group.

"We've been in this hell-hole of a tank for three days; I can't stand it any longer! It stinks in here, and I'm hungry and thirsty."

"I can't take it anymore either Mom, Bruce, Rich, and Dave are starting to get a little ripe," Jacob added. "I don't care what the rest of you do, but I gotta get out of here, and soon."

Jacob was 16 going on 46 thanks to the apocalypse. The plague, or virus, or whatever it was, had cheated him and his brother out of some of their childhood and they were never going to get it back, and there was nothing that I could do about that.

So I taught him and Billy as much as I could about everything I knew, from foraging for food to torturing (yes I said torturing) prisoners for information, and just let them become whatever they were going to become, and hoped that it would help them survive the rigors of this new and extremely unpleasant zombie filled world.

"A *little* ripe? These guys reek enough to puke a maggot off a gut wagon," Billy stated, interjecting his own colloquial phrase.

"I hate to bring everyone down with the facts, but I think it probably stinks just as much out there among the piles of rotting eater corpses as it does in here, most likely even more," I said. "There're thousands of dead and mutilated bodies outside fermenting in the sun. But, you're right, we can't stay in here much longer, we definitely need food and water."

"We haven't heard any sounds out there for quite a while, at least twenty-four hours, except for that incessant sound of flies buzzing around the stacks of bodies," Billy said. "I vote we bail out of here and take our chances outside."

"All right, I guess we've got no other choice, besides some of the flies are starting to make their way in here, but I'll go first," I insisted.

******

Jack usually went first when there was any kind of danger lurking about. It's not that he particularly wanted to go first, but he felt that with his combat experience he had a better chance of surviving (or killing) anything that he and his family might come in contact with. Even though his family were becoming quite good at killing zombies (and crazy humans), Jack still thought that it was better if he took the point (the lead) most of the time. After all, he was the *Alpha Male* of the group.

******

Stumbling around in the semi-darkness of the crowded tank, I made my way over our former friends who would had been rotting away before our very eyes, that is if it had been light enough within the confines of the tank for us to see them.

Pushing the hatch up and over its apex, the sound of a dull thump was barely heard over the millions of flies buzzing around, as the heavy cover plopped down on the severed head of one of the thousands of dismembered and decomposing corpses that littered the surrounding countryside and our tank. The large steel cover for all intent and purposes flattened the skull and caused the liquefied contents within the rapidly decomposing cranium to ooze out of several of its orifices and run down the side of the tank's turret, staining it with a putrid yellowish-purple gelatin like substance.

I waited at the top of the turret for a few moments to allow my eyes to adjust to the sunlight that they hadn't seen in days. Then when I felt that my eyes had gotten used to the abundance of light and I would be able to see any danger lurking outside of the tank, I continued on with my mission.

I slowly raised my head out of the tank's turret, stopping as my eyes crested the rim of the hatch. Turning my head to the right and then to the left, my eyes panned the 360 degrees of decaying fly infested carnage that lay before me.

"The only things that are moving are the flies and the *snappers*, and a whole hell of a lot of *twitchers*!" I whispered down to my family, coining new names we could use to describe the decapitated heads of the zombies that were still trying to bite whatever they could reach, and the spastic squirming bodies of the now dead undead, just before inhaling a vast, however, unknown number of flies with my next breath.

After flailing around for what seem like an eternity while choking on the squishy wriggling bodies of the multitude of nasty insects that had invaded my mouth, I somehow finally cleared my mouth and throat of most of the distasteful arthropods and began to breath somewhat normally again with my hands cupped over my nose and mouth, allowing just enough of a gap between my fingers to let some air in and keep most of the flies out.

My unabridged oxygen intake was short lived, as one way or another I still had to communicate with my family.

So I widened the gap between my fingers slightly and braved the relentless onslaught of the unruly menacing flies as I spoke to my family once again in a now muffled voice.

"There are too many flies out here," I said, as I slid back down into the tank. Then contorting my face, I used my tongue to scrape the last remaining pieces of the now mutilated intrusive flies from between my cheek and gums, before spitting them out onto Bruce's headless body. "We're going to need something to cover our mouths and noses to keep the flies from creeping in them."

"You mean again?" Jacob asked with a slight smirk on his face.

"Yes, again!" I said, making a gagging sound to clear my throat, as I hocked up an insect wing covered lugee and spit it on the floor at my youngest son's feet for a visual effect, and watched the smirk slowly fade from Jacob's face.

"I don't have a scarf or a rag," Gin said. "I guess we could use some of these dead guy's clothes?"

"I guess we'll have to," Billy said, pulling on Dave's shirt hard enough to rip the fabric and send buttons soaring in different directions around the interior of the tank.

With the morning light shinning in through the open hatch, Jacob spotted a metal storage box tucked neatly away behind where Bruce's headless and spat on body laid.

"Hold on a minute, look at this," he said. "Gas masks! This box has gas masks in it."

Packed tightly in the box were four gas masks (one for each of the tank's regular crewmembers) complete with chemical hoods; which Jacob quickly handed out to each family member before quickly covering his head with his own.

"These are really cool," Jacob said, *his* voice now muffled through the mask.

The rest of us donned our gas masks as each of us tried to mentally prepare ourselves to go into one more sphere of horror this world had to offer that was surely and anxiously awaiting our arrival.

"All right lets go outside," I ordered, my voice also muffled once more.

As I began to climb out of the tank, leading the way again, I heard Billy say.

"Grab your guns!"

I stuck my head back down the hatch and told them.

"Leave the AK's we're out of ammo for them, just bring the 9mm weapons, the pistols and the Sub-2000, we'll get ammo for them in the armory, there's still plenty of ammunition left in there, and plenty of M-4's in there too."

One by one, we crawled out of the tank, the rest of my family squinting as their eyes struggled to adapt to the brightness of the sun that they hadn't seen for three days, and that was now temporarily blinding them.

"Holy crud!" Gin screamed, as her eyes adjusted to the daylight and she witnessed the full scope of the slaughter that surrounded us.

"Quiet, keep your voice down, are you trying to get us killed?" I whispered, paranoid that the noise might bring more zombies, or worse, raptors.

"Sorry!" Gin moaned, distraught by the surrounding landscape.

During the three days in the tank, they had all forgotten just how brutal the massacre they had escaped from had been. Or maybe they all just wanted to forget the vast amount of carnage that they had previously witnessed.

Whatever the reason for their temporary amnesia, the scene they were now being forced to endure, was so horrific that we all knew that none of us would ever be the same again.

Piles of the zombie bodies that had been torn apart by the raptors and the T-Rexes' were everywhere, their rotting carcasses were stacked one on top of the other, sometimes as many as twelve bodies high. If we hadn't of had to kill so many, and hadn't grown to hate them so much for their insatiable appetite for our flesh, we might have felt somewhat sorry for them.

However, as things were, we felt no remorse for the hundreds of zombies we'd killed and burned that now lay in the piles before us. Or for the ones that we'd killed all along the way since the undead began their attack upon us at our home.

Neither was there any remorse forth coming for the ones that were torn apart by the giant lizards, the ones that we now had to climb over or step on to get to what we were hoping would be the safety and security of the armory.

The sickening squishing sounds of bloated intestines squirting out their feces and different colors of fermented juices, along with the sliding sensation of rotting muscles and tendons tearing away from the bones as we used the severed limbs of the formally undead as steps to elevate us over the decomposing mounds of remains were bad enough.

However, couple that noise and feeling together with the crunching sound of the bent and broken teeth of the ever vigilant snappers as the decapitated heads gnashed their teeth and fervently chomped at their elusive meals while we trudged over the stacks of convulsing dismembered torsos and slippery disemboweled organs.

Now, imagine if you will how the cacophony was only made more odious by the never-ending sound of the innumerable flies circling the seemingly endless mounds of degrading bluish-green corpses.

These sounds echoed in our minds for weeks after, bringing back the memory of the short but what we regarded at that time, as an un-ending journey to the weapons cache we so desperately needed.

"Good call Dad," Jacob said, as he kicked a biting head to the side, knocking several of its teeth down the open hole where its throat should have been.

"What good call?" I asked. "You mean going back into the armory?"

Jacob laughed softly through his now fly incrusted gas mask.

"No, I mean calling these heads snappers, because that's exactly what they're doing, they're snapping at us."

"Everyone stay alert, just because we don't see any *live* eaters, that doesn't mean that there aren't any nearby. And watch out for those heads, I mean snappers, you get bit and you die," I warned everyone, knowing that there was really no need to.

"Watch out for raptors too!" Jacob warned. "They're a lot faster than the eaters are!"

During our trek to the front door of the armory, we saw no sign of *live* zombies (just *live* heads), or of the prehistoric monsters that had destroyed their massive horde and inadvertently and ironically saved our skins at the same time.

When we finally made it to the entryway of the armory, our clothes were adorned with small chunks of festering flesh, and dripping with rotting blood, feces, and several bodily fluids that none of us had any idea of what they might be, and really weren't itching to find out.

And as if that weren't enough to make us sick to our stomachs. To highlight the decaying mess that befouled our clothing, our garments were peppered with a generous amount of hitchhiking maggots that wiggled excitedly as the flies that accompanied them continually swooped down and landed nearby, and then took off again, never venturing to fly too far away from their descendants.

"We've got to get out of these clothes, at least the pants, they're slimy, and they stink," Gin announced with a sour look on her face as she peeled away her gas mask.

"How can you tell that it's your clothes that sink? I mean with all of the rotting corpses lying around all over the place, you've narrowed down the source of the smell to your pants?" Jacob asked, with a teenage sarcastic smile on his face.

"Well you can keep your foul-smelling clothes on if you want to, but I've got to get out mine," Gin answered, not much in the mood for levity after scaling the mountains of decaying corpses in the street.

"First things first, we need to get the guns and ammunition, then maybe we can either wash our uniforms, or find some others here in the armory," I ordered, as I began to make my way to where the M-4 rifles were stored.

"First things first, we need to get these maggots and pieces of rotting skin, and whatever this other stuff is off of us," Gin insisted, as she brushed the putrescent body parts and fly larvae from her clothes.

"Good idea Mom," Jacob said, as he too wiped the decomposed body parts and little white grubs from his uniform.

"You talked me into it honey," I said, as I brushed a clump of maggots off my left forearm and watched them pepper the floor in front of me.

"Me too," Billy proclaimed, as he too wiped some rancid discolored skin and several maggots from both of his trouser legs and from the top of his boots.

After we had skimmed off our outer layer of disgusting putrefied flesh and maggot infestation, which had magnified our experience to a great extent, we continued into the bowels of the armory to collect the much-needed weapons that were stored there.

The huge zombie horde that had attacked us had been drawn to our location by the sound of the buildings crashing down and the cannon fire that caused them to fall, so inside the armory was mostly devoid of zombies. Some of the raptors, which luckily for us were no longer present, had summarily dispatched the few zombies that had infiltrated inside the building, leaving it a *zombie free structure*, at least for the time being.

Although at the time of the massive invading horde's attack upon us, we hadn't seen any of the raptors or the tyrannosaurs devour any of the undead legion, however, their tell-tale calling card was evident in several spots throughout the inside of the armory.

"Watch out for the dinosaur shit, it looks like they pinched a couple of seriously heinous loafs before they skedaddled out of here," I warned, making my way into the M-4 storage room. "I don't know what in the hell they've been eating, but it looks pretty obnoxious; I don't think that you want to step in it. It doesn't smell all that good either…go figure?"

Once we were all inside the weapons storage room I said.

"Everyone grab two rifles, and let's get to the ammo room, we'll need as much 5.56 and 9mm ammo as we can carry," I informed them as I picked up two M-4 carbines that the Sarg had left behind after freeing them from their locked rack.

"Why two rifles?" Gin asked.

"Because we don't know exactly what we're going to run into out on the road, but from our experiences out there we all have a pretty good idea of what to expect," I answered grimly. "And whatever we run into, one thing is for sure, we don't want to be caught short of firepower when we encounter it."

Gin and the two boys each grabbed two rifles from the same rack, and we continued to the room where the ammo was stored, watching our step as not to inadvertently tread in any of the several piles of expelled feces that the raptors had graciously left behind.

"It's all still here!" Jacob shouted, seemingly surprised.

"It should be, zombies and prehistoric lizards don't use guns," Billy quipped, as he rolled his eyes at his brother's naive statement.

"Billy you stay here with your mother, Jacob you come with me," I said. "We're going to see if we can find some new uniforms and maybe a shower, and anything else we can use. You two stay here and see if you can locate something we can use to carry the spare magazines for these guns."

Taking the 9mm pistols and our edged weapons, Jacob and I proceeded down the hallway in search of much needed assets.

"Keep your eyes peeled for the office where they keep the keys to the vehicles. Before Bruce died and the tank blew up, we thought that there might be some Hummers parked in the back where they found the tank, we need the keys to one of them," I said, reminding Jacob.

"I know Dad, we were on our way to look for one when that sniper opened fire on us and blew Bruce's head clean off his shoulders," Jacob added without emotion. "I got the pleasure of sitting on his headless body's lap for the last three days; I'd like to thank everybody for that one."

During our three-day stay in the tank, we all had the opportunity to become very intimate with the slowly decomposing bodies of our three former friends, so I wasn't surprised to hear Jacob *reminisce* about his stay at the hotel Abrams.

It wasn't long before we stumbled across some clean uniforms, a small locker room with a shower, and an office where we found a small brown metal box full of keys.

"The showers work, well kind of," Jacob said, as he turned the handle on one and a small trickle of water dribbled out. "It's not much, but if it lasts we can take a cold shower."

"Any shower is better than no shower!" I exclaimed nodding my head in agreement.

It had been four days since we had left the YMCA, and all the comforts of home that it had provided for us. The Sarge and his people had turned the abandoned club into a sanctuary, an oasis in the middle of a zombie desert.

While we were there, we had grown used to things being a little like they were before the apocalypse, before all of the death and destruction. We had grown used to the hot meals and the hot showers, the clean sheets and the warm beds.

It seemed that those days were over now, and we would have to make do with what we had and what we could find, no matter how meager.

"Look what I found while you were gone, magazine pouches for the M-4 mags," Billy bragged, holding up a pouch in each hand as Jacob and I rejoined him and his mother. "And we loaded this cart with ammo, and since the Sarge broke down the front door with his giant crowbar, we should probably move to another room, one that has a door."

Nodding in agreement once again, and motioning for them to follow me, I said. "Good idea, let's go, I'll show you what Jake and I found."

After leading my family to the showers and letting them pick out their new uniforms that the National Guard generously provided us with (*Army Digital* camouflage pattern), I told them that we would all clean up right after we secured a new vehicle for our future journey into hell.

There was no use in taking a shower and putting on clean outfits, and then going outside and having to slop through a bunch of blood and guts to get to a vehicle. It made more sense to do the dirty work while we were still dirty.

It was too dangerous for one or two of us to go outside alone in search of some means of transportation; whoever braved the outside world would need someone to watch their backs while they looked.

Taking the box of keys in tow, along with an old tarp we had found, Jacob and I cautiously made our way out the back door of the armory, while Billy and Gin stood watch over us.

The carnage at the back of the building was not as bad as it was in the front of the building. The high fence that surrounded that part of the armory had kept most of the marauding zombies at bay, the one's that did find their way in were lying in several pieces which were scattered throughout the parking lot by the prehistoric beasts that had ripped them to shreds, and saved our lives.

We meandered through the parking lot avoiding stepping on most of the rotting body parts, and at the same time, hopefully avoiding any rogue sniper's bullets that might be aimed at us.

"There's a bunch of Hummers back here Dad," Jacob acknowledged, tossing the tarp onto the seat to keep it clean before jumping into one of the vehicles. "Hand me a key and I'll see if it works.

I handed Jacob four keys in a row, none of which would start the Hummer, however, as Jacob turned the fifth key, the military vehicle turned over and then started with a roar.

"Can I drive Dad, I can do it," Jacob begged, smiling and gripping the steering wheel.

It was only a few yards to the back door of the armory, and there wasn't what you would call a *whole lot* of dead bodies to drive over. Besides, he needed the practice; we were sure to need him to drive at some point in the future.

"Sure pull it up as close as you can to the back door, then get right back here."

Jacob followed my orders to the letter and parked the Hummer close the rear entrance of the building without incident. Then he joined me again as I had requested with the tarp in hand.

"What now Dad?" Jacob inquired eager to drive again.

"I think this time we're going to take two vehicles and travel in a caravan. Every time we get on the road, something happens to our transportation. So this time, since we have two military vehicles at our disposal, we're going to try something different, and maybe we'll have better luck.

I dug through the box of keys once more, handing them one by one to my son who promptly inserted them into the ignition of the second Hummer.

"Bingo!" Jacob yelled, as the second Hummer spewed smoke from its tail pipe and began to rumble.

"Pull it up behind the other one, not too close though, we need to be able to load supplies into both of them," I informed Jacob, as he slowly drove the olive-drab colored truck over a bloated carcass that was doubling as a speed bump, and moved the motor vehicle into place.

"Good enough," I said. "Let's hit the showers!"

Gin was pleased that the armory had showers; however, she wished that the hot water had been working. Nevertheless, things being as they were, she agreed with me that any shower was better than no shower at all.

Once we had cleaned the dried cadaver juices and lingering stench of the festering bodies off of our own carcasses and slipped into our new uniforms, we secured one of the rooms that had two exits and began to gather as much ammo as we thought we could pack into the two Hummers, and then we loaded every magazine that we had.

"When are we leaving," Gin asked.

With all of the horrific occurrences that had happened in the last few days, I hadn't considered what we would do, or where we would go.

Hell, I didn't even think we would live through it, let alone make plans for what we would do if we did.

"I think we should spend the night here locked in this room; while we figure out what we're going to do, where we're going to go, you know, make a plan."

"We could try and make it back to the YMCA?" Gin suggested.

"We could, but the Sarge left us for dead, he left all of us here and he could have waited, he should have waited, I would have waited for him.

So I put a few rounds in the back tires of the bus as he drove off. Therefore, if we go back to the Y, and him and Beth didn't make back we'll be fine. That is unless they show up later, then I'll have to kill him.

On the other hand, if we go there and he and Beth made it back in one piece, he's not going to be too pleased to see us, and I'll have to kill him.

Or, if we show up there and he welcomes us with open arms, I'm still going to kill him, it'll just be a little easier that way.

Either way, if I end up having to kill the Sarge, and I *will* end up having to kill him, it's the principle of the thing you know. I don't think his people are going to take too kindly to that, do you?"

"No, probably not," Gin answered.

"Maybe we can find another YMCA, or something like it," Billy contended.

"Or maybe another box store, like before," Jacob added.

"Well we'll just have to figure it out, but for now the Sarge's YMCA is not an option," I stated firmly. "Is everyone in agreement?"

"That sounds fine to me," Gin agreed casually.

"It's all right by me," Billy answered.

"We'll find some place just as good as the Sarge's place sooner or later," Jacob said optimistically.

"And if we run into the Sarge at anytime in the future, he's going to be dead before he hits the ground; nobody is going to run away and leave me and my family to die, not and live to tell about it anyway, at least not if I can help it," I mentioned nonchalantly as I racked a 5.56 NATO round into the chamber of my M-4 rifle.

We spent the rest of that day planning our next move, filling up the Hummers with extra rifles, pistols, and ammunition, filling some containers with water from the showers, and generally making ready for the next day's trek.

Fortunately for us, the former Sergeant in charge of the motor pool had been on the ball and kept the cluster of vehicle's in his care fueled using the gas pump located on the property. This kept the stable of Hummers and other transportation ready to move out at a moment's notice, and gave us one less thing to worry about before we departed on our next journey into the zombie wilderness. It also saved us the trouble of stomping over a myriad of decomposing body parts in our clean new uniforms while we prepared for our upcoming departure into what would surely be a horrific apocalyptic odyssey.

As far as eatable provisions were concerned, we were lucky enough to find a soda and snack machine in the building, but not lucky enough to find either one of them unmolested.

It seemed obvious that early on in the zombie invasion, the troops that were staffing this armory left in a big hurry. Only stopping to raid the machines and then to lock the doors behind them.

Who knows whether they panicked and ran for the hills, or set out to face the invading hordes as a disciplined military unit? However, disciplined military units don't usually pillage their own installations before heading out on a mission, no matter how dangerous they feel that mission might be. So my guess is that command and control broke down here, just as fast as it had everywhere else, and an everyman for themselves scenario took place.

Whether or not my guess was right or wrong, how and why they left was of no consequence, the fact was that they had emptied the machines before they did so, leaving us without any of the much-needed sustenance to get us by until we were able to forage for some real food.

But that's the way it is in the middle of a zombie apocalypse, some good, some bad, some ugly... mostly the bad and ugly.

THE JOURNEY BEGINS! AGAIN!

"Wake up everyone, rise and shine, the sun is already up, we're burning daylight," I cheerfully announced while strapping on my Glock 19.

"I'm awake, and ready to go!" Gin stated grumpily. "I'm so sick of the smell around here, the sooner we leave the better."

"That's my girl, rough and ready," I kidded.

My good mood could have only been brought on by the fact that we were about to leave this god forsaken hellhole of a place. However, even though we were still about to journey into the vast unknown of the living-dead apocalypse and that thought left little room for happiness, at the time my focus was on leaving the stench of the multitude of rotting corpses that surrounded us, at least for awhile.

"Boys, get up we're leaving in just a few minutes," I said, still adjusting my gear.

Slowly both boys started to stir, rubbing the sleep from their eyes and making moaning noises as they stretched.

"What about breakfast?" Jacob asked.

"What about it?" I answered back. "We don't have any food remember, and even if we did, I personally would like to eat somewhere that doesn't smell like road kill, we did enough of that on the Morphodite."

"Me too!" Gin added. "Let's go, the sooner we leave the sooner we can find some food and eat."

The three of us picked up our brand spanking new M-4's, and Jacob grabbed his trusty pistol caliber carbine in the 9mm variety, and we headed outside to our newly acquired Hummers.

"Billy, you and Jake take that one," I said, pointing to the rear vehicle. "Your mother and I will take the lead, stay close, but not too close, maybe about ten or twenty yards behind us. Billy you drive, Jacob, you ride shotgun, and I mean ride *shotgun*, keep your gun ready and your eyes peeled."

With our guns fully loaded and in hand, and our Hummers fully loaded with extra rifles, ammo, and fuel, we slowly pulled out of the armory's motor pool area.

With mangled corpses covering the ground in every direction, we heard the sound of rotting flesh and intestines being squeezed and squished, and the bones of the undead cadavers being broken and smashed under our tires as we traversed across the gruesome landscape, weaving back and forth around the larger mounds of eviscerated, and decapitated corpses, and just plowing over the smaller piles of bloated carcasses and assorted body parts.

There was no sign of the raptors or of the T-Rex's, only the dismembered twitching corpses and the snapping heads of the zombies that had fallen prey to them.

Several hundred yards of what you might call a killing field had to be crossed before the bodies began to thin out somewhat and we no longer had to grind our way through, ripping sinew and muscle from bones as we attempted to gain traction on the slimy pieces of atrocious body parts of the fallen undead cannibals.

Once clear of the mass of swollen remains and most of the still biting heads. I stopped our small caravan and got out of the truck, then announced to my family.

"We need to dig out some of this gore from inside of the wheel wells, some of the eaters clothing among other things has gotten wrapped around stuff; we need to get it out before it messes something up. Plus, we'll never get away from the smell and these damn flies if we don't clean this mess up."

"By all means then, let's clean up this mess," Gin said, without hesitation.

"Gin, hand me one of those spare rifles, I'll use it to pull this crap out."

Seeing me using the barrel of one of the surplus M-4's to clear my vehicle of zombie remains, the boys followed suit and began digging at the oozing sub-human debris that was also stuck in their wheel wells.

After pulling a hand, two mutilated feet, half of an arm, two blood soaked shirts, and something that resembled part of a ground up internal organ from the wheel wells, along with unwrapping a small intestine that was twisted around one of the front shock absorbers, we soon had the hitchhiking residue of the once ferocious cannibalistic monsters removed from the underside of our vehicles and we were once more on our way.

We were able to make our way to the freeway, and with the bodies of the dead zombies now becoming more random, traveling was easier and much faster.

It had been about twenty-five minutes since we had left the armory when I looked in my rearview mirror and saw Billy and Jacob smiling and waving trying to get our attention, when I waved back, they both pointed at some zombies that were several hundred yards away walking through a field.

None of us had ever thought that we would be happy to see a live zombie roaming around the countryside, but considering the alternative of seeing a prehistoric beast that was supposed to have been extinct for millions of years, one that could easily out run us and rip us to pieces, we would take what we could get.

After that, we began to see an occasional group of zombies wandering around in search of food, or us, depending on how you look at it.

"There're some more eaters Jack," Gin pointed out. "We're seeing more and more of them now; I wonder why we haven't seen any of those other creatures since they forced us into that tank?"

"I have no idea, but if I never see another one of them again, it'll be too damn soon," I answered. "I mean unless they show up and save our asses again, and don't eat us afterwards."

"Right!" Gin replied, and then asked.

"What are we going to do if we do see them again?"

"I guess if they're close and pose any kind of a threat, we'll see how effective our weapons are against them? I wish we still had our AK's, bigger bullets ya know."

Gin didn't look too happy with my answer, but there wasn't much we could do if we were attacked by the ravenous gigantic lizards except test our weapon's effectiveness.

We certainly couldn't out run them on foot. We might be able to outdistance them riding in our vehicles, however, from what we've already seen of them, they are very quick and nimble, able to jump, trot, run, and still turn on a dime and give you nine cents change, so who knows what else they can do; climb, crawl under, slide down, etc.? They may be able to go any number of places that our vehicles are unable to traverse? They might be able to easily "*head us off at the pass*" so to speak, especially if there's more than one of them. Our only option might be just to stand and fight, or to find some place to hide until it is safe to continue to travel.

In either case, at this moment our chances of surviving an attack by the merciless oversized reptiles seemed rather grim.

"What do think is going on, I mean there's not supposed to be raptors running around out there?" Gin asked, as if I was supposed to have an answer to her question.

"I don't know what's happening. We've got dinosaurs roaming the planet, at least our portion of the planet. We've got dead people roaming the planet with them. Who knows what else the *Gods* have in store for us?" I answered, knowing that my answer had done nothing to help ease the emotional stress that was consuming her.

We drove all day down highway 77, sticking to our plan that we had made the night before, which was to make our way a little south of Corpus Christi, and see if we could find a spot somewhere around Baffin Bay. Several small towns are close by and might offer food and possibly a permanent sanctuary, if there *was* any such thing anymore.

We would stay well clear of big cities if possible, our experience with them in the past had not been too pleasant, and the overwhelming number of zombies that tend to inhabit large metropolitan areas makes it impossible to ever clear all of them out and make the region reasonably suitable for the living.

As usual, we traveled on the highways or interstates; they had their own challenges but were still much faster and seemingly offered a better margin of safety than did the smaller roads.

The zombie population was becoming more and more visible as the hours passed; however, there was still no sign of dinosaurs, although occasionally we would run across pockets of mutilated undead that had been torn apart and scattered about just like the scene around the armory.

"Looks like they've been here too, that's another group of eaters we don't have to worry about," Gin said, as she pointed in the direction of a pile of fermenting body parts, partially cloaked in a swarm of flies. "Some snappers too! They've been here all right!"

"We don't have to worry about *them* now, but we still have to worry about the raptors," I stated, scanning the area for any sign of the prehistoric reptiles.

At that very moment, Billy beeped the horn to get our attention.

"Is he crazy?" Gin shouted. "He'll get us all killed!"

With no zombies near, I pulled over to see what my son thought was so important that he felt he needed to honk the horn and alert every undead sub-human within earshot of our vehicle that we had arrived, and that dinner was about to be served.

34

As I stepped out of the vehicle, I saw Billy and Jacob pointing into a field. When I looked in that direction, I saw the first dinosaur that we'd seen since we were forced into that Abram's battle tank almost five days before.

"It's a raptor, and he's about three hundred yards away, I don't think he's seen us yet," I said, looking at my wife.

After seeing with my own eyes what one of these prehistoric reptilian beasts could do to a human body in a matter of seconds, I decided to take no chances.

I reached into the Hummer and pulled out my M-4, there was no need to rack a round into the chamber because we always carried our guns with a round in the chamber, locked and loaded, or cocked and locked if you prefer, but I decided to do a press check anyway just to make sure.

I ordered my family to do the same, and they complied with my mandate immediately by pulling the charging handle of their weapons back slightly and checking to see if a live-round was being pulled out of the chamber by the gun's extractor.

I looked around the surrounding landscape and could see only the one lizard and still no zombies close enough to be a threat, and decided to try a long range shot to see the effect it would have on the monster reptile.

I shouldered my rifle and looked through its iron sights at the distant meat-eating dinosaur, and told my family.

"I guess this is as good of time as any to find out if these rifles are up to the task of putting down one of these killers. I'm going to take a shot at him, if he doesn't go down and charges at us, we'll all open fire on him and shoot until he does go down. Then we'll get the hell out of Dodge before the noise brings a horde of eaters our way."

I slowly flipped the safety on the M-4 to fire, took careful aim, and slowly pressed the trigger to the rear.

A loud bang exited the muzzle of the gun and a small jolt pounded into my shoulder as the 5.56mm projectile sped toward the over-grown lizard at nearly 3000 feet per second.

My aim was true considering that this was the first time that I had fired this particular weapon, and I wasn't sure how well the sights had been adjusted by the previous shooter. The shot wasn't a clean kill shot, but I'd managed to hit the animal just below what you might consider its armpit, that is if the raptor's talon laden upper extremities could be called arms.

The wounded raptor began to hop around, sometimes falling down, but getting up immediately after doing so.

In its agony, the now wounded and highly pissed-off giant marauding lizard somehow managed to spot us and made a beeline directly for the four of us.

I began firing at the charging creature, and out of the corner of my eye, I saw Billy and Gin raise their rifles and begin to shoot at the beast as well.

I guess it was fortunate for us that the National Guard armory had been stocked with an older model of the M-4, the type that incorporated the safe, semi, and the *full-auto* selector switch, and not the newer models that replaced the *full-auto* function with a *three round burst*.

As the ravenous monster lizard came closer at a remarkably fast pace, I switched my rifle to full auto, and when it had closed the gap to about forty yards (now sporting several more bullet holes I might add) I emptied the remainder of my thirty-round magazine into its chest in under a half a second.

Gin was firing on semi-auto, as was Jacob now that the beast was well within the effective range of his 9mm carbine; however, Billy had switched his gun to full auto from the start and was riddling it with 5.56mm projectiles too.

We stopped shooting when the well-perforated carnivore tumbled to the ground in front of us and dropped dead at our feet.

Jacob started counting the bullet holes in the animal's carcass, which totaled fifty-two that he could see, four of which were headshots, but only one had penetrated the skull and punctured the animal's brain. The other three had broken several of the enormous lizard's teeth and shattered its jawbone.

"Holy shit in an argyle sock, that was a close one," Gin panted. "I know I hit that thing at least five or six times, and it still landed four feet from us."

"Most of our shots were at a distance, I think the one's that killed it were probably inside fifty yards, it was most likely the head shot that finally did it," I surmised, as I dropped the empty magazine from my gun and inserted a full one.

"Lucky that thing wasn't one of the T-Rex's, I don't think we would have been able to stop one of those gigantic beasts," Billy added. "At least not with these puny weapons."

"I think you're right." I agreed. "Our guns were made to kill human's not hulking mammoth lizards. We probably should try to avoid them at all costs, and from now on, head shots for the lizards too!"

Just then, Jacob hollered out.

"Eaters!"

We turned and saw ten or so zombies descending upon our position from the opposite side of the road.

"Okay, here we go again, this is just like old times, all of that gunfire is bringing in eaters," I said.

"Yeah, just like old times, these bastards came out of nowhere," Gin agreed, dropping the empty magazine from her rifle too.

"I'll get these dirty rotten bastards," Jacob announced as he raise his Sub-2000 carbine. "I only shot seven or eight rounds at the raptor, so I have plenty of ammo left to take care of this group of undead stinking scum suckers."

"Take it easy son, I'm beginning to think you don't like uninvited eaters, and besides you might hurt their feelings if they hear you talking like that," I said, figuring that a little humor might be good for everybody at this point.

"Hurt feelings is soon to be the least of their worries," Jacob answered smiling.

Boom! Boom! Boom!

Jacob's gun sounded three times, and three of the zombies shed their maggots into the air like rice at a wedding, as they dropped to the ground with hunks of their skulls missing due to the impact of his bullets.

Several more shots fired from Jacob's weapon, and several more diseased brains oozed out onto the ground; and our immediate and latest zombie problem had been extinguished.

"I told you I'd take care of them," Jacob bragged. "One shot, one kill, just like in sniper school."

"Shut up, your sixteen, you've never been to sniper school," Billy taunted, as his younger brother gloated.

"You shut up, I watched it on TV, and that's what they always say," Jacob responded.

"It was still good shooting Jacob, keep up the good work," Gin added, as she climbed back into our Hummer and smacked the bottom of her fresh magazine, making sure it was seated firmly in her rifle.

Climbing back into the Hummer myself, I recommended.

"Let's get out of here! More eaters are coming! Let's not waist all our bullets here, I'm sure we're going to need them later."

I looked into my rearview mirror as we drove away from the carnage left by our most recent harrowing episode, and I could see a number of zombies making their way onto the scene that we had just left.

"From the looks of it, eaters seem to crave dinosaur flesh too; most of them walked straight passed the dead eaters on the ground and began to devour our lizard friend. Maybe the downed eaters were a little too ripe for their discriminating palates."

"That was no friend of mine," Gin stated emphatically. "I hope we never see another one of those monsters… ever."

Trying to be realistic, I told her.

"That's highly unlikely; I don't know what we're going to see? But I bet we'll see more of those at some point. In this hellish world it seems like if there's one, there's always more than one, no matter what it is. Unless it's something that we want or need, and then those things seem to be in really short supply."

It wasn't long before my prediction came true.

We had not gone more than five miles when Jacob spotted the silhouettes of three dinosaurs on the horizon. Sticking his head out of the window, he shouted at us and pointed in their direction.

"There're three of them, looks like two raptors and one T-Rex. They're running parallel to us."

At that point, we all saw the three lizards Jacob had spotted. They weren't just running parallel to us; they were chasing down a medium sized horde of freelancing zombies.

That's probably why they didn't pay any attention to Jacob hollering out of his window.

"Look, they're after that group of eaters!" Gin said, pointing to the same gaggle of carnivorous bipedal beasts.

"Better them than us," I said, pushing down on the accelerator pedal and feeling our Hummer lurch forward.

With their superior speed it didn't take long for the dino's to reach the group of staggering living dead, and with their superior ability to rip things apart, it wasn't long before the zombie horde was lying in pieces on the distant hillside.

We kept moving in an effort to put some distance between the killer beasts and our small caravan, and despite their keen eyesight, hearing, and sense of smell, the distraction of tearing their quarry limb from limb gave us ample time to separate ourselves from the potential danger that they posed.

As we rode along the freeway dodging the undead pedestrians, and abandon cars, I began to wonder if traveling in separate vehicles was such a good idea.

If the people in the other Hummer were just a group of guys we had met along the way there wouldn't be a problem. If we got separated, we could always find them later and get back together, and if we never saw them again, so what, nobody would really give a shit.

Since this zombie apocalypse began, there had been many people and many things that we were never going to see again, we'd get over it.

But they weren't just a group of guys we happened to run into, they were family, they were our children, and we didn't want to get separated. If those dinosaurs had finished off those zombies back there and then came after us, how hard would it have been to stay together with a bunch of giant man-eating beasts chasing after us?

"Honey, I think it might be a good idea to ditch the other Hummer and have the boys ride with us, if we get separated somehow, we may not be able to find each other again," I strongly recommended.

"That sounds like a good idea to me," Gin concluded as her motherly instinct kicked in. "Besides; we can cover each other better if we're all in the same place, and less chance of one of us being hit in a crossfire."

"Yes, that's all we need, to get hit by friendly-fire," I responded as I pulled our Hummer to the side of the road.

The boys pulled their vehicle up behind us, and after checking to make sure that no threats were in the vicinity, they got out of their truck to see why I had stopped.

"Boys, we decided that we should probably all travel in the same vehicle, less chance of being separated or catching friendly-fire," I explained.

"Oh man, now I'll never get to drive," Jacob said with a frown.

"You'll get to drive," I told him. "And you just might end up breaking the record for the most felony hit and runs."

"That's never going to happen, not after the mass quantity of eaters that Dave mowed down with the bus." Jacob asserted. "Not unless I'm driving something just as big."

"Most of my *accidents* were accrued in civilian type vehicles. The old school bus that Dave used to plow down hundreds of the undead is in another class, I believe it falls into the super-modified public transportation category, so it doesn't count," I facetiously explained.

"Cool!" Jacob exclaimed as he stepped toward the driver's seat.

"You're not going to let him drive *now* are you Dad?" Billy asked, not happy with the prospect of his younger brother driving him through a world filled with ravenous zombies and other heinous nemeses.

"No, not right this second," I said. "First we have to transfer what we can to this vehicle, and then he'll drive. He's going to have to sooner or later; it might as well be now.

"That's just great, first eaters, then dinosaurs, now this, we're doomed for sure," Billy said, shaking his head in disgust.

What's that old Indian saying? I asked rhetorically, and then answered my own question. "It's a good day to die?" Then without hesitation I pulled my tomahawk out and waved it above my head, letting out a savage and prolonged *Indian War Whoop*.

Gin never did get my sense of humor, and this time was no exception.

"That's not very funny, we've almost died about a thousand times since this whole thing started, and now you're making jokes about being killed," she said, glaring at me.

"Sorry honey, it's a gift," I insisted, still trying to be funny and not being very successful at it.

We transferred as much ammo as we could fit into our lone Hummer, there wasn't much room to carry anything else, as we had loaded up both vehicles to near full capacity before we left the armory.

"Jump in the vehicle, I'll grab one more case of ammo, I think we can fit it in somewhere," I said to my family, as I leaned far into the rear of the soon to be abandoned Hummer to drag the last case of ammo to the back of the truck, not knowing that it would be the last thing that I would ever say to them.

Suddenly I heard Gin scream. It was a loud but short scream, as if she had stopped in the middle of her yell. Then one shot from Jacob's carbine sounded as I saw the flash from his rifle's muzzle reflect off a velociraptor's body.

Then I watched in horror as my wife and two sons were literally torn apart right before my eyes.

The last thing I remember, I pulled my M-4 rifle sling from my shoulder and began walking toward the lead truck firing the gun from my hip at the raptor that was halfway inside the Hummer and still clawing at my family.

In a torrent of rage I blacked out, when I regained consciousness I found the remains of Gin, Billy, and Jacob still inside the Hummer along with the bullet riddled raptor still clutching one of Gin's severed arms in its blood stained jaws.

Another raptor was lying across the hood of the Hummer with several gunshot wounds to its head and body.

Various empty M-4 magazines were scattered around the vehicle, and the bolt on my rifle was locked to the rear, displaying the empty magazine through the ejection port in my gun.

Tears welled up in my eyes and my knees grew weak as I stood there helpless, surveying the hideous scene of my families brutal death.

Rage began to overtake me as I watched a group of ten zombies approach, intending on having my dead family and me for brunch.

The feelings of hopelessness and helplessness that had initially swept over me and utterly consumed my very being, leaving me incapacitated and dejected, quickly gave way to blind rage.

I knew it was too late to help my family, but I *could* take out my wrath on the small advancing zombie troop, and that's exactly what I did.

Without a moment of hesitation, I tossed my rifle onto the hard concrete road and pulled my tomahawk from my tactical vest.

I waded into the slobbering mass of ravenous cannibalistic undead with a vengeance.

Hacking wildly at them, I made my way to the back of the mob, hewing off their limbs and cleaving their heads as I went. Then I turned around and marched back through the ones that had been spared in my first assault, and decimated the remaining zombies one by one, as they approached me.

As I killed the zombies, visions of Gin and the boys flooded my mind, and a bizarre and gruesome phenomenon began to play out.

As I zealously attacked a female zombie, I saw Gin's blue eyes staring back at me through the murderous fury on the face of the undead woman.

At that moment in time something inside me snapped.

I grabbed the female zombie (which in my mind had chosen to impersonate my now dead wife), by the back of her long dark maggot infused matted hair, and plucked out her left eyeball with the pointed end of my weapon.

As the gelatinous bulb quivered on the end of my tomahawk, dripping blood from the ripped out veins that dangled below it, I showed the extracted left eye to her still attached right one seconds before cramming it back into the eye socket from which it had came.

By driving the eyeball and the spiked end of my bloody tomahawk back into the socket and deep into her brain, I finally put her out of everybody's misery.

Billy was next in my mind's eye, as a young male zombie wearing the same type of army shirt as my slaughtered son had previously worn, stumbled toward me with a hungry *thousand yard stare*.

With all of the power that my adrenalin-filled muscles could muster (which also had the tendency to throw my aim off slightly), I swung the blade of my razor sharp tomahawk down vertically so hard into the middle of the juvenile zombie's forehead, that it violently split the younger looking monster's face and skull open. Flinging each side of its head several inches apart and exposed his throbbing greenish-gray maggot infested brain, but did so without destroying it.

After splitting its skull, the downward thrust of my weapon was hard enough to sink the *hawk* deep into the bone of the upper portion of the zombie's rib cage.

With my edged weapon stuck in the undead cannibal's chest, and with its brain still active, this Billy look-a-like proceeded to claw at me in an attempt to grab my arms and pull me to his malfunctioning disjointed mouth.

My tomahawk had barely scraped the zombie's brain so its hunger for human flesh was still its only priority.

Even though its face was in two distinct pieces and it was unable to bite me, it was obvious that the zombie didn't see it that way.

With my life still in grave danger because of the other, yet to be fed zombies approaching me with the intention to feast. I pulled my Glock 19 from its holster and shoved it into the facial gap my tomahawk had made, and fired six or seven shots with the muzzle of the gun touching the frontal lobes of the zombie's pulsating brain.

The first two shots sounded muffled. However, the blasts from the gun and the bullets that preceded them quickly opened a hole the size of a baseball in the back of the monsters head, and it fell to the ground as I continued to pull the trigger and pump hot lead into its throbbing gray matter with the greenish tint.

As for the zombie that my mind's eye saw as Jacob, my youngest son who had been butchered in front of me only moments before?

Well, what I did to it is too nauseating, too disgusting, and too abhorrent to share with one who has such a delicate stomach as yours.

Therefore, for the sake of your mental stability and well-being, and because I am kind, I will do you a favor and forgo the lurid tale of that particular zombie's ultimate demise, thereby sparing you the explicit *splatterpunk* description of the event, along with any mental images that you might conjured up during my telling of that episode which would surely be seared into the dark crevasses of your mind for eternity, and I will continue on with the rest of my story.

After I regained my sanity, or what was left of it, I harvested the remaining zombies as brutally as time would allow, and then returned to the truck that housed my dead family.

As I returned to my family I realized that the next horror in the long line of never ending horrors awaited me. My wife and two sons had been killed, literally ripped apart limb from limb, however their skulls had remained intact, therefore as I approached the vehicle where my loved ones bodies were waiting, I could hear the sounds of teeth grinding and slapping together, and gurgling sounds emitting from the bodies that still were privy to their lungs. The horrendous sight of my dead family snarling and snapping at me was almost too much to bear. I had only one option now, and that was to put them out of their misery by putting a bullet into their brains. That chore was by far the hardest thing that I had ever had to do in my whole miserable life; and as I leveled my gun at each one of my family member's heads and fired the gun at point blank range into their skulls one by one, my sorrow was so great that I didn't even notice their blood splattering on my face. However, I did notice that the hate that I had accrued for the Sarge had increased exponentially, as had my resolve to find him and make him pay.

Never in my life had I felt as sad as I felt that day while burying my wife and two sons in that roadside ditch.

I slept in the clean Hummer that night, and stayed in that place probably longer than was prudent, while watching over the graves of my family. I was determined to make sure that no rogue zombies that might smell the alluring aroma of fresh meat, would claw at the newly dug graves, and end up digging them up in the middle of the night to satisfy their heinous desire to have a midnight snack.

Early the next morning with a host of zombies on the horizon and heading in my direction, I pulled the "*Death Hummer*" over the graves of my family, took Jacob's 9mm folding carbine and machete out of the doomed truck, dowsed the vehicle with gasoline, and set

48

it on fire as a finally safeguard against any of the undead attempting to rob the graves of my beloved family.

As I broke the mesmerizing trance of the burning vehicle in front of me, I turned the key and started my ride, put it in gear, and I began my quest to find the Sarge, the man I was convinced had caused the death of my family by his chicken-shit ways, having left us alone to fend for ourselves in the zombie wasteland.

Then as fate would have it, a couple hundred yards down the road, and to their chagrin, I encountered the first of many more zombies that would be added to my ongoing total of felony hit and runs.

MEANWHILE ABOARD THE MOTHER SHIP

"Lieutenant Commander Jol!"

"Yes Captain Xarr?"

"It has been brought to my attention that test subject group 32452013 has been attacked by some of the pre-extinction bipedal carnivorous creatures that *you* released onto the planet to save test subject group 32452013 from the overwhelming numbers of the control group that had them surrounded," Captain Xarr stated, raising his voice with every word spoken.

******

Lieutenant Commander Jol had not been informed by his *underling* of this new development in the current events concerning the test subject group 32452013 (Jack and his family).

The *underling* that was responsible for relaying such news to his superior.

The *underling* that was scheming to be promoted and replace Lieutenant Commander Jol at his station as second in command.

The *underling* that would resort to any means that he deemed necessary to accomplish his ultimate nefarious goal.

That diabolical *underlings* name was.

******

"My subordinate officer, 2nd Under Prime Lieutenant Commander Zeem has informed me of no such event Captain Xarr!" Lieutenant Commander Jol passionately insisted.

"Informed or not, test subject group 32452013 has been attacked by one of *your* pre-extinction bipedal carnivorous creatures.

I can only surmise that you failed to have the genetic differentiation microchip properly adjusted to insure the success of this particular part of our mission," Captain Xarr barked loudly at Lieutenant Commander Jol.

"No Captain Xarr, I made all of the proper checks and followed proper protocol to the letter to insure the success of that portion of this mission."

"So am I to understand that you adhered to all of the checks and balances, observed all of the proper procedures and proven methodology without fail Lieutenant Commander Jol?" the Captain barked again.

"Yes Captain Xarr!" the Lieutenant Commander responded adamantly.

"Yet you still managed somehow to *not* be informed of the heinous attack on test subject group 32452013? The heinous attack on test subject group 32452013 that I have been told decimated their ranks and left only the progenitor of test subject group 32452013 alive to carry on with our experiment and to help complete our mission successfully."

"Sir, 2nd Under Prime Lieutenant Commander Zeem has been derelict in his duty by not bringing this issue to my attention!" Lieutenant Commander Jol whined, as he glared at his underling.

"Captain Xarr, if I may interject?" 2nd Under Prime Lieutenant Commander Zeem interrupted.

"What is it Lieutenant Commander Zeem?" Captain Xarr demanded harshly, glaring at both of his subordinate officers.

"It is true that only the progenitor of test subject group 32452013 is still alive; however that is only because of the swift action taken by me during the attack of the pre-extinction bipedal carnivorous creatures," the subordinate Lieutenant Commander boasted.

"What swift action would that be?" demanded the Captain once more, the look on his face telegraphing an insistence on a swift and concise answer.

"Well Captain Xarr, while I was diligently observing the movements of many of the test subject groups down on the planet, and monitoring the activities of the beasts that had been released onto different regions of the planet from all of the other Annunaki ships assigned to your fleet.

I noticed a small drove of the pre-extinction bipedal carnivorous creatures that Lieutenant Commander Jol had inserted the *proper* microchips into and *supposedly* correctly calibrated them for the particular assignment in which we are scrutinizing at the moment.

They were seemingly driving themselves on their own initiative toward the test subject group in question, while ignoring many of the control subject groups within their immediate scope, which I found to be very odd behavior considering that the animals were *allegedly* programmed to only attack groups of control subjects.

Being aware of the possible interaction that might take place between the two groups if they were to meet, and the actions that would need to be taken under such circumstances to curtail any calamity as a result of both groups colliding. I ascertained that any decision to rectify the matter was well above my personal pay grade.

So with all of the factors in mind, I made a concerted effort to appraise Lieutenant Commander Jol of the situation unfolding on the planet's surface," the gloating 2nd Under Prime Lieutenant Commander answered.

"And what exactly was Lieutenant Commander Jol's response?" the Captain inquired angrily.

"Captain Xarr, after repeated attempts to contact Lieutenant Commander Jol, and numerous inquiries as to his whereabouts on the ship, I received no response at all from Lieutenant Commander Jol.

Later however, the scuttlebutt around the ship was that he was busy cavorting with the gynandromorph that calls itself, I mean herself Patty," 2nd Under Prime Lieutenant Commander Zeem answered, smirking at Lieutenant Commander Jol.

"That is a complete falsification Captain Xarr, nobody tried to contact me. It is true that I was on deck sixty-nine with the gynandromorphs, but I was not cavorting with them, I was administering their medicine to them. And the one that calls herself, I mean itself Patty was giving me a hard time as usual, and at the same time to use one of the planet's more popular vernaculars, *creeping me out*.

I mean have you seen that gynandromorph? Yikes!" Lieutenant Commander Jol cajoled adamantly in his defense, as he denied Lieutenant Commander Zeem's statement while trying to be as convincing as he possibly could.

"That is what they all say when they get caught Captain Xarr, deny, deny, deny," Lieutenant Commander Zeem responded quickly, still gloating.

"Indeed they do Lieutenant Commander Zeem, indeed they do," Captain Xarr agreed.

"Well Captain Xarr, as I was unable to retrieve any guidance from my immediate superior and as time was at a premium. I had no other choice but to take it upon myself to try to salvage what was left of this portion of our mission, and save the remnants of the test subject group 32452013 if there was still time enough to make that goal possible. That is if there was any remnants of the test subject group left to save after having to waste so much time endeavoring to hunt down Lieutenant Commander Jol as he clandestinely cavorted with that gynandromorph on deck 69." Lieutenant Commander Zeem eagerly explained to his Captain.

"I have noticed a flair for the dramatic in your story of Lieutenant Commander Jol's incompetence," Captain Xarr noted suspiciously.

"Yes Captain Xarr," Lieutenant Commander Zeem admitted. "However, in this case Lieutenant Commander Jol's actions, or should I say inaction is rather dramatic."

"Just make sure that your flair does not border on fabrication Lieutenant Commander, or one of the indoctrinating persecution chambers will have your name above the door, minus your rank. Is that clear Lieutenant Commander Zeem?" Captain Xarr asked, as a slight smile crept onto his face.

"Yes sir, Captain Xarr, perfectly clear."

As Lieutenant Commander Zeem answered his superior, he thought.

"If the real truth were ever known, I would be spending the rest of my miserable existence on a maximum security hard labor penal colony planet somewhere in the Qualone Nebula sector, and that is after a very long stent as a VIP guest of the Annunaki Confederation where I would be occupying my own private indoctrinating persecution chamber just as Captain Xarr had alluded to."

******

The *real truth*, as 2nd Under Prime Lieutenant Commander Zeem had aptly put it, was a fact that he had conveniently left out of his discourse. Which was that he had taken it upon himself as part of his plan of ascension, to secretly readjust the genetic differentiation microchips in a small gaggle of the bipedal predators sometime after Lieutenant Commander Jol had them released onto the planet, making sure that they could be traced back to Lieutenant Commander Jol using a remote control mechanism onboard the ship.

This nefariously devised readjustment ultimately caused the attack on as they are referred to by the alien beings, as the test subject group 32452013.

The planned attack was meant to discredit his superior Lieutenant Commander Jol and cause him to be replaced as second in command of the starship by… the one and only… 2nd Under Prime Lieutenant Commander Zeem.

Unfortunately for Jack, his family was thereby inadvertently and unsympathetically sacrificed as collateral damage in the process.

******

"But Captain, he's lying, *can't you tell* by looking at his face?" Lieutenant Commander Jol implored, as he noticeably dropped the authoritarian military protocol and the linguistic dialect peculiar to the specific region within the Anunnaki Confederation and surrounding quadrants.

Captain Xarr ignored the blatant lapse in Anunnaki military protocol for the second time, and the lack of regionalism in the speech patterns within the insubordinate plea from Lieutenant Commander Jol.

In his mind, the Lieutenant Commander's appeal was a pathetic sign of weakness, a trait that he had never tolerated in any of his officers, and he wasn't about to start now.

"Go on Lieutenant Commander Zeem, what did you do after you decided to take matters into your own hands?" the Captain asked, still glaring at Lieutenant Commander Jol.

"Captain Xarr, by the time I had made repeated attempts to receive orders from Lieutenant Commander Jol on the matter at hand and received no satisfactory results, the pre-extinction bipedal carnivorous creatures were almost upon test subject group 32452013, and the group had not yet seen the animals approaching.

In the time it took me to acquire the proper coordinates, and to descend a survival team equipped

56

with the appropriate paraphernalia to successfully complete the task of saving test subject group 32452013, all but one of the members were already dead.

The remaining member, the progenitor of the group, was placing himself in grave jeopardy in what would have surely been a futile attempt to seek revenge upon his group's attackers that would have certainly resulted in his death also.

The descended survival team quickly put the lone survivor into a syncope trance and exterminated the pre-extinction bipedal carnivorous creature that had annihilated the other members of his group, and also put down all of the other reptilian carnivores in the general area of test subject group 32452013.

Then as per directive P2134, the survival team transformed the scene of the incident to depict a contrived falsehood that was derived from the facts that the survivor would remember from before the syncope trance was initiated, and would recall after his consciousness was reinstituted." Lieutenant Commander Zeem recounted in detail.

"Has the progenitor of the now demised test subject group 32452013 any recollection of the events that took place?" Captain Xarr asked, his unrelenting harsh stare remained fixed on Lieutenant Commander Jol.

"Captain Xarr, the progenitor's only recollection is that of the fact that the pre-extinction bipedal carnivorous creatures attacked without warning and with malice aforethought, *most likely due to the miscalculated settings in the microchip implants*, and that their premeditated massacre left his family traveling along another plane of existence somewhere in the vast reaches of the unknown cosmos," the 2nd Lieutenant Commander answered.

"So Lieutenant Commander Zeem, am I to surmise that during the time that you claim to have tried to contact Lieutenant Commander Jol, a claim in which he tenaciously denies I might add. And while you were addressing the problem that arose due to the malfunctioning implanted microchips, that Lieutenant Commander Jol was cavorting with the gynandromorph named Patty on deck 69?" Captain Xarr demanded an answer, as he slammed his fist down on the arm of his command seat.

"Not exactly Captain Xarr, the genetic differentiation microchips that were implanted in the earther's prehistoric beasts were not malfunctioning, they were *mis*-programmed. Although maybe a more precise analogy is that they were *dis*-programmed.

Dis-programmed by a staff officer that was more receptive to the needs of a nymphomaniacal gynandromorph named Patty, than to the needs of our mission," Lieutenant Commander Zeem clarified, as he once more smirked at Lieutenant Commander Jol with a look on his face of one who could be smelling one of his *own* farts.

The Captain nonchalantly leaned back in his command chair and looked at both of the lieutenants for a moment, and with a smug look on his face, he then asked.

"Lieutenant Commander Jol, do you remember when the test subject group 32452013 was facing the overwhelming numbers of control subjects, and I told you that I didn't come half way across this galaxy, all the way to the Saxfox Major constellation, leave my female companion and our off springs, spend the last three Kronal sections setting up this *experiment* on this ugly green and blue rock, just to see test subject group 32452013 eliminated prematurely?"

"Yes Captain Xarr, I do remember that statement," Lieutenant Commander Jol answered, thinking that the temperature control setting on the bridge of the mother ship had been raised to an uncomfortable level, as beads of perspiration formed on his brow. "However Captain, technically test subject group 32452013 has not been prematurely eliminated, the progenitor of test subject group 32452013 is still alive, you said so yourself."

To address an Annunaki *superior* officer by only their rank was a grievous breach in the standard military edict, however, once again Captain Xarr seemingly chose to ignore the blatant lapse in Anunnaki military protocol.

"Lieutenant Commander Jol I think I was wrong about you," Captain Xarr said as he smiled in an irritatingly smug and conceited way.

"Yes Captain Xarr," Lieutenant Commander Jol answered once more, feeling a sense of relief knowing that he had violated a stringent rule of the Annunaki military and apparently gotten away with it.

"Do you also remember when I told you that under my tutelage you just might make it to the rank of Sub-prime Lieutenant Commander one of these days?"

"Yes, Captain Xarr," Lieutenant Commander Jol answered enthusiastically, as panic and blind fear caused the delusion of wishful thinking to encompass his thoughts, and he now naively anticipated what he believed to be a long overdue promotion.

The smirk quickly left Captain Xarr's face as he abruptly stood up and shouted.

"Guards, take Lieutenant Commander Jol into custody!"

The false enthusiasm quickly drained from the Lieutenant Commander's very being, like air being released from an overly inflated balloon.

As quickly as Lieutenant Commander Jol's dreams of promotion were ripped to shreds by his Captain's voice, they were immediately replaced by a queasy feeling in his stomach and visions of the reality of what was to surely become his very painful future.

As the soon to be *former* second in command stood quivering and weak-kneed in the firm grasp of the ship's security guards, he could feel his feces liquefy within his small intestine and his sphincter muscle controlling his rectum involuntarily flex several times before relaxing.

The bridge crew grimaced and moaned as they heard gurgling and squirting sounds emanating from the direction of Lieutenant Commander Jol, as diarrhea ran down the inside of both of his legs and quickly filled his boots, in essence, he had shit down both legs.

"2nd Under Prime Lieutenant Commander Zeem!" Captain Xarr shouted, as he again sat back in his command seat.

"Yes, Captain Xarr," 2nd Under Prime Lieutenant Commander Zeem answered briskly, springing to attention.

"You are no longer 2nd Under Prime Lieutenant Commander, you will take former Lieutenant

Commander Jol's station and rank as 1st Under Prime Lieutenant Commander. Is that clear Lieutenant Commander Zeem?"

"Clear, Captain Xarr," answered the gloating and newly advanced officer, realizing that his nefarious plan had come to fruition.

Glaring at, and also smelling the now shit stained former *number two* (no pun intended, of course now he was really #2), the ship's Captain ordered.

"Guards, take *Private* Jol to the indoctrinating persecution chamber in Bay 5, and inform the persecuting officer in charge that a senior medical aid is to be assigned to him to prevent any premature demise on his behalf. Is my order understood?"

"Indeed Captain Xarr!" the guards answered in unison, as they both snapped to attention as well, still holding the now *Private* Jol in their vise-like iron grips.

"Then proceed, and get that stinking incompetent out of my sight, unless you would like to join him in the chamber for his indoctrination and persecution?"

"No, Captain Xarr!" the guards replied in unison once more, as they hurriedly escorted the soiled and miasmatic Private from the bridge of the mother ship and out of the view of its commander, being careful to avoid stepping in the puddle of anal expulsion left by the former Lieutenant Commander.

Captain Xarr turned to his still gloating subordinate and gave the newly promoted officer his first order as 1st Under Prime Lieutenant Commander.

"Lieutenant Commander Zeem, recall *all* of the pre-extinction bipedal carnivorous creatures and reset their genetic differentiation chips to the proper settings, and keep them aboard their respective transport ships until further notice.

And keep in mind Lieutenant Commander, the indoctrinating persecution chamber in Bay 5 is our largest chamber, and still has room for several more incompetent crew members if you so choose to join your former superior."

"Yes Captain Xarr!" the newly appointed Lieutenant Commander answered. "I mean no Captain Xarr!"

"And Lieutenant Commander Zeem, get someone up here to clean up that mess, it seems that Private Jol has leaked some of his inner being out of his boots and onto my deck."

"Yes Captain Xarr, I will see to it immediately."

"See to it that you do Lieutenant Commander, Private Jol's miasma is beginning to give me a headache."

"Aye Aye Captain," the new Lieutenant Commander responded loudly.

"Oh, and Lieutenant Commander Zeem!"

"Yes, Captain Xarr?"

"If I hear, or if I hear of, even one of the crew referring to the bridge of my ship as the poop deck, I will have them, one of the gynandromorphs housed on deck 69, and *you,* drawn and quartered, and I will have all of your spines disassembled geometrically, and not necessarily in that order.

Is that clear Lieutenant Commander Zeem?"

"Perfectly clear Captain Xarr!" the Lieutenant Commander shouted, feeling *his own* sphincter muscle controlling *his own* rectum begin to involuntarily pulsate then relax, as he felt the desperate act of unintentional defecation knocking at his back door as well.

"One more thing Lieutenant Commander," Captain Xarr noted, with a solemn and scrutinizing gaze.

"Yes, Captain Xarr," Lieutenant Commander Zeem answered, feeling his sphincter muscle now beginning to palpitate.

"If you ever find yourself derelict in your duty by not bringing *any* issue to *my* attention, you'll find yourself being derelict of everything except for screaming agony for next fifty or so Zytor cycles. Do you understand?" the Captain cautioned, spewing his warning with a maniacal rectum twisting stare.

"Indeed Captain Xarr," Lieutenant Commander Zeem answered in a high-pitched squeaky voice, as he felt the muscles in his throat contract in conjunction with his sphincter, and a small amount of liquefied feces fluxing out of his flexing hemorrhoidal anal canal.

THAT WAS THEN, THIS IS NOW

"Son-of-a-bitch, another hot day in the Texas panhandle, I need to find a vehicle with working air conditioning," I thought, as I walked at a slower pace down south Georgia St. in Amarillo, sweating like a two-hundred dollar whore on buck night.

After having lost yet another vehicle during a sneak attack from a small gang of roving road warriors, and barely escaping with my miserable life, which is more than I can say for most of them, I again found myself hoofing it along the Texas streets in search of yet another means of transportation.

Seeing a small storefront sign in the distance with crossed pistols painted on it, I made my way toward the building that it was promoting, quickening my pace with every step.

"What have we here? The first gun shop I've encountered that isn't surrounded by a bunch of eaters, I hate those bastards," I whispered to myself. "Now's my big chance to pick up a silencer for my M-4 and maybe a couple of other choice items while I'm at it."

The door to the gun shop had been broken open signaling that I wasn't the first intruder to enter the former business, and it looked like whoever had been here before me wasn't much of a so called "gun-nut".

From the condition the place had been left in, the earlier trespassers were most likely a couple of amateurs or group of such that had little or no knowledge of firearms, but in their panic to stay alive during the onset of the uprising of the undead, had ventured into this gun store in search of some lethal means by which to defend themselves, which they up until Armageddon came knocking at their door, had not felt the need to become acquainted with.

The shop had been ransacked but most of the inventory was still intact, not on the racks or in the display cases, but scattered all over the floor.

More than likely a few guns were missing and probably some of the ammunition too, but for the most part, it looked as though the business' inventory was still inside the store, it had just been haphazardly tossed all over the place as if whoever had done it was in a big hurry to just grab something, and not too choosy about what it was that they were taking.

There were still a number of guns lying on the floor, and the original burglars had left many boxes of ammo with them as well, ripe for the taking. You just had to dig through the mess to find what you needed.

My main concern at this time was not to salvage more firearms or ammunition, it was to secure a silencer for my rife, or find a pistol that would accommodate a suppressor, or both if I could manage it.

Kicking aside the abandoned accessories such as holsters, cleaning kits, and other assorted firearm related articles that covered much of the gun shop's floor, I was lucky enough to locate a Beretta 92 with a threaded barrel that was made for what I was looking for. I crammed the pistol in my belt and continued to search for a silencer for my long gun and my new Beretta.

Beneath a pile of broken glass from one of the display cabinets, I found one of the silencers that I had been searching for.

Before the end of the world as we knew it, the display case had housed several suppressors of different makes and models that were manufactured for a variety of different guns, rifles and pistols alike.

There before me was an M-4 sound suppressor with a dark earth finish. It didn't match the color of my 5.56mm rifle, but color coordination wasn't my highest priority at that moment.

I picked up the newfound asset and stuffed it into my pocket, and continued to dig through the pile of broken glass which was mixed with other goodies that had little or no interest to me at the time, looking for a silencer for my new 9mm pistol.

As I perused the stockpile of what would have been ill gotten gains a couple of years ago, I heard a noise coming from outside the front door. I knew that it definitely wasn't the police or a security guard, as the laws that had been legislated regarding looting no longer applied, and even if they did apply, there was nobody around to enforce them, at least nobody that wouldn't get their head blown *clean off* for trying.

"Probably eaters," I muttered, as I reached for my tomahawk without stopping my search for the elusive 9mm suppressor.

Suddenly, the noise got louder as the door to the shop was pulled open farther; however, I still could not see anyone (or anything) in the doorway.

I was too far from the door for my combat hatchet to be of any use to me if the noise was being made by anything besides eaters, such as someone with a gun.

Quickly, and none to silently, I dropped my tomahawk to the floor and raise my rifle.

I flipped the safety lever onto *semi*, and I slid my finger onto the trigger of the weapon and gently put pressure on it.

Still crouching down I whispered.

"Who's there?"

Waiting for a reply and not receiving one, I whispered again with more authority.

"Who's there?"

"It's me, don't shoot, or stab, or hit, or whatever, don't hurt me, I'm not dead," a man's voice whispered back.

"You're not dead yet, come out into the open so I can see you or you will be," I answered back, aiming my M-4 at the doorjamb knowing that my rifle could easily shoot through it.

"Ok, I'm coming in there, I don't want any trouble."

"You won't get any if you don't start any," I said. "So let's go, come out where I can see you, and keep your hands where I can see them too."

A shadow cast by the noonday sun first inched its way into the doorway, and then the silhouette of a man holding a rifle in his hand took its place.

The man was holding the gun by the end of its barrel, so there was no need to have him drop it and risk the sound of it hitting the floor, or worse, accidentally discharging and attracting more unwanted company.

Both of his hands were well away from the weapon's trigger, and I knew I could easily kill him long before he could even get the gun aimed at me.

However, if he had chosen that method of self-destruction, I was willing to risk the sound of an *intentional* discharging of my firearm attracting that unwanted company that might be in the area.

"Step in here so I can get a better look at you mister," I ordered, still pointing my gun at the man, with the mindset to stitch him up if he even looked at me sideways.

The man took several steps inside the shop and stopped.

"I'm just looking for some ammo, I'll take what I need and leave," he said, as he held up his own M-4 type rifle in his right hand. "Like I said before, I don't want no trouble."

The man looked haggard, and his age seemed to be somewhere around his late fifties, but looking through the dirt and grime on his face and the scruffy salt and pepper beard it was a little hard to tell.

He was dressed in blue jeans with a big rodeo belt buckle and a dirty white Stetson hat. All of which went well with the cowboy shirt he was wearing that was reminiscent of something that Randolph Scott might have worn in one of his western movies.

"Like I said before, don't start any trouble and you won't get any trouble," I reiterated to the man, still slightly pressing on the trigger of my M-4 which was now aimed at the man's head.

I really didn't give a shit about whether or not I needed to kill him. It didn't matter to me if he started trouble or not, I'd just as soon blow his head off his shoulders as look at him.

The only thing that was stopping me at the time was that I didn't want to take the chance of drawing a bunch of zombies into the shop before I had found what I was looking for.

By this time in my journey I was more than a little skeptical, and my attitude was completely cynical.

"Are you completely out of ammo?" I asked suspiciously.

"Totally dry, thought I might find some in here," the man answered.

Well Mama *Doom* didn't raise a total fool, and I wasn't about to take this man's word for anything at this time. I'd known him for every bit of two minutes and would kill him in a heartbeat if he even looked cross-eyed at me, zombies or no zombies.

"Put your weapon down on the floor and turn around," I ordered. "And do it quietly."

"I told you I'm out of ammo, and this rifle is the only weapon I have," he insisted.

"Shut your trap, drop the gun, and turn around. You've got three seconds before I separate your head from your neck, two... one..."

The sound of the man's rifle hitting the floor echoed off the empty back wall of the gun shop as he turned and faced the front door.

"Okay, okay, I'm turning around," he said, as he raised his hands in the air.

"Failure to follow simple directions, strike one," I whispered, glaring at the man. "If that noise draws eaters in here, you're the first one I'm going to kill."

"You said to drop the gun," the man retorted, with a panicked sound in his voice.

"I'm going to come over and search you," I told him. "If you make another sound, or if you as much as even flinch, I'll drop you like third period French, do you get me?"

"Yes sir," the man answered, as he interlocked his fingers on top of his head without a directive from me.

As I patted him down for any hidden weapons he might have had on his person, I asked him.

"What's your name mister?"

"Jason, my name is Jason Bla..."

I interrupted him.

"Last names don't mean *dick* anymore, most of the people I've run into don't live long enough for me to bother remembering their last names anyway. So save your breath Jason."

Having Jason at a great disadvantage, and after having found no more weapons on him, and after checking to make sure that his gun was as empty as he claimed, I thought that it might be fun to mess with him a little.

After all, the noise of the dropped rifle had not attracted any eaters, and fun was a commodity that was not very plentiful during these arduous times.

"My name is Jack… Jack Doom!" I said smiling, divulging my old Marine Corps moniker to him and waiting for his response.

Given that I had just told him that last names didn't mean *dick* anymore, and then proceeding to tell him mine, well kind of, I expected him to project an air of confusion, and maybe stutter something indiscernible in kind.

However, his reaction to my name was anything but what I had expected it would be.

"Ja... ack Do... oom?" he stammered, as he turned toward me.

"Yes, Jack Doom," I answered. "Do you have a problem with that?"

"No sir, not at all Mr. Do... oom," he stammered once more.

"Then why are you acting so scared?"

"It's just that I've heard of you, heard about some of the things you've done, some of the things that you might do."

******

Jack had never met this man before in his life, and nobody had called him Jack Doom since he was serving overseas in the Marine Corps. So for someone to say that they've heard of him could mean only one thing. Someone he had been in combat with had talked to this man, and that person could only be the Sarge.

******

With the smile now completely gone from my face, I insisted the man give me some answers.

"Where did *you* hear the name Jack Doom?" I queried, glaring at Jason once more.

"From a man I met a few weeks ago."

"What man?" I demanded.

"Just a man, I run into people every once in a while. I mostly try not to get killed by them, and I try not to have to kill them either, although it doesn't always work out that way. I mean the part about not having to kill

them, not the part about me not getting killed by them."
Jason began to meander.

"I figured that out all by myself, I'm kind of smart that way," I told him.

"I'm just trying to be clear Mr. Doom."

"Well Jason, what did this man look like?" I asked, sensing that I had a lead on the ever-elusive Sarge's whereabouts.

"Well, he was kind of stocky, and he had red hair... and he was traveling with a girl," Jason answered.

"What did this girl look like?"

"She was a blonde, nice to look at, even though she had a black eye when I saw her.

I still wouldn't mind wallowing naked on top of her if you know what I mean," Jason admitted, as he raised his left eyebrow several times rapidly.

"Yeah, I know what you mean," I answered, nodding.

"And she carried a .22 rifle, looked almost like our guns, and she called him Ron."

"Did he have a name for her," I asked, now trying to get the vision of what I imagined Beth's naked body to look like out of my mind (but not trying too *hard*, no pun intended).

Jason put his fingers to his chin and thought about my question for a moment, and then answered.

"He called her Bev, no wait, he called her Beth, that was it, Beth. I mean when he wasn't calling her *you little bitch*, or *you fucking whore,* or something like that."

"When did you run into those two?" I asked.

"It was about a month ago I think, it's a little hard to keep track of time these days, but I think it was four or

72

five weeks ago," Jason answered, feeling a little more relaxed now as I had yet to kill him.

"Where?" I inquired, still glaring at Jason, but now mostly just for show.

"East of here, somewhere in Oklahoma," was Jason's answer.

"Somewhere in Oklahoma? Where in Oklahoma?" I asked angrily, and not at all just for show.

"It was just outside Oklahoma City, near a little place called Shawnee. There's a compound there made up of a bunch of shipping container stacked on top of each other and laid out in a square so that the guards posted on top can see down on every side," Jason answered, fearing that he'd upset me (and he had).

"Are they still there?"

"Probably not, nobody stays there for very long," Jason answered.

"Did they say where they were going?" I asked, still pointing my weapon at him.

There was no doubt that Jason was afraid of me, so I saw no reason not to exploit his fear for the benefit of what I now saw as my mission in life (the painful death of my old *friend* the Sarge).

"They didn't say where they were headed and I didn't ask. But my guess is that they were going to go east, because they hung around with a bunch that kept talking about joining a band of survivors that's hold up somewhere they called the *Badlands of Indiana*, even though people kept telling them to beware of the Indiana Badlands.

Some guy they called *The Caucasian* is supposedly the leader of that group."

"The Caucasian in Indiana huh, sounds like a really fun crowd," I said chuckling, figuring that I had Jason completely cowed, but still not letting my guard down.

"If the Shawnee site is so safe and secure, why would anyone want to leave there and go to a place called the *Badlands*?" I asked suspiciously.

"That compound in Shawnee is just a way station, the people in charge only let you stay there for a few weeks tops, and then they send you packing, they need the space for the next group of weary travelers that might happen by," Jason answered, forcing a smile to his face. "By the end of a few weeks they usually have all of your assets, you know, anything that you've got that's valuable, and then they don't want to be host to a bunch of freeloading squatters that want to take up permanent residents. You know, new arrivals have new stuff that might be valuable. So out with the old and in with the new."

"So are you saying that they steal your stuff and then kick you out?" I asked.

"No, no stealing is aloud, and you better not get caught stealing, especially from the compound owners. People lose their things gambling on fights or whatever, whoring with women… or men, and any number of things that the compound has to offer. But however they lose their stuff, most leave with a lot less than they arrived with," Jason answered.

"And what if somebody doesn't want to leave, then what?"

"I don't know, I was only there for about two weeks and then I left on my own."

I had gleaned all the information I was going to get out of Jason, so I smiled and told him.

"You can put your hands down now, that is if you're going to stay calm and not do anything stupid?"

"I'm not going to do anything stupid to you Mr. Doom, you'd kill me, like I said before, I heard of some of the things that you've done."

"Good, because here's the way I see it. Either you're with me, or you're against me, nothing in between," I told him, as I lowered my gun from his face.

"I'm with you Mr. Doom, I truly am."

"Then stop calling me Mr. Doom, my name is Jack," I said still smiling, although still ready to kill Jason anytime at the drop of a hat. Any hat!

"Okay Mr. Doom, I... I mean Jack," Jason said nervously, still not ready to accept the fact that I wasn't going to kill him where he stood.

"Relax Jason. If I were going to kill you, you'd already be dead," I said, smiling again as I lied to his face.

"Now since we're going to be all friendly like, you can help me find a suppressor for this gun," I told him, pulling out the Beretta that I had stuffed in my belt, and again pointing a gun at his face.

"Sure thing Jack," Jason answered, as he began to nervously look around the room, not realizing that my new Beretta was not loaded.

After searching Jason and knowing that he had only the M-4 type rife as his only weapon, I suggested to him that he might consider grabbing another gun, since after all, he was in a gun shop.

"You could probably use another gun Jason; I prefer a 9mm pistol. Ammo is much more plentiful and it's lighter than the .45 stuff. And 9mm does an adequate job on the eaters, and anybody else for that matter."

"What's that weird looking gun you've got strapped on your back, I've never seen anything like that before. It is a gun isn't it?" Jason asked.

"This was my youngest son's carbine, it's a 9mm rifle, it's called a Sub-2000 and uses Glock mags," I told him. "It looks weird because it folds in half for transport. Pretty *zoot* uh?"

I couldn't resist showing Jason the carbine that Jacob had used to kill so many zombies, so I laid my M-4 down on the floor beside me and pulled the rifle off my back.

Because of the way the Sub-2000 was designed, you could carry it folded, with a fully loaded 33 round magazine inserted into its magazine well, and that's exactly how I was transporting it.

Like I mentioned earlier in the apocalypse, "Mama Doom didn't raise a total fool".

Jason had yet to make any sudden moves to alarm me, or show me in any way that he was a danger to me (that's why he was still alive), and I wanted to keep it that way. So I figured another little scare, just to keep him honest might be called for in this case.

I took the small carbine by the pistol grip of the weapon with my right hand, I released the locking latch with my left hand and flipped the barrel up and forward, snapping it into place. Then I twisted the gun to the left and I slapped the bolt handle down feeding a round into the chamber of the carbine.

The whole operation from the time I had the rifle in my hands, to the time I pointed the loaded weapon at Jason's face (again), took less than three seconds from start to finish.

"That's very impressive, but could you point that thing somewhere else?" Jason asked politely, not sure if I was going to pull the trigger or not. "Pointing guns at me seems to be becoming a habit of yours."

"Like I said before, if I were going to shoot you, you'd already be shot," I answered smiling, as I once more committed willful perjury.

******

As Jack leaned down to pick up his tomahawk, he noticed a silencer lying under it. He had inadvertently dropped his combat hatchet right on top of the very suppressor that he had been searching for before Jason had entered the shop.

******

"Here's what I've been looking for," I said, as I ripped the package open that held the silencer.

"And here's what I've been looking for," Jason announced, as he waved a box of ammo over his head.

******

The two men spent the next hour fitting their firearms with sound suppressors, and gathering ammunition for their guns. Jack kept a close eye on

77

Jason as they did so, still not trusting the man he had just met.

As the two men worked side by side, Jason's curiosity finally got the best of him and he just had to ask Jack the question that had been eating at him (no pun intended).

******

"Hey Jack, I don't mean to pry, but why are you so interested in that guy Sarge and his girl friend?"

"I never said Beth was his girlfriend."

"Come on Jack, a guy traveling around the country in the middle of an apocalypse with a good looking female, she's his girlfriend, *one way or another*," Jason stated, as a maniacal smile crept onto his face.

"Maybe?" I said. "I guess I'll find out when I catch up to them."

"She's not your girlfriend is she? Did the Sarge run off with your girlfriend, and now you're going after them to get her back?" Jason asked excitedly.

"Beth has nothing to do with it, at least not yet anyway, I hardly know her, so calm down and keep your dick in your pants," I answered, thinking that Jason was going to need a cold shower if he kept thinking like that.

"So if Beth isn't your girlfriend, and you're not chasing after them to get her back, why are you chasing after them?"

"I don't remember saying that I was *chasing* after anybody."

"I saw the look in your eyes while you were asking me about them, you're chasing after them all right, and I wouldn't want to be this Sarge of yours when you catch up to them," Jason said, smiling even bigger now.

"You must have misread the look I was giving you. That was the look I use when I'm trying to decide whether or not to kill someone like you." I said smirking, while watching Jason's smile fade away.

"The Sarge is an old friend, we fought together in the sand box, and we met up some time ago here in Texas and then got separated. I'm just trying to find him and get back together again," I told Jason.

I certainly didn't want to tell Jason the truth, which was what he had already guessed. So I told him a half truth and hoped that he would drop the subject.

My dealings with the Sarge, past or future was none of his business, and if we did end up traveling together, when we caught up to the Sarge and Beth I didn't want him saying something to either one of them that might give away my true intentions.

My answer satisfied Jason's curiosity, at least for the moment, but I was still left wondering why I was bothering to tell this perfect stranger anything.

As we scavenged up as much of the new supplies as we could carry, I had a thought.

"I wonder if Jason has a vehicle, he never did mention how he got here from Oklahoma?"

Jason now was sporting his original rifle, and two 9mm pistols he had appropriated from the gun store, all with silencers attached, and several boxes of ammo for each of the three guns.

"That's quite a load to carry, it's almost as much as I've got," I said. "You wouldn't happen to have some kind of a vehicle parked near here would you?"

"I have an old pick-up truck parked a few stores down the block, I didn't want to just drive up here and stop in front of the gun shop not knowing if anyone was inside," Jason answered, seeming not to understand what I was getting at.

"Well, my ride ended up down the road a piece with three flat tires, it was a nice ride but spare tires were a little hard to come by at the time, so I had to leave it behind," I told him, not bothering to mention exactly how my ride had ended up with the flat tires, or the body count that I had left in the vicinity of the vehicle. "Maybe we could ride together in your truck?"

"There's nothing that I'd like better Jack, but we're going in opposite directions," Jason answered, oblivious to my hint.

"No we're not, I'm going to Oklahoma to find the Sarge, aren't you coming with me?" I asked, now staring at Jason with a blank look on my face.

Before Jason had a chance to answer my question we heard a noise coming from outside the building.

"Quiet! Eaters," I whispered, pointing to the front door.

I hoped that it was a couple of picaroon zombies and not a pack of feral dogs on the prowl that was making the noise. But I'd take the dogs over a raptor or two.

"It's been a while since I've seen any of the dead walking around, that's a good sign, right," Jason concluded.

"I've noticed that the lack of eaters in a given area usually means that there's a pack of feral dogs nearby, or worse," I informed him as I slowly made my way toward the front of the shop.

"Feral dogs? That doesn't sound good," Jason declared, as he too moved in the direction of the front door.

As I approached the door, I could see two mutts running south down the street, then a moment later another three dogs passed by the doorway on the other side of the street, all heading south.

"Stay still," I order Jason. "They haven't seen us yet."

Being fortunate enough not to have crossed paths with any of the feral dog population as of yet, Jason should have done as I ordered and froze in his tracks.

However, never having seen a pack of the roaming curs, and not realizing the danger that these vicious mongrels posed, he continued to walk forward to my position.

Strike two!

"Freeze you dumb-ass, you'll get us both killed," I barked in my best drill instructor whisper as I set my M-4 to full auto.

But it was too late, a straggler that had allowed the main pack to advance a couple of blocks ahead of it, had caught a glimpse of Jason's movement as it passed the doorway.

The malicious K-9 abruptly skidded to a halt, and turned its full attention to the doorway of the gun shop. Then, in a split second it bolted toward Jason and leaped into the air with the intention of implanting it's fangs into my new found partner's face.

Standing only a few feet from Jason and the malevolent attacking dog, I leveled my suppressed M-4 at the lunging crossbreed and pulled the trigger.

At somewhere between 600 and 800 rounds per minute, my rifle spit out a fusillade of full metal-jacketed projectiles of the 5.56 variety into the attacking animal in mid-flight.

The effect of such a myriad of bullets hitting the beast almost simultaneously was to slam the vile critter against the doorjamb just inches from Jason's face, killing it instantly.

Apparently, Jason still hadn't learned his lesson; the dog I had just killed had barely hit the ground when Jason sprang out the front door of the gun shop to see where the other dogs had gone.

Strike three!

"Look, I think they're after that group of dead!" he shouted, pointing at a small clutch of zombies in the distance.

"Better them than us," I whispered back to him, as I pulled him back inside the shop by the collar of his shirt. "I've never seen any live dogs and eaters together, but in this crazy world who knows, there's a first time for everything I guess."

At this point, with three strikes under his belt, I realized that Jason was a little too high strung to be traveling with me. He didn't seem to be able to follow simple instructions (like stop moving), and immediately after almost being ripped apart by a feral dog, he had jumped out into the open and started shouting.

Fortunately for us, the main pack of dogs were busy a few blocks away running around doing whatever it is that feral dogs do when they're not attacking *me*, and they didn't hear him yelling at the top of his lungs.

It was only a matter of time before his antics would get him killed, and I didn't want to be his conjoined twin when it happened.

I felt that in the light of what had just taken place, I had only two options to choose from.

Option number one (my preferred option), I could ask Jason nicely for the keys to his truck, and then send him on his way. I would take his truck and follow the Sarge's and Beth's trail into Oklahoma, and Jason could continue his journey south on foot until he found himself another vehicle, or was torn apart by zombies, feral dogs, or raptors, whichever came first.

Option number two (not my preferred option, but still on the table), I could ask Jason nicely for the keys to his truck, and if he refused, I would kill him and leave his carcass to be torn apart by the zombies, feral dogs, or the raptors, whichever came first. Then I would take his truck and continue to follow the Sarge's and Beth's trail into Oklahoma, while he was slowly being digested by whichever pack of carnivores decided to choke down his dumb ass for lunch.

Whichever option was to be chosen, the choice was going to be solely up to Jason.

I had no intention of presenting his two options to him before the fact. He could choose to cooperate, and allow the Zombie Apocalypse to choose the time, place, and method of his ultimate demise. Or, he could choose not to cooperate, and to die a quick and relatively painless death in Amarillo Texas by my more than capable and willing hand.

Either way was fine with me, but one way or another, I *was* going to take possession of his truck and head into Oklahoma in search of my prey.

"That was pretty stupid of you Jason, first you didn't stay still like I told you to, and then you went outside and started shouting," I asserted, still whispering angrily.

"I just got excited, that's all," he replied. "I didn't mean no harm."

"No, you didn't get excited, what you got was us almost killed," I challenged. "That's all I need, is a letter sent back to my family that reads; *Jack Doom was killed because he befriended an idiot named Jason.*"

Jason had no idea whether any of my family was alive or not, but the curious look on his face when I stated that a letter might be sent to them announcing my premature death, was almost worth the price of admission.

"Letter?" Jason asked curiously.

"Never mind, I need the keys to your truck, hand them over," I sternly ordered.

"That's okay, I don't mind driving," he replied.

"No, it's not okay, you won't be coming with me, give me the keys," I demanded once more, slowly turning my rifle in his direction.

"I don't have the keys, I left them in the truck, take the truck, just don't shoot me Mr. Doom," Jason pleaded, now visibly afraid again.

"I intend to do just that," I said, now pointing my rifle at his chest.

"Th... th... that's fine, y... you take the truck, I... I'll find another truck, or a car, or som... something," Jason maintained, as he began to stammer again.

"I'm glad you see it my way Jason, now let's go get *my* truck, and for your sake when we get there the keys better be in it," I stressed firmly, secretly hoping that he was telling me the truth about the truck's keys.

We cautiously retreated from the gun shop with Jason leading the way. He claimed that his vehicle was only two blocks away, so I allowed him only one knife to fend off any peril that we might encounter along the way, or that he might run into on his way back to the gun store to retrieve his other weapons after I had gone.

"There it is; the primmer gray one parked by the curb."

"As soon as I confirm the keys are in it and it starts, you can go back to the gun shop and pick up the rest of your weapons," I affirmed.

Jason now began to act strangely, turning his head back and forth as if he were looking urgently for something.

I had seen this type of behavior before, in Afghanistan. Some of the Hajji's we had captured had exhibited this type of behavior when they were close to panicking and trying to decide whether to make a break for it or not.

I quickly tossed my paraphernalia into the bed of my new gray truck and glanced inside, and seeing that the ignition had no keys dangling there.

"Son-of-a-bitch Jason, I tried to be nice," I grumbled.

85

At that moment, Jason turned and began to run back toward the gun shop.

"Damn it Jason, I really didn't want to shoot you in the back," I mumbled to myself, as I took aim at Jason's lower spine.

My M-4 let out four quick muffled pops as I pressed the gun's trigger to the rear. My shoulder felt a mild shove from the recoil of the weapon as I watched Jason fall to the sidewalk just yards from me with four bullets in his back.

I had forgotten to put my rifle back into semi-auto mode before shooting Jason, so the quantity of bullets entering his body disjointed his spine on impact, splintering several of his vertebras and severing his spinal column, killing him instantly.

Fearing the smell of blood in the air would hasten the return of the feral dogs, or bring in any wandering zombies, raptors, or worse, Tyrannosaurs that might be patrolling the adjacent streets; I quickly rifled through Jason's pants pockets searching for the keys to my new truck.

"Ah, here they are," I said quietly to myself as I pulled a blood soaked keychain out of the dead man's pocket.

I had killed Jason with a quick twelve-yard volley to his backbone, which had severed his lower spine. As I stood up to walk back to the truck, I flipped the control on my rifle to semi-automatic and pulled the trigger once more, putting a single bullet into Jason's head to prevent him from becoming one of the living dead.

I thought I at least owed him that much, as payment for the truck if for nothing else.

I had searched Jason earlier, and had missed the truck keys, but in my own defense, I was searching him for weapons not for keys.

Upon returning to the pick-up truck, I inserted the key into the ignition and heard the engine turn over, sputter, and then start up.

In moments, I was on the road once again and making good time, I was headed into Oklahoma and back on the trail of the Sarge.

However, as I pushed northeast in the new and unfamiliar ride, I couldn't resist adding two more of the living dead to my tally of felony hit and runs by sideswiping a couple of hitchhiking corpses and sending them spinning clear off the road, and temporally clear of their adopted flies.

At the same time, I managed to do minimal damage to *my* new truck.

As I drove past the city limits sign of Amarillo I increase my score one more time by veering slightly off the road to clip the hips of another unsuspecting pair of zombies, I left them with some exposed broken bones and secreting some of their spoiled juices as they wallowed and twitched in the nearby roadside ditch, hopefully suffering greatly.

I had developed a viable technique for accruing a large number of zombie hit and runs after losing a sweet little ride I had acquired some time ago in west Texas.

After butchering several zombies execution style just outside of Pecos Texas, I ran across a classic car dealership that had a fully restored 1969 Mach 1 Mustang setting in its showroom.

This little gem was maroon with dirty piss-yellow racing stripes and sported a 351 cubic inch Cleveland engine under its flat black pinned down hood. It also had a 4-speed manual transmission along with a posi-traction rear-end and original Goodyear poly-glass tires.

Sweet!

This little honey was faster than a coon dog chasing a bitch in heat. And that's where the problems for me began to surface. My new hotrod brought out the teenage boy in me and I just couldn't resist sticking my toe down the throat of the carburetor every once in a while.

Well, as fate would have it, I was driving way too fast up interstate 20 after checking out one of the countless dead end leads that I had been chasing, this particular one had dried up just east of El Paso.

After stopping for a well-deserved urination station break (I had to take a piss), I had just reinserted my toe back into the carburetor when I spotted an obese male zombie staggering across the freeway and figured I could dust him off with the right front fender of my "Stang" and no one would be the wiser.

I didn't take into consideration that this particular undead hunk of shit was rather new to the world of the walking dead, and its flesh had not decomposed enough to just slide off the bone like a well cooked rack of Louisiana ribs when scraped by my speeding sports car.

When I hit the monster at around 55 M.P.H., I receive a clue rather quickly about the viscosity of the chunky cannibal. It happened when I saw the fender of my vehicle fold up like an accordion, and I heard the right front tire pop as the metal exoskeleton of the car carved its way through the vulcanized rubber surrounding the wheel and sent my speeding childhood wet dream careening into the safety guardrail that lined the side of the road.

It was at that point when I realized that I had hit a newly initiated member of the zombie tribe. When the sickening crunch of the fender rendered no maggots onto the hood or windshield of my car, I knew that this citizen of the dead had not been *undead* long enough to even begin to host the fly larvae that most of its fellow zombies were sponsoring.

Although I had literally knocked the shit right out of the "Mustang Killer" and broken nearly every bone in its flesh seeking body, watching it squirm on the ground in front of me in its shit-smudged trousers did nothing to change the fact that I was again on foot.

After that incident, I decided to change the rules of my felony hit and run quest.

While I would still endeavor to stain the nation's roadways with the entrails of the marauding zombie hordes, I would slow the accosting vehicle down to about 15 miles per hour. Just fast enough to still smack the crap out of the savages and break a few bones, thereby leaving them sloshing around in their own fecal matter and other rotting juices, yet do only token scarring to my ride, lest I end up walking again.

OKLAHOMA IS OK

Six weeks earlier in Shawnee Oklahoma...

It was a cool but not cold evening as the Sarge and Beth sat around their campfire amid the group they had been staying with for the past week.

"Beth, go get me another beer, and then get your ass back over here you little bitch," the half-drunk former sergeant barked, as he crushed an empty beer can and tossed it to the ground. "I had a long hard day out killing those diseased sons-a-bitches, or as Jack's kid called them, *Eaters*.

At any rate, killing those bastards has made me mighty thirsty, so you'll make it quick if you know what's good for you."

"Okay Ron, I'll hurry," Beth said, as she left the campfire and proceeded to fetch the Sarge a beer.

When Beth returned with the beer, she found another woman (also drunk) sitting on the Sarge's lap with her arms wrapped around his neck.

"*Good, maybe he'll sleep with her tonight and quit pestering me, I can only hope,*" Beth thought, tired of fighting off the Sarge's unwanted drunken sexual advances.

"Here's your beer Ron, Jimmy said it's the last one you get tonight, and he sounded kind of pissed."

"What? Now there's a two six-pack limit around here? What the hell?" the Sarge questioned, as he snatched the beer from Beth's hand. "And what's he got to be pissed about? I'm the one that's going to need another beer."

Beth took her seat beside the two groping drunks and pretended to ignore their obvious moans and groans as she watched the Sarge's right hand make its way into the woman's blouse to fondle her left breast.

"I hate to break up your little wrestling match, but before I left to get you a beer, you mentioned Jack's kid, Jacob was the youngest one. Do you think that Jacob and the rest of Jack's family made it out alive?"

Just as Beth spoke the last word of her question, the back of the Sarge's hand that was still warm from the breast he had been coddling, landed across her mouth, knocking her backwards onto the ground and out of her chair.

"I told you never to mention that," the Sarge shouted, as the woman on his lap laughed, not bothering to even make an effort to cover her now completely exposed left tit as she looked down at Beth lying on the ground,.

Getting to her feet, Beth wiped the trickle of blood from her bottom lip onto her sleeve, picked up her chair, and sat back down.

"I'm sorry. It'll never happen again Ron," she pledged, feeling her lower lip swelling as she licked the remaining blood from it.

"It had better not ever happen again, especially while I'm having a well deserved beer and trying to get a little even more well deserved nooky from a lovely little lady like this one," the Sarge bellowed loudly, as he again groped at the inebriated woman who sat on his lap pretending to slap his hands away as if they were two 9th grade school kids having their first sexual escapade.

91

After scolding Beth, the Sarge took the liberty of opening his drunken wrestling partner's blouse wider and totally exposing her naked chest, he salivated over her tits as his warm alcohol laced breath questioned the woman.

"What was your name again darling?" the Sarge slurred, while looking down at the drool that he had just slobbered onto the woman's mammary glands.

"Anna." the half-exposed woman answered smiling, as she watched the Sarge gaze at his saliva as it creped down her breast and dripped off her left nipple.

Beth turned away from the two fondling lushes and stared into the campfire, no longer listening to their alcohol-induced banter.

"Don't worry Ron, I give you my word, it will never ever happen again, because as soon as I find the right people, I'm going to kill you just before I leave with them," Beth thought, as she rubbed her swollen lip before taking a sip of her own beer that she had been hiding from Ron.

******

Before Beth, along with the Sarge, Jack and his family, and the men that were killed on the mission to procure more powerful weapons for their group had left the safety of the YMCA compound and drove their modified school bus to the National Guard Armory. She had been known as somewhat of the resident psychopath, a psychopath that you would definitely want on your side in a fight.

Her petite stature combined with her uncanny prowess with the .22 rifle she wielded, along with many other zombie killing techniques she had mastered, as well as her nerves of steel under fire, were becoming the stuff of legend around the Y.

Her fabled status among the folks at the compound almost rivaled the legendary chronicles of Jack Doom in Iraq and Afghanistan. *Almost* being the key word here.

After abandoning Jack and his family, Beth and the Sarge had returned to their YMCA stronghold only to find it burned out and deserted, with the dead bodies of zombies and many of their friends lying in the hallways torn to pieces and charred beyond recognition.

As they surveyed the sickening carnage, they weren't quite sure what had taken place during their absence.

All they knew for sure was that the building had been burnt from the inside as if gasoline had been poured down the hallways and then ignited, all of the supplies and equipment were ruined, and there were mass casualties consisting of both their fellow comrades and members of the zombie hordes scattered all through the interior of the building.

In addition to the grisly scene of dead bodies everywhere, of course the building was filled with the ever-present undaunted flies, and smoke and fire damage was ubiquitous. On top of that the smell of smoldering rotten corpses, burnt plastic, and gasoline fumes made the stench over powering and the air in the building possibly conducive to short and long term diseases, all and all making the structure unlivable.

With the YMCA rendered no longer fit for human habitation, the two had no choice but to trek back into the zombie abyss.

Beth was now traveling with the Sarge only because she didn't want to be left alone in the middle of the new and dangerous reality that this zombie world offered, and although they had ran across a few small groups of people after leaving Jack and his family; she had not felt comfortable enough with any of them to part with Ron. But now the beatings he was inflicting upon her were becoming more frequent and more severe, so she began to rethink her decision to stay on with him and to continue their pilgrimage together.

However, being the alleged psychopath that she was, she wasn't about to forget the way the Sarge had been treating her, and no matter how long she traveled with the man, or how many times he may have saved her from as he so aptly put it, those *sinister sons-a-bitches*, she was still determined to get even with him sooner or later, one way or another.

******

Barreling (if you can call 29 mph barreling) east on interstate 40, in his gray pick-up truck, Jack see's that the vehicle's fuel gauge is starting to point a little south...

******

94

"I need to stop for gas the next chance I get," I mumbled to myself. "And maybe pick up a map of Oklahoma and the rest of the country too."

About six miles inside the Oklahoma border from Texas, sat the once sleepy little town of Erick Oklahoma. I say once sleepy little town, because like most if not all towns in the country and probably the world, Erick Oklahoma had died in its sleep.

After seeing the sign that signaled a prime spot for collecting a tank full of gasoline was just ahead, I took the next exit ramp off the interstate and pulled a hairy right turn into a truck stop that sat right off the freeway.

"Eaters in the parking lot, I hope that means no feral dogs," I said aloud, as I aimed my truck at the nearest zombie.

A metallic thumping sound vibrated through the truck as a tall slim female member of the rotting dead bounced off the right front fender, scattering maggots across my windshield and disseminating the covey of flies that surrounded feminine homicidal maniac.

"Chalk up another one," I yelled, hoping to attract as many of the undead in the immediate vicinity as I could.

The remaining two zombies in the parking lot were joined by three more that came from around the back of the building. I aimed my now slightly dented truck toward the four that had ambled toward each other and solidified into a pack, and stepped down hard on the gas pedal.

With the accelerator pedal mashed against the floorboard, the truck lurched forward and moved in the direction of the slow moving crowd. I only had about forty yards to gain enough speed to accomplish the maneuver that I had in mind.

By the time I reached the mob of zombies, the truck was traveling at close to thirty miles per hour, and just before running into the maggot-infested corpses, I turned the steering wheel hard to the left and slammed on the brakes. The lightweight rear end of my vehicle began to slide toward the four zombies as I braced for the imminent impact (hopefully a 15 mile per hour impact, the new rule you know).

When the side of the bed of the truck struck the approaching horde of zombies, the result was not exactly what I had intended.

I had hoped that by skidding the side of my vehicle into the group, they would have been mangled to the point that I wouldn't have to deal with them and could focus my attention on the single diseased savage that was apart from the group.

However, that was not the case; two of the undead had been severely mutilated to the degree that I had planned, but the other two were hardly even scratched in the process, leaving them still on the attack and very close to me.

With no other choice, I pulled the suppressed Beretta 92 I had appropriated from the gun shop in Amarillo, and pointed it at the face of the ugliest monster and pulled the trigger.

Now you might think why I would bother to waste time trying to figure out which of the zombies was the uglier of the two before sending a bullet down range to enact its ultimate demise.

Well the truth is, most of the undead, especially the ones that have been trotting around since the green flag dropped signaling the start of the zombie apocalypse, are so ripe, so decomposed, and so degraded, not to mention so disgusting, that to call one of them uglier than another is just plain ludicrous.

So there's really no time wasted or hesitation involved in picking out the ugliest one; the closest one to you is always the ugliest one, and usually the first one to get shot or hacked to death.

Please, just humor and bear with me, and try to keep up while I get on with the story.

The silencer did its job, and the gentle popping sound of the pistol didn't alert any nomadic fiends in the neighborhood of my presents, it just announced in advance the bullet that was about to smash through the teeth of the walking dead man and exit out the back of his head, subsequently scattering the hovering flies along with pieces of skull and hair that was mixed with white fly larvae and hunks of green-tinted diseased brain.

With one more ravenous zombie by my truck and the other one closing in on me fast, I jumped out of the vehicle and shot over the roof of the cab at the nearest flesh eating monstrosity, catching the top one eighth inch of its cranium with my first bullet, and peeling back some of its scalp as my bullet skidded along the crown of its skull.

My second shot missed (which I could hardly believe considering how close the attacker was to the barrel of my gun, however, shit happens), but my third bullet drilled its way through the middle of the monster's forehead and literally exploded its brain, momentarily

97

causing its head to expand by one third as if it had been quickly pumped full of air. Then just as fast as it had expanded, the head imploded back to its original size as the zombie dropped to the ground.

The last transient corpse that was in the parking lot was nearly upon me as I turned away from the one I had just dispatched. I swung my pistol toward the head of the remaining vagrant, and leveled the muzzle about five inches from the bridge of the snarling cannibal's nose.

With absolutely no time to spare, and with just inches between me and my sudden and untimely death, I squeezed the trigger on the Italian made pistol and forced the zombie's brain out the back of its skull with the utmost efficiency.

"Holy fuck in a cardigan sweater, that was a close one," I said aloud, as I stood alone in the gas station parking lot among a swarm of flies that were hovering over the five rotting corpses at my feet.

I quickly surveyed the surrounding area looking for zombies, feral dogs, or anything else that might be approaching, and was relieved to see nothing but empty streets and vacant lots in every direction, and all were devoid of any movement.

I pulled my dented gray pick-up truck close to an SUV that was parked near the front door of the truck stop. Then I checked to see if the SUV had the keys in it, but no such luck. I then unscrewed the vehicles gas cap and pushed hard several times on the side of the SUV causing it to rock back and forth while I listened for a splashing sound made by the gasoline sloshing around in the fuel tank.

"Sounds like there's plenty of gas in this one," I mumbled to myself.

I then went into the truck stop's merchandising area to look for something to siphon out the gasoline with.

As I walked toward the building, I thought.

"I wonder how many of these eat'in sons-a-bitches are walking around with car keys in their pockets?"

But I wasn't about to start searching every dead man that I killed in the hopes that one of them just coincidently would have the keys to a vehicle that was close.

After all, some of these bastards had been walking around the country for over a year, who knows where in the hell they had left their cars.

Inside the building, I encountered two more of the undead brutes stinking up the joint rather thoroughly, and summarily executed both of them with extreme prejudice using a swift downward swing of my hatchet onto the top of their putrescent craniums and into their brains.

Unable to find what I required to siphon the much needed fuel from the vehicle inside the shop, I made my way out the back door of the store where a found a garden hose that was used for watering the plants decorating the perimeter of the building.

I chopped a seven-foot section from the hose, and then headed around front to where I had parked my truck.

Upon arriving back at my vehicle, I stuck one end of the pilfered garden hose into the gas tank of the SUV and began to suck on the other end of the hose, bringing the vehicles fuel through the lime green plastic tube.

When the gas reached my end of the hose, I carefully inserted it into the tank of my truck, making sure not to lose the flow of gasoline during the procedure, and the refueling process had begun.

After affording myself a generous supply of the SUV's gasoline, I pulled the improvised virescent siphon hose from the two vehicles, drained the residual fuel from it, and tossed it into the bed of my truck; I tightened the gas cap and jumped into the cab.

I wasted little time getting back on the road, for I was on the trail of my *so-far* elusive prey, and was following the first solid lead that I had had in months.

I wasn't about to give the Sarge a chance to give me the slip. I was only a few hundred miles away from his last reported location, and if the *Gods* were on my side (that will be the day); I'd be having breakfast with the Sarge in the morning.

After leaving a few *dead* zombies at the truck stop, as I drove away I saw several more of the undead barbarians moseying onto the property, ever so eager to take their deceased comrades place.

So just for fun (as I said, a rare commodity), I waved my trusty tomahawk out the driver's side window and let out the loudest *Indian War Whoop* I could muster on such short notice, but sadly I got the attention of only a scant number of newly arriving hungry pagans.

However, while doing so, I did manage to ram into two derelict cadavers that were blocking the entrance ramp back onto interstate 40 and send them limping back to hell, as I once more added to my felony hit and run total (abiding by all of the current laws, rules of the road, and safety regulations of course).

Then as soon as I was back on the interstate gazing down the long stretch of highway before me, I was reminded that in all of the excitement at the truck stop, I'd forgotten to pick up a road map? Not wishing to waste precious time by going back, and risk letting the Sarge's trail grow cold, I figured I would be able to find a map down the road somewhere, maybe at a somewhat less populated establishment.

THE SHAWNEE COMPOUND

Less than 40 miles from Erick, and after dispatching three more of the unhinged ravenous savages to gain entrance to the building, I acquired an Oklahoma road map at a gas station in Elk City Oklahoma.

Subsequently, I kept on the road as much as possible, stopping only to take a sincere squirt or to drop a seriously heinous deuce or two when the need arose.

I didn't bother to search for food or supplies along the way, as I was pretty well stocked with everything I needed at the time (guns and bullets), and I was far more interested in catching up to the Sarge than doing any grocery shopping.

I even took a hiatus from slapping the living shit, or un-living shit, maybe I should just say maggot infused shit, out of the miscreant road zombies with my truck for a while; for fear I might damage my vehicle and give the Sarge a bigger head start than he already had.

So I force marched so to speak, through every little town, burg, village, hamlet, and whistle-stop the western part of Oklahoma had to offer, on the way to my fateful rendezvous with the one-time friend I intended to kill on sight.

Traveling at the apocalyptic break-neck speed of a blazing 25 miles per hour, give or take a mile an hour one way or another, I covered the vast distance of 120 mile or so in a record breaking time of only five and one half hours, and found myself on the outskirts of Shawnee Oklahoma as the sun began to set in the western sky.

The compound that had been given the name *Way Station* by its founders, had posted signs every few miles in every direction, so it wasn't very hard to find once you got within ten miles of the place, no matter where you were coming from.

The Way Station was enclosed by a five-foot cattle fence that didn't do much for security, it mostly just marked off the boundaries of the place and afforded people a place to park their vehicles if they were lucky enough to have one.

However, with a rotting zombie snapper (head) on every fence post adorning the perimeter of the property, there was no doubt that you had found the place when you finally arrived.

The doubt was whether or not you wanted to be admitted to a place that used human heads to announce its existence.

As I approached the main gate at the compound's entrance, a short man with an AK-47 greeted me and informed me that I could keep my weapons, but that they had people watching, and the penalties for killing someone without do cause were very harsh.

I figured that the fly engirdled rotting snappers on the fence posts all along the perimeter of the property that the man alluded to with a slight sideways head gesture and a quick glance, might be one of the harsh punishments that he was referring to.

He did however, fail to inform me on just what *do cause* might consist of, but I figured that if I found the Sarge hanging out here at the Way Station, that his mere presents would be *do cause* enough for me, and I would deal with the punishment if any, when the time came.

Another man sporting a similar rifle as the short man at the gate guided me to the spot that he wanted me to park my truck. So, not being one to ever want to cause anyone any trouble, I obliged him in his efforts to do what he probably thought was his apocalyptic calling.

As I shut my truck's engine off, the man approached me and pointed to the storage containers that Jason had mentioned before he had forced me to kill him.

"Go over to the black container, that's the main door, the guard there will tell you where you can stay until you leave, and take anything that you don't want stolen with you. Cause I'm not here to guard your shit," he said, not knowing that hidden under the jacket that I was carrying was my suppressed Beretta which was pointed at him the whole time.

I carefully collected my belongings (the ones that I didn't want stolen) and headed for the front door of the station, being careful not to let the man see my pistol that was still pointed in his direction.

The Way Station as it was called was a bunch of shipping containers placed in a square configuration with twenty containers on each side and stacked five high. Jason's description of the place didn't do it justice.

I had envisioned the Way Station as just a little fort that could house a couple of dozen people and supply them with a meager excuse for safety and some semblance of *peace of mind* for a short time.

What I found was more like a small town set up like a mall, with a carnival like atmosphere.

However, one thing about the Way Station was very clear from the start; circus ambience or not, their security was anything but meager. With armed guards patrolling on the roof of the makeshift metal city, one guard on the top of every upper level container, and a fabled John

Browning .50 caliber M2 machine gun at each corner of the compound, they seemed to be more than prepared for any type of threat. Dead or alive!

In fact, they were prepared enough to cause me to rethink my previous mindset about dealing with the punishment if any, when the time came.

Even if I could make it outside the compound after committing something that they considered a crime, there was no way that I would be able to make it across one hundred yards of no man's land to my truck without being ventilated by several different calibers of bullets, most of which were somewhat large.

Therefore, I decided that if I did find the Sarge inside the Way Station, I would play nice for the time being, and act like all was forgiven and I was so happy to see him that juice was literally running down my left leg.

Then as we traveled together as the best friends that we used to be, and when we were far from this place or any other place that might be able to save him. At that point, I would take great pleasure in watching him squirm as I carved him up from ass hole to belly button with a dull elk antler; and that's just for starters.

"How long do you plan to stay?" The gruff man at the entrance to the black container, who hadn't shaved in months asked.

"Not long, I'm just looking for a friend, I heard he might be staying here," I answered. "Maybe you've seen him; he's traveling with a girl that has blonde hair."

"Lots of guys are traveling with girls, lots of girls are traveling with guys, some have blonde hair, and some don't," he answered somewhat cryptically.

"Go straight down there and go up the stairs, you'll find an empty compartment where you can sleep for a couple of days," the man said, pointing to a stairwell at the far end of the compound. "You can fight all you want, but no killing, we take a dim view of kill'in around here unless it's a sanctioned event."

"I wouldn't think of killing anyone, I even have a hard time putting those poor dead souls that are out in the wilderness to rest, even when they're trying to kill me," I told him, conjuring up the most pathetic look of a beat down sissy that I could put on my face without bursting out laughing.

"Keep moving then, you're blocking the doorway," the man said, just before he put a *"you pussy's make me sick"* smirk on his face. You may know the kind of look I'm talking about, a look that just screamed "I'd like to beat the living fuck out of you just for the hell of it" kind of look.

Sometimes a humble demeanor is the best way to stay out of trouble when you find yourself in a new and unfamiliar place that has a fair amount of alpha males on the prowl.

However, you've got to be careful not to show too much weakness, or some of the predators will think that you're an easy mark and kill you just for the fuck of it.

Or you might get lucky, and they'll try to make an example out of you by beating the holy piss out of you, just to show everyone just how tough they think they are (if you can call that luck).

In any case, the *I'm a badass* look on the doorman's face was all he had to provide at the time, so I decided to let him off easy and just keep my eyes open and my

106

mouth shut, except of course when I asked about my best-est friend in the whole wide world, *the Sarge*.

Although with that said, I wasn't about to let some overly aggressive dick-head wolf on me for their own personal sadistic pleasure. So as I ambled through the festive sanctuary searching for *my* prey, I kept my pistol hidden but at the ready to do my bidding at a moment's notice, ready to stitch up *Chinese gangland style* if necessary, anyone that needed a strict lesson in apocalyptic life that might feel froggy and decide to jump.

My guess was that I wasn't the only one in the joint that was ready, willing, and able to ignore the no killing without do cause rule, and cack someone for giving them the toad eye. The biting heads (snappers) on the fence outside would probably attest to that; that is if they could talk.

The Way Station, as I said, was nothing like I had pictured it would be. The big-top-like milieu of the place reminded me of some of the post-apocalyptic movies I had seen before the real apocalypse had darkened our world.

Some of the entertainment that the station offered during your stay there was rather tame, and some was downright brutal.

There were club fights where you could bet on which man or woman was going to *club* the living shit out of the other one first, using a real club of course.

There were several naked women dancing saloons, and some naked men dancing saloons too (if that's what you're into).

Many whorehouses were available for a price (everything had a price); they weren't really houses, just a shipping container with dividers to separate the horny as they fornicated to their heart's content.

They had a movie theater that played everything from porno flicks to kiddy films (the kiddy films weren't much of a draw, most of the younger children on the planet were dead by now).

In addition, two live freak shows were available for your perusal.

There they had some captive freaks, geeks, and a few other aberrations (mongoloids, human oddities, mental midgets, weirdoes, birth defectives, etc., that sort of thing, you know the types) they were attending to a couple of wayward zombies as part of the show. Which for a small extra fee you could beat to death with your choice of weapons, or with only your fists, if that was your type of entertainment (the zombies that is, freaks and geeks are too hard to come by these days to kill just for sport).

You could do any one or all of these things, or much more if you wished, that is if you felt that the outside world wasn't supplying you with enough carnal violence to suit your needs, and you had an ample amount of *stuff* to barter with.

Even though I had come to thrive in this type of environment, I wasn't looking to kill anyone unnecessarily, or as they told me outside, *without do cause*, at least not at the moment anyway.

Not even the temptation of beating a zombie to death with my bare fists could sway me from my self-imposed mission (the truth is, I was pressed for time or I would have succumbed to that temptation).

Hell, the real truth is, I'd fight Helen Keller if the price was right! But like I said, I was pressed for time, and Helen is never around when you need her to go a few rounds with you.

You could buy most anything at the Way Station, everything from sex to weapons to you name it were available to anyone, if you had the right currency to close the deal.

Which brings me to the people who thought that gold and silver were a good insurance policy in case of a societal collapse; they had a rude awakening when the *real* world dropped the hammer down on top of them.

Gold and silver bars, as well as coins made of the same expensive rare metals were now melted down for their metallic weight and made into bullets, then sold or traded the same as the common lead projectiles.

As it turned out, the precious metal hoarders who once had visions of wealth and prosperity during the end times do to their shrewd dealings and clever foresight of envisioned future events, ended up only being the proud owners of the most expensive bullets on the planet, bullets that really weren't worth any more than any other conventional firearm ammunition.

Paper money was good for starting fires, lighting cigars, and wiping your ass, and that's about all.

The real currency that had value was whatever you had that someone else wanted, and was willing to bargain for, or kill you to get.

After a day and a half of staying out of trouble (and not killing anyone), and several propositions for sex (one from a skinny yet pushy male who now is nursing a broken nose and two bent teeth), and several more offers to trade Jacob's Sub-2000 that I had strapped on my back, my inquiries into the whereabouts of the Sarge were reaping little bounty.

Then totally by accident during one of the sanctioned beat downs on the second level, I overheard a man mention that the fights that the Caucasian put on were much bloodier and far more violent.

"Excuse me sir, but did I hear you mention the Caucasian?" I asked nicely.

"Yeah, what about it? You got a problem with what I talk about?" the man answered back, not so nicely.

The man was in his early thirties and bigger than I was, and looked as if he had been eating fairly well throughout the apocalyptic food shortage.

He also, along with his large friend who sat beside him, acted as if they were both used to getting their way, one way, or another.

Looking for information and not a fight, I kept my mild outward demeanor as I ramped up my inner combat mindset, and said to him.

"No, not at all, talk about anything that you'd like, I just heard you mention the Caucasian and I think a friend of mine is on his way to join up with him, and I thought you might have seen my friend."

"I don't give a fuck about your dumbass friend, and I don't give a fuck about *your* dumb ass. So shut the fuck up, and get the fuck out of my way, you're making me miss the fucking fight," he said loudly, as he stood up and leaned toward me, encroaching into my personal space while doing his best to lay his version of the toad eye on me.

Sensing that this man had some information about the Sarge and Beth, and that he was the alpha male I had mentioned earlier that was willing to *wolf* on me for his own personal pleasure, I felt that it was my duty to myself to beat the information out of him.

I figured that this behemoth of a man was dead set on teaching me a lesson for interrupting his sporting diversion (the sanctioned fight) with a sporting diversion of his own, by beating me half to death in front of the already gathered, lathered, and cheering audience.

Without hesitation, I twisted myself sideway into the larger of the two men, and employed a small-circle Jujitsu technique that flung him to the floor in a blink of an eye. Before his friend could react, I kicked *him* in the teeth with the heel of my boot and knocked him backwards off his seat.

The crowd cheered as the sanctioned fight halted and they began to watch the fight between myself, and my two larger opponents.

With three of the formally seated man's teeth lying on the floor in a pool of blood beside the larger aggressive Neanderthal, I could see the rage in the caveman's eyes as he struggled to stand. Seizing the opportunity to take a cheap shot at this *want-to-be* alpha male, I plonked my foot down hard on the big man's mouth while he was still down (did I mention that I cheat real good), tearing his bottom lip down passed his chin. Then I retracted my foot and forcefully reapplied it to his face one more time, planting the steel toe of my boot deep into the mouth of the oversized goober I had dropped to the floor first.

His boot muffled screech sent the applauding onlookers into somewhat of a feeding frenzy, as several of them blindsided their fellow sports fans with sucker punches.

A full-on melee ensued as I continued to stomp in the faces of the two men that I considered to have started the un-sanctioned physical altercation in the first place.

After my boot heel had broken a few of the men's teeth and tenderized their faces, I bent down over my bloodied foe and asked him one more time.

"Now that you've had your fun, I'm going to ask you again. Have you seen my friend? He is loud, has red hair, and is traveling with a good-looking blonde girl with big tits. Have you seen either one of them?"

The man spit a mixture of blood, saliva, and his two front teeth onto the floor, then while holding his bottom lip in place and dropping one more loose tooth out of his mouth, he replied.

"Yes, I saw both of them, maybe a month ago, and my friend over there," he slobbered, pointing to the other man on the floor with missing teeth. "We saw them arriving at the Caucasian's camp the day we left there. The girl looked kind of beat up and sad, but the red haired man was laughing and carrying on as if he had just returned home from a long restful vacation."

"Where exactly is the Caucasian's camp?" I asked the now profusely bleeding man.

"Indiana!" he replied.

"Where in Indiana, you fuck?" I asked, gritting my teeth.

"In the *Indiana Badlands*," he answered, spitting out more blood.

"Okay, I see you want to do things the hard way," I said, as I slapped down on his right eyeball with the palm of my hand, causing the back of his head to bounce off the mental container's floor; which helped to jar his memory and convince him to cooperate a little more.

"A little town in the heart of the Indiana Badlands, I don't know what it used to be called before the outbreak; now the Caucasian's followers call it *Hell*. He named it himself just after he set up camp inside the gym of an old high school at the eastern edge of the town," the pounded bully finally confessed. "But you don't want to go there, the Caucasian eats people like you for breakfast."

Shut up! If I want yours or your girlfriend's opinion," I told him, pointing to his still unconscious male friend I had pummeled. "I'll beat it out of the both of you."

Then the reality of the situation struck me.

"Never mind!" I told him with a smug chuckle. "I already did!"

As the violent clash of fisticuffs continued between the patrons of the sanctioned fight, I thought that it might be a good time for me to bid my fond farewells to the bully's and to the Way Station, and continue on my journey. After my little information session with the two oversized barbarians, I didn't think that it would be too awful wise to over say my welcome; you know, everybody has to sleep sometime, and after a good night's sleep, I didn't want to wake up dead.

So as I stood up over the cowed bully that had thought he would use me as his personal punching bag, I set the sole of my boot at the corner of his left eye socket and pushed down hard, scrapping a large chunk of skin down the side of his face, peeling it away and exposing the man's cheek bone.

His loud girlish scream, served to not only cause a break in the action of the ongoing brawl as participants stopped momentarily to see what had caused the feminine shriek. But also awakened the man's partner from the kick induced slumber I had produced just seconds after flinging the larger man to the floor.

Being a fair and just man, I thought it only right to allow the second man to share some of the fun his mountainous friend was hoping to have at my expense.

But before I kicked the man in the mouth again, knocking out four of his molars and causing him to bite off a small section of the tip of his tongue on my way out the door.

I leaned down once more and whispered in the ear of the man that proclaimed he didn't give a fuck, and reminded him of one of life's truths.

"Remember asshole! It's not the size of the dog in the fight; it's the size of the fight in the dog!"

Toting my possessions back to my truck as I was leaving the Way Station completely unscathed (however, I can't say as much for some of the pilgrims that I had encountered there), I tried not to look like I was in a hurry to leave the outpost. Not being familiar with all of the rules and regulations of this bastion of sanctuary and sin, or of the punishments for non-compliance with its unknown stipulations, I wanted to nonchalantly depart

114

from the premises to avoid any unnecessary indiscretions that might delay my hunt for the Sarge, or render me mostly lifeless with my snapping head on a pole.

To my surprise, upon arriving at my vehicle, I found it in exactly the same condition that I had left it. Apparently the parking lot attendant's warning to take what I didn't want stolen was unsubstantiated in this case.

"You've got a real nice place here, sorry I have to leave now, but I've got places to go and people to see," I told the parking lot guard as I jumped into my truck and started the engine.

The man opened the gate and waved me through, not bothering to say anything as I drove by him and the body-less snappers wobbling on the fence posts on both sides of the gate.

Even though the gatekeeper had told me that I could fight all I wanted too, as I shooed some of the unwanted hitchhiking flies that had chosen to abandon their staked out heads on the fence posts and ride along with me out to the cab of my truck, I had to wonder if there would be any kind of an alarm sounded to stop my departure, considering that some people might be under the mistaken impression that it was *me* who started the melee that was still in progress inside the Station.

After all, I had beaten the living shit out of two of the Way Station's pilgrims. But let's face the facts; it wasn't like they weren't begging for it. In fact they should be happy, after all, they were looking for trouble and they found it. So all in all they got exactly what they wanted.

However, as I drove down the road away from that apocalyptic refuge, leaving all of the shopkeepers, whores, fighters, trouble makers, freaks, geeks, and whatever else, to their own mechanisms, no alarm was sounded that day, and maybe any day (unless you killed someone without do cause, whatever that is).

For fighting and brawling, stealing and whoring, and just plain beating the fucking hell out of somebody just for the fun of it was a way of life in that small oasis in the middle of our zombie infested world, and I was just another passerby in a long line of people looking for whatever it was that we were all looking for as we continued to march across the landscape, incarcerated on this planet of the living dead.

INDIANA WANTS ME

Beware of the *Indiana Badlands* were the words that kept popping up all along the trail to my destination.

First from Jason, then from the boisterous bully at the Way Station that had begged me for, and promptly received, the excellent thwacking that he so richly deserved.

And indeed, that's what the three hillbilly men in Arkansas told me just before they tried to take me prisoner and I was force to separate the top of their skulls from the rest of their bodies (well two of them anyway).

They weren't the easiest kills that I had under my belt, but they weren't the hardest either.

After the sun went down on the day we met, we were all sitting around the campfire that the three of them had blazing inside an old rickety barn.

We were celebrating not getting ourselves killed by a medium sized horde (twenty-five to thirty of the undead grisly cannibals) that happened to stagger onto the freeway close to their camp that afternoon.

You see, I had just come out of Oklahoma, still driving along interstate 40, and minding my own business I might add.

I was cutting through their lovely scenic state on my way northeast to rendezvous with that Caucasian crowd I had heard so much about. You know… the group that the Sarge and Beth might be in cahoots with.

I rounded a curve in the road and found myself face to face with that medium sized horde I previously mentioned.

The members of that horde were not only blocking my way, but also had three strangers surrounded and backed up against a wrecked truck that had been hauling cases of soda and water before the end of the world scenario put an abrupt halt to normal interstate commerce, and pretty much everything else that was normal as well.

Ordinarily I would have just driven around the whole bunch of them and let the three men fight it out on their own, for I had pressing business to attend to in Indiana. However, the water truck had stopped in the middle of the road because of a fiery crash of two semi-tractor trailer rigs sometime in the distant past, and had been abandoned there.

Most likely the undead uprising over a year ago had caused the crash, but whatever the reason for the burnt and mangled wreckage, the fact was that the derelict debris along with the water truck and the horde of pagan flesh eaters had the road blocked, at least for the moment, and the steep inclines on both sides of the road prevented me from driving around the blockage on the soft shoulders.

I could have waited out the life-threatening melee, and if the *living* citizens had won the fight, they would probably be pissed that I just sat there and watched what could have been in their minds their unnecessary and ultimate demise taking place. And if one or two of them were killed in the process, the survivor or survivors would no doubt consider me at fault for their friend's death. Nonetheless, no matter how many of them did manage to survive the deadly encounter, the remainder of the group would most likely be pissed off at me for not helping them.

On the other hand, if the ravenous horde of the dead won the battle, the three men that had lost the fight would not provide enough meat on their proverbial table to feed the mass of undead former humanity, and they would without a doubt come after me to complement their four-course meal, and I would have to fight them alone or retreat and put a *serious* dent in my time schedule by trying to find another route around the mechanical and sub-human obstructions that were blocking the road.

Delaying my trip to the Indiana Badlands by following an unknown detour was not an option at this point in my quest to hunt down the former Marine Corps sergeant I had been searching for.

So with retreating from the scene not a viable alternative, I figured that one way or another I was going to have to fight someone or something no matter what, so I might as well side with the living and spend my bullets on the dead.

Besides, I was running low on water and could use a couple of cases of the precious liquid to get me through to Indiana.

The crowd of fuming zombie beasts that were attacking the three men by the water truck was sporting as many maggots as they were the hovering flies that they paraded around themselves, which only added to the unsavory and ghastly chore of dispatching them.

And while we're considering the revolting chore of zombie dispatching, I might as well share with you an unscientific observance that I had made over the past several months of tramping through the zombie apocalypse.

It just might answer a question that had plagued (no pun intended) many before, during, and maybe even after the zombie upheaval, that is, *if there is an after*.

As many watched movies and TV shows, bought and rented DVDs, read books and comic books about zombie invasions taking over the planet (before they actually did take over the planet), and as some were even participating in zombie runs in full make-up and costume, one question about the walking undead was never actually answered, and not even really addressed, not to my knowledge anyway.

The question was either never brought up at all, or skirted around and left to the audience to contemplate without any real facts or clues to guide them.

Well, with the endless meandering around the zombie infested countryside that has led me to this place and time. I can assure you that I do have the answer to the allusive question, although maybe not completely conclusive on the subject, and probably not the answer that you would like to hear. Nevertheless, the answer is the reality that we have to live with.

What is the question, you ask?

The question is.

"Do zombies defecate?" That is the question.

Do the undead discharge feces from their anus on a regular basis?

Do these insane rotting cannibals have a bowel movement at any time in their miserable existence?

The answer is... unfortunately, a resounding yes.

Yes indeed, they do shit their pants at certain intervals. These intervals seem to be about once every three months. Because the undead rot slower than normal dead things decompose, their metabolism slows at a comparable rate.

Apparently the virus, or whatever causes them to reanimate and walk the earth craving the bodies of the living, and of the dead if no living entity is available for immediate consumption, slows their metabolism down to the point that they only need to discharge their waste products at a rate about 100 times slower than the living do, even though they tend to want to eat about 100 time more.

I say the answer is *unfortunately* yes, because (as you may have already guessed) with the overwhelming stench of their rotting carcass's, along with the smell and sight of hundreds, if not thousands of maggots dripping off them, not to mention the flies that are constantly taking off and landing on them and their putrid discharges, things can get really ripe smelling in a big hurry.

Now you throw in several pounds of fecal material (shit), some of which has been dried for weeks or months, and some that they might have just loaded into their underwear recently (depending on the date of their zombiefication and their last unholy meal), being hauled around all over hell's creation in the seat of their pants.

What you end up with then, is a bunch of undead cannibalistic savages that are not only looking to eat you alive, but also have the capability to stink up the place to the point that your eyes water so much that it's hard to see the dirty bastards to kill them.

This of course is a double-edged sword; you have to deal with their combination of fecal fetor and rotting reek when you get close enough to them to hack them to pieces with an edged weapon of your choice, like a tomahawk or machete.

However, on the flip side of the coin, much of the time you can smell their approach or hear the swarm of flies that are escorting them and avoid them altogether, thus sparing yourself the possibility of being killed and eaten, and then later being toted around in the seat of their pants stinking up the joint to high hell. Or possibly joining their ranks as one of the surviving bitten or scratched and marching around the heartland of America killing and eating the living, and embarrassingly shitting your own pants at the same time as you excrete your unfortunate victims into your trousers and haul them around all over hell's creation.

Granted, there are many of the undead maniacs galumphing around the countryside that are so horrifying that they might, and probably without a doubt have, made some of the living humans survivors shit their own pants on the spot.

However, for the most part, we among the living aren't prone to running around with a lump of half-processed smelly shit in our britches. And even if we do take a dump in our drawers because we had the shit scared out of us, we still have the mental capacity to change our underwear from time to time; and most of us actually do.

So let's look on the bright side of the matter.

These continually starving morons running around the country soiling themselves at every opportunity, is just one more good reason to put an end to their miserable existence as soon as humanly possible, before they stink up the whole planet with their poor hygienic practices. Not to mention, humanely relieving them from what has to be a monumental case diaper rash.

Now back to the rescue attempt...

Not wanting to damage my truck in a full head-on assault of the horde of ravenous monsters that were blocking my way into Indiana, I stopped my truck and got out to lend the overwhelmed rednecks a helping hand.

Only one of the men had a weapon of any consequence.

He was wielding a four-pronged pitchfork against the crowd, and I noticed that all three of the men had pistols strapped on, but their sidearms were all holstered.

This along with several dropped zombies on the perimeter of the skirmish told me that they were not only out of ammo, but were all smart enough to re-holster their weapons for use at a later time (after they had found more ammo).

They were smart enough, or experienced enough, not to throw the empty pistols at their enemy in a panic during a futile endeavor to stave off the aggressors, as so many people in the movies had done.

After stopping my vehicle and pulling out my suppressed M-4 rifle that had already killed dozens of the dead and at least one of the living, with my best sarcastic voice I yelled to the men as I configured the weapon for battle by flipping the thumb safety onto semi-auto.

"Have you girls seen any eaters around here?"

Releasing the bolt and letting it fly forward thereby inserting a round into the rifle's chamber was not necessary because I always traveled with a bullet in the tube of all of my firearms, in case of just such an emergency, as did everyone that wanted to stay alive in the zombie apocalypse.

When zombies attack, and a fraction of a second can mean the difference between living to fight another day, or being chewed up and *shit* out; I usually opt to fight another day. But hey, that's just the way I am.

I chose the suppressed gun because of the open area and the probability that the sound of my 9mm Sub-2000 would only serve to draw more of the undead that were surely within earshot into the fight.

The sharp crack of the silenced M-4's supersonic bullets traveling at somewhere around three times the speed of sound, could only be heard for about seventy yards in every direction as they broke the sound barrier.

Whereas the loud unencumbered muzzle blast of the Sub-2000 as it spits out its projectiles could be heard for more than a mile in all directions.

So my choice was simple.

In a zombie apocalypse, silence is golden, so always choose the quieter weapon if possible when dealing either with the living or with the dead, unless of course for some reason you want to attract the dead or let the living know your whereabouts.

Two of the men thought that my sense of humor and timing was impeccable and smiled as I approached, probably out of relief that someone had come to help them.

However, the third one, who I would later find out that he went by the name of Eric, looked a little pissed as he gouged out the eyes of a tall stout female zombie in a tattered wedding dress with his pitchfork.

As the prongs of the primitive farm implement penetrated the zombie bride's brain, her mouth was so close to his face that he could smell the monster's fetid breath as it growled, snapped, and puked up a few choice maggots onto his shirt before dropping onto the road and quickly dying at his feet.

As the horde slowly advanced on the three men, I decided that it would be prudent to begin shooting the zombies closest to the hillbillies first, and work my way to the rear of the crowd, just as I would if they were attacking me.

Although shooting the zombies that were within arm's reach of the men increased the chances of me hitting one of the hillbillies by accident, it was a risk that "*I*" was willing to take.

After all, if I hadn't happened along when I did, they would most likely have been killed and eaten anyway, so if I would inadvertently dust one of them off, their death would be far quicker and much less painful than being an entree for the midday gathering of the savage hordes.

I had been experimenting with a tactic that I was trying to develop, when the situation was conducive to employing such a tactic, and this looked to me like the perfect time and place to further test this process of zombie eradication.

The stage was set, I didn't know or really care about the men I was getting ready to save, there was a target rich environment well within the range of my weapon, and I had plenty of bullets in case things went sour.

Moreover, if things really got bad and the horde turned on me, I always had the option of flipping the selector switch on my gun to its full-auto mode and employing a spray and pray tactic without too much regard for anyone's safety but my own.

Like I said, I didn't know the hillbillies, and I really didn't care about the hillbillies, so give me a break.

The method that I chose to test in this situation was what I called the multiple head shot technique.

It goes like this.

You take aim at your target (a zombie head in this case), and you try to hold off on your shot until one or two more zombie's heads (if that's your target) are in line with the bullet's future trajectory.

Your goal is to splatter at least two of your targets back to the lower depths of hell where they belong (living or dead) with only one bullet, and send three or more of the barbarians to their *doom* (pun) if possible.

It sounds easy enough to do if all of the targets are willing to collaborate, and happen to fall into a single line in front of your gun, but the reality of this type of approach is that most of the time you have to be patient and wait for your targets to unwittingly cooperate.

That's the main reason that you wouldn't try this particular method while trying to rescue someone that you actually gave a shit about.

Anyway, back to the story.

So I let loose with my M-4 utilizing the method that I had been experimenting with and just finished explaining, and watched through the iron sights of my rifle as its bullets caused slobbering menace after slobbering menace to hurl their ensconced maggots and pieces of their rotting flesh, matted hair, and chunks of their degenerated brains onto the three men that I was trying to save, as I aerated the skulls of the attacking zombies in front of them.

Although not getting the massive body count that I was hoping for with my new experimental approach, many of the attacking zombies that were nearest to the imperiled hillbillies did *bite* the dust; which was a refreshing change from biting everything else within their grasp.

After exhausting the first 30 round magazine (not clip, there's a difference), with less than satisfactory results using the *experimental* tactic, I dropped the empty spring-loaded sheet metal bullet holder to the ground and inserted a fresh, fully loaded replacement into my rifle.

Then with all three of the hillbilly's life spans becoming shorter by the second, I abandoned the multiple head shot with one bullet strategy, and adopted the more efficient technique of one shot one kill as a matter of policy.

Halfway through my second magazine and with most of the pack of zombies ravaged and weighted down with lead, the remainder of the horde was a simple mop up operation.

After devastating most of the remaining festering throng of cannibals with well placed head shots and a couple of sharp force trauma inserts to the brain with my trusty battle hatchet. As a gesture of good will, I saved the last survivor of the deadly legion of undead flesh eaters for the hillbilly with the pitchfork to dispatch.

Seeing my intentions were honorable, he gave me a knowing nod and then wasted little time planting the long spikes of his farming tool deep into the skull of the last of the raw-flesh eating connoisseurs.

Immediately after the monster hit the ground, the man stomped his foot onto the side of its head and jerked firmly upward on the handle of his pitchfork, prying it from the brain of the still twitching body of his latest extermination victim.

After pulling the farming utensil out of the zombie's skull and leaving four perfectly round 1/4 inch holes which allowed the maggots that occupied the outer circumference of its brain to crawl out through the small openings.

Several squirming fly larvae oozed out in single file, leading the way for a small surging stream of dark red, almost black colored blood to empty onto the road.

"Thanks mister," the man said, no longer seeming irritated by my presents, as he propped himself up leaning on the handle of his fork like he had just finished a day's worth of hard labor filling a barn's loft with hay.

"Any time," I answered, thinking that the road being blocked was the only reason that I had bothered to stop and help.

Besides the realization that the reanimated corpses had a tendency to take a deep meaningful crap in their drawers on occasion, the older, or should I refer to them as the more mature of the walking dead, seemed to be evolving a new attribute as part of their ongoing distasteful and visually disgusting death ritual.

I had seen a glimmer of this trait on the bus as we plowed through the gigantic horde that almost stopped us in our tracks on the way to the armory.

After Jacob and Beth had shot off some of the probing fingers of the zombies whose hands were intruding into the bus through the gun slits made in the side of the bus. We noticed, but weren't concerned at the time about the severed fingers that squirmed and flexed on the floor of the vehicle after being dislodged from their recently *nubbed* hands.

However, their evolution, or de-evolution, had now increased to the point that many of their body parts seemed to have a life of their own after being disjointed from the parts of the body that they had been previously attached too.

Although, this was a common occurrence from the beginning of the zombie takeover of our world when appertaining to the decapitated heads of the undead troglodytes, and a sight that every survivor was growing accustom to seeing.

It was an occurrence that my family and I had been privileged to witness firsthand, as this phenomenon was present from the very start.

When the glass from our broken patio door cleanly sliced off the head of our neighbor Julie, her severed skull had rolled underneath our kitchen table still snapping at us and foaming at the mouth, until I oxygenated the hostile cranium with a neatly placed 9mm slug.

Now, as me and the three strangers introduced ourselves, the convulsive bodies of some but not all of the former undead, which were now presently completely dead, twitched harmlessly, yet eerily at our feet.

Tim, Eric, and Matt were their names, and I could tell by the way they casually spoke their backwoods slang and carried themselves, that they were uneducated and had probably been financially poor their whole lives.

However, now that the alleged civilized world had come to an abrupt end, they no longer had to rely on the meager wages from their haphazard menial labor jobs to support their wants and needs. Now they had just been taking what they wanted from wherever or whoever they wanted to take it from, just as most everyone else was doing.

Unfortunately for them, this time they had decided to take from me, even after I had saved their asses from the imminent *doom* (no pun intended, that was earlier) that was about to befall them. I guess that old saying is true. "No good deed goes unpunished."

Anyway…

After stopping my vehicle in the middle of highway 40, and making light of the hillbillies situation before butchering my fair share of *their* deadly menace that blocked my way. I told them my plight (I needed to get to Indiana by driving through the mess we had just created on the roadway), their willingness to help was without hesitation (supposedly as a partial payment for saving their sorry asses), and we began to move some of the oscillating corpses to the shoulder of the road to make enough room for my vehicle to pass.

After we had cleared a tract through the now harmless but still undulating bodies that cluttered the freeway, there was plenty of leeway for me drive my truck between the wrecked vehicles and the dispatched zombies so that I could resume my trip north on my chosen route.

However, soon after the grisly work of moving the twitching corpses was finished, the three men invited me to join them at their campsite for some libation and relaxation (as further payment for saving their useless and unknown to any of us, their soon to be *short* lives) before I continued on my journey toward the Badlands of Indiana.

******

Now as Jack has stated in the past, Mama *Doom* (not her real name) didn't raise a total fool. With his experience on the river with the cabin cruiser cannibal, and countless other encounters along the way, Jack was already leery of the three men's overly congenial attitude and willingness to be friends so quickly after they had met.

Their fine new clothes didn't match their accents or their use of the English language. It was quite clear from their Pigeon English and colloquial regionalisms that they weren't used to hobnobbing with the rich and famous.

However, their possession of some things that didn't quite match, well let's just say, their personalities, was

131

nothing out of the ordinary now days. For in these troubled times people were forced to make do with whatever they could find as they scavenged through the deadly wilderness that was teeming with zombies, crazies, murders, maniacs, and of course all around good guys like Jack Doom.

But when Jack spotted one of the men slip something into a bottle of whiskey just before handing it to him, he felt that his suspicions about the men were justified, and the future outcome of their meeting was of their choice. It seemed that the three were itching for a fight; and Jack was just the man to scratch that itch for them. It was not going to be a fair fight, one way or the other, but the three hillbillies were begging for it, and Jack Doom was going to give it to them.

So, when Jack refused to take a drink from the tainted bottle, the outward demeanor of the three men quickly changed from a happy go lucky mood, to a dead serious type of temperament.

Fortunately, Jack was prepared for the change of heart that the men were now displaying.

******

"Friend, are you sure you'z wants to go up into the Indiana badlands? I'z hear-ed some nasty stories bout dat place. Beware of da badlands up thar in Indiana, that's what's I'z hear-ed. You knows they don't call it da badlands for nutten," the younger man they called Tim warned.

"I've got business in Indiana," I responded.

132

"Must be some business to take you-uns into dat place," my new *friend* Tim replied.

"Drink up friend," the tall blonde man said to me, not knowing that I'd seen him put something into the bottle that he had handed to me. "Dis shit'll help take da edge off after a hard day of kill'in."

"No thanks, I'm trying to quit, you know, drinking and driving don't mix," I replied.

"One drink won't hurt, dis here is a celebration, we all lived through that zombie attack," the man said very convincingly.

"You know how it is, with practically every state having that ridiculous .08 limit; you can hardly have one beer before you're over the limit. You don't want me to get arrested for drunk driving do you," I said smiling, hiding the movement of my right hand with the whiskey bottle as I slid it down the front of my pants where I had stuffed my Glock 19 just in case. "Besides, I'm not much of a whiskey drinker, too much Indian blood in me ya know."

I had chosen my Glock to cram down the front of my trousers because of its short barrel. It was easier to conceal and I could still sit down without it jabbing into my legs. Not to mention there was less of a chance of me shooting my dick off with that particular weapon because of the way the safeties were built into it.

The blonde haired man either couldn't seem to grasp my sense of humor, or else he was just in no mood for levity as he prodded me with his pitchfork.

"Okay friend, now I'm not asking you'z to take a drink, I'm telling you'z to take a drink," the blonde headed hillbilly named Eric now shouted while menacingly poking his pitchfork in my direction.

"Okay, okay, I didn't mean to offend anyone," I said, as I raised the bottle from my lap that was stealthily concealing my 9mm pistol.

I had only brought my tomahawk, M-4, and Glock with me to the barn, and with my M-4 resting against the hay bale beside me, still within reach, but not likely to be grabbed before Eric could easily plunge his pitchfork into me. And with the distance between me and my opposition far enough away to yield the same results if I tried to pull out my tomahawk, I opted to used my pistol to try and get out of this potentially, and most likely soon to be fatal situation.

Since the bossy man named Eric had pissed me off by demanding that I drink from his tainted whiskey bottle, not to mention he was standing over me brandishing his primitive weapon just inches from my face. I decided to give them no quarter or mercy, because I knew that they had planned to give me neither as well.

Meanwhile the other two men were busy laughing and drinking from their own bottles of libation, thinking that it wouldn't be long before what was mine was going to be theirs.

Considering all of the variables that I could process in the split second that I had to reconnoiter my precarious circumstances, I felt that I had to choose to deal with the more aggressive one named Eric first, and take him out of the picture before he drove his pitchfork into my face. Then I would take care of the other two, hopefully before they even realized what was happening.

That seemed to me to be the most logical avenue to pursue at the time. After all Eric was the closest to me, making him the ugliest one of the three.

So I raised the bottle to my lips, and began to tilt it upward giving the illusion of allowing its liquid to drain into my mouth.

However, just before the whiskey reached the neck of the bottle, I pulled my Glock from behind the whiskey bottle that was obscuring it, and shot Eric in the middle of his forehead right at his blonde hairline.

My bullet split his skull open at the top and splattered part of his brain onto his friend Matt who was seated directly behind him.

With the whiskey bottle still in my left hand, I swung around toward Tim, who was sitting just to the right of Matt, and on my left side.

While Eric's falling body still shielded me from Matt I swung my pistol toward Tim.

Not expecting me to do anything but take a drink of whiskey, and surprised by my rapid movement and the sound of the gunshot, Tim choked on the alcohol he was drinking and spit it onto his friend Matt.

Now seeing Matt drenched with whiskey and his face sprinkled with pieces of Eric's head, Tim contorted himself back awkwardly trying to reach the rifle he had leaning on the arm of his aluminum framed lawn chair.

Thrown off balance by his quick movement and the full fifth of whiskey he had in his right hand, he almost fell completely off of the already unsteady seat he was perched on.

As he regained his balance on the tilting chair and came back forward with his long gun in his left hand, he

135

didn't have a chance, for I already had my pistol leveled at him for at least two seconds before he even turned back around.

Before he was even aware of his dire predicament; his forehead came into contact with the second bullet that departed from my Austrian build firearm which crushed the front of his thick hillbilly loser skull, sending him backwards once more, this time all the way to the ground.

Now two were dead at the scene, and the third man was technically on life support and didn't even know it, still wiping the remnants of his buddy's brains out of his eyes.

Eric's dead body had totally collapsed onto the floor of the barn and was no longer blocking Matt's view of me, or mine of him.

While Matt was still unable to see clearly, I sprang over Eric's limp carcass and began to pistol whip him to the ground with the heavy steel slide of my gun.

While he lay stunned, bruised, and disorientated with his back hugging the dirt floor of the barn, I forcefully shoved the neck of *my* whiskey bottle between his lips, chipping two of his teeth on its way in.

With the booze bottle draining into his mouth, I jammed the muzzle of my pistol unreasonably hard into the man's right nostril and order him to swallow the alcoholic beverage.

"Drink up dumbass," I screamed, poking the barrel of my gun even harder into his nose.

A gurgling sound spewed from him as the caramel colored whiskey mixed with the greenish-yellow snot that had the vague appearance of mother-of-pearl as it erupted out of his unimpeded left nostril and slowly slid down the side of his battered face as he gasped for air.

"I said drink, shit-hook, I want to see what this shit does to you," I screamed, as I watched his eyes slowly close as the drug tainted liquor quickly began to take its desired effect.

As the man passed out from the "Mickey Finn" that was intended to incapacitate me, I pulled the bottle from the unconscious hillbilly's mouth and screwed the cap back on the bottle.

"I had better hold on to this for awhile, it just might come in handy at some point," I mumbled to myself.

Then I reached for the bottle of booze that Matt had dropped as the slide of my Glock 19 introduced itself repeatedly to him on and about his head and shoulders.

I slammed the almost full bottle of liquor as hard as I could against his cheekbone and collapsed the orbital cavity of his left eye socket as the bottle shattered across his face.

Then using the razor sharp edges of the broken neck of the glass container as a *scalpel*, I proceeded to peel back his *scalp* from the top of the bridge of his nose to the hairline at the back of his neck, fucking him up *Indian style* (I wasn't kidding about my Indian blood), making sure to extract as much of the cranial skin as I could pull off his head.

"Talk about a quarter inch on top and white sidewalls," I again mumbled, this time with a smirk, as the bloody white bone of Matt's skull revealed itself just above both of his ears.

"When you wake up, you'll wish I had killed you like I killed your asshole friends," I muttered, as I picked up my two guns and the drug-contaminated bottle of intoxicant and prepared to walk back to my truck.

I really didn't know exactly why I had chosen to scalp the hillbilly named Matt before I left the barn; it just seemed like the right thing to do at the time I guess.

After all, I really only wanted to see what the whiskey that they were trying to make me drink would do to a person.

Of course on the other hand, they did piss me off, so they all got what they deserved.

"Oh well, better him than me," I said aloud, as stuffed my pistol back in my pants (get your mind out of the gutter, it was my Glock, remember I said "it" had a *short* barrel), and tossed my M-4 and whiskey bottle onto the seat beside me.

After loading three cases of bottled water into the back of my pickup truck, I decided to go out of my way to use one of the unfortunate road kill zombies that I had rescued the hillbillies from as a speed bump (because it had pissed me off too).

However, I didn't bother to add the horizontal cadaver to my ongoing felony count, even after hearing its bones snapping under the weight of my vehicle, because it was already deceased. No sport!

I departed the gruesome scene, and drove through the gap of corpses avoiding any further contact with the macabre remains, and continued on my trek toward the so-called *dreaded* Badlands of Indiana, tossing Matt's bloody scalp out the window to two hungry wayward zombies that were patrolling the roadside at the time; in lieu of running them over with my truck. Then I let out

one of my loudest *Indian War Whoops* as I drove away:
it seemed like the right thing to do

THE SISTERS TOO

Somehow I had managed to make it through Little Rock without incident and was still cruising along interstate 40 at the phenomenal speed of close to 18 mph as I approached Memphis Tennessee.

Out of boredom, and in an effort to kill as many of the rotting sons-a-bitches as I could without damaging my vehicle. I began to take potshots at the heads of the dead who were unfortunate enough to wander onto the highway and be close enough as I drove by them to take a bullet in the skull without me having to exert much effort.

However, when a well-dressed male zombie wearing what looked to be a very expensive gray pinstriped suit along with a solid red tie and patent leather shoes to complete his ensemble, stumbled too close to my truck as I squeezed the trigger of my pistol and sent a speeding round-nose cylinder of copper jacketed lead smashing into its face. Pieces of its brain and cranial juices rained down on the windshield of my vehicle and all over my exposed left arm that was dangling out the driver's window brandishing my weapon.

"Fuck me raw doggie style all the way to hell!" I yelled, as I watched through my side view mirror as the offending zombie splattered on the concrete roadway behind me.

"Damn eaters, I already smell enough like road kill to make somebody barf up a lung, and now this!"

Crossing the Arkansas, Tennessee state line, as well as the Mississippi River at the same time as I blew into

Memphis, I looked down at the river and saw that it was still polluted with hundreds of dead bodies, just as it had been in the beginning when my family and I had fled our home and trekked down the massive waterway when society first went tits up.

The smell of the river had subsided little from what I could tell. Even though it was hard to discern the differences between the smell of the river below me and the funky stink of the surrounding air within the cab of my truck, as I inhaled the stench from my past zombie encounters that had accumulated on my clothing and on the inside of the vehicle. I was relatively sure that the intense reek that was permeating my surroundings was a mix of both contributing factors as I bolted across the bridge and through the rising air from the warm water in the river below.

The visual aspect had changed slightly from the time of our original voyage down the mighty river, although its banks were still cluttered with hundreds of dead bodies, many of the original carcasses of the dead were no longer bloated and floating in the water as before. They had either made their way down to the Gulf of Mexico, been eaten by the wildlife that lived in the water, or totally rotted away and their bones had sank to the bottom of the river.

So more than a year after this whole thing started, the Mississippi River was hosting slightly less bloated floaters than in the beginning.

However, the older bloated cadavers that had been beached on the banks of the river and stuck in the mud somewhere along the way, had finally dissolved through the process of putrefaction, and been replaced with the

141

now sun-bleached skeletal bones that had been housed inside their former selves.

Crossing that river had brought back a stream (no pun intended) of memories from the past, some good and some bad.

I remembered my loving family and the life we had before the apocalypse.

It also brought back memories of past days when we fought together side by side against the dead and the living alike.

Whether the memories were of the good times we had, or of the bad times we endured, it saddened me to think that they were all dead now.

Crossing that atrocious river had reminded me of the death of my family, but more importantly, it had again reminded me of who the blame for their deaths lied, and what my mission in this miserable life was, and it strengthened my resolve to catch up to the Sarge.

Renewed resolve or not, I still smelled like death warmed over, and I needed to clean up as soon as possible.

So I made my way through north Memphis as fast as I could and was lucky enough not to run into any unsavory characters that wanted to physically change me, my truck, or my outlook on life.

My map of Oklahoma had a small U.S. map on the reverse side, but it was big enough that I could follow the interstate system without having to carry a map of every state with me. After a quick glance at my map, I stayed on I-40 as it jogged due north, and I was going balls to the wall on the outskirts of town when I came to a nice little waterway called the Wolf River, a tributary of the Mississippi, which seemed like a prime bathing area for me to scrape some of the rancid death off me.

The freeway crossed the river as it meandered past the north side of Memphis, but there were no exits off the road at that spot. So I figured that I would take the next exit off the throughway and back track to the river.

The next exit took me to N. Watkins St. where I turned right and headed back south.

Luck was with me so far in my quest to cleanse the dead skin and goo from my own carcass and clothing, for the Wolf River was just five-hundred feet ahead.

As I approached the river, I could see what seemed to be a very nice little sandy patch on the other side where a low point in the terrain had caused the overflow of the river to empty into it and form a small lake.

I drove back across the *Wolf*, and parked my truck in the emergency lane on the east side of the road.

With none of the undead in sight (which was rare) I grabbed my two suppressed firearms and exited my vehicle. I made my way down the side of the hill toward my own private beach, which was about a hundred yards away, give or take a few feet.

To get to the beach, I had to wade across a small tributarian creek that had helped to form the lake, but once I was there, I found it to be the perfect place to wash up and launder my clothing.

I quickly peeled off my soiled and smelly duds and took them with me into the water, keeping them down stream of me so as not to bathe in the remnants of the dead zombies that were being washed from my laundry.

I hadn't bothered to stop for, or for that matter even think of pilfering some soap from someplace before I headed for the river. Considering that it was too late to worry about it, I decided to just enjoy myself and let the river water do the cleaning on its own.

This was the first time in a very long time that I had stopped and been able to relax, not to mention go swimming too.

The Wolf River was definitely not comparable to the swimming pool at the Sarge's Y, but it was better than nothing, and the warm water; compliments of the summer sun seemed to be doing the trick.

When my clothes were as clean as they were going to get, I rang them out and found a nearby tree with an overhanging branch to hang them up to dry.

With the balmy summer sun beating down on my fully exposed body, I decided to lie on the sand, absorb some vitamin D, and wait for my things to dry.

Well, you've all heard the old saying.

"If it sounds too good to be true, it probably is!"

Well, it was too good to be true all right.

Just as I got comfortable and began to let my head air-out a little.

In the distance, I heard dogs barking.

"Well shit the bed," I complained softly as I stood up. "And just when I was beginning to relax."

It didn't take long for the sound of the barking to get closer.

In fact, I *barely* (again, no pun intended, remember I was still naked) had time to pick up my M-4 before I saw a girl break through the bushes on the ridgeline of the riverbank as she ran toward me.

She was wearing blue jeans and a bloodstained white t-shirt. If she had a weapon of any kind, I didn't see it.

When she saw me standing on the shore she screamed.

"Help me!"

That was just before she tripped and tumbled down the steep muddy bank, ending up sprawled out in the sand with her head inches from my bare feet.

Spitting some sand out of her mouth, she looked up at me standing in front of her *stark raving naked*, and repeated her urgent request.

"Will you please help me?"

I didn't have time to answer her question. The dogs that I had heard that were chasing the girl, now had caught up to her, and me.

Two of the feral dogs had been flanking her and now were trotting along the edge of the bank, one coming from the right side and one coming from the left side.

However, our main problem at that instant was the two vicious dogs that were attacking us head on.

I seated my rifle into the small of my shoulder and pointed the muzzle in the direction of the charging K-9's.

The crack of the supersonic projectile sounded the timely demise of the lead dog, but didn't detour the malevolent mutt that followed.

Taking aim at, and just before I put a cap in the second hound, an old adage came to mind and it goes something like this.

"If you can't run with the big dogs, stay on the porch!" I thought, as my bouncing genitals gave the girl at my feet a meter to accurately measure of the pounding recoil of my rifle as it weighed down the rapidly approaching mongrel with lead.

Now with two of the feral curs out of the way, I gave my full attention to the two that were closing in on us fast from each side.

I quickly swung my rifle to the right and drew down on the dog on that side first.

As it leaped into the air off of the cliff like river bank and started its downward trajectory toward us, I shot a bullet into its mouth that followed the backbone of the animal clear to its tail, and the dead dog plowed into the sand between the legs of the girl that was still lying at my feet.

I had chosen to shoot the dog on my right side first, because I knew that I could swing my gun around faster to the left side and get a quicker sight picture on the last of the malevolent pooches that was rushing toward us.

I did just that, and with one final shot, I ended the canine's attack at the riverbank.

"Thank you," the girl that was still lying at my feet said, looking up at me past my manhood that was still swaying from the rifle's recoil.

I held out my hand and helped the girl to her feet.

Not out of kindness, I wanted her to stand up so I could search her for weapons, even though I hadn't seen any up to that point.

I wasn't about to turn my naked back on some hyper-active, man-hating, psychopathic whore that I didn't know (and I have known some from time to time),

146

that might have been ready, and more than willing to turn my lights out at a moment's notice without as much as saying fuck to me.

Especially, just because I was too lazy, stupid, or too busy drooling over her tits to check the fucking cunt for weapons first.

Not that I was being judgmental mind you, I was just being cautious, and there was no way in hell that we were going to continue our conversation any further without me frisking her first.

As the young woman got to her feet, her toned body and curvaceous features did not hesitate to revel themselves to me, so I quickly took inventory of her, visually at first, and then I thought that a hands on method of searching would probably be a bit more *protracted* but yield far more information about the female's possible if not probable risk to my health.

The girl stood about five foot five inches tall and weighed in at somewhere between one hundred and fifteen pounds and I wouldn't kick her out of bed for eating crackers.

She looked to be somewhere in her early to mid twenties, which was younger than I was, yet she was still legal in every state and most civilized countries around the world.

Her short brown hair although relatively clean except for the beach sand she had just plowed into, looked like someone had trimmed it with a malfunctioning weed-cutter with an automatic centrifugal clutch.

She wore a clinging blood stained white short-sleeve t-shirt that very effectively put her shapely jiggling twins on display, and with her skintight designer jeans adhering to her pelvic region as if they had been painted onto her body, I didn't need to hear anything that she had to say, because I could read her lips without really even trying.

However, wearing her color coordinated blue high-heeled sneakers that laced up passed her ankles, it was a wonder that she wasn't being toted around in the south-end of someone's (something's) underwear by now.

How in the living hell she was able to stay out in front of that pack of feral dogs while wearing those shoes was beyond my comprehension.

Looking at the girl, even with her punk-like haircut and being as semi-dirty as she was, I wouldn't have called her homely by any stretch; even without makeup I think she rated on a scale of 1 to 10, somewhere around... *Plain Jane*, certainly no lower. At least from the neck up I mean. Below the neck was an entirely different story. There she climbed up the scale quite dramatically.

"Hold still, I'm going to check you for weapons," I told her, in the harshest voice I could convincingly muster standing before her in my birthday suit, thinking that I wouldn't mind checking her for ticks either.

"I don't have any weapons, I dropped my knife somewhere back when the dogs were chasing me," she insisted.

"Good move, dropping your only weapon while being chased by a pack of hostile dogs," I declared sarcastically.

"I couldn't help it, I tripped and fell, and the knife flew out of my hand. The dogs were already gaining on me, so I didn't have time to retrieve it. You saw how close they were, if I would have stopped even for a moment, they would have surely caught up to me and killed me.

Hey, if you hadn't have been here, I would be dead by now anyway.

There's no way I could have fought off all of those dogs with just my knife.

You can go ahead and search me if you want, but I'm telling you that the knife I lost was the only weapon that I had," the girl said, as she continued to whine.

"I'll be the judge of that," I said, remembering the keys in Jason's pocket I had missed, as I patted the front of her body down, even though I had not seen any *unnatural* bumps.

Doing a swift groping search by checking her *natural* bumps (which quickly and pleasure-fully, considering she wasn't wearing a bra at the time), revealed that she was hiding no *lethal* weapons above the waist.

Then by feeling around her shapely hips and slightly down into the waistline of her skintight jeans, I found no weapons below her waist either.

Well, no *lethal* weapons anyway! Just a single house key buried deep in her right front pocket.

"*Nice set*, now turn around," I ordered, complementing her on her hormonal growth as I spun the buxom woman's backside toward me.

I made one final check of the back of her waistband, and with a gentle pat on her callipygian butt, I communicated to her that maybe sometime in the future we might be able to become *friends*. Or at least, check each other for ticks.

After searching the woman, I deemed that she was telling me the truth and that she had no weapons on her person (except for those two locked and loaded torpedoes that she had strapped on her chest and was lugging around all over fuck's creation).

"Okay, you're clean," I announced, as I spun her back around to face me again, and brushed some of the sand off her shoulders. "Well kind of."

"I told you I didn't have anything that could hurt you," she asserted with a smile, as if she had just won an argument.

"I know you did, but I can't take any chances, I've seen too much out here to trust someone that I don't know. Even someone as innocent and harmless looking as you," I maintained, making no effort to hide the *naked* truth.

"Well anyway, thank you again for saving me from those damn dogs."

"You're welcome, I guess," I answered, as I picked up my pistol and walked away. "Let me get some clothes on, and then we can get properly introduced."

I pulled my damp clothing from the tree branch and proceeded to put on my pants.

The girl slowly brushed the sand off her clothes, and began to shake her head wildly.

"I'll never get all of this sand out of my hair," she complained, running her fingers through her hair.

When I was all dressed, and the girl I had saved was done shaking the sand off her, we introduced ourselves to each other.

"I think you know me a little better than I know you," I said, with a slightly embarrassed smile on my face. "My name is Jack, what's yours?"

"I'm Cassandra," the girl answered.

"Well Cassandra, it's nice to meet you, but I've got to ask, what in the hell is a big tit-ed woman like you, doing running around this paganistic savage land all by yourself?"

"I was out looking for food and weapons, and not having much luck finding either one when I saw those dogs you just killed. They were quite a distance away, but heading in my direction. So I began to run away to try to maintain the gap and avoid them, but no matter which way I turned, or how fast I ran, they were still behind me.

Well, one thing led to another, and before I knew it, I was pretty far from my sister's house, and the dogs had almost caught up to me. So I ran as fast as I could to the river thinking that I'd have a better chance of fighting them off if I jumped into the water. But instead, you were here and saved me," Cassandra explained.

"Yes I did, I saved your life, now you owe me everything you've got... pay up!" I teased jokingly. "But seriously, I think we had better get the hell out of here. I mean if you're coming with me. I'm not an expert on those damn canines, but I've never seen a pack of feral dogs that small, they usually run in bigger packs, so there's probably more of them traipsing around here somewhere.

Nevertheless, it's up to you, you can travel with me for awhile if you'd like, or we can go our separate ways right now, it's your call.

However, if you're going to go with me, then wiggle your pretty little butt in this direction, because I'm getting the heck out of Dodge as we speak.

Before more dogs show up, or eaters, or whatever in the hell might show up that I'm going to have to kill," I told her, as I trudged back through the muddy water of the small runoff, and began the short walk back to my truck.

"I need to get to my sister's house; it's not too far from here. Do you think you could take me there?" she asked, as she followed me to my vehicle.

"Where exactly does this sister of yours live, and what's she going to say when you drag a strange man into her house?" I questioned, trying to see what I might be getting myself into.

"She won't say anything, she never says much since our sister Pam died." Cassandra answered, looking forlorn.

"I'm sorry to hear that, what happened to her," I asked, as if I didn't already have a good idea, and really gave a shit about her sister which I never knew.

"It's a long story," Cassandra answered sadly.

"Well considering that you've had the distinct pleasure of seeing me buck-ass naked, i.e. full frontal male nudity, I think you can take the time to share your story with me," I said smiling, still a little embarrassed by the incident.

Smiling back at me as she climbed into the truck, Cassandra began to tell me the lurid tale of how her sibling paid the ultimate price.

"Well it wasn't all that long ago, my sister Pam, her new baby Kyle, and I were hiding out with her boy friend Dick in this metal warehouse like place after being run out of my home by a bunch of the resurrected ones.

We were trying to get to my other sister's house, Carla; she lived several blocks away, that's where we're going now, to Carla's house."

"You call them the resurrected ones, that seems like a mouthful to say when you're in a pinch. I mean, what do you do when one of those sons-a-bitches is about to eat one of your friends? Hey lookout, the resurrected ones are attacking you," I said, laughing. "I just call them eaters; it's short, sweet, and to the point. All you have to do is yell out "Eaters" and get down to the business of killing the dead bastards."

"That makes sense, maybe I'll start calling them that too," Cassandra, concurred.

"Which way is it to your sister's house?" I asked, as I started the truck and put it into gear.

"If you go straight down this road for about two miles and then hang a left and go a couple more blocks we'll be there," Cassandra answered, pointing the way.

"Then we move," I said, pushing down on the little pedal on the right. "But don't let me stop you, please continue with your story."

"Well, on the way to Carla's house we were attacked again, that's when we ran inside the warehouse to hide. It was kind of small, but with the metal walls and roof, it was pretty secure from the resurrected ones, I mean eaters, and from the dogs, and we hadn't seen any normal people for awhile so we felt kind of safe there.

I don't know what kind of business used to be in it, it was empty when we got there. Just a couple of workbenches and an old refrigerator filled with mold.

We couldn't go outside to gather food and water or anything else. So we spent most of the time just sitting around inside that big metal shed.

After a couple of days we needed food and water really bad, especially the baby, he wouldn't stop crying. And his constant screaming was the reason that the resurrected ones. Damn, I mean eaters, stayed in the neighborhood for so long, and literally had us trapped in the building."

As Cassandra relayed the story to me, tears began to run down her cheeks. I wasn't quite sure why at the time. Her story so far sounded like a typical zombie apocalyptic nightmare that we had all been going through for over a year now.

Everyone had been surrounded by a pack of bloodthirsty dead demons in a feeding frenzy at one time or another, it sounded pretty normal to me.

However, I was about to find out what had her so upset.

"On the third day we decided to make a run for it, and that's when it happened.

Besides the constant badgering outside by the resurrected ones... eaters, the never ending howling and screaming by my sister's baby had us all at our wits end.

That's when Dick, my sister's boyfriend, but not Kyle's father said."

******

Several weeks earlier...

"Will you shut that brat up, it's going to get us all killed," Dick yelled, over the baby's screams.

"He won't be quiet, he's hungry and thirsty, he hasn't had anything to eat or drink in days," Pam said, flustered.

"If he would just shut the fuck up for a couple of minutes maybe the zombies would go away, and we could get the fuck out of here, did you ever think of that?" Dick screamed, as his rage became apparent in his eyes.

"Well I don't know what to do, we don't have any food or water to give him, and that's why he's crying, he's starving and dehydrated," Pam screamed back.

"I heard you the first time bitch, now did you hear me?" Dick demanded, still screaming. "The little bastard is going to get us all killed if he doesn't shut the fuck up!"

"Both of you shut the fuck up, before *you two* get us all killed," Cassandra interrupted in a loud whisper.

"Well then, if you don't get Kyle some food and water, I guess we'll all just get killed then," Pam stated to Dick in a snotty tone.

"I'm not going sit in this metal container like spam in a can waiting to get eaten by the undead, just because you can't control that God dammed screaming bastard of yours!" Dick now whispered loudly as well, just before snatching Pam's baby from her arms.

Now Kyle screamed even louder as Dick pummeled the child with his open hand, slapping the holy shit out of the kid and screaming in his face.

"Shut the fuck up!"

"What are doing to my baby?" Pam yelled, as she lunged forward and tried to pull her baby from Dick's arms.

Dick side stepped the charging women and shoved her to the floor.

"I'm gonna shut this fucking brat up, somebody has to, and since you and your stupid-ass sister over there won't do it, I guess it's up to me to do the heavy lifting around here," Dick snarled, gesturing toward Cassandra.

"Shut up Dick, and give me that baby before you really hurt him," Cassandra ordered the infuriated man.

"Fuck you Cassandra, I told you two I'm not going to die because of some out of control brat," Dick shrieked, tucking little Kyle under his left arm and grabbing a hold of the crown of his little head with his right hand.

By now Kyle had reduced his caterwauling to a mere whimper, because even at his young and tender age of only a couple of months, he had sensed that the severe pain associated with the proper beat down that he was receiving from Dick, was correlated to his incessant howling.

However, being clenched under the hairy arm of his pissed off knuckle-dragging attacker, the baby Kyle was helpless to do anything except realize that without a doubt, he had fucked up royally.

Unfortunately for Kyle, the realization of his situation came too late, and although he had now completely stopped his unsettling yowling and adopted a demeanor of total calm and silence, Dick had already began his grisly deed.

The two women watched in horror; as Kyle's eyes began to bulge out of their sockets as Dick slowly twisted the baby's head clockwise one hundred and eighty degrees.

A sickening and slight crunching sound was heard as Kyle's immature neck bones were stretched past their limit and began to separate from one another.

Kyle had died almost instantly when his head reached 94°, his almost non-existent neck muscles being no match for Dick's strong twisting grip.

However, Dick didn't stop there.

Letting go of Kyle's limp drooping head, which was now 180° awry. Dick quickly renegotiated his grip on the small head and began twisting it another 180° further.

Then with a forceful tug on Kyle's light brown hair, the maniacal bruiser wrenched the child's head from its body and a muffled popping sound ushered in a split second of total silence inside the warehouse.

Kyle's lifeless small frame that was being cradled in Dick's left arm like a football; leaked his life's blood onto the floor, and his decapitated head that Dick now held in right hand similar to the way a basketball player palms a basketball; was dripping the same crimson liquid onto the floor as well.

Within seconds, the headless body of the eight-week old child began to squirm in Dick's grasp as the toothless jaws of the infant started to open and close and its glazed over eyes rolled up and down and back and forth; glaring shortly at each adult before moving on to the next one.

Cassandra, speechless and paralyzed with shock, stood there with her mouth hanging wide open.

Pam on the other hand was now hysterical with grief; first letting out a blood-curdling scream and breaking the momentary quiet, and then she yelled.

"What have you done to my baby? You monster!"

Dick, startled by Pam's sudden high pitched squeal and the feeling of Kyle's bobbing head trying to escape the hold he had on it, released his grip on both the dead baby's body and head and let them drop to the floor as he stepped back.

Kyle's head dropped straight down and landed neck first on the smooth concrete floor of the warehouse.

A low bass-toned squirting sound reminiscent of a fat woman's diarrhea fart shot out into the room as the air in the small neck was forced out between the concrete floor and the torn flesh that comprised the rim of what was left of the little baby's neck.

The release of the bubble of air out of the neck caused a vacuum that attached the ogling infant's head to the floor like a suction cup.

Pam who was beside herself and not thinking clearly, allowed her maternal instincts to skew her clarity in the matter just as most mothers would, and almost before her bone-chilling screech had stopped echoing throughout the empty warehouse, Pam dove to the floor toward Kyle's decapitated head like a professional baseball player might slide into second base headfirst.

As she scooped the head between her arms and drug herself to Kyle's face using her elbows to pull her along the floor and the vacuum-sealed skull as an anchor, the chomping head attached itself to Pam's lower lip by clamping down on it with its toothless gums, as it would have done with a nipple during breast-feeding.

Now, with Pam and her baby seeing eye to eye (do I have to say it?), Pam's maternal instincts turned to panic and she stretched her captured lip to its limit as she tried to pull away from the anchored head that was determined to suck the life from her lower lip.

However, Dick was still pissed because even though the kid had stopped howling, he felt that his girlfriend had taken up where her little brat had left off.

So, Dick took a half step forward and kicked the seven pound wallowing infant's carcass (with the head attached it would have been closer to ten or eleven pounds) toward Cassandra.

With his other foot he proceeded to launch a full soccer style kick to the back of Kyle's small head, detaching it from its hold on the floor and forcing it to smash hard into Pam's face, breaking her nose and flattening it against her face, while splitting both her upper and lower lips in the process.

The powerful kick crushed the soft bones of the baby's skull, allowing the toe of Dick's boot to penetrate into part of the neonate's brain, killing it dead, and sending Kyle to the train station with a one-way ticket to hell.

The broken bones in the back of Kyle's now caved-in head were crunched together by Dick's impromptu boot battering, causing the tiny jaws to clamp down even harder and lock into place on Pam's swelling bottom lip.

The impact from the collision when the two faces collided, caused not only Kyle's head to be mutilated even more, but also did serious damage to Pam's face and lips as well, leaving both her and her baby with open lacerations on their faces, and unintentionally trading bodily fluids with each other.

Even more panicked now; with the crumpled head of her dead baby seemingly permanently latched and dangling from her broken and bleeding face and lips. Pam stood up and began to swat at the crinkled head, bitch slapping it back and forth as if she was playing tetherball, Kyle's head being the ball, and her lower lip being the tether, and her body serving as the pole.

The horrendous sight of Kyle's crushed skull being swung around and spattering blood in all directions, along with pieces of his small pink brain that wasn't stuck to the top of Dick's boot, snapped Cassandra out of her shock induced trance as she watched Pam wallop the swinging cranium, trading hands with each whack, like a New York City pimp slapping the shit out of one of his stable whores for trying to hold back a fifty-dollar bill on a Saturday night.

As Pam pummeled the lip-locked head around the room, both Cassandra and Dick realized that the saliva coming from the dead baby zombie's head, mixing with the open cuts on Pam's bruised and battered face, and especially her split lower lip, was akin to her being bitten by one of the undead.

As a result of the infant's spit entering her blood stream, it wouldn't be long before she too would turn into one of the diseased cannibals that she was busy slapping silly as they watched.

Soon after that she would turn to *them* for her first meal in three days.

Dick who was still angered by the continued noise that Pam was making as she screamed and relentlessly continued to slap at the head of her dead son. Now was fearing that he might lose his life to his (now former) girlfriend, didn't hesitate to step up to the plate so to speak, and put an end to the macabre display of mayhem.

Grabbing the arm flailing Pam by the hair on the back of her head with one hand, and lifting up on the back of her pants using her belt with his other hand, he lifted her feet off of the ground, and as her legs wiggled and kicked trying to reach the concrete surface of the floor to gain traction, Dick used her face (and Kyle's still attached head) as a battering ram, running it headlong into the skinny side of one of the I-beams used as part of the structure's supports.

The bones in Pam's face were crushed, her forehead was split open like a ripe watermelon that had been hacked in two with a large butcher knife, and now she too was dead.

Cassandra had feared for her life as well, not only from the likely forthcoming zombie sister that was soon to be present within the walls of their sanctuary, but also from the crazed baby killer in her midst.

Now with one of the potential threats eliminated by the other, Cassandra knew that she would have to act fast if she wanted to live.

After all she thought.

"If he would do that to a defenseless baby just because it was crying, what does he have in store for me?"

As Dick dropped Pam's limp body and watched it collapse downward, the two sides of her brain squeezed the steel beam as it swelled, causing her to slide slowly towards the floor. The slow movement of her sister's body slipping down the support, gave Cassandra enough time to rush toward Dick with her knife in hand, (the knife she had lost just before meeting Jack).

Waving her knife over her head to compensate for the height difference between the two adults, Cassandra attacked her would be murderer with a violent fervor.

Dick never saw his demise or Cassandra coming.

As he watched the fingers on Pam's lifeless body beginning to twitch, while both hemispheres of her dissected brain still squeezed the thin side of the vertical steel I-beam, the last thing he remembered seeing was two inches of Cassandra's eight-inch butcher knife blade which she had stuck through the back of his skull, now protruding out of his forehead.

******

Several weeks later...

"And after I stuck my knife through Dick's head, I had no choice but to sit in that warehouse and try not to pay attention to the three dead bodies that were squirming around on the floor.

So I waited in that god forsaken warehouse and stayed quiet until I stopped hearing the resurrected ones... damn it, I did it again, I mean the eaters. Anyway, I waited for what seemed like a lifetime for them to stop moaning and groaning, scratching on the side of the building, and milling around outside, when they finally did leave, that's when I left the warehouse and made my way to my other sister's house," Cassandra described, wiping her tears on her sleeve. "With nobody crying or

162

screaming inside the building I guess the *eaters* lost interest after awhile."

******

While listening to Cassandra's story, I was reminded of a theory of mine relating to the emergence of the almost instantaneous body movements of anyone or part of anyone that has been killed, or dismembered after the fact. Because I've not had the satisfaction of seeing my theory demonstrated on an appendage cut off, torn off, or in any way removed from a living person like myself, I'm not sure if it applies to limbs that once belonged to living humans who may have lost an arm, leg, hand, foot, or finger etc. and survived.

In the beginning, only the severed heads of the dead were still active after their owner's demise, as long as they hadn't received enough blunt or sharp-force-trauma to destroy the brain inside.

However, as time passed (well over a year now), the bodies of the twitchers, or the severed body parts thereof, began moving almost immediately after the brain had been killed or the head had been separated from the body.

My theory on this subject goes something like this.

The virus, which is apparently lying dormant in everyone, incubates for an unknown period of time, which seems to be getting much shorter, then at some point in the fermentation process it begins producing positive charged ions which titillate the nerve endings and makes the muscles in the body (or body parts) involuntarily flex. The result of this process is the bizarre phenomenon of twitchers.

******

"Well Dick sounds like a fitting name for the asshole," I claimed. "I mean considering everything that you've told me."

Cassandra nodded in agreement as she pointed to a white house with a big front yard that sat on a corner lot.

"That's my sister's house right over there."

I pulled my truck over the curb and into the yard and drove it close to the front door of the building like I always do, parking it close just in case a timely exit is called for.

After hearing the story of how Cassandra's sister Pam had met her maker, and how the boyfriend Dick had tweaked the kid for lathering up the zombies that had them surrounded, I thought.

"I probably would do the same thing if the need for such activity ever arose. Only I'd do it without all of the feminine bitching and moaning that this Dick character had done."

"Would you like to come in for a while, you can if you want to, maybe have a drink or two, and who knows, maybe I'll take you up on your offer to ride along with you," Cassandra invited with a smile. "There's really not much left for me around here anymore and I really would like the company, my sister Carla isn't much of a conversationalist."

"Sure!" I responded cheerfully to the gracious invitation. "It's been a long time since I had a drink with a pretty girl."

Needless to say, I kept my thoughts about Dick's behavior to myself as I prepared to meet Cassandra's other sister Carla.

Thinking that I probably wouldn't be very long inside her sister's house, one drink was going to be my limit, because I wasn't about to get slobbery drunk in a strange house that I hadn't secured for myself, pretty girl or not.

So I stuffed my Glock 19, and tomahawk under the seat, and crammed my Sub-2000 along with my M-4 and tactical vest into the small space behind the seat where I had stored the tainted bottle of whiskey, and took only my machete and suppressed Beretta with me.

As we bailed out of the truck and jogged the three yards or so onto Carla's porch, I asked.

"Are you sure your sister won't mind you bringing a strange man into her house with you?"

"Oh she won't mind at all, she's been dead for quite some time now," Cassandra answered, showing no emotion.

I found it odd that Cassandra hadn't mention to me earlier that her sister was dead. Even when I had asked her back at the river if her sister would mind her bringing a stranger home with her, she made no mention of the death of her sister Carla. All she said was that her sister doesn't say much since the other sister had died.

With all of the killing and dying that she relayed to me in her tale of the little baby Kyle and her sister Pam's ultimate demise, it seemed to me to be a rather easy segue to transition to.

On top of that, she had been blubbering like a schoolgirl all the way from the river as she told me how she managed to escape the zombie entrapment at the warehouse; all at the expense of three other people, one of which she cacked herself because she felt that he needed to be cacked I might add. Now she didn't even blink an eye at the mention of this other sister being dead.

Maybe she was immune to all the killing and death this world had to offer, I know I was getting to that point myself. And all the sniveling in the truck was just a relapse into previous emotions.

Or, maybe she hated her sister Carla's guts, and never really gave a shit about that particular sibling.

Of course, the reason for her uncaring attitude might have been because she has so many brothers and sisters, aunts and uncles, mothers and fathers, cousins, dogs and cats, not to mention gold fish, that she feels that she can spare a few from time to time if the occasion calls for it.

A little sarcasm to lighten the mood, it's one of my best distinguishing characteristics you know.

Whatever the reason for Cassandra's emotional perspective, something didn't seem right to me, so I decided to maintain my usually combat ready situational awareness until I was completely sure that Cassandra posed no danger to me.

Cassandra led the way, unlocking the door with the house key that I had found during my search of her personal assets.

We entered the house which looked a lot bigger on the outside than it did on the inside.

"Make yourself comfortable and I'll get those drinks I mention," Cassandra said, as she disappeared into the kitchen. "Sit on the couch, it's way more comfortable than the chair is."

I took her advice and planted my slightly sunburned butt in the middle of the couch that she had recommended, placing both my pistol and my machete on the couch cushion at my right side. That way if Cassandra chose to sit beside me, she would be free to sit on my left side, leaving my right hand available to do any pleasurable work that might become necessary. Such as another impromptu weapons search.

I mean if the evening went in that direction.

After all, she had already seen me naked as a Jay Bird, and who knows, maybe she liked what she'd seen.

And besides, a consensual cavity search of the woman would go a long way in convicting me that she was harmless.

It wasn't long before Cassandra returned to the living room with a bottle of wine and two glasses.

"Sorry I don't have any wine glasses, I hope you don't mind," she said, with a somewhat artificial smile on her face.

I had seen the fake smile that Cassandra had plastered on her puss (*puss* fits better than mug, or face, in this particular narrative). It was the same fake smile that strippers used to get guys to pony up bigger tips at the titty bars where they danced; strippers in every city in the world used the artificial smile tactic, before the end days that is (see what I mean about puss).

Cassandra stood in front of me pouring equal amounts of wine into the generic glasses that she had sat on a coffee table that separated the two of us.

167

"Before we get started partaking in this complementary libation that you've so generously offered, I have a question about the warehouse and the starving baby," I said, canting my head to the left.

"Sure, go ahead and ask," she said, as she finished pouring our drinks. "I've got nothing to hide."

Now, I really wished that she hadn't made that comment, because everybody knows that people that find it necessary to announce that they don't have anything to hide; usually have a hell of a lot to hide.

With my senses now heightened to possible danger, I proceeded to ask my question.

"Well as you, and your sister which had recently had a baby, were trapped in that warehouse, surrounded by ravenous eaters, with said baby starving and crying for food, did it ever occur to anyone that one of the two of you girls might want to flop out a tit and feed the kid? Or at the least, cram one of your natural pacifiers into his mouth to calm him down?"

A confused look swept over Cassandra's face momentarily wiping away her smile.

Then as fast as her smile had disappeared, it was back, and the look in her eyes was like someone had illuminated a light bulb over her head.

"Speaking of breast feeding, that reminds me, I need to change my shirt," she replied, as she lifted the bottom of her muddy bloodstained shirt and pulled it inside out over her head.

Now as the shirtless woman with what I guessed to be a choice set of 38 D's, wagged her impressive pair of juicy exposed breasts at me from across the room as she

168

began a slow, rhythmic, and methodical dance; even though the room was completely devoid of any music.

You might think that I would sit back, drink my glass of warm wine, and enjoy the show. After all, I had placed my paraphernalia on the couch in a place that would free me up in hopes of just this type of event.

However, I still had this nagging feeling that something wasn't quite right.

So with a smile on my face, I took what was the first sip and what was to be the last sip of my wine as I nonchalantly reached for the handle of my machete.

I picked up the *bush*-trimming tool (under the circumstances, no pun intended) and began to tap the flat side of the blade on the couch in time with a chorus of imaginary music that Cassandra was dancing to.

As the blade bounced higher with each strike on the foam rubber couch cushion, the dull reflection on the blood stained steel blade reflected an image that was moving behind the couch, which confirmed the ominous feeling that had been pestering me was well founded by revealing the danger that was lurking there.

Seeing the startled look on my face that I was unable to contain, even though I had been leery of my new *would-be* girlfriend from the moment we walked through the front door, Cassandra screamed out.

"Now Carla, now!" as she quickly slipped her stained t-shirt back over her head and pulled it down, once more hiding her exposed tits from view.

Sensing that there was no time to try to contort my neck to the right and tweak my body in the direction of the sinister reflection to get a better look at the perceived threat. I instead, leaned forward on the couch and twisted my body the opposite way to try to create some distance between myself, and the person I now knew to be Cassandra's *not* so dead sister Carla.

Now in full twisting mode I dropped the generic glass of wine and stood up. The momentum of my adrenaline powered pirouette spun me around to the left so quickly and so forcefully that if I hadn't have grabbed the double barreled shotgun that Carla was brandishing in my direction with my left hand, I would have completed a full 360° rotation and ended up with my back to the maniacal sister and her 12 gauge riot gun again.

With my hand midway down the barrel of the gun, I pulled the muzzle passed the left side of my body and cradled the shotgun under my left arm.

Carla's index finger (trigger finger) had been gently caressing the forward edge of the gun's trigger until I yanked the firearm to me. Her finger placement on the weapon's trigger in conjunction with my violent tug caused enough pressure to be applied to the firing mechanism to produce a discharge of the firearm.

The noise of the shotgun's blast not only signaled that the double barrel weapon had now spent half of its ammunition, but together with a shrill scream that came from behind me, helped announce that two fingers on Cassandra's right hand were now missing in action.

I tugged further on the barrel of the gun dragging Carla halfway over the back of the couch where she had been hiding.

As she squirmed helplessly, bent at the waist over the couch, and struggling to retrieve the gun from me, she tilted her head up to see her sister sitting against the living room wall clutching her bleeding three-fingered hand.

Carla was much huskier than Cassandra, taller and built like a professional football player. She had the same garden tool haircut, and it was apparent that she was no stranger to a fork entering and exiting her mouth.

I didn't know if they were really sisters or not, and at the time I didn't care, nor was I in any mood to ask.

With Carla's head two feet from my crotch, I heaved up one more time on the barrel of the gun under my left arm, raising her head as I did so, and with one smooth and coordinated motion, I parted the chubby girl's oily hair three inches into her brain with a swift downward stroke of my machete.

Then I quickly turned around to face Cassandra (if that was her real name) anticipating her attacking me too, only to find her still huddled against the wall squeezing her wounded hand and sobbing from the pain.

I unloaded the shotgun, stuck the single remaining un-spent shell into my pocket, and let the gun that was still held in the clenched fist of the deceased sister drop onto the couch beside her dead body as I shared my thoughts with Cassandra.

"You fucking cunt," I said to her calmly and in a monotone voice. "I was thinking about making you my *main* squeeze, taking you to Indiana with me, the whole nine yards, but you've ruined that for yourself, you fucking cunt.

If you and your sister, or lover, or whatever in the hell that "Bull Lesbian" looking thing is over there twitching on the couch hadn't tried to go all Dick Cheney on me with that coach gun. Well you'd still have

171

all of your fingers, and Carla wouldn't be draped over the back of that sofa with a new part in her nasty custom haircut, thrashing around and thinking about where she went wrong in life as her brains leak out onto the floor.

Now let me guess, I'm supposed to just take this despicable and heinous act of treachery in stride and blow it off, after all, I lived through it, so no harm no foul right?" I asked, as I pointed to the middle linebacker flopping up and down on the couch."

Reeling in pain Cassandra cried. "I'm sorry, it was my sister, she made me do it, I didn't want to, she made me."

"Bull shit," I maintained, still in a low monotone communication.

"No really, she has been a little off for over a year now.

A few months after people began to rise up and walk around dead, Carla swore that she had seen dinosaurs roaming the countryside. She claimed to have seen a T-Rex and two velociraptors while she was out alone trying to find us some food.

I never saw any such thing, but I was sequestered in Pam's house during that time and we were both too scared to go outside, even to look for food.

I don't know what Carla saw that day, as if seeing dead people walking around trying to eat you wasn't enough, but whatever it was that she saw, dinosaurs or not, it seemed to put the zap on her head. Because when we finally met up she wasn't the same as she used to be," Cassandra remembered, as she cringed from the pain of exposed raw nerve endings caused by her absent digits.

172

As Cassandra continued to try to convince me that she had not been a willing participant in the planning or the execution of the failed ambush that had ultimately extracted two of her fingers from her hand and her alleged sister from the living, her eyes became glassy and began to roll back in her head.

"Oh, now you're going to pass out on me, what, the pain is too much for you?" I asked, sarcastically.

******

Jack hadn't been this pissed-off in a long time. He had befriended this woman, saved her life, offered to team up with her and travel together, and had not really asked for anything in return.

Although he had figured that sometime in the future they might get acquainted a little better and maybe even do some *naked wallowing* down the road somewhere, and even though she had seen him close up in the raw, and turnabout is fair play, he wasn't in a big hurry to jump her bones before she was ready.

And what was his reward for all of his hard work, bravery, patience, and kindness?

He thought it was the proverbial sharp stick in the eye, and he was sick to hell of people poking him with sharp sticks.

From the start, he didn't completely buy Cassandra's story about the baby Kyle, and how he met his demise.

Although it wasn't all that farfetched considering everything he'd seen since the undead began to walk the earth.

173

The excuse she gave him about not wanting to be a part of her sister's bushwhacking attempt didn't wash either.

On their way to *Carla's* (supposed) house from the river, she could have easily said, *"Can I go with you?"* and never even mentioned Carla or the house where she was hiding, and none of this would have happened.

They'd be on their way to Indiana together.

She would still have ten fingers attached to her hands.

And her so-called sister Carla wouldn't be twitching on the couch in dire need of seven hundred stitches in the top of her skull, along with an emergency brain transplant.

Yes, Jack was really pissed off at Cassandra, so pissed off in fact that his angry brought back memories of Matt the hillbilly he had scalped as he passed through Arkansas, leaving the man alive, bald, and most likely waking up with a horrendous headache.

******

"If it's good enough for Matt, I think that's it's good enough for you," I said, as I walked toward the front door.

"What?" Cassandra mumbled, just barely conscious.

"I've got something for you, it's out in my truck," I answered. "You know; the truck that we would have been, could have been, and should have been driving up to Indiana as we speak."

"Oh, that truck," Cassandra acknowledged; murmuring as her eyes again rolled back into her head.

After making sure that the coast was clear, I sprinted out the door and off the porch, scurrying to my truck to retrieve the bottle of whiskey that I had stashed behind the seat.

In the distance I could see a small cluster of zombies making their way west down a side street four or five blocks away, and another group that was much farther away coming toward the house.

Due to the absence of the brain-eaters close to the house, the sound of the shotgun blast inside the home had been muffled enough that the undead a few blocks away hadn't been attracted by the noise.

However, their presents told me that feral dogs roaming in the neighborhood were probably nonexistent; at least that was still the ongoing theory up to that moment.

Dogs move in, zombies move out. Zombies appear, and dogs disappear.

Who knows what that's all about, but everyone that's still alive has already figured out that in this hellish new world you had better be ready for anything, because sooner or later, whatever anything is, it's probably going to show up at some point and try to kill you.

In any case, the zombie population was beginning to multiply in the neighborhood and I would need to be quiet and try not to attract uninvited guests to Carla's house.

With whiskey bottle in hand, I bolted back onto the porch and back into the house.

Cassandra hadn't moved from the spot where she had squatted the moment her finger's departed from her hand.

With Cassandra still on the verge of passing out, I held the tainted bottle of booze up to her mouth.

"Here you cunt, drink this," I offered politely, knowing that she would take a drink, *whether she wanted to or not*. I would make sure of that.

"What is it?" she asked groggily swaying from side to side.

"It's what you're going to need to kill the pain, it's whiskey," I answered. "It's the *really* good stuff."

In shock and sitting on the border between consciousness and blacking out, Cassandra thanked me and took a sip from the drug-laced bottle.

Little did she know at the time, but it was the last sip of anything that she would drink as a full-fledged woman, for school was in session and I was the teacher, and I intended to teach the little bitch a hard lesson that she wouldn't soon forget.

It was apparent from her recent actions that she liked surprises; after all, she surprised me by showing up at my private beach unannounced with a pack of feral dogs in hot pursuit, begging me to help her. Then she and Carla didn't hesitate to surprise me with a double-barreled shotgun pointed at my back.

Therefore, I figured who was I to deny her what seemed to be one of her favorite pastimes, which was obviously to blind side people with surprises. So I intended to give her the surprise of her life, and she'd get it as soon as she woke up from the drug induced stupor that I was about to inflict upon her.

176

"Take another sip, I think you're going to need it," I insisted, as I pressed the neck of the bottle between her lips. "Pretty good stuff isn't it?"

My question was to go unanswered as Cassandra's eyelids slowly dropped over her eyes as the knockout drug quickly took control of her conscious-will and plunged her into a deep slumber.

"Well Cassandra, if that's your real name, this is your lucky day, you're lucky I like you and decided to give you something to put you to sleep first," I told the unconscious woman that was slumped over at my feet.

I pulled my four-inch folded skinning knife from my front pocket and flipped the blade open. I had yet to kill or maim a zombie with this specific knife, I had only used it to slice the food I was eating and to cut rope and other relatively clean inanimate objects that needed to be cut, sliced, diced, or trimmed, and sometimes even julienned, so I deemed it safe to use to maim Cassandra without the fear of infecting her with any latent germs from the undead and thereby causing her to prematurely join their ranks.

After kicking her two slothfully inactive ejected fingers out of the way and noticing that their apathetic attitude toward any movement answered my question pertaining to my theory on motion after separation in the living (in which there was none), I shoved Cassandra's limp body from its sitting position to a recumbent posture on the floor, and rolled her over onto her back.

I put my pocketknife up to her throat, and with the blade turned upward, I jabbed the point of the blade through the top of her shirt being careful not to poke her skin, and used a sawing motion to cut the thick material at the neck of her garment.

Then after turning the knife over, I continued to slit her bloodstained white shirt down the middle, again being careful not to nick her skin with the sharp blade, or slice through any of the dried blood on the shirt.

With Cassandra's shirt now resembling a vest more than a shirt, I peeled back both sides of the ruined apparel revealing her hefty set of major league yabos once again.

Tearing a thin strip of relatively clean cloth from her shirt, I wrapped it around her wrist, making a tourniquet to stop the profuse bleeding from her wounded hand.

I left the girl who once was my *would be* girlfriend, lying bare-chested and unconscious on the living room floor, and made my way into the kitchen.

I collected a hodgepodge of flammable items such as paper towels, wooden spoons, and anything else that would burn, piled them into the right side of the double sink, and opened the kitchen window above it several inches to vent the forthcoming smoke.

An eight-inch iron skillet hanging with a four-piece set was perfect for the job at hand.

A box of kitchen matches above the stove was the final component needed to begin the first phase of Cassandra's learning process.

As flames rose from the right side of the sink, I filled the left side with water from Cassandra's bottled water stash that she and Carla had no doubt pilfered from somewhere or somebody, and searched the kitchen cabinets for a container of salt and a large freezer bag.

After locating a 12-inch plastic bag and cardboard container of salt with a girl on the label that was too stupid to get in out of the rain, I poured the entire contents of the heavy-paper canister into the bag which I sat on the counter on the left side of the sink.

Before I returned to Cassandra in the living room, I tossed two more wooden spoons, several more paper towels, and a box of breakfast cereal onto the fire. Then I carefully placed the black cast iron frying pan on top of the cereal box.

The fire in the sink was burning nicely and its smoke was being sucked out of the kitchen window as planned, so I hurried back into the living room knowing that Cassandra would be anxious to receive her surprise.

Cassandra hadn't moved an inch and had even begun to lightly snore under the influence of the drug she had ingested.

The tourniquet was doing the job that it was intended to do, which was to stop the flow of blood and allow it to coagulate.

I knelt down beside the unconscious woman with my skinning knife in hand, and began to have second thoughts about what I was about to do.

My hesitation lasted only a moment as I began to think.

"Fuck this bitch, she had her chance, she made her choice, she chose poorly. And if she and that bull on the couch had had their way, I'd be the one flopping around on the other side of the room picking buckshot out of my ass."

"And besides, I need something that will be a constant reminder of all the horse shit that seems to keep spewing out of every orifice of the people that I meet," I said, aloud to myself.

With that, I straddled the woman's stomach as if I was climbing into the saddle of my favorite filly, and I began a surgical incision around the circumference of Cassandra's left tit.

Of course, I mean as *surgical* as one can be using a folding pocketknife that's been dipped in whiskey for sterilization as a scalpel.

Her pair being symmetrical, I chose her left breast only because I'm right handed and thus from my point of view it was the easier of the two to extract from her chest.

As I cut the skin around the large mammary gland, I tried to be as precise as I could be using the primitive tool at hand, and make the circle as perfect as possible.

When the circular cut was completed, I lifted the edge of the lacerated skin and sliced the flesh that was still connected to the tit holding it in place.

I pulled Cassandra's severed breast from her chest and held it nipple down in the palm of my left hand as I wiped the blood from the blade of my skinning knife onto the leg of the patient's designer jeans.

As these events unfolded, a strange thought crossed my mind, which made me smile.

"No doubt several warrants had been issued for my arrest for past felony hit and runs, not to mention leaving the scene of multiple fatal accidents, I wonder if now I'll be charged with practicing medicine without a license?"

Juggling (no pun intended… again) Cassandra's left tit in one hand, and my knife in the other, I dashed into

180

the kitchen and threw the separated yabo along with my skinner into the cold water in the left side of the sink, and grabbed what was left of the roll of paper towels I had used to fuel the fire.

Sticking the handle of the hot frying pan into the cardboard center roll of the towels, I crushed the flimsy roll against the handle of the pan using it as a homemade potholder.

I ran back into the living room and knelt down beside Cassandra as she continued to snore, unaware of the operation that I had just performed.

As I put the bottom of the hot iron skillet on the gaping wound left by the boobular extraction, I saw steam rising from the girl's chest and heard the sizzling sound of flesh being seared as the wound was cauterized to stop Cassandra from bleeding to death.

The drug-laced whiskey was far exceeding expectations, and Cassandra had hardly moved from the time I had stretched her out on the floor to prep her for her boob-job, to the time I placed the hot iron frying pan on her chest.

With her wound cauterized and the bleeding stopped, I removed the skillet from her chest and went back into the kitchen.

The fire in the sink was almost out and was beginning to emit more smoke from the embers, even though the kitchen window was open and disseminating most of it outside, the residual fumes were beginning to sting my eyes.

I dipped the frying pan into the sink where the solitary twin was soaking, and filling it with some of the marinating liquid (H2O), I doused the smoldering embers in the adjoining sink.

I knew that the zombies that I had sighted when I fetched the whiskey from my truck must be close by now if they had stayed true to their course, and a sense of urgency began to set in.

"I don't have much time, I've got to make this quick, I don't want those eaters out there trapping me in this house," I muttered, as I dipped my hands into the cold water and pulled the sunken pocketknife and amputated breast out of the sink.

Fortunately, the short blade on my folding pig sticker was perfect for hollowing out the mango-orange colored core of Cassandra's cut off chesticles, and in addition, the rounded portion of the blade worked well to scrape off the left over fatty tissue from the skin, so that part of the preparation went quickly.

With the breast now hollow and the inside devoid of excess fat and gland, I inserted the prepared skin into the plastic bag of salt.

Salt serves to draw all of the moisture out of the hide, thereby tanning it and turning it into a fine leather product.

Although non-iodized salt works best for tanning, the kitchen salt was all I had, and it would have to do. It would take longer, but I had all the time in the world, that is unless I got myself killed running around this planet from hell.

With the one of Cassandra's twins bagged and salted, I wiped down my knife and stuck it back into my front pocket, then returned to the living room and to the *one tit wonder* still sound asleep on the floor.

I tucked the tanning tata underneath my arm and unlaced the white cord from one of Cassandra's afore mentioned high-heeled sneakers. Later I would use it for the drawstring of my new leather diddy bag, or *titty* bag, whichever you prefer.

Stuffing the shoelace into my pocket, I conducted a quick search of the house for Carla's stash of 12 gage shotgun shells, which I found rather quickly hidden behind the same couch she had laid in wait behind to ambush me, and was now slumped over.

It wasn't much, just a couple of boxes, but it was enough to justify dragging the double barreled shotgun with me.

I wrenched the coach gun from Carla's rigor mortis grip and collected my machete, pistol, and whiskey, then headed for the door, stopping briefly to take a furtive look through the curtains decorating the front window to make sure that I wouldn't run head-long into a swarm of ravenous maggot magnets malingering by my truck.

With the coast as clear as it was ever going to get, and Cassandra beginning to stir, I bid her a fond farewell just before I bolted out the front door and jumped into my truck.

"Goodbye Cassandra or whatever your name really is. Remember, I just wanted to *play doctor* with you, not become your doctor, but don't worry, no matter what happens from here on out, I'll keep abreast of the situation for you."

As I tossed Cassandra's salted gazonga onto the passenger seat along with my pistol, donated shotgun, and the rest of my stuff, and started my getaway vehicle, I realized that I didn't want Cassandra waking up

183

screaming in pain or screaming just because she was no longer symmetrical, or maybe a little bit of both, thereby inviting every undead and unfed flesh eater that was within earshot of Carla's house in for dinner.

I mean, how in the world is she ever going to learn her lesson if she doesn't get to walk around one tit lighter and maybe slightly off balance for at least a month or two?

I spotted a couple of small hordes of the undead that had seen me make my exit from the house and that were approaching my location as rapid as their unstable staggering could bring them. So I decided to lure them away from Cassandra to give her a fighting chance to enjoy her newly balanced life.

I put the truck in gear and drove out of Carla's front yard and onto the street, where I slowly drove back toward the river honking the horn and shouting.

"Fuck you eaters, come and get me, you disease-ridden pieces of shit."

I have to admit; sometimes I can be quite the charmer.

My ploy worked as my engine idled and pushed the truck down the street at a speed equal to that of a normal adult's pace that was briskly walking along.

With the horn bellowing out its harsh and annoying sound at equally timed intervals, along with a few choice words yelled from the cab of my truck, I led several of the gathering hordes, and many of the smaller groups of two or three (their flies included) down the road behind me in pursuit of what they hoped would be their next unholy meal.

As a last ditch effort to make a distracting noise in the opposite direction from which I'd come, and before continuing on to interstate 40. I stopped the truck about a mile into my journey back to the river because I just couldn't resist taking a couple of potshots at the lead zombies in the growing herd that was following.

My choice of weapons to carry out this task was the trusty Kel-Tec Sub-2000 which I pulled from behind the seat where I had stashed it.

The Sub-2000 is an inexpensive, but difficult to obtain (at least it was before the zombie plague decimated our world) high capacity 9mm carbine.

And like I told Jason, it's a non-assuming yet effective pistol caliber weapon; the Sub-2000 folds in the middle and locks in place at half its functioning size for easy and safe transport, while standing ready to be called into action at a moment's notice.

By sliding a latch and flipping the barrel back into its firing configuration, with one slap of the bolt handle, or charging handle if you prefer, a round is chambered and the rifle is ready to be fired.

The whole operation can be accomplished in well under five seconds.

This impudent little firearm is lightweight, rugged, reliable, and was my deceased son Jacob's favorite gun, which he used very successfully in the ongoing war against zombies and reprobate humans alike.

"Okay ladies, come and get it," I yelled at the mix of male and female zombies nearing the tailgate of my truck, as I flicked the blued barrel of the folded rife into zombie killing mode.

I popped off two full metal-jacketed lead projectiles of the 9mm type into the head of the undead walking corpse nearest to me (about twenty yard away), and watched as my bullets penetrated its face and slammed into the back of its cranial cavity, causing the usual large chunks of diseased brain to be ejected out of the back of the head, along with generous portions of hair-laced skin and shattered bone.

My generosity stopped after the first zombie collapsed in the middle of the road, two bullets per zombie was not only a waste of ammunition, but a waste of my valuable time as well.

For this particular crowd of flesh eaters, from this point on, I would allocate only one headshot to each of the remaining trailing zombies that I chose to put down.

Unless one or two of them begged for more than a solitary shot to their cranium, and because I am a kind and generous man, then of course I would be more than happy to oblige them.

Although I enjoyed watching every one of the zombies that I shot die just feet away from me, my plan was not to spend a lot of time annihilating this horde of the starving undead that I had led away from Cassandra.

The main purpose of leading the zombies away from the house, was to try and insure that Cassandra could live to enjoy the surprise that I had *left* for her, the surprise that in my opinion she had begged for, and that I was congenial enough to give to her free of charge.

I was anxious to leave the scene and continue on to Indiana in pursuit of my former friend the Sarge, especially considering that I had wasted so much time in pursuit of a possible female *traveling* companion, ok, or just a female companion. Either way I had wasted too much time, so I incorporated extreme prejudice as I weighted down five more of the walking cadavers with hot lead, and was back in my truck before the last one hit the ground.

ADJUSTMENTS MUST BE MADE

"Lieutenant Commander Zeem!"

"Yes Captain Xarr?

"Your report Lieutenant Commander!"

"As per your request Captain Xarr, I have compiled a list of recommended adjustments in the experimental groups that I think will enhance the outcome of our mission," Lieutenant Commander Zeem answered.

The Captain of the interstellar spaceship stared at his new Lieutenant Commander with a curiously angry look on his face.

"So far Lieutenant Commander, your report consists of only one sentence, and I have already found issue with two of your statements within that sentence," Captain Xarr complained.

"Captain Xarr, please illuminate me," Lieutenant Commander Zeem begged with as much dignity as he could muster, as his thoughts turned to the previous officer that had been 2nd in command.

"First of all Lieutenant Commander Zeem, do I look like the type of Ship's Captain that might *request* something from one of my crew members?" the irate Captain inquired.

"No sir, Captain Xarr," Lieutenant Commander Zeem answered, his eyes bulging as he looked from side to side hoping to get some kind of sign from another member of the crew on how to handle this frighteningly awkward situation.

However, all members of the bridge crew now focused intently on the mechanism in front of them, pretending that they were busy doing their jobs and not listening in on the conversation between their Captain and his newly appointed 2nd in command.

All except the security detail, they stood at attention, poised and ready to take Lieutenant Commander Zeem into custody if the ship's Captain so ordered.

"Pardon me Captain Xarr, I did not mean any disrespect, it was a figure of speech," Lieutenant Commander Zeem whined, as he lied through his alien teeth. "I am still attempting to master the vernacular of the language in this sector of the planet."

"Then I suggest you spend a vast amount of your off duty time in the ship's library getting familiar with the speech patterns of the inept indigenous people of this world."

"Yes Captain Xarr, I will take your advice under consideration," Lieutenant Commander Zeem answered.

"I see. Well thank you so very much for considering my unassuming and deficient attempt to counsel you in the ways of improving yourself. Which by the way, *would* make you a better staff officer under my command, and thereby make you *much* more fit for duty as second in command on my inadequate little interstellar spaceship," the Captain stated in a monotone voice, as he glared at his newly appointed underling.

"You are most welcome Captain Xarr," the unwitting officer answered, as the bridge crew looked at each other and cringed.

"Lieutenant Commander Zeem, would you like to know the other issue I have with your report so far?" Captain Xarr asked, gritting his teeth.

"Yes sir, Captain Xarr!" the young office answered loudly, seemingly oblivious of his captain's ire.

"Well *Lieutenant Commander* Zeem, you stated earlier, and I quote."

"I have compiled a list of recommended adjustments in the experimental groups that *I think* will enhance the outcome of our mission."

"Yes Captain Xarr, those were my exact words," Lieutenant Commander Zeem boasted. "I have researched the past performance of all of the experimental groups, and I believe that I can recalibrate our instruments both aboard ship and the microchips implanted in the experimental groups to the proper adjustments, which might greatly enhance the outcome of our mission.

Tired of the language games, and wondering if the up and coming officer's promotion was one of the few mistakes he had made in his career, Captain Xarr blurted out.

"I think, I believe, it might, I keep hearing these words that reek of insecurity, words that cause me to believe that you're not too sure of yourself, yet you seem to expect me to risk the success of this mission on your obvious self-doubt."

"Yes sir Captain Xarr, I mean no sir Captain Xarr," Lieutenant Commander Zeem gasped, involuntarily exercising his already strained sphincter muscle once more.

"Lieutenant Commander Zeem, the aura of complete ineptitude that you have chosen to display to myself and the other members of this crew is of monumental proportion.

Normally I would have already had a security detail taken you into custody and you would be joining *Private*

Jol in his indoctrinating persecution chamber as we speak.

However, due to the unique circumstances that surround your particular case, I feel that a small and very rare dose of leniency is called for."

"Yes... Captain Xarr," Lieutenant Commander Zeem stammered, not yet feeling totally relieved.

"Lieutenant Commander Zeem, you will accompany me to the indoctrinating persecution chamber in which Private Jol is occupying," Captain Xarr exclaimed.

"Yes, Captain Xarr," the Lieutenant Commander barked, his body becoming rigid as he sprang to attention.

Lieutenant Commander Zeem, although he did feel somewhat relieved that he was not being escorted to join Private Jol in the indoctrinating persecution chamber by members of the ship's security force, and instead seemingly taking a tour of the chamber with the Captain, he still felt uneasy about the impromptu visit.

"Number 3, take the helm, Lieutenant Commander Zeem and myself will be on deck 13, Bay 5, indoctrinating persecution chamber 35 until further notice," Captain Xarr ordered. "That is unless Lieutenant Commander Zeem decides to resign his commission and make his visit with Private Jol a permanent one."

"Aye aye Captain Xarr," the ships third in command responded as he too sprang to attention and clenched his sphincter taut.

A unified sigh of relief gushed onto the bridge of the alien ship, as several command officers released the breath that they had been holding in anticipation of being on the receiving end of Captain Xarr's rage, and the possible forthcoming demotion of the new Lieutenant Commander in charge.

"Heisaf dojjie stilel fornakate," (Translation: He is fucked doggie style) one bridge officer remarked to his colleague in his native tongue.

"Are you insane, you know that Captain Xarr ordered all crew members to speak in the language, dialect, and vernacular, of the semi-intelligent indigenous creatures on the land mass of which we hover over?

Hell, even the gynandromorphs contained on deck 69 are being made to comply with that decree, there are no exceptions," another bridge officer reminded. "If Captain Xarr hears you speaking Annunaki, if you're *lucky* your new quarters will be on deck 69 with the gynandromorphs, and luck isn't something that you want to count on around here."

"Thank you comrade for the reminder, I hope my indiscretion will go no farther than this bridge," the offending officer begged, as he looked around the bridge to see if his remarks in his native Annunakian tongue had been overheard by any other crewmembers.

"We will see, indeed, we will see," was the cryptic reply from one of his shipmates, as he began to consider ways of turning his fellow space-mariner's slip of the tongue to his advantage.

Upon arriving in Bay 5, at one of the indoctrination and persecution areas of the ship, Captain Xarr addressed the enlisted guard securing the door of chamber 35.

"I do not hear Private Jol, he is stationed here in Bay 5, Chamber Number 35 is he not?"

"Yes Captain Xarr, Private Jol is stationed right behind this door," the guard answered.

"Then why do I not hear the private? If the persecuting officer is not malingering, I should hear Private Jol being indoctrinated," Captain Xarr insisted. "Do not you agree Lieutenant Commander Zeem?"

"Absolutely Captain Xarr, we should defiantly be hearing the sounds of former Lieutenant Commander Jol's rehabilitation," Lieutenant Commander Zeem concurred.

"You see sergeant, Lieutentant Zeem agrees with me because he knows that we will be able to hear his rehabilitation in progress if he continues to... how do those Americans down on the planet's surface say it, oh yes, if he continues to *fuck up*," the Captain warned, raising his voice and leaning in close to his Lieutenant Commander's face.

"Isn't that right Lieutenant Commander?"

"Yes... Captain Xarr," Lieutenant Commander Zeem hesitantly confessed.

"The persecuting officer assigned to this bay is Rylo Kesbvoff of the Science Academy on Tarsa II," the sergeant at arms told the Captain. "He has been decorated many times for his unwavering devotion to his duty *and* his attention to detail."

Captain Xarr gave Lieutenant Commander Zeem a knowing look as he nodded his head, revealing his confidence in the persecuting officer behind the door of chamber 35.

"Open the door sergeant," Captain Xarr ordered.

"Yes, Captain Xarr," the sergeant replied, as he pressed the protruding octagonal mechanism that operated the chamber's door.

The indoctrinating persecution chamber door opened and the former Lieutenant Commander Jol, now Private Jol was seen sitting perched several feet off the deck in a shiny metal chair that was suspended from the ceiling and which resembled what one might describe as an early twentieth century art deco battery-operated execution chair.

The state of the art Annunaki rehabilitation seat came complete with a riveted reinforced skull cap that sprouted from the back of the seat and curved back down to encapsulate the upper portion of the victim's (the one being indoctrinated) cranium.

The heavy metal straps that pinned Private Jol's wrists firmly to the arms of the chair reflected the dim greenish-yellow light that flooded the chamber as the two Annunaki officers entered the room.

"Rylo Kesbvoff of the Science Academy on Tarsa II, it has been many cycles of Oraiya since we last served together," Captain Xarr said gleefully, as he greeted the persecuting officer in charge of Bay 5.

"Pacal Xarr my old friend who's name reflects his storied ancestor Admiral Pacal Xarr from our distant Anunnakian past." Rylo Kesbvoff stated, as he greeted the ship's Captain with the traditional Annunaki military salute.

******

The traditional Anunnaki military salute is performed by standing at attention with the heels of the feet together and toes pointed out at a 45° angle. The left arm is held stiff, straight down along the left side pressing against the body with the left hand clenched in a fist, and with the knuckles pointing to the left of the military personnel doing the salute. At the same time, the saluting subordinate bends the right elbow at a 90° angle, and places the right forearm into a horizontal position across the front of the body just below where the rib cage comes together in the center of the body (also known as the sternum, or breastbone). With the right hand bent upward at the wrist at a 90° angle to the forearm, and with the thumb touching the sternum and all of the digits pointing straight up, the soldier stands rigid and does *not* look at the superior officer, even if eye movement is necessary to adhere to that regulation. If moving the eyes left or right away from the higher-ranking officer is not possible for some reason or does not accomplish the mandatory task, in such a case the saluting soldier would simple close their eyes.

Then a slight bow of the head to show the proper respect and admission of subordination within the military hierarchy is required, which completes the salute.

Done properly the soldier should look like he or she is standing at attention and momentarily praying to the Anunnaki Gods with only one arm. Similar to what it would look like if one could hear the sound of one hand clapping.

However, if the soldier's right arm has been severed from their body, then the maneuver is performed using

195

their left arm, provided it is still attached to the soldier's body.

The only acceptable way a militarily ensconced Annunaki can lose their limb and still maintain their status in the current branch of the Annunaki armed forces, is to lose said limb during an active combat role in the service of the Annunaki Confederation.

If the soldier looses an arm or a leg in any other way, such as an accident, that soldier would be immediately drummed out of the Annunaki military and placed in a civilian organization for the remainder of what would have been their military service contract.

In the rare case that a soldier has been unfortunate enough to have had both of their arms dismembered from their body during combat, then he or she is deemed unworthy to serve the Annunaki cause and is summarily executed on the field of battle by his comrades.

The slightest failure to comply with the ancient Anunnaki military protocol of saluting, under any circumstances, even on the battlefield, is looked upon as a sign of disrespect to the superior officer and so deemed an offense that is punishable by death if the offended officer considers the execution of the perpetrator necessary for any reason whatsoever.

Most soldiers that *are* found guilty of this offence hope that they are going to be the one that is lucky enough to receive the summary death penalty as their punishment.

For those that do not, *will* without a doubt end up in a place somewhat similar to the place that Private Jol now occupies.

******

"I see that the powers that be in the *upper* echelon have been wise enough to promote you to Captain, and not only given you an interstellar spaceship of your own to command, they have chosen to honor you with the command of the flagship of the Annunaki fleet," Rylo Kesbvoff the Captain's friend flattered. "However, I am slightly surprised that the Captain of the pride of the Anunnaki expeditionary fleet was not aware that I was aboard his ship."

"Rylo Kesbvoff of the Science Academy on Tarsa II. While you are slightly surprised and apparently overly concerned at my *assumed* lack of situational awareness concerning my crew and my command, I, on the other hand am not only very surprised and overly concerned, I am disappointed as well. That *you* of all Annunaki's have surmised that *I* of all Annunaki's, would be so flagrant in disregarding my duty to the Supreme Being of our planet," Captain Xarr retorted, with a smirk. "While you busy yourself with dissecting the Captain's responsibilities, you seem to be failing in your conjecture to ascertain the identity of the person who was responsible for your assignment to this particular vessel and mission."

"Still the same Pacal Xarr, all business, and no sense of humor," Rylo jested.

"You are wrong about that Rylo Kesbyoff; I do have a sense of humor. Did I not petition for you to be allocated as the overseer of the indoctrinating persecution chambers not only on Bay 5, but of all of the rest of the persecution bays on deck 13 as well?

197

Or did you think that you were placed in charge of all of the rehabilitation chambers on this craft because of your merit?" Captain Xarr joked. "Besides, if I did not have a sense of humor, I would have already had you taking Private Jol's place in that high-tech rehabilitation chair of yours."

His Captain's remark amused Lieutenant Commander Zeem and a slight smirk broke the stiff horizontal line of his mouth.

"I stand corrected Captain Xarr," Rylo admitted, snapping to attention and saluting just in case, as trading places with Private Jol was not high on his list of accomplishments he was trying to achieve during the mission.

"And speaking of Private Jol, have you authorized a break in his indoctrinating persecution regiment? Lieutenant Commander Zeem as well as myself have been here for at least four of the earther's minutes, and we have yet to hear him beg for mercy, or even heard the slightest screams of agony coming from the direction of Private Jol," Captain Xarr inquired, pushing three of Private Jol's severed toes toward Lieutenant Commander Zeem with a sweep of his boot.

"I'm afraid I'm going to have to add the charge of dereliction of duty to the Private's list of offenses. It seems that during the separation of the interphalangeal joints of those three toes you just kicked over to the Lieutenant Commander, Private Jol passed out from the minimal pain of that process.

This action taken by the Private causes me to believe that he is either malingering, thereby being derelict in his duty, or as I suspect, he is no braver than a

198

uniformed Annunaki school girl who sits crying in a puddle of her own urine after getting caught cheating on a final exam.

In either case, I am adding an additional charge to the Private's ever-growing list of transgressions, and several more digits will be removed from his extremities in accordance with the proper protocol for that additional violation.

How an Annunaki with as low of a pain threshold rating as Private Jol has professed to have by his recent actions, has somehow managed to get into the military service of the Annunaki Confederation, let alone become an officer on a fleet interstellar spaceship assigned to carry out a mission as important to the Fatherland as the one we are now conducting, is well beyond my humble and meager comprehension," Rylo announced, again snapping to attention.

"I have brought Lieutenant Commander Zeem to your indoctrinating persecution chamber in hopes of giving him a glimpse of his future if he keeps insisting on... let's just say, bending the rules," Captain Xarr claimed, as he inspected some of the persecutor Kesbyoff's instruments of indoctrination.

"I will be more than happy to instill instruction to the Lieutenant Commander in a way that he will remember for at least 16 cycles of Oraiya, and that is after we return to our home planet," Rylo offered, after noticing Lieutenant Commander Zeem smirk at the thought of him replacing Private Jol in the chair.

Pulling from a hook on the wall a hammer that looked like it was made to tenderize meat (and it was), Captain Xarr walked over to the unconscious Private Jol.

"Please join me if you would Lieutenant Commander Zeem."

Without hesitation the Lieutenant Commander followed his leader to the gleaming metal chair where his predecessor, who was now oblivious to his surroundings after being *indoctrinated* senseless, was seated.

Captain Xarr handed his young subordinate officer the meat hammer, and with a pleasant smile on his face, he cocked his head and gave the order.

"Strike Private Jol on the left hand as hard as you can!"

"Sir?" the Lieutenant Commander questioned.

"It was your report that was *Lieutenant Commander* Jol's ultimate undoing, so I think that it is only fair to the *Private,* that you are the one that wakes him up so as to avoid further charges that will no doubt result in a longer stay in this chamber and facilitate additional digital extractions," Captain Xarr explained, as he prompted his subordinate to carry out his latest order with one more warning. "And Lieutenant Commander, if you question my orders one more time, I promise you that it will be your toes that get kicked across this room. Is that clear?"

"Absolutely clear Captain Xarr!" Lieutenant Commander Zeem replied, shouting out his answer.

Moving into position to make sure that Lieutenant Commander Zeem could see him, Rylo Kesbyoff smiled at the Lieutenant Commander while nodding his head slowly to remind the young officer that he was anticipating servicing the Captain's second in command sometime in the near future.

With visions of himself sitting under the greenish-yellow light in the metallic recliner, Lieutenant Commander Zeem raised the heavy spiked hammer over his head, and with as much force as he could summon from his dominate arm, he smashed the head of the heavy tool down onto the top of the unconscious former officer's left hand.

The former Lieutenant Commander was rudely awakened as the flesh tearing hammer impacted his hand, and what was left of Private Jol's good eye bulged out of its socket as he tried to scream through the thick cloth gag that had been wedged into his mouth.

"Is that a new technique, using a gag?" the Captain asked.

"Yes, it muffles the sound of the weaker ones, cutting down the decibel levels and eliminating the need for the indoctrinating persecutors or their staff to wear audio frequency protection," Rylo answered.

"Hit him again Lieutenant Commander!" Captain Xarr barked. "I don't think he is completely awake yet."

The hammer fell onto the hand of the constrained ex-officer once more, and again a muffled scream echoed throughout the chamber.

"Please enlighten me Rylo Kesbyoff, does not the restriction of the mouth for the purpose of lowering the decibel levels affecting the disciplinarians also impede the process of the personnel being disciplined from exercising their normal penchant for begging for merciful tolerance?" the Captain thoughtfully inquired as he once more ordered.

"Again, Lieutenant Commander!"

As it had done twice before, the heavy spiked meat mangler fell barbarically hard upon the left hand of Private Jol, shattering bone and tearing through multiple layers of skin, muscle, and tendons.

"Their pathetic whining and their pitiful cries for mercy are of no concern to me. If I were to give mercy to all of those that begged for it, discipline would not be able to be instilled, and rumors of my generosity would spread like wildfire through the Annunaki Confederation of planets and beyond. Those rumors would not only place doubt in the eyes of my commanders, and give a glimmer of hope to my future clients, but also propagate a firestorm of disciplinary voids of which I would be held responsible for," Rylo said, in answer to his Captain's question.

"I understand your concern, and your lack thereof, and with that said, I shall now try to get my point across to the young Lieutenant Commander here," Captain Xarr, grunted.

"Are you sure you don't want me to teach your Lieutenant Commander the lesson?" Rylo asked willingly, again making sure that the young Lieutenant Commander could see him smiling maniacally and nodding his head.

"Not at this time, however, if Lieutenant Commander Zeem fails to understand the gravity of the situation, you will be his next teacher," the Captain promised, as he glared at his newly promoted officer.

"I am sure I won't have long to wait," Rylo commented, as he too glared at Lieutenant Commander Zeem.

Holding his hand out, Captain Xarr ordered Lieutenant Commander Zeem to surrender the meat mallet to him.

"Hammer please, Lieutenant Commander Zeem."

Lieutenant Commander Zeem relinquished the tenderizing gavel at the same time his sphincter relinquished its strangling iron grip on his anus.

Thinking that he had not only dodged the proverbial bullet, but he had also had the pleasure of practicing some of the fine art of indoctrinating persecution on the innocent officer he had nefariously replaced, he shared his thoughts with Captain Xarr.

"A career in the subtle yet ever illusive art of indoctrinating persecution might be something that I might look into sometime in the future Captain Xarr."

"Well as Captain of this ship, I would not want to discourage any of my officers from expanding their horizons so to speak.

However, I would caution you or anyone considering a change in career choices not to take the leap blindly.

Therefore, as your superior I feel that it is not only my obligation, but it is my duty to help inform you of all aspects of the change in venue that you are now contemplating," Captain Xarr schooled, as he gently tapped the bloody head of the teaching mallet in his hand.

"Thank you Captain Xarr, any advice you could give me would be greatly appreciated," Lieutenant Commander Zeem added, not noticing the gleam in Rylo Kesbvoff eyes as he listened to their conversation.

"I am glad that you feel that way, it shows me that you have initiative and that I have picked the right Annunaki officer for the job at hand," the Captain boasted. "Now put your left hand down on top of Private Jol's left hand and don't move or flinch, and you had better not under any circumstances scream in my ear. Is that clear Lieutenant Commander?" Captain Xarr ordered, as he raised the metal hammer over his head.

"Yes Captain Xarr," the Lieutenant Commander answered, his sphincter muscle again gripping his rectum tighter than a gnat's ass stretched over a rain-barrel.

The pain from the hammer slamming down on the top of his hand was immense and Lieutenant Commander Zeem's eyes protruded out of his eye sockets just as Private Jol's one good eye had done just minutes before.

However, he held his hand steady, and did not flinch. And the only noise that was heard echoing around the chamber were the muffled screams of Private Jol, as the sharp edges of the broken bones in his left hand gouged through the skin on the top of his hand, and through the palm of Lieutenant Commander Zeem's hand as well; and of course the smug snicker of Rylo Kesbvoff of the Science Academy on Tarsa II.

"That is your lesson for today Lieutenant Commander, and if there is a need for another lesson that has to be taught to you, the pain involved in that lesson will be raised to a level that you cannot at this time comprehend," Captain Xarr proclaimed. "Is that clear Lieutenant Commander Zeem?"

"Perfectly clear Captain Xarr," the cringing Lieutenant Commander answered, as he tightly grasped his bleeding and mutilated hand.

"Now enough playing around, get to sick-bay and have that hand taken care of, then get back to the bridge, we have a mission to complete," Captain Xarr ordered.

"Yes Captain Xarr," Lieutenant Commander Zeem responded, as he saluted with his right and as of yet uninjured hand.

Passing the guard and leaving the chamber, Lieutenant Commander Zeem had no doubt that his Captain had chosen his left arm as the teaching tool, keeping his right arm intact and able to perform the proper protocol that shows respect for superior officers during a salute.

However, no matter how much he tried, he could not imagine how there could possibly be more pain than he could comprehend.

Then the graphic memory of Private Jol's dismembered toes bouncing off the top of his boots flooded back into his brain, and he no longer questioned his Captain's comments.

With Lieutenant Commander Zeem on his way to visit the ship's doctor to have his injured hand attended to, and well out of earshot, a seething Captain Xarr irately questioned his confidant.

"Rylo Kesbvoff! Where is the senior medical aid that I ordered assigned to Private Jol to prevent any accidental or purposeful premature demise on his behalf?" Captain Xarr angrily interrogated his chief indoctrinating persecutor and old friend.

"She stepped out moments before you and Lieutenant Commander Zeem entered the chamber Captain Xarr," Rylo answered, sensing his superior was in no mood for banter. "We had run out of smelling salts here so I sent her to Bay 2 to retrieve more. That is why Private Jol was not conscious when you and Lieutenant Commander Zeem entered the chamber."

"Who did you assign to fulfill the post?"

"3rd subordinate medical aid Suni sir," Rylo quickly answered.

"3rd subordinate medical aid Suni, she is not the one that was brought up on charges of cavorting with two naked gynandromorphs at Fleet Admiral Kiiney's party celebrating the Annunaki Confederation's victory in quadrant 42 over *Krhul* the "Butcher of Tikyor" is she?" Captain Xarr asked, unable to contain a smile.

"No Captain Xarr, that was 3rd subordinate medical aid Suin, I heard she is aboard, but I don't want her on *my staff*, figuratively speaking of course.

"You are correct, she is aboard this ship, I had her transferred from the A.S.S. Uranus (Annunaki Space Ship Uranus) to my vessel prior to lift off.

I felt she might be good for morale.

I mean anyone that was not intoxicated and would willingly, and knowingly commit gynandromorphy at a *Fleet* Admiral's party with not one, but two naked gynandromorphs is bound to keep morale high, at least at a recreational level don't you think?" Captain Xarr speculated with an even bigger smile.

"I have no doubts she will be a true asset to the wellbeing and morale of this ship's male crew members, but if I were you I would keep her away from the gynandromorphs, I hear you have a couple of the meaner ones on board, up on deck 69. Mean or not, gynandromorphs when mixed with regular Annunaki's can be quite a handful, naked or with their clothes on," Rylo warned, sporting a smile of his own.

"I'm quite aware of the dangers of gynandromorphs.

I am holding one of them on charges of unauthorized use of its *mesmerizimic gland* in an effort to further its own agenda of receiving unlawful carnal knowledge of at least one of the male earthers.

It enraptured and then had clandestine illicit galactic interspecies sexual relations with the employer of one of the test subject group's progenitors before our experiment commenced," Captain Xarr informed Rylo.

"Sickening, damn gynandromorphs!" Rylo exclaimed, as the smile faded from his face.

"Yes, sickening is one word for it, *yikes* is another if you know what I mean?

Anyway, that particular gynandromorph will be handed over to the proper authorities upon our return to our glorious home planet. The remaining gynanromorphs, if they do not cause any problems on the return voyage, will be drafted into further service for the good of the Annunaki Confederation in some worthy capacity, and probably stationed somewhere on the outer planets of the Confederation's dominion," Captain Xarr assured his friend. "Meanwhile have 3rd subordinate medical aid Suin checked for parasites and tested for any and all recreational transmitted diseases that might be residual from any of her past indiscretions.

Then have her report to my sanctum sanctorum tonight at the earther's time of 8 o'clock pm central daylight savings time, and see to it that she brings a bottle of Artillian fermented berry juice with her.

At that time I will conduct a *personal* interview for a possible field promotion in lieu of a conventional time in grade preferment in rank, that is, if she passes all of your tests and is found to be, let us just say… *bug free*."

"Certainly Captain Xarr, I will attend to that matter personally as soon as 3rd subordinate medical aid Suni returns with the smelling salts."

"And pick up those disjointed toes before someone slips and falls, you might as well have titanium ball bearings rolling around on the deck," the Captain ordered, as he departed the indoctrinating persecution chamber in Bay 5.

******

Later that day...

After a brief stint in the ship's Sick-Bay, and a couple of dozen lies later (Lieutenant Commander Zeem couldn't have rumors of his outlandish stupidity and lesson in Annunaki discipline floating around the ship; it was bad for his image), the Lieutenant Commander was back on the bridge of the mother ship awaiting orders from Captain Xarr.

"Captain on the bridge!" an Ensign yelled, as Captain Xarr crossed the threshold of the hatchway onto the bridge and made his way to his command chair.

"Lieutenant Commander Zeem, report!" The Captain shouted with authority.

"Captain Xarr, I have observed that most if not all of the members of the control groups (zombies) are beginning to become lethargic and inert in the manner that their attacks are being executed.

Furthermore, the inactivity of the canine population (K-9, feral dogs), except for a few isolate incidences seems to be becoming almost epidemic, if you will pardon the pun sir," Lieutenant Commander Zeem, reported.

"Your recommendation Lieutenant Commander Zeem?"

"Captain Xarr, I recommend that the genetic differentiation sector found in the DNA of the main constituent of the chromosomes that abounds in all of the species that are germane to this operation be altered to better fit the dynamic criterion of our experiment, to help insure the success of our main mission to this planet," the Lieutenant Commander answered abruptly. "Similar to the adaptations that were made at the beginning of our mission which slowed the physical decomposition process in the body's of the control groups."

"Please continue Lieutenant Commander, and tell me your recommendation of which calibration changes should be made in the chosen DNA that should be prosecuted to further fit our needs," Captain Xarr exhorted.

"The configuration of the pestilence implanted into the control subjects and canine corps during the evaluation period prior to the inception of our experiment, was intended to repulse both groups, making them repugnant to each other.

That configuration had a success rate of 98.9310482658% and only a handful of the control group members or feral canines attacked and devoured each other, and an even smaller percentage pleasured themselves by consuming the dead bodies known to the earthers as road kill," Lieutenant Commander Zeem explained.

"Your point Lieutenant Commander?" Captain Xarr asked, stroking his chin.

"Captain Xarr, I am sure that if the science engineers were to skew the DNA of both the members of our control groups, and the remainder of the feral canine packs with scanning directional electromagnetic plasma-pulse reconciliation beams, set to tweak that DNA 180°. It would not only erase the repulsing factor within them, but at the same time instill a loathing of monumental proportion for each other, thus avoiding the current issues that could affect the success rate, or even possibly cause the failure of our mission.

If the level of the DNA modification is set high enough, blind rage at the sight of the opposite groups or entities within those groups would be the outcome.

Of course, all of the test subject groups would inevitably be directly or indirectly affected by this measure.

Directly they would be affected in a twofold manner.

One being that the earthers would be attacked more vigorously by the members of the control groups and by the feral dogs; and two being that smaller numbers of the control subjects and feral dogs would be attacking them because of the higher attrition rate among the two groups caused by their constant vicious attacks upon each other."

"And why would the earthers be attacked more vigorously Lieutenant Commander Zeem?" Captain Xarr asked, still stroking his chin.

"Well Captain Xarr, overall the control groups in conjunction with the wild dog population would be thinned out some by their mutual hatred for each other, making the planet's surface less perilous for the test subject members per say. However, the increased ferocity of the adversarial groups will offset the drop in population of both groups, meanwhile still affording us the accomplishment of the prime directive of our mission.

You see Captain Xarr; an air of over confidence is beginning to be observed in many of the members of the test subject groups. These members are finding the control group's lethargic demeanor less threatening, partially because of the earther's new physical prowess that their constant activity has awarded them, and partially because of their newly acquired fighting skills. The emergence of their behavior has taken place over such a long period, that the living earthers are so far unaware of the change and thus becoming bolder and less cautious in their battles with the members of the control groups that they call *zombies*; among other things.

I purpose that the new alteration within the DNA of the control groups should also be configured to change the lethargy characteristic of the control subjects, which would not only help to heighten their senses slightly, but it would also give them an enhanced equilibrium shift that would promote a swifter and more dangerous adversary for the earthers to combat.

The enhancements in the 180° switch will be noticed immediately by the members in the test subject groups, and force the surviving earthers to fight to their full capability, and live up to their full physical and mental combative potential," Lieutenant Commander Zeem proclaimed.

"Make the changes Lieutenant Commander, but be sure that *you* don't kill off all of our test subject groups," Captain Xarr replied.

"Captain Xarr, there is one more adjustment I would like to make to the DNA," Lieutenant Commander Zeem indicated.

"And that is, Lieutenant Commander?" the Captain inquired.

"Captain Xarr, up to this moment, the members of the control groups have been traveling in no less than arrays of two or three.

I purpose that we reconfigure the their DNA components to allow them to travel in a singular manner if they so choose or are otherwise prone to do, not being restricted to pairs or larger groups as they venture around the planet's surface in search of the earthers," Lieutenant Commander Zeem suggested. "That new configuration would leave less of a chance of accidentally annihilating the test subject groups under the revised ferocity factors implanted into the control groups and their feral affiliates."

"An excellent idea Lieutenant Commander Zeem, a kind of insurance policy for you, you keep the test subject groups intact, and at the same time you keep yourself from joining Private Jol in his chromium plated vat of *deep kimchi*, if you know what I mean," Captain Xarr explained.

"Yes Captain Xarr, a kind of double indemnity or dual redundancy policy."

"By all means Lieutenant Commander Zeem, make the necessary changes to the control groups and to the canine corps that you have purposed, and ready the pre-extinction bipedal carnivorous creatures for deployment at a moment's notice in case their dispersion becomes necessary for any reason.

Also, add a remotely activated extinction microchip to the beasts, with an additional automatic mechanism for activating the microchip at a preset time (a timer) that will be determined at a later date" Captain Xarr ordered. "Indeed, you still may avoid Private Jol's fate after all!"

"Yes Captain Xarr, that is definitely one of my goals which is high on my list of achievements while serving as your second in command sir," Lieutenant Commander Zeem admitted, while he wondered why Captain Xarr kept insisting on bringing up his predecessor's ghastly fortune, as he again felt his sphincter muscle unilaterally begin to involuntarily strangle his rectum.

THINGS CHANGE

I was finally back on the road again after dodging the bullet one more time, the bullet in this case was really a bullet and not just a figure of speech, and it came in the form of a bull dyke wielding a double barreled shotgun. More accurately, it was double ought buck that the bull lesbian with the weed trimmer hair cut was getting ready to pepper me with, but you get the picture.

I had lucked out one more time and as I drove along the freeway avoiding the usual masses of wrecked and abandoned vehicles, stumbling cadavers, and road kill speed bumps, I wondered just how long my good luck was going to hold out.

Traveling alone through the zombie apocalypse was quite different than making your way through the devastation with a group.

One of the first things that my family did when the dead population rose up and began to hunt down the living, was to make a list of things that we deemed necessary to survive in the zombie ravaged world.

I still carry a copy of that list with me, although some of the conceptualizations listed are not feasible or indeed even possible when traversing the wastelands of a zombie Armageddon all by your lonesome. Therefore, I took it upon myself to modify them to fit my solitary needs and still try to not get myself killed.

Below I have submitted for your consumption, the rules, or rather guidelines to live by that my family tried to adhere to during their time in the zombie nation.

Keeping in mind of course that this list was constructed during an episode of mass panic, in the middle of a pandemic of biblical proportion, while in the midst of hundreds of flesh eating dead human's hell bent on making us the main course of their next meal.

We did not have as much latitude to leisurely lounge around partaking in such decadent pastimes as reading post-apocalyptic science fiction/horror novels as one might think.

No, our main goal was to survive, second by second, minute by minute, hour by hour, well you get the idea.

Our list of things to do to help us avoid being...

EATEN, DISMEMBERED, DISEASED, SHOT, BITTEN, MUTILATED, or otherwise KILLED, CAPTURED, or MURDERED by zombies, normal humans, insane maniacs, ruthless reptiles, or other diverse mentally deranged entities etc.!

1. Watch for eaters (zombies) and rogue humans! Always assume that one is near.

2. Never have less than two (2) guns on your person! Fully loaded!

3. Always, have a gun within reach, always!

4. Never, go anywhere alone, anywhere! Ever!

5. Always, carry a backup weapon, i.e., knife, hatchet, sword, bat, etc., always!

6. Always, keep a lookout on duty, day and night, all of the time, 24-7!

7. Never camp out in an open area, unless it is unavoidable, if unavoidable, refer to the first six rules!

8. Gather as much ammo as possible, check everywhere you go.

9. Look for and take, as many guns and high capacity magazines as possible, always check!

10. Take anything you think might be useful in the future, if possible, but don't over burden yourself, you still might have to move fast.

11. Look for food and water all of the time!

12. Learn as much about the enemy (eaters or non-eaters) as possible, and share the information!

13. Watch your back! Watch everybody's back!

Number 1 needed to be modified to read; always assume that *something* that wants to kill you is nearby.

And right off the bat you can see that number 4 and number 6 are absolutely out of the question.

Number 4 says never go anywhere alone, you are alone, so to follow the rule (guide), you either have to park you ass and never go anywhere, or do what I do and go everywhere alone (as if I have another choice).

As far as staying awake 24-7, well you try it and tell me how that works out for *you*.

I had grossly violated rule number two when I took only my machete and suppressed Beretta with me into Carla's house, and though a second gun would not have helped me in that case, I still should have respected every rule on the list that was possible to adhere to. However, fortunately I lived through the ordeal… barely, and going forward, I endeavored to do my best to make sure that a mistake like that would never happen again.

The day was ending and I figured that I had maybe an hour and a half left of light to find somewhere reasonably safe to bed down for the night.

I had been sleeping in my truck the past three nights, and doing it one more night just wasn't going to work for me if I could help it, I mean not only was it too cramped for a good night's sleep, but it could be potentially dangerous as well.

Zombies could possibly conspire to break a window out and get into the cab, but that was highly unlikely, as they seemed to be too stupid to plan anything as elaborate as picking up a stone and hurling it through a window, although earlier in my journey, some had managed to climb up the rungs of a water tower's ladder, so highly unlikely or not, it was definitely possible

Of course, there was always the possibility that in their zeal to get to a free meal at my expense, one of the festering undead apex predators might stumble and fall headlong into the window, smashing it and gain access to the cab of the truck in that manner.

Another scary possibility was that a large horde of the diseased beasts would smell the delicious aroma of my pristine flesh, and surround me during the night with enough dead bodies that my truck could not plow through their masses, and I would be trapped in my vehicle for the rest of my miserable life. However long that might be?

Another situation, although not nearly as likely, however, still possible and just as frightening that *could* come about, is the scenario of the rogue human or gang of humans that might happen on to me while I slept, and I would wake up surrounded by a group of most likely pissed off shit-bums with nefarious intentions toward my physical and mental health.

So, I decided to slow down a little and look for an out of the way place to bed down for the night; a place that might shield me until morning from all of the possible untold dangers that could be lurking in the dark.

Looking back on the last few days, I saw that I was becoming rather caviler in my method of zombie killing, and lackadaisical in my physical security, and that wasn't sitting too well with me.

I had once told my boys not to become apathetic in this world of the dead we now inhabit, for lethargy leads to carelessness, and carelessness will get you killed.

And like it or not, I was getting too careless for my own good, and sooner or later my failure to give sufficient attention to avoiding harm and or errors was going to put my ass in a sling, one way or another.

If I found myself being toted around in defecation form by some uncouth, unwashed, unwept, undead disgusting sack of maggots, and traveling all over fucking hell's creation in the lower portion of his or hers soiled and twisted tighty-whities, well the odds of me ever catching up to the Sarge was somewhat astronomical to say the least. Unless sometime later in the course of events, he too had been munched on by the same undead sack of *shit* (which was now *me*) that had devoured my body in the first place, and then we could meet up somewhere in the gastrointestinal tract of the offending zombie thug, but what would be the point.

So without farther ado, I decided to find some reasonably secure digs and rethink my approach to exterminating both menacing zombies, and humans of all different varieties.

Unbeknownst to me at the time, but the timely rethink of my *modus operandi* was going to save my life before nightfall.

I was coming up fast on Nashville Tennessee as the sun was beginning to set. I wanted to bed down for the night and tackle the unknown dangers that Nashville had to offer in broad daylight, instead of risking traveling through a large metropolis during the night.

Journeying even close to a large city was dangerous enough during the daytime, but to try to traverse a major metropolitan district in the dark was a death wish waiting to happen.

Although I had done it on several occasions, traveling at night in any area was not something that I would endorse. It's a good way to get yourself killed, and I only did it then because of the life and death circumstances at the time. In other words, I had no choice.

I slowed my truck down to a crawl and began to search the landscape for a suitable place to spend the night.

My idea of a suitable place to spend the night was a mobile home, a manufactured house, a trailer, what some might call a tornado magnet.

Many times, they are isolated to some extent, and being in a rural locality, the odds of that were pretty good.

They are built flimsy (especially the older ones) when compared to a building with a foundation under it, and considering that I would be spending only one night there, flimsy was what I was looking for.

You see trailers (except for the doublewide ones) are just a long rectangle with one exterior door. Although not very good for deflecting the unwanted advances of rogue humans (that's where the isolation comes into play), but when zombies pay you a visit in the middle of the night, it is rather simple to kick or chop a exit portal through the back wall while your uninvited and hungry company is busy beating down your front door.

Believe it or not, finding a mobile home in rural Tennessee is not really too hard to do.

Therefore, my search had ended within a couple of miles as I spotted a nice cluster of three trailers perched on top of a small hill among some trees, and setting back off the road a hundred yards or so.

An access road, which was really only two dirt tire tracks mostly covered with weeds, led me passed an old dilapidated barn and a few rickety livestock shelters that had long since lost their odor of the animals that they had once housed.

"Probably abandoned years before the eaters came along," I mumbled to myself.

The evening was well into dusk as I parked my truck at the far end of the first trailer.

Vowing to clean up my act and be more vigilant of my surrounding and less apathetic in my efforts to stay alive, I gathered up some of my equipment that I had let be scatter around the cab of my truck, and I began to try to get organized.

My Glock was still under the seat on the passenger's side, along with my reliable tomahawk, and my tactical vest and M-4 were still crammed behind the seat, all were where I had stashed them before entering Cassandra's sister's house.

I retrieved my rifle and then my vest; I put on the vest, then pulled my two weapons from under the seat and placed my Glock into the integrated holster on the front of the vest and slid my trusty tomahawk through the makeshift wire loop I had manufactured for quick access to that weapon.

With my right hand firmly clutching the pistol grip on the suppressed M-4, my left hand seized the machete that I had used to put down the raging bull earlier in the day, and I set out to clear the trailer and the area around it of any and all unwanted trespassers.

I had hoped that being as far off of the road as this batch of tornado magnets was, that the only thing that I would have to deal with would be the occasional hoot owl or two interrupting my sleep, and *maybe* a small cluster of undomesticated forest zombies making their way amongst the scattered trees.

However, as usual my hopes and dream were quickly dashed on the rocks below. For as I exited my vehicle and rounded the corner of the first trailer (my chosen sleeping quarters), I ran head long into a solitary female zombie.

This member of the legion of the undead looked malnourished (of course most of the seasoned ones do), although there was a clue that this particular piece of rotting meat had once eaten its fill many times over.

With its crestfallen look and sunken indigo colored cheeks, I figured that it had been dormant for quite some time now, but as I approached, it became very excited to see a free meal consisting of fresh raw meat wandering by.

I had inadvertently supplied the stimulus to motivate this ravenous undead maniac by accidently slamming the door of my truck, and it wasted no time taking advantage of my careless presents.

Besides the fact that this particular ghastly female cannibalistic fiend was not wearing a shirt, and her sagging bluish-green tinted tits with dark, almost black spider veins reaching out from her mold covered nipples were hanging down and flopping against the full and leaking colostomy bag that was hanging off her right side. Which by the way, looked as though it should have burst three weeks earlier?

Seeing a flesh eater in the flesh is of no consequence.

Pay no attention to the odd occurrence of seeing a *lone* zombie on the prowl.

Forget about all of that, and remember this.

Miss Constipated Colostomy was moving fast, faster than I'd ever seen a zombie move, except for the few that had inadvertently landed in water for one reason or another and were flailing around wildly while trying to remove themselves from the liquid; and it was patently obvious that this raunchy cunt was *jonesing* for my tasty flesh covered bones.

Her lanky stature and her rotting muscles and tendons were not hindering the pursuit of her prey (me) in any of the usual ways.

Although she still stumbled and swayed as she approached me, just as hundreds of the undead had done prior to her arrival, this one was different.

222

The maniacal murderous rage in her eyes was the same as I had seen countless times before, and the swarm of flies that encompassed her stench like an aura was still abundantly apparent as well.

The elongated maggot filled drool that oozed from this thing's mouth was nothing that I hadn't had to deal with many times in the past either.

However, the speed mixed with the smooth supple movements at which this attacking monster was descending upon me was something that I'd not previously had to contend with.

Closing the fifteen-yard gap between us swiftly, and almost before I knew it, the ravenous female cannibal was upon me.

I leaned back, and with a quick twist of my body to the right, I narrowly avoided the feminine cadaver's first deadly lunge.

As the zombie whizzed by me close enough to pepper me with her contrail of orbiting flies, the adrenaline fed muscles in my hand tightened even more on the pistol grip and trigger of my M-4 causing me to unintentionally light off a 5.56 caliber round into the living corpse's hip.

The bullet slamming into the zombie's pelvis bone and collapsing part of the skeletal support structure on the right side of its body caused the running road kill to dip down slightly as it passed by me.

The new angle of the half-naked female's body generated even more of a pendulum effect on her sagging shit stained tits that bounced against her over inflated and dripping colostomy bag as she turned and galloped back toward me.

The consequence of this new physical imbalance being demonstrated by the shirtless monster; was as the swaying breasts wagged toward me, the horizontal hold I had on my machete across the front of my body was at just the right angle to cleanly slice off one of the attacking cannibal's swinging mammary glands.

Even as the epinephrine coursed through my veins at the moment of the attack, the whirling tit spiraling around as it headed for the ground, reminded me of Cassandra, and the salted tit in the plastic bag I had left on the seat of my truck.

"*Hewed another one off at the root*," I thought, as a slight smile crept onto my face as I stepped backwards to regain my own balance.

However, my nostalgic memories were short lived as the severed booby hit the ground and belched out a clump of wiggling fly larvae onto the grass.

Not to mention the fact that the extra weight had now been lifted from the collapsed side of the furious womanly stiff, and she had regained her newly acquired speed and hunting prowess.

Her almost perfectly performed pirouette in the fading sunlight brought me back completely from my session of reminiscing, to the dire straits at hand.

The increased speed that this zombie was demonstrating was nothing to be trifling with, so I flipped the selector switch on my M-4 rifle to full auto and quickly raised the weapon and pointed it at the charging zombie.

I employed the spray and prey method of annihilating the enemy, not necessarily through instinct or choice, but mostly because of the lack of time that I had to deal with the rapidly approaching threat and the *rare* panic that had gripped me.

In the low light of the fading day, I could see the dim flashes of expanding gases from the ignited gunpowder as they exited the suppressor that I had attached to the muzzle of my rifle.

I watched the excessively packed colostomy bag explode, flinging in all directions (including mine) the fermented and discolored zombie feces that was inundated with some kind of plump round discolored worms that resembled pale-white night crawlers as my bullets ripped through the somewhat opaque flesh colored plastic shit container.

The worms had been encapsulated in the colostomy bag and most likely in the zombie's intestines too; they were still alive and feeding on the female's fecal matter as they were unknowingly being marinated at the same time by the food source they so dearly craved.

They were bigger than the traditional maggots that were prevalent in the older zombies, and had the yellow tint of a tapeworm.

Their skin, if that's what you want to call it, had bumpy ridges on it like a grub worm, and was wrinkled like finger tips that had been submerged in water too long.

However, the most disturbing thing about these burrowing invertebrate animals was the fact that now they were crawling on me and still nibbling on the splotches of undead's diarrhea that dotted my clothing.

Unfortunately for me, hurling zombie shit all over myself *and* fuck's creation didn't do much to stop the onslaught of the overly aggressive dead body that was now at arm's length from me.

My finely honed reflexes were the only thing that was to come to my aid that night, as I jammed my rifle into the charging beast to block its arms from reaching me.

Even without a bayonet attached to the front of the gun (I don't think one would be of any use with the silencer sticking out a good nine inches passed the bayonet lug anyway) I could feel the suppressor imitate one, as it sank several inches into the rotting flesh where the sagging right yabo had been extracted.

The M-4 stuck in the chest of the zombie slowed its momentum and kept the fiend at bay long enough for me to raise my machete and part her hair, just as I had done to Cassandra's bull dyke-ish alleged sister.

Miss Colostomy dropped on the grass in front of me like the afore mentioned high school class, taking her swarm of flies with her, at least the ones that weren't swarming around my shit splattered carcass.

"God damn it, talk about holy shit," I whispered, not wanting to attract any more dormant zombies that might be skulking in the area, as I looked at the speckled pattern of defecation that now adorned my uniform. "Leave it to these fucking eaters to fuck things up for me again. How in the hell am I supposed to sleep now, hell I can't even get back into my truck and leave until I clean this stinking shit off me, God damn it."

It was bad enough just to have shit slung all over me, but the slew of crap that was splattered all over my equipment and me was not just ordinary shit. This stuff was *premium* zombie shit, made from the finest human

226

body parts this undead and now single-titted female cannibal could ingest.

Just the thought of this sickening shit being sprinkled all over me (not to mention the worms) was enough to induce me to upchuck the meager meal I had consumed earlier in the day, but somehow I managed to chock back the vomit and continue my quest for a good night's sleep.

With night now upon me I walked to the front door of the chosen trailer.

"I guess I can clear this cracker box and see if there is a change of clothes inside," I murmured to myself as I shooed away some hovering flies.

I twisted the doorknob and pressed against the door, a crackling sound was heard as the door peeled away from the weather stripping that sealed it to its frame.

The sound of the sealed door being opened told me that nobody had entered or exited through that opening for a very long time, however that didn't necessarily mean that the humble abode was devoid of danger.

"Watch for eaters Jack," I mumbled softly, as I leaned on the door, and peeked through the ever-widening gap made by my pressure against it.

I could smell a vague musty odor through my own shit stained stench, however, there was no sign of movement that I could see, and no resonance of flies buzzing throughout the dwelling, except of course for the stragglers that were trailing in behind me.

I shooed the flies away one more time before I shut the door behind me and flipped the brass bolt to its locked position.

Although I had yet seen any sign of trouble, I was not about to let my guard down for a moment, not until I was sure that I was alone.

The trailer was small, only about forty feet long by twelve feet wide, so it didn't take me long to check every nook and cranny and deem it relatively safe for the night.

After wiping most of the zombie shit off my M-4 with one of the pillow cases from the bed, I was able to find a scanty selection of clothes to change into after taking a minimal but effective bath, or shower if you prefer, using what was left of the stagnant water in the toilet's tank.

I found a bottle of *Brut* cologne in the bedroom, signifying that the trailer trash that once lived there was a real class act.

Fortunately, for me, most of the shit from the colostomy bag had splattered on my clothes and not on my face, thus I avoided getting any in my mouth or eyes. So it was a simple, but no less gross of a task to clean myself up before I doused myself with the fragrant liquid from the tall green bottle and poured myself into the oversized pajamas that the former tenant had left for me (I told you it was a scanty selection).

From what I could ascertain from the physical evidence left in the trailer, the former owner had bugged out at the beginning when our world went tits up.

They took what they thought they would need to avoid the first wave of the undead that appeared so suddenly that fateful day, and apparently all of their clothing was at the top of their list.

Some pictures were also missing, made obvious by the empty nails that had been pounded in the walls, and their kitchen drawers were emptied and the contents tossed onto the floor in their haste to leave their home.

However, in their rush to abandon their home, they did manage to take all of their guns, how many I did not know, but I was able to scavenge a few boxes of assorted ammunition that I found under their bed, so I surmised that they had several different types and calibers of firearms with them when they fled.

I guess all in all, they weren't a whole lot different from me and my family when we were force to abandon our home.

Nobody knew what was going on at first, and nobody had much time to plan or prepare for what turned out to be a game changing apocalypse.

In fact, the only real difference that I could really see between us; was that my family and I lived close to a river and had a 15-foot utility boat named Morphodite in which to make *our* hasty escape down the nearby waterway.

Morning came too soon as it usually does, and at first light I dragged myself out of the first bed I had slept in, in what seemed like forever.

I found some thirteen gallon garbage bags under the sink and stuffed my feces ridden digital-camo pants and shirt into one, along with my tactical vest and camouflaged hat. My Glock 9mm pistol, machete, and tomahawk, I put in a separate bag.

Still wearing the borrowed PJ's, I peeked out the windows in all directions around trailer, and not seeing any perceived danger, I made a break for it out the front door to my truck clutching my garbage bags in one hand, and my M-4 rifle in the other.

I tossed my dirty laundry on the floor of the truck on the passenger's side, and laid the bag containing my feces laden weapons on the seat atop the bag that contained Cassandra's salted down tit.

I started my truck and as I reached for the gearshift lever, I spotted a tool that if it were in working condition just might come in handy at some point.

With rule number ten instilled in my brain, I slammed my foot down onto the parking brake and bolted out of the truck.

Rule #10. Take anything you think might be useful in the future, if possible, but don't over burden yourself, you still might have to move fast.

Beneath the trailer under a weathered blue tarp, the two-foot guide bar of a small gasoline powered chainsaw had caught my eye.

I ripped the tarp from over the saw and grabbed it by the front handle, it was lighter than I had expected so the chore of retrieving the power tool was quick and easy in the absence of any ravenous dead people stomping around, or rogue humans taking pot shots at me.

Tossing the power tool in the bed of my truck, I jumped into the cab, released the parking brake, threw the truck into gear, and in no time I was back on the road again heading north toward Nashville on my way to the Indiana Badlands.

REUNITING WITH THE CLUMP

After my last harrowing episode at the Wolf River, I was a little leery of stopping at another river or stream to wash my soiled clothes and equipment.

But then again, I was always a little leery of stopping anywhere to do anything. Because experience had taught me that no matter where I stopped or what I did when I stopped, there was always the potential to get myself killed in any number of horrific ways. Not that you had to stop somewhere to get yourself killed, death was stalking every road and street as well as every house and building, and everywhere else for that matter. But for the most part, for me anyway, there seemed to be a slight illusion of safety and being somewhat in control whenever I was traveling from point A to point B, although an illusion was all it was.

So about 25 miles out of the heart of Nashville I opted to stop at the Red River (ironic don't you think), it was clear of bodies as far as I could see, both up stream and down from my position, so I decided to do some cleaning up.

This time things went as planned for a change and I didn't have to kill anything, and nothing tried to kill me.

How refreshing.

So, after another laundry day at the beach, this time using soap that I had scrounged from the trailer, I was clean and smelling like the *Brut* that the *Zombie Gods* had turned me into. My weapons were clean too, and I was hauling ass up interstate 65 north at a blazing speed of 25 mph in the scorching heat of the midday sun, hell bent for the Badlands of the Hoosier state.

After opting to stick with the truck that Jason had donated to me, the truck that wasn't equipped with factory air conditioning; eluding wrecked and abandoned vehicles and most of the feral zombies I was encountering along the way was beginning to be quite a chore in the summer heat and putting a serious crimp in my calm demeanor. So it didn't take long before I was cussing out loud to myself and sweating profusely like a whore in church, and wondering how long it would be before my own B.O. would require me to take another dip in a meandering stream, or again shower, utilizing stagnate commode water as my liquid cleaning medium.

Keep in mind of course that I still had a felony hit and run score to upgrade, all of that dodging around most of the reanimated sub-humans to keep my vehicle in one piece was starting to put a crimp in that endeavor too.

However, remembering the advice that I had given my youngest son Jacob moments before he was killed, as he readied himself to take over the responsibilities of driving our vehicle and *us* into the zombie wastelands.

"Plow into them (the zombies) if you want to son, one of them can be your first confirmed felony hit and run. Just make sure that you don't hit anything but the eaters. Eaters probably won't hurt the Hummer too much, but don't get greedy trying to hit them all or you'll end up hitting a parked vehicle, and that *will* damage our Hummer, and then we'll be on foot again.

Remember, your first priority as the driver, is to get us out of danger, not into it, and then to get us to our destination wherever that might be, and you can't do that if you hit every parked car and truck along the way."

232

Taking my own advice and passing up a multitude of undead road targets, mainly because I wasn't driving the sturdy Hummer anymore, kept me on the road, mostly out of danger, and still heading to my next destination.

However, the lack of exertion afforded to me by the absence of some of the steering wheel movement, did nothing to keep me from using the idiom, *"sweating like a whore in church"* multiple times as I felt over heated and suffocated inside the cab of my under equipped vehicle (no air conditioning and no power windows).

Even with the driver's window rolled all the way down and the passenger window slightly open allowing *some* air flow, but not down far enough to allow unwelcome passengers admittance to the cab of the truck on that side, the inside of the vehicle was like a Lakota sweat lodge, so the whore in church analogy rang true in the sweltering heat.

Although I was traveling at only 25 mph, I was still making good time coming out of Bowling Green, Kentucky, and I had just crossed the Barren River when I spotted a place called "The National Corvette Museum" on the left side of the road.

I had been driving for quite some time and besides being low on gas, I needed to take a break, stretch my legs, and get out of the Detroit built sauna for a while.

I figured that I might be able to siphon some gas out of one of the abandoned cars that were scattered around the property, so I took the exit and in a matter of moments I found myself on the museum's parking lot.

Even though I knew there had been plenty of fuel in Nashville, I had opted to pass on through that place as fast as I could, being a large city, the danger level was not worth taking the chance of stopping for gas there unless I absolutely had to.

Instead, I chose to jump onto northbound interstate 65, which was a straight shot up into Indiana, and hopefully to the Sarge, and I would take my chances looking for gas somewhere else.

Hell, I was just relieved that I got through Nashville without being attacked by something.

Well it didn't take long to find a car at the museum that had enough fuel in it to mostly fill up my gas tank.

After I was finished with that chore, and with my butt still feeling like a pincushion from the long hot and sweaty ride, I thought that I might take the opportunity to scrutinize the museum's wares. Even though after my earlier Mustang experience, I had no desire to try to satisfy my boyhood need for speed by commandeering some factory produced racing machine similar to that '69 Mach I.

Although, if I had had the need for that boyish pleasure, that would have certainly been the place to satisfy it.

After I had taken a quick tour of the museum, I was heading back outside to my truck, when out of the corner of my eye I caught site of two buck-zombies escorting one female of the undead persuasion, all of which were trudging onto the parking lot faster than your usual staggering corpses, and heading in my direction.

For some reason it always seems that when zombies appear, no matter where you are they always have a tendency to get between you and the place that you want to be, and this time was no exception.

"All right eaters, I guess you want some of this today?" I said to them as we converged, and I pulled out my tomahawk, making ready to send the three zombies to their ultimate *doom* (no pun intended; okay the pun was intended this time).

I quickly thrust my miniature bone splitter into the top of the leader of the pack's head, and twisted it sideways with a jerk, popping the skull like a ripe watermelon, thereby releasing part of its abnormal pulsating brain into the open air.

Not only did I release some of its brain to the surrounding atmosphere, but at the same time, I managed to release the horrendous smell into the air that its cranium had been cloaking as well.

The smell was so strong and vile that many of the flies that the other two zombies were harboring jumped ship and landed on the now exposed encephalon.

With one down and two less insect-circled flesh eaters to go, I turned my attention to the female of the group who was next in line to be sent back to hell where she belonged.

I needed to get back on the road, and felt that I was burning daylight dealing with the dumbass duo that was still blocking my way, so I pulled my battle hatchet from the oozing skull of the downed undead one, and I stepped forward and transplanted the small ax into the forehead of the meandering girl's corpse.

She (it) dropped straight down to the asphalt instantly, only stopping momentarily to crush her tail-bone as it hit hard on the blacktop surface, and then the female monster toppled over, scattering her fair share of maggots onto the parking lot on impact. Then shaking off several more as it (she) shook violently at my feet during her post undead convulsions.

That time my firm grip on my tomahawk helped it peel out of the zombie's forehead as it (she) dropped to the ground, and I stood there with it in hand ready to bury it into the next and final undead cannibal that was quickly closing the gap between us.

Even though I was slightly distracted by the sound of some of the maggots hitting the blistering asphalt and sizzling as if they had been tossed onto a greasy spoon's hot griddle, I raised my weapon to split the third skin craver's skull and destroy its diseased brain. But at that point I had to do a double take, because the stumbling flesh eater that was eyeballing me for a mid-afternoon snack looked very familiar.

Even with a swarm of flies hovering around it, and some of its skin discolored to match the nasty baby shit pastel green tint of the rotting meat that inundated and hung from its teeth, the scab filled face of the ungainly cadaver before me finally rang a bell.

All at once, the face of the once well-known and familiar slobbering man-eater that was doing its best to stand in front of me brought back a flood of memories from my past life.

This now rotting and stinking maggot trap that was staggering toward me, intent on making me its mid-day meal, was my former boss *Batshit Bobby*, from the hellhole where I worked before the zombie outbreak caused civilization to go belly up.

"So there really is a God," I said aloud, as we closed the narrow gap between us.

236

I could have walked up to Batshit and instantly blown the top of his head clean off using one of my 9mm firearms, and got back into my truck and drove away, leaving his now *totally* dead festering body to rot away in that parking lot.

I might have advanced toward ole Bobby and planted my tomahawk deep into his brain (*about twenty times*), putting him out of mine and *everybody else's* misery, forever, and again leaving him to be consumed by the maggots that seemed to be so fond of him (*nobody else is*).

I could have ran screaming and crying into the nearby woods and pissed my pants like a six-year-old girl (that's not going to happen by the way), and hope that Bob wouldn't follow.

Or, I could have even just got back into my vehicle and drove away, allowing Batshit Bobby to live out the rest of his slowly decomposing undead life in peace while wandering through the Apocalypse searching for his next abhorrent meal.

However, my former boss who got the name Batshit Bobby because we all figured that he was crazier than... how did we used to say it... oh yes... crazier than a clump of dried *bat shit on a proverbial stick*, didn't deserve to be treated in any of those common, uncaring, pedestrian ways by me or by anyone else. No, I had something better in mind for my ex-boss Bob.

Unfortunately for Bob (while he was still alive, as opposed to undead, he liked to be called Bob, he thought it made him sound more human) too many of the memories that flooded back into my head and took me back in time to my old place of employment were not *fond* memories. They were reminders of how Batshit Bobby and his little concubine fucked over most of the people there on a daily basis, including me. That is, while they weren't busy just plain fucking each other in the *naked nasty* way. You know, "Parking the bus in tuna town", "Cattle prodding the oyster ditch", "Bumping uglies" that kind of stuff. At least that was the rumor at the time.

"Well, well, if it isn't Batshit Bobby my old boss," I stated, not really expecting a practicable answer from the maggot-seething maniac.

"Raaor...eerr...sheeaor," Bob the zombie slobbered his answer back, not recognizing his former minion.

"Bobby, don't you recognize me," I asked. "You should, you fucked me raw so much when you were my boss, that at times I thought we were married."

"Arrraagga...uuch...barruu...ieerr!" Bob this time slobbered back in response to my inquiry, as he labored to slurp a lump of coagulated fly larvae that was dripping down his chin back into his mouth, and still not remembering me.

"I'm hurt Batshit, and I thought we were friends," I said smiling, as I stepped back from one of his staggering lurches toward me.

"Uraaup...cauugh...pwiih," the pugnacious zombie wheezed, as he choked back into his throat the drooling wad of escaping maggots.

"Bobby you should take better care of yourself, I mean look at you, Bob you look like shit.

Your clothes are dirty and torn and you've got pieces of rotting skin hanging off you, not to mention the scabs and open lesions all over your face and arms, and who knows where else.

Bob, let's do you a favor and keep this next assessment of your personal hygiene just between us shall we?"

"Woreee...aaarroo!" Bob grunted in agreement, as he lunged at me again.

I sidestepped Bob's unwanted advances, and began to elaborate on my impromptu assessment of his lack of cleanliness and his nonexistent sanitary practices.

"You fucking stink Bob!

You have flies hovering all around your dumb ass. When you walk, if that's what you call that staggering stomping you're doing, you leave a contrail of *vectors of disease* flying along in your wake.

You can come clean with me Bobby; did you shit your pants too?" I asked, laughing as I dodged another one of Bob's untimely advances.

Paying no attention to my critique of his personal hygienic practices, the marauding epidermis eater, and former supervisor burped up a clutch of his favorite little white worms mixed with a bundle of incubating fly eggs onto his bottom lip, and then announced just before they dribbled down his chin.

"Eeaaap... juwwr... aawwooa... oorge," he said, no longer able to hold in the deluge of wiggling entities as he expectorated the mixed cluster of house fly larvae, eggs, pupa, and whatever that blue stuff was out of his mouth and onto his waiting chin.

As the sickening concoction of maggots and other insect spawn were being expelled from his mouth to make room for my tastier body parts, Bob began to salivate even more in anticipation of feasting on me for a late brunch.

Upon the ejection of the distasteful blend that Bobby had discharged in my direction and that had ultimately came to rest on top of his right shit covered shoe, Batshit lunged at me once more.

"Well, if that's the way you feel about it Bob, I guess our friendship is over," I answered, pulling my underused machete from its sheath.

It was time to give Batshit some of his own medicine. Although I would have preferred to give him his dose of payback while we were still back at the old *Buffoonery* where we both worked, but I guess any payback is better than no payback at all.

However, before I got started dismantling my old boss, I just couldn't resist asking him one last question, a question that I'd been dying to ask for years, and this looked like the perfect time to ask it. I mean after all it wasn't like I was going to let Baitshit off the hook with just a warning, so I said to him.

"Bobby old pal, before we get down to the business at hand, I want to ask you something."

"Orragagi...poawtha!" Bob replied, stepping toward me quickly.

"I'll take that as an okay," I answered back, raising my machete as I sidestepped another one of the zombie's unwanted advances.

"Grrooltha!" the zombie Bob said, confirming his earlier affirmative answer.

"Okay Bobby, here goes.

On the day the world went to shit. Just how high was the *blowjob* count that your ballsy masculine looking little concubine had been dispensing to you? I mean the total from the day that you hired that little cunt?" I asked, harshly. "One...two...three hundred? Don't be shy Bob; we all knew what you two were up to.

As a matter of fact, most of the people that worked for you thought that it was a miracle that as much as her head was bobbing up and down in your lap, that she didn't compress a couple of vertebra in her neck, or develop a severe case of chronic whiplash."

I knew it had to be a coincidence that Baitshit Bob scowled, then grimaced and stumbled toward me quicker than he had before.

I'm sure the maggots gushing from his mouth as if he were trying to spit them at me was nothing more than a brain dead maniac accidently ejecting his vile contents as he opened his mouth wide enough to take a big bite of me as he lurched forward.

Nevertheless, his reaction to my question was so well timed, along with the expression on his scab covered greenish-blue tinted face, that I couldn't help but to laugh in his face while he charged at me. His coincidental facial contortions coupled with his unintended body language was just too convincing, as I imagined his anger was the result of my query into his past sex life with the odd looking co-worker that he had once lavished so many unearned promotions onto.

I mean, I'm sure they were *earned*, just not in the normal sense that one conducts a professional business, unless of course your professional business happens to be a prostitution ring.

With my question satisfactorily answered by the look on Bobby's rotting face, I decided to proceed with administering Baitshit's well-deserved medicine.

Without hesitation, however still chuckling, I systematically began to carve protuberances from Bob's lurching cadaver, starting with his fingers.

I swung my machete in the manner that I thought a very successful, yet highly underrated pirate such as Black Bart would have swung his saber while boarding one of the many ships he ravaged during his under publicized, yet illustrious career.

Visualizing myself as Black Bart I swung my machete at Batshit's hand.

The fingers on Bobby's right hand were tossed into the air briefly as the upward diagonal cut from my pirate saber (my machete) sliced them off cleanly while taking the lower half of the hand that they were attached to with them.

I then concentrated on my former boss's left hand, trying to be a bit more precise while cleaving off the fingers on that side.

The degree of refinement of a precision operation of this type is critical to its success, and would have been a bit easier a week earlier, before the undead got what seemed to be their second wind and began to move at a higher rate of speed and with a less gangling gate.

With that said, I managed to endeavor to persevere, and I was much more successful in my undertaking (need I say it) to hew *only* the digits off the left hand, as I watched all four fingers and the tip of Bobby's thumb being hurled into the air and ultimately landing at his feet.

The process of carving my ex-employer up like a Thanksgivings Day turkey, at first had little effect on his will, or his cravings to have me for lunch, as he continued to stumble toward me with his arms outstretched and his fingerless hands dripping blood that was quickly coagulating.

However, after I had managed to cut off both of his arms at the shoulders, the look on the ghoul's face was priceless as his armless torso leaned in my direction in a futile attempt to grab me, only to find that his squirming arms were lying on the ground blindly groping at his own ankles.

After seeing the confused look on Batshit's decomposing mug as he momentarily stared at his arms wiggling on the ground unwittingly groping at his feet, I began to think.

"Maybe these zombies aren't as brain-dead as I thought! Maybe Bobby was really pissed about me questioning his integrity in his past dealings with his oddly masculine looking concubine?"

Then it occurred to me, who gives a shit what these sons-a-bitches think, or how they feel, or even if they think or feel. They are here to do two things as far as I am concerned.

1. They are here to eat humans, dead or alive. That's why my family called them Eaters.

2. They are here for me and people like me to kill, and honing my fighting skills to a fine edge in the process is just another perk this world offers to the living.

Without further ado, I sashayed to the familiar zombie's right side and knelt down; swinging my machete downward and casually hacked off part of Batshit's excretion covered right foot (Bob had apparently *shat* (past tense of shit) down at least one leg during his stint as a zombie, and some of the residual ordure that hadn't stuck to his inner thighs and lower leg, had been burped out of his pants leg and onto the top of his shoe at one point), slicing through one of his $350 Florsheim shoes, his foot, and in the process, several drooled out maggots that had inadvertently landed on Bobby's foot during one of his gagging and heaving fits sometime prior to meeting up with me on that day.

By now, I had abandoned my pirate fantasy which went 180° in the opposite direction of my rethink of my rather caviler methods of killing zombies, although I still found myself adhering to my old modus operandi a little too much given the fact that I was by myself in the midst of a world filled with ravenous living corpses. Nevertheless, I just couldn't help myself when it came to getting even with my former boss and nemesis.

After all, it was payday for Bob, and I was the paymaster.

However, although I was concentrating more on dismembering my old boss, I did try to keep a watchful eye out for other zombies in the area that might be aware that it was not only high noon, but also lunchtime, and as usual, I was the prime cut at the top of the menu.

And while we're speaking of *keeping an eye out*.

Before I cut the head off the wandering corpse that had once ordered me around with impunity while he and his manly looking concubine reveled in my misery, I raised my machete into the monster's line of sight, and with a quick jab, I shoved the point of my weapon into its eye socket. I followed the thrust with a swift clockwise twist, thereby extracting the stiff's dominate eyeball and flinging the gel filled ovoid orb onto the ground.

No matter how I decided to leave this poor excuse for a former human being, who I felt was apparently a substandard excuse for a zombie as well. I wanted to make sure that as long as he and his severed body parts twitched and convulsed on the tarmac, his visual cortex would still be able to process the view of the surrounding area that was cluttered with his own disconnected remains, and hopefully add to this piece of shit's slowly rotting torment. Therefore, I left his remaining eyeball intact.

With no arms and only one and a half feet, Bob wavered in front of me dripping his vile smelling juices onto the ground. And just before I separated his head from his neck, I flipped my machete upside down and with both hands I drove it hard into the former *man's* (and I use the term loosely) lower abdomen and began a sawing motion as I lifted the long razor sharp knife up the living corpse's belly.

My machete quickly unzipped Batshit Bobby's gizzard, allowing his semi-bloated viscera to be belched out of his body cavity onto the hot noonday sun-heated blacktop, and unfortunately onto my boots as well; giving a new meaning to the term *spilling your guts*.

The sizzling sound of my former employer's internal organs being seared by the blistering sun baked parking lot, along with the smell of those simmering organs on the ground, made me gag as steam from the zombie's boiling bodily fluids rose up from the hot black surface.

I kicked the zombie's disemboweled guts off my boots before slashing Bob's neck into two pieces with a horizontal swipe from my machete and watched as his head flip over a couple of times, flinging maggots in a spiral formation on its way down to splashing into the pile of slowly cooking innards at our feet.

It was at that time that I thought, even though I was still trying to *involuntarily* gag up the back of my tongue into my mouth.

"This is the putrid stench of sweet revenge!"

What was left of Bobby's body soon followed his head into the malodorous mound of his former inner self.

Now as my ex-manager's divided body parts quivered and quaked in the middle of the museum's parking lot, bloating somewhat more in the heat of the day as his internal gases expanded, each severed part seemed to take on a life of its own, as per the further evolution of the zombie hordes.

On the blistering asphalt, the slimy gut pile slowly churned, looking as though a can of giant worms had been emptied onto the ground and now the worms were trying to find a place to hide.

It was just another sickening sight in a long list of sickening sights that I had become desensitized to, as the entrails undulated and twisted, intertwining in the pile, deforming and reforming the shape of the slippery mound in a grisly *blob-like* display.

"Wow, talk about gut-wrenching, uh Bob?" I jested, glancing at his fluctuating decapitated head slowly oscillating back and forth and up and down on the churning mass of extracted internal fortitude.

"Clack, snap, click, click, click, clack," Bob answered back, as his jaw was thrusting upward sending the bottom row of his teeth slamming into the upper row of his discolored choppers repeatedly, in a futile yet unfaltering attempt to still feast on my delectable, although out of reach living flesh.

Smacking, clacking, and clicking with his teeth was the only sounds that Bob's mouth could make now, considering that his lungs were dangling out below his rib cage and lying roughly four feet away, completely separated from his vocal cords.

However, the postmortem contractions of Bobby's heaving lungs, continued to send air wheezing in and out through his loosely connected and rotted trachea. Causing the flesh by his *neck-hole* to act as lips, which flapped and vibrated against each other, making a *juicy* farting sound both when the air entered and when it was expelled from his bronchial tubes.

Besides the sinister sound of teeth clattering on the gut pile, mixed with the sounds of someone taking an acutely significant dump in unison with the rattling. Batshit's skull ejecting maggots orally and being bounced up and down driven by the force of his thrusting mandible, gave the freakish illusion that Bobby was agreeing with my every word while he puked up a zombie apocalypse version of Uncle Ben's *perverted* rice at the same time.

"Well I guess they don't call them choppers for nothing," I replied to the detached chomping head that was still intent on having me a la carte, even though it seemed not to be able to keep down its earlier meal of rice pudding.

The severed fingers of the zombie twitched quicker than the unconnected arms flexed, as they meandered in circles like wounded inch worms near the heap of squirming guts.

Meanwhile, the half of the hand with the fingers still attached, roamed the parking lot a little farther from the chaotic scene, resembling a crippled tarantula on the prowl.

The weight of the arms flexing on the tarmac, left them skidding back and forth on the torrid surface, peeling off layer after layer of flesh that was quickly singed and curled up into little balls of scorched skin, as they inflicted a serious case of road rash onto themselves clear down to the bone.

After I had completely and to my high standards, satisfactorily butchered my former overseer, I saw that my job there was done, and I thought that it was about time to return to the task of hunting down my old friend the Sarge.

After all, there was still much more work that needed to be done in that particular arena.

I left Batshit Bobby in somewhat of a pile in the middle of that parking lot, that is, in as much of a pile as undulating limbs, and twisting intestines will stay in as they typically and unwittingly try to inch their way away from the center of the assemblage.

As I pulled off the lot, my rearview mirror reveled that Bob's snapping head was rolling from the top of the heap (most likely helped along by his squirming entrails) onto his flexing right leg (I only knew it was his right leg because I could see that half the foot had been removed; and I had left his other foot intact and firmly attached to his left leg) and there it settled in for a good impromptu gnawing.

Unaware that it was his own leg that he was chewing on (I mean if zombies are actually aware of anything but their voracious appetite), Bobby's head continued to bite away at the relocated leg even as it seemed to be trying to escape his menacing brownish-green snapping teeth as it wobbled back and forth on the automobile museum's parking lot.

As I left the parking lot to get back onto the main road, I watched gleefully as Batshit's quivering severed leg wormed itself away from the main mound of stacked flesh and churning internal workings, and dragged Bob's munching decapitated ravenous brainpan along with it.

Even after *witnessing* all of the aforementioned butchery and subsequent slithering and wriggling of my ex-boss's disemboweled internal organs and dislodged appendages, I'm still not convinced that the increase in the after-death movement of the so-called dead zombies is a product of *zombie evolution*, although that term is as good as any.

I figured it this way, because the walking dead cadavers never seem to be interested in anything except choking down anything with meat on its bones, and of course avoiding water as much as possible, to think that their primal brain functions could cultivate anything as advanced as evolution, just does not compute.

My theory on this particular phenomenon is quite simple and makes much more sense to me than something that under normal circumstances usually takes millions of years to come to fruition. Not that I was living under normal circumstances by any stretch of the imagination.

In conjunction with my positive charged ion theory of early twitcher movement, I have incorporated my concept of the reason that the undead and their body parts continue to struggle even more in a grotesque ballet of twists and turns *long* after their twisted souls have been sent back to hell (where they belong), it is loosely based on the reason that Mexican jumping beans move around after being jostled.

Within the Mexican jumping beans are tiny worms that wiggle when they are disturbed and thereby cause the bean to move as if it is alive.

When movement occurs in the dead (really dead) zombie population, it is caused by the interaction of the ravenous fly larvae gnawing on the raw nerve endings within the muscles and tendons. This gnawing titillates the nerve endings causing the contraction of said muscles and tendons, causing the disjointed limbs and various other affected parts of the corpse to flex awkwardly, and thus giving the illusion of life after *undeath* well after the ions have lost their positive charge; except for the zombie's head of course.

Because the head houses the diseased brain that is in control of the organism, it still is possessed with an insatiable appetite for flesh (preferably living human flesh and brains, but in these times of trouble they'll take whatever they can get), unless blunt or sharp force trauma has been inflicted upon the skull thereby penetrating into and killing part of the brain.

Whether it is the cerebrum, telencephalon, cerebellum, diencephalon, mesencephalon, or the whole encephalon (a little medical terminology to lighten the mood) that is destroyed doesn't seem to matter.

To make a long story *even longer*, if any one of the parts of the brain are destroyed, or if all or any number of the parts of said brain is devastated, at that point the foul reanimated cannibalistic road kill is terminated and ceases to plague the earth any further. Then its ensconced maggots take over the mechanics of body movement from there.

I also believe that the reason that the older zombies have a tendency to move a lot more than the newly inundated ones, is that they have more maggots that are incorporated within their stinking carcasses, and the more maggots they have gnawing on their frayed nerves, the more movement they will display upon their final death.

Why these nerve endings don't seem to be affected before the undead meet their maker is a bit confusing, however, there is always the chance that they *are* affected and thus *are* the cause of the newly found athletic ability of the walking dead.

Now, in the beginning, why the fingers moved immediately after they had been cut from the hands of the undead no matter how long the zombie had been enrolled in the zombification portion of our program is beyond me. The best explanation that I have been able to come up with is, "*shit happens*".

Well, anyway.

I don't know how Bob found his way to that Corvette Museum. The last time that I saw him was the day the world spiraled into a graveyard spin.

He had left work just a few minutes before I had, and driven off in the opposite direction. He must have run into the same kinds of mayhem that I had seen on the road that day.

Possibly he and his family had tried to make a run for it, and didn't make it. However, knowing him as the coward that he was, he might not have even tried to get to his family and take them to safety (at that time everybody thought that there was such a thing as a safe place).

The most likely scenario that Bobby had chosen to pursue that got him so far from home, being the chicken shit, candy-ass punk that he was.

Was when the shit hit the fan, he bolted from the buffoonery and ran screaming and crying into the zombie wilderness, pissing his pants along the way like the previously mentioned six-year-old girl.

How my previous foreman found his way to the Corvette Museum is of little consequence. The main stipulation is that he will spend the rest of eternity fermenting on the parking lot of that abandoned classic automobile facility.

That is, if some feral dogs or coyotes, or maybe some of his own ilk (zombies) don't come along and devour his entrails, trot off into the wild, and shit him out by a tree stump somewhere. Or in the latter case, maybe just tote him around in the seat of their britches until hell freezes over and we get written confirmation from the *Gods* that it happened.

252

By the way, either scenario works for me.

Just before bidding my last fond farewell to my old boss, I thought.

"It's too bad Bobby's odd looking masculine concubine wasn't with him, I could have killed two birds with one stone so to speak."

"Fuck you Bobby, and the *whore* you rode in on," I yelled, slightly changing that well know phrase to match Batshit's prior workplace indiscretions, while waving my tomahawk out the window.

Then my last words to my old boss, if you can call them words, was my usual loud *Indian War Whoop*, just to set the tone for the activities that would surely be a part of my journey sometime in the near future.

DEREK THE RED

Traveling on long trips by yourself can be lonely, and loneliness can lead to boredom, and keeping with my new resolution to not become apathetic and end up getting myself killed and eaten for no good reason (fucking with Batshit Bobby was a good reason), I altered my former modus operandi to an even greater extent.

With that in mind, I decided to increase my awareness during my trek to Indiana by employing a new tactic against the walking dead army that seemed never to tire of trying to make my life more miserable than it already was.

At certain times earlier, I had fired my weapons out of the driver's window at what I refer to as road zombies.

Picking them off one by one as I drove passed, not worrying about attracting more of the rotting sons-a-bitches with the noise the firearm was making, because by the time any curious flesh eaters could make it to the scene of what would have been a crime a couple of years ago, I was long gone.

Drive-by shootings of pedestrian zombies was not only good sport, but with the movements of the cadavers combined with the movement of my truck, and my rule that only head shots counted (and only head shots do count), it also helped hone my shooting skills to an even finer edge.

However, that too began to become boring after awhile, even with extending the range of my shots from between point-blank range (which had a tendency to expel their vile juices all over *me*) or a few yards, all the way out to almost twenty-five yards.

Therefore, I made the decision to do a little maiming on the side to liven things up a bit.

You know as well as I do that there's nothing that makes you feel better in a zombie apocalypse than a good *dead body mutilation* from time to time to take the edge off.

Therefore, I began to lower my aim and started taking out clavicles and knee joints and an occasional spine when I felt the need arise.

In doing so, I left a trail of crippled zombies limping around, or incapacitated and wallowing in their own feces; from just north of Nashville all the way to the Indiana border and beyond.

When I was picking off road zombies from the comfort of my truck as I passed, I would blow out a leg joint (knee or ankle, sometimes both) to slow the swifter aggressors down some, to a more malleable, safer speed.

Then on occasion, I would stop momentarily and carve some of the mean off the dirty deteriorating bastards with either my tomahawk or machete, and leave them to somewhat safely spook the next live human to come along. I kept that practice to a minimum though, for I still had a reunion to attend up north in the badlands.

Although, when I did stop to mutilate one of the *grim reapers*, hacking their hands off with my edged weapons became a mainstay in my quest to neutralize the undead without killing them, making them comparatively less menacing and far less dangerous before I began the ritual of manually disassembling their good looks.

This process was usually done first for my own safety, even though I had already crippled the monsters with a 9mm slug in one or two critical skeletal junctures, and then chopping their jaw off to curtail their habit of biting was normally the second thing on the list.

Don't get me wrong, I didn't spend too much time cleaving pieces of their decomposing flesh off of the dastardly man-eaters, I still had pressing business in Indiana to take care of, but once I started to whittle one down to size, I felt that it was only fair to everyone (and everything) involved to finish the job.

Even though the job didn't take that long, that's not to say that every zombie that I started to transform, got the finishing touches, sometimes circumstances dictated that I leave the scene prematurely so as not to be carted away in the pants of a horde of the ravenous dead.

You may find it hard to believe, but given half a chance, those devious monstrosities will sneak up on the unwary, and carry out their unethical atrocities without a second thought.

Before I am judged too harshly for my indiscretions toward the monstrous beasts committing unspeakable acts against the remainder of the human race, keep in mind that everything that had meaning to me had been taken from me because of the zombie uprising.

Although these hideous brutes were not directly responsible for the death of my family, they are definitely a major factor in the bigger picture of what has happened and what is still happening to our world.

If I can't get my hands on more of the prehistoric beasts that were directly responsible for the demise of my beloved wife and children, I can certainly dish out some pain and agony to some of the salivating abortions that cross my path.

So I feel a little pay back from time to time is justified and deem it as therapeutic.

Besides, if *your* God didn't want me wandering around the zombie wastelands dishing out punishment for past offenses against nature, *she* certainly wouldn't have turned me into the predacious creature that I am today.

Nevertheless, with my awareness of the new fleet-footed abilities of the zombies, along with their contemporary solitary ways, and still keeping a weather eye out for raptors hunting in the area (one can't be too careful you know), I continued northward up interstate 65 to rendezvous with the undetermined trouble that awaited me in Louisville Kentucky.

Passing the Louisville city limits sign reminded me that this wasn't the first time that I'd been to Louisville.

Twice I'd taken my youngest son Jacob there to compete in the national archery tournament held there annually.

Although he had done very well at the state level, his lack of desire to practice for the big contest came back to bite him in the ass both times that we were there.

Something about how he didn't need to practice, and wasn't I aware of how well he had done at the local and state tournaments?

Anyway, Louisville was the last stop before crossing the Ohio River and the Indiana border, and I was still making good time on my journey through the Bluegrass State despite the occasional stops for my barbarism therapy, and by keeping a weather-eye out for danger during those therapy sessions, I had managed to avoid any delays of any consequence.

So I was driving along thinking about how in the past, my family and I had had run-ins with numerous groups of people and zombies alike, all of which were trying one way or another to bring us to the end of our road so to speak.

Then as if I had tried to put a hex on myself, I began to wonder when my good fortune was going to run out, and that's when it did.

Just like in the past, I rounded a curve and found the freeway blocked. Ahead of me on the highway were two large box trucks from a now defunct rental *enterprise*.

The trucks were parked perpendicular to the road and blocked every lane and about half of the emergency lanes on both sides.

Dozens of cars and trucks were haphazardly filling the ditches on either side making it impossible to drive around the back of the rental units.

They were positioned so that the two men standing between the trucks could easily walk out from behind them for a parley if they chose to. Yet the trucks still afforded cover for the two of them if the feces was going to be flung into spinning rotary blades, and trust me, a copious amount, a superabundant amount of shit was about to hit this fan. At least for some it was.

This wasn't my first rodeo, and just because I couldn't see any more than two men standing in the road, didn't mean that there wasn't more hiding somewhere nearby.

It was too late for me to stop and turn around, even at the apocalyptic hyper-speed of 22 mph that I was traveling at the time. I was well within the range of their weapons the moment they came into view.

If I stopped and tried to make a run for it, I would surely die of lead poisoning if the two men were so inclined to inject me with a fatal dose of the heavy metal.

I figured my best chance to make it through the roadblock and into Indiana, was to try to negotiate with the probable road agents.

I slowed to a stop a couple of yards from the rental trucks and yelled to the two men that had cautiously moved from behind the trucks in my direction, pointing their assault rifles at me as they did so.

"Howdy fellows, how may I help you?"

"First of all you can put your hands where I can see them," the taller man ordered.

"Well sure, I can do that," I answered, leaving my suppressed pistol on my lap as I grasp the steering wheel with both hands.

"What brings you down my road, and where are you headed stranger," the other man gruffly asked.

"It's the shortest distance between two points is why I'm on *your* road," I said with a plastered on smile. "I'm headed into the Indiana Badlands."

"Well stranger, you've got more hair than I do, hell more hair than me and Tony here put together, wouldn't you say so Tony," the shorter man insisted.

"Hell yes Danny, you gotta have a huge pair of furry cojones to go up into Indiana. Mister, you might be okay on this side of Indianapolis, but any farther north and you'll be in the shit for sure.

Danny and I were up there once about five months ago, just in time for the spring thaw. Zombies were coming back to life everywhere, their blood and muscles unfreezing, hell, we just barely made it out alive; we'll never go back up there if we can help it. Right Danny?"

"You got that right," Danny agreed.

"Tell me mister, why in the fuck would you willingly want to go into the Badlands of Indiana?" Tony inquired with a steely eyed gaze.

"I've got business there," I answered, still faking a smile.

"Business, in the Badlands, don't make me laugh," Tony said chuckling.

"Yeah, don't make us laugh," Danny agreed, his demeanor becoming solemn.

From past experiences, when somebody's demeanor changes from cheerful or congenial to solemn or harsh, it is usually not too long before bullets start flying.

"What kind of business might you have that would take you into the Badlands by yourself?" Tony asked suspiciously, still glaring at me.

With my fraudulent smile fading, I answered Tony's question.

"I'm going into the Indiana Badlands to find a guy that calls himself the Caucasian; he's the leader of a group of people up there."

When I mentioned the Caucasian, Tony and Danny both hesitated for a moment, and I could see the unmistakable look of fear on their faces as their jaws dropped slightly pulling their lips apart, and their eyes bugged out uncomfortably from their eye sockets.

Then Danny stammered as he asked.

"Are... you... friends with the Caucasian?"

"Yeah... are you... a friend of the Caucasian?" Tony chimed in, also stammering.

The look of fear in the two men's eyes told me that they felt that they had more to lose than I did. That gave me a distinct advantage over them in a fight, so I thought that it was time that I took control of the situation.

"Lower your weapons," I ordered, as I slowly reached for my Beretta, hoping the two men were scared enough not to call my bluff.

To my surprise, the men immediately lowered their rifles, and their body language told me that they had assumed that the answer to their question about my relationship with the Caucasian was yes.

With their weapons no longer pointed at me, I grabbed my M-4 to complement my pistol, and with a gun in each hand, I got out of the truck.

"Are you two all alone out here?" I inquired, re-plastering my counterfeit smile back onto my face.

Tony and Danny looked at each other as if they were confused and trying to figure out how to answer my question.

Then Danny spoke up.

"No, we're not alone out here, we're not completely stupid."

"Well, I'm not anyway," Tony added, with a vague smile.

"We got a couple of guys hiding out there in the bushes with high powered hunting rifles just in case our roadblock stops a vehicle who's occupants are too much for the two of us to handle," Danny confessed, scratching his nose with his middle finger which was pointed straight up and directed at Tony.

Danny was smiling at his friend as if to get the other man's approval of his admission and of the obscene gesture that was brought on by the *stupid* implication, when his face exploded into Tony's.

Temporarily blinded by his blood, hair, skin, middle finger, and part of the cartilage that once supported Danny's nasal cavity, and stunned by the horrendous noise from the big bore gun that had just killed his friend, Tony never saw the man I would come to know as Derek.

Derek had sneaked up behind the two men, blown Danny's face off with one of the biggest and most powerful handguns ever produced, and then slashed the upper part of Tony's skull off with a large meat cleaver.

"Not any more they don't! I took care of them first while you guys were down here giving each other hand jobs," the man dressed in a blood red mechanic's jumpsuit announced, as I raised my rifle in his direction. "Calm down, I could have killed you first if I had wanted to."

Now standing in front of me and over the two dead men that he had just killed, stood a man in his mid-twenties, six feet tall with sandy brown hair and a mustache to match. He was dress in a red jumpsuit and he was holding a meat cleaver dripping with Tony's blood in one hand, and a big-ass stainless steel .50 cal. S&W (Smith & Wesson) revolver with an 8 inch smoking barrel in the other.

Figuring that the man may have just saved my life I said to him in a loud voice.

"What in the fuck is wrong with you? Put a silencer on that cannon before you draw every eater for a hundred miles."

"I'm sorry! I didn't think of that while I was busy saving your ass," the man in the scarlet coveralls explained sarcastically.

"What?" I said loudly again. "I think your howitzer broke my ear drums."

"Hey, I said I was sorry," the man said smiling as he holstered his gigantic revolver.

"Explain yourself!" I demanded, pointing my M-4 at the man. "Why did you kill those two?"

"These two clowns... well four clowns, had every intention of robbing you of everything you have and then killing you if the mood struck them," the man answered. "They pulled the same shit on me seven days ago, and the only reason that I'm talking to you today is that there used to be five of them, I had to kill one of them to escape."

Not being one to take anyone at his or her word in the zombie apocalypse (remember Cassandra) I said. "Well that's very convenient, you just happen to be their only victim that got away?"

"Yeah, pretty much," the man answered. "Take a look over there."

The man pointed down to a concrete culvert that ran under the freeway behind the rental trucks.

"Lead the way," I ordered, ready to blow this man's head clean off if he looked at me crossways.

263

The man turned around and began to walk in the direction of the drainpipe.

"My name is Derek if you give a shit," he said.

"I don't," I answered abruptly.

"Well you might after I show you this," Derek responded.

Derek galloped down the grassy slope beside the freeway almost giddy as he dodged the abandoned vehicles and led me to the hidden concrete channel under the throughway.

In the sun, his bright red jumpsuit contrasted with the overgrown blue grass of the states nickname sake, and he stuck out like a sore dick in a snowstorm (even though it was the middle of the summer).

As I watched him almost gleefully scoot down that small hill bouncing off the fenders of some of the cars, I had to wonder how he had managed to stay alive as long as he had.

He stood at the opening to the drainpipe and waited as I cautiously ambled down the grassy incline.

As I approached the concealed conduit, a familiar odor began to permeate my nose, and a well-known sound accosted my ear drums.

The usual disgusting stench of rancid flesh pervaded the air in and around the opening under the highway, and as I got closer, I could just barely see dozens of mutilated rotting bodies stacked on top of one another through the almost opaque black curtain of swarming flies.

"See what I mean?" Derek said, holding both hands in a gesture depicting a game show host offering up a prize. "And if you look in the back of those two trucks,

264

you'll find all of the ill gotten gains those assholes took from all of these people... and me."

Braving the stench and the multitude of flies, I moved nearer to the pile of human remains, and upon closer examination I could see that most of the bodies had multiple bullet holes in their torsos, and all had at least one gunshot wound to the head for the prevention of reanimation.

"Okay, I'm convinced," I admitted, still pointing my gun at Derek. "Let's get out of here before we go deaf from this incessant buzzing."

"I'm going to get my shit out of their truck," Derek proclaimed, as he walked back up the hill, ignoring the fact that my M-4 was leveled at his back. "I'd take back my car too, but those dirty cocksuckers wrecked it when they rolled it down the hill and it slammed into the other side of the ditch."

Derek opened the back door of one of the box trucks and began to dig through its cargo.

"I'm only going to take what those highway men took from me, the rest of this stuff belongs to those poor bastards down in the pipe," he announced, as he fished out a Bowie knife that had a buffalo engraved on its deer antler handle.

I climbed into the back of the truck with Derek after I secured one of the doors to the outside wall of the vehicle with a piece of wire and lodged a small rock between the other door and the frame of the cargo hold, heeding a warning that an over-the-road truck driver named Clyde had given me.

During the early days of the outbreak, my family and I had met Clyde at a rest stop on our way to Texas, and he was adamant about making sure that you never get into the back of a truck without making damn sure that nobody can close the back doors and lock you in.

That was a warning that I took to heart and had immediately began to practice religiously while scrounging through semi-trailers and any other vehicle that could ultimately end up being a metal sarcophagus with no way out.

Picking up a bag of what turned out to be *stale* marshmallows (big surprise) I told Derek that he could do whatever he wanted, but unlike him, I had been mercifully spared the ravages of a conscience and would be partaking in the so-called spoils of war if he had no objections.

After all, those poor bastards rotting away in that culvert would no longer have a need for anything in either of the trucks, and to leave it there under a false pretense of some misguided ethical bull shit; would just be leaving the generous bounty to the next undeserving human that happened along, while you did without.

I took a bite of one of the stale marshmallows as my comment brought a smirk to my newfound friend's face, and we both continued to rummage through the contents in the back of the rental truck.

Being in Louisville Kentucky, I found it rather ironic that buried deep within the pile of pilfered goods I discovered a baseball bat, a Louisville Slugger.

As I picked up the wooden bat, it brought back the memory of months passed.

"Look at this Derek, boy does this bring back memories," I said, clutching the bat with both hands.

"Did you play baseball in high school or college; coach a little league team or something?" Derek asked, looking up from the pile.

"Hell no, I hate baseball, it's a slow and boring sport," I answered, mimicking swinging the bat at a fastball.

"Then, why the memories?" Derek asked, looking a bit confused.

"Once during a search of a home by me and my family, we were looking for supplies, you know how it is.

Anyway, this ninety-something year old woman came busting into the room with the intent of doing us bodily harm, and I was forced to give her the righteous beat down that she was begging for, that is after wrenching her Louisville Slugger from her frail, arthritic grip," I explained chuckling. "Those were the good old days, back when we only had eaters and rogue humans to contend with, no massive amounts of flies hovering over the dead, the ones that walk around anyway, and no other unbelievable... things."

I stopped myself before disclosing the fact that I'd seen dinosaurs roaming the fruited plains, not to mention that a pack of the rogue prehistoric beasts had killed my wife and two sons.

I had just met Derek and thought it might be prudent at this time not to come across as a *complete* raving lunatic.

"Stop right there! *Unbelievable things*? What could possibly be more unbelievable than dead bodies standing up and attacking people for their brain matter?" Derek asked, being careful not to disclose an unbelievable secret of his own.

"Are you trying to tell me in your own rather cryptic way, that I've got more to worry about than just zombies, wild dogs, rogue humans, and the average ordinary bullshit this world seems to conjure up on a daily basis?" Derek asked, as he continued to dig through the items in the back of the truck.

"Oh, no, I think you've covered it pretty well, especially the bullshit part," I retorted, looking at him with raised eyebrows.

Before Derek had time to quiz me further on my enigmatic statement, and long before we finished inventorying the items in the truck (we hadn't even looked in the second vehicle yet) the sound of hundreds of swarming flies hovering around the approaching zombie horde alerted us of the impending danger and hastened our retreat.

"I hear eaters coming, it seems that hand cannon of yours rang the dinner bell, and I'm sure we're on the menu," I warned, as I jumped to the ground. "Come on, let's go, leave all that stuff; it won't do you any good if you're churning around inside some eater's gizzard."

Derek jumped to the ground and joined me at my truck.

"Fuck!" he yelled. "We gotta move one of those trucks."

Running back to the truck that we had just abandoned, Derek jumped into the cab.

"Hey, the key is in it," he shouted.

"Well move the fucking thing then," I shouted back, as I sent a 5.56mm round diagonally through the skull of the first walking dead man to make it onto the scene. "Quit fucking around and hurry the fuck up dumbass."

"Roger that," Derek answered, turning the key and starting the engine. "I mean about hurrying up, not the dumbass part."

Derek slammed the truck into reverse and it began to roll backwards; he then jumped from the truck without attempting to stop it.

While he was running back toward me, I took the liberty of blowing the top off another zombie's head that had stopped to snack on Tony.

Then I watched as the truck that had been blocking our way, rolled off the shoulder of the road and careened down the hill toward the drainage culvert that was doubling as a sarcophagus for the pile of human bodies Tony, Danny, and their two unseen friends had waylaid and then killed.

It spilled some of its contents along the way, and took out several hungry zombies that were approaching from that direction, before coming to rest wedged between two overturned cars; this helped to clear the way for Derek and me to make our escape before we became surrounded by the looming horde.

"Damn it, you might know the fucking truck would slam into my car," Derek complained, shaking his head from side to side.

As I stomped my foot down on the accelerator pedal and felt the truck lurch forward pressing me against the seat, two of the undead ungracefully walked in front of us.

With no other options at my disposal, I continued toward the two with the hopes of doing no or just minimal damage to my getaway vehicle.

One of the wayward decomposing pedestrians that had inadvertently wandered into my speeding truck's crosshairs was a lanky male dressed in a lime green jogging outfit complete with matching expensive, not to mention trendy, running shoes.

His stature along with his position relative to the front of my truck, afforded his leg between the left knee and hip to be the prime target for the right front fender of my vehicle to strike.

Although the truck was traveling at only twenty miles per hours (5 mph over the hit and run speed limit) at the point of impact, the angle and contour of the leading edge of my vehicle, together with the monster's gate, sent the ungainly dead man flipping head over heels ten or so feet into the air.

The collision broke both of his legs and left him sprawled out in the ditch at the side of the road squirming and oozing a dark liquid out of most of his orifices; and encircled by a gaggle of his most loyal flies.

The second target that my truck had picked out to obliterate was a little more disturbing, that is if one were to be disturbed by such an escapade.

It was a nine or ten year old boy suited up in a Cub Scout uniform, troop 495 if I recall correctly.

Yes, troop 495, that number was sewn on the sleeve of his dark blue uniform, it was momentarily pressed up against the windshield in front of me when the little boy's arm was disjointed by the impact and tossed onto the hood, then rolled up onto the windshield blocking my view.

That was the number that was being dragged in front of me several times, along with several trailing hemorrhaging veins, as my windshield wiper raked the bloody stump that was enclosed in the sleeve of the youth's blue shirt back and forth in front of me before peeling it off my front window.

I remember watching that number spiral down as the amputated arm slid across the fender and fell to the ground.

"That was a close one, that little fucker almost broke my windshield!" I thought at the time.

It was hard enough as it was, driving through a zombie apocalypse, dodging abandoned cars and trucks, trying to increase your felony hit and run count without becoming a fatality statistic yourself.

Trying to accomplish all of that, and doing it in a safe and unobtrusive manner with a broken windshield obscuring your view of the outside world would be verging on the impossible.

As we sped away, I could see in my rearview mirror that three zombies were taking advantage of the exposed brains that Derek had so generously provide for them by forcefully opening up Danny and Tony's craniums, and that they were busy fighting over chunks of the two men's brains that they had extracted from each of the skulls: it reminded me of a pack of stray dogs fighting over scrapes of food in a pile of garbage.

CRIPPLING TIMES

Along with the guy who called himself Derek riding shotgun, and Cassandra's tanning severed breast riding bitch, the three of us had shot the gap between the remaining parked rental truck and the zombie horde that was quickly filling the landscape, and were heading north toward the Ohio River and the Indiana border.

We had no choice but to leave the cargo left in the trucks and littering the countryside to the multitude of marauding monsters that had chased us away, escaping with our lives seemed more important at the time, and we both knew that we could find needed supplies somewhere in a less *populated* area.

"Did those fuckers seem faster than normal to you?" Derek asked, as he leaned back and put his feet up on the dashboard.

"I think that *is* the normal nowadays. I noticed their new agility a couple of days ago," I informed him, keeping my eyes on the road while groping for the bag containing the salted booby, as I narrowly avoided an overturned armored car. "The good news is, even though they're faster and more agile, they still stagger around somewhat with a gaggle of buzzing insects announcing their arrival, and a well placed 9mm slug or a tomahawk blade has the same effect as before."

"I prefer this here meat cleaver," Derek said, holding up his blood stained rectangular-bladed hatchet. "The thick heavy blade on this bastard sinks into their skulls right nice, cause I keep it sharp enough to slice down the middle of a nun's cunt-hair and separate it into two distinct pieces, even the thin blonde ones."

"Each to their own, my tomahawk has served me well on numerous occasions, although I've never tried slicing a nun's cunt-hair in two before, not even one of the blonde ones," I told him vehemently, thinking that I wouldn't mind trying it if the opportunity ever presented itself. "But it has split the craniums of many of those repulsive maggot wagons, and if I live long enough, it'll crack the skulls of many more to come."

"Indeed," Derek agreed.

Within minutes, we could see the bridges that spanned the Ohio River; two were dedicated to automobile traffic, one for trains, and oddly enough, one was solely for bicycles and pedestrians.

As usual, traffic on all of the bridges was inadequate for the purposes for which they had been constructed, taking in consideration that they were now serving only the population of a zombie apocalypse that had been inflicting a high attrition rate upon its members for quite some time, both living and dead.

As we crossed the river, we were in the only moving vehicle on the I-65 Bridge, and that was no big surprise, hell, we were in the only moving vehicle period; be it on a bridge, road, trail, or river, we were in the only moving vehicle for miles around.

I had not seen a moving train since this whole dead people coming to life thing began, and although there were some pedestrians traversing the walking bridge, as one might guess, they were all zombies searching for their next *human* meal.

A few minutes later we were in what was once referred to as the state of Indiana.

Of course, all of the states were no longer states as we remembered them, having no centralized government in existence; they were now just lines on maps and borders marked by welcoming signs, most of which depicting the state's nickname.

Nevertheless, calling them by name gave everyone who referred to them as such, a way to designate a plot of land that was familiar to most of the people still living.

Welcome to Indiana, the Hoosier State, the small, almost apologetic sign attached to the bridge read as we crossed the now meaningless border into Indiana.

Once in Indiana, and relatively safe from harm, that is as safe from harm as one can be while traipsing through a zombie filled world on their way to a place called the *Badlands*, Derek spoke up.

"What's with the tit riding bitch?"

"It's just a trophy given to me by a traitorous conniving cunt that needed to be taught a good lesson in the ways of a doomsday lifestyle," I answered snidely, remembering how Cassandra had betrayed me.

"Oh... by the way, I never caught your name," Derek said, without revealing any emotion from my response to his inquiry.

"My name is Jack," I said, as I kneaded Cassandra's salted down tit with my right hand to spread the sodium chloride into every pore.

"And what's with the salt Jack?" Derek asked in a monotone voice. "You're not planning on eating it are you?"

"Hell no, I'm not planning on eating it, I prefer my tits attached to the women that grew them, they taste better that way don't you think," I answered laughing. "Besides, I think we've got enough cannibals stalking around the planet the way it is, don't you?"

"Indeed I do, that's why I take the opportunity to kill as many of them as I can, every chance I get," Derek proclaimed.

"Good, then we're going to get along just fine," I declared, as I dropped the seasoned yabo back onto the bitch seat and picked up my Beretta.

"Watch this!" I said, sticking the gun out of the driver's window.

Up ahead was a lone zombie hitchhiking on the wrong side of the road. I rested my pistol on the door and waited until the barrel of gun came into line with the zombie, then I pressed the trigger softly to the rear and felt Isaac Newton's third law of motion take effect.

The bullet from my 9mm pistol slammed into the left side of the chest of the stumbling corpse, dislodging at least two of its ribs and sending them through its tattered shirt, following the projectile out the backside of the its body.

The zombie faltered for a moment, then leaned forward and continued to stumble toward us. We drove by the profusely bleeding walking carcass, narrowly avoiding the aura of flies that encompassed it, and watched as it tried to catch up to us stumbling even more than before.

"Holy fuck Jack, you sure are a lousy shot. Hell, I could have put a round right through its eye from that distance," Derek insisted.

275

"You're missing the point," I told him with raised eyebrows.

"What point is that? You can't hit the broad side of a barn if your life depended on it?" Derek contended, as he began to chuckle and shake his head back and forth in disbelief of my pathetic shooting prowess.

I spotted another creepy cadaver ambling along the side of the road, and again stuck my pistol out the window.

As we approached the second roadside maniac who was several feet farther away than my first target, I quickly raised the gun, aligned the front sight with the rear sight, and lit off two 9mm slugs in the direction of the stinking mutation.

The two rapidly fired successive shots sent the bullets hurtling into both eyes of the staggering dead man. The result of which was, before either eyeball had completely exploded, the twin full metal jacketed projectiles had ripped a five inch gaping hole in the back of the brain-dead beast's skull, and insisted that a large amount of its diseased gray matter exit the spheroid enclosure with them.

"I stand corrected Jack, you do know your way around a firearm," Derek shyly confessed.

"Just a lucky shot," I admitted sarcastically.

"Well if that's the case, I would prefer to keep on the good side of your *luck*," Derek knowingly indicated. "But tell me, why the atrocious shooting display if you're able to shoot the balls off a bull-gnat at fifty paces?"

"I decided some time back, that those eaten sons-a-bitches weren't the only ones that can run around the country and maim people, and then go about their business as if they don't have a care in the world," I explained. "So I made up my mind to do a little substitute teaching out here in the land of the free and the home of the brave."

"You're wounding them on purpose, is that what you're saying?" Derek asked, shaking his head and giggling.

"Ding, ding, ding, we have a winner ladies and gentlemen, *Derek the Red*, you may go to the head of the class," I jested, as I too giggled.

"You're one sick psychotic son of a bitch Jack," Derek said laughing.

"It's a gift, but you don't have to sugar coat it, we're friends, you can tell me what you really think of me," I prompted, still giggling like a schoolgirl removing her prom dress in the back seat of her dates car.

"Well let me give it a try, I'm in the mood to do a little teaching today myself," Derek stated as he pulled his huge revolver from its holster. "Any particular place that you like to hit them?"

"I prefer knee joints or collar bone, but I've been known to drop one or two of them with a bone splintering shot to the femur or the pelvis from time to time," I informed Derek, as he made ready to try his hand at crippling a zombie instead of killing it. "But those shots usually leave the eaters in the middle of the road, sploshing around in a pile of their own excrement, and cause a road hazard to anyone that might be traveling that route behind you."

"Safety first eh Jack?" Derek quipped, as he spotted his first target up ahead.

"Absolutely," I quipped back, pointing to the next zombie in a long line of zombies that Derek and I would be attempting to incapacitate that day.

Derek stuck his massive firearm out the window and pushed the muzzle forward of the windshield, he carefully aimed the weapon from the other side of the glass, and shot the pedestrian corpse in the foot as it stumbled onto the road from the shoulder.

"Nice shooting Tex, I think I saw some toes fly off his foot when your bullet tore through the shoe," I said, complimenting Derek's shooting.

"Toes hell, half his foot flew off into the ditch," Derek argued as he laughed.

"Yeah, that was some mighty fine shooting all right, but next time make it the whole foot," I beseeched. "They have a harder time walking with one foot missing."

"The whole foot it is then," Derek agreed, as he again took aim at a bloated roadside corpse that was moseying along the highway.

"KaBoom!" Derek's S&W revolver reported.

"How's that Jack, did you see that foot fly into the air?" Derek the Red asked confidently.

"I think you might have taken out some unsuspecting flies with that airborne foot," I added. "It looked like it made a temporary hole right through the middle of the swarm."

"Well, I meant to do that," Derek bragged still laughing.

"I'm sure you did," I agreed, thinking that my new partner Derek was so full of shit that his eyes were turning brown.

Derek and I popped bullets into almost every walking, stumbling, or staggering dead body that we came across from the time we left Louisville until we were forced to curtail our endeavors do to unforeseen technical difficulties.

Before my shooting partner ran out of .50 cal. ammo for his hand cannon, I loaned him my Glock 19 so he could continue to impair the movements of the undead that frequented his side of the interstate highway, and save some of his larger caliber ammo for something a little more serious that we might encounter along the way.

However, rationing his handgun ammunition apparently was not part of Derek's plan, and he began to switch back and forth between the two guns.

Before anybody gets themselves all lathered up over my quick acceptance to the partnership of Derek and myself, try to stay calm. As he proclaimed at the onset of our relationship, he could have killed me first. On the other hand, he could have killed me second or third, but he didn't, he made no aggressive moves toward me whatsoever.

He said nothing when he holstered his gun and I raised mine.

He led me to the culvert where the dead bodies were hidden to show me what might, and probably would have happened to me if he hadn't been there.

He didn't even have a problem with me when I told him that I had no qualms about taking everything in both of the trucks, no matter who the stuff once belonged to.

Moreover, when I told him how the old lady had begged me to administer my own brand of a proper

279

thrashing using her own Louisville Slugger, that ultimately led to her untimely and grisly death, he didn't even blink an eye.

And if he was trying to be sneaky and gain my confidence, all the while working with another person or two with a plan to waylay me sometime in the future, well then he left his cohorts in the dust many miles behind us in Kentucky.

With all that said, I've said it before, and I'll probable say it again.

Mama Doom didn't raise a complete idiot.

I was keeping a hairy buffalo eye on my new found friend, and if Derek had decided to make a threat, toss a threatening look in my direction, or if he had chosen to make any kind of threatening or aggressive move towards me whatsoever, I was ready to send him to hell with the rest of the ungrateful dead I had sent there previously. At least that was my plan, and I was sticking to it.

We had only gone a few miles after leaving Tony and Danny to make their way through the twists and turns of the diseased and maggot clogged intestines of the marauding undead that were joining them for dinner (literally).

That's when I noticed that the heat gauge on the dash was beginning to indicate that the engine temperature was rising to well over the manufactures suggested acceptable limit.

Derek had been rotating the use of my Glock 19 pistol and his S&W .50cal revolver to pop caps into the wandering zombies on his side of the road, and had just finished empting the 15 round magazine in the Glock.

He was in the process of trading the auto-loading bottom feeder for his huge wheel gun, and had decided to see if he could take the *whole* head off the next zombie that meandered across his side of the northbound freeway with his last fifty cal. round.

It wasn't long before his next target came into view, and firing his weapon from a few yards away, he easily managed to accomplish his self-imposed task.

The large bullet shot from Derek's stainless steel hand cannon not only decapitated the monster instantly, but also scattered small chunks of the zombie's head in a ten-yard radius from the point of impact, thereby littering the road and our truck with indiscernible pieces of what was once the ravenous cannibal's cranium, along with a multitude of dead and wounded flies and their larva.

The pressure pushing outward from the middle of the unfortunate monster's head caused by the large caliber bullet, had turned what would have been a temporary wound cavity had the projectile impacted somewhere in the body, into a permanent wound cavity that had obliterated the skull.

The forces interacting inside the skull had been so great, that all that remained in the space that the head had once occupied, was a cloud of pinkish-green mist that had helped to disperse with extreme prejudice the congregation of swarming flies that had been hovering around it.

Now the only thing that was hovering over the headless twitching corpse that had collapsed on the freeway was a quickly fading cloud of tiny diseased blood droplets which were suspended in the warm summer atmosphere above it.

We slowly rolled passed the decapitated body that was oozing some kind of yellowish jelly looking goo (a new look) out of its tattered neck hole, as steam from our overheated engine began to seep up through every seam in the forward compartment of the truck's body.

We were both still laughing about how the skull had exploded and rained down an array of minute pieces of bone, brain, skin, and what was left of the hair on the balding cadaver, onto the hood, windshield, and top of the truck as I gently pushed on the brake and brought the truck to a stop.

"What are we stopping for?" Derek asked, as he pointed to an overweight male zombie that was struggling to climb up the small embankment next to the road on his way to invite us to lunch.

"Oh I don't know, you think it might be because of all the smoke pouring out of the engine compartment," I asked sarcastically.

Derek still laughing replied.

"Uh... maybe?"

"Kill that one with your cleaver," I firmly suggested, referring to the obese walking corpse that had made it to the top of the earthwork that supported the parkway. "We've got mechanical problems and we may be here awhile, not that it really matters at this point, considering that your gun just rang the dinner bell for every eater rambling about in the greater part of southern Indiana... again!"

"Roger," Derek answered, as he exited our vehicle with his meat cleaver in hand and headed for the hungry corn-fed deviant beefeater. "I've got to take a serious squirtation break anyway."

I got out of the truck and stretched my legs, then plodded forward to inspect any damage that I figured we had incurred earlier by turning the Cub Scout into a mushy speed bump in the middle of the freeway.

When I rounded the front fender and saw the extent of the damage, I turned toward Derek and whispered as loud as I could.

"Hold off on that serious squirt of yours, we've got a serious problem right here."

Bending down to take a closer look, I could see radiator fluid spraying out around what I believed to be the young scout's front teeth.

The kid's teeth had penetrated the front grill and were now lodged in the truck's radiator causing some of the liquid to leak from its cooling system.

That along with the top half of his torso minus his head, and what remained of his torn and bloody shirt (less the numbered sleeve and of course his severed left arm that went with it), which was stuffed into the fins of the radiator, were stopping the airflow and causing the engine to overheat.

After clobbering the nearest menacing monstrosity (the fat one) with a swift downward hack to the top of its skull with his trusty meat cleaver, Derek rejoined me at the front of the truck.

"Trouble boss?" he asked, putting his hands on his hips while still clutching his heavy meat ax that was now dripping with mutant blood.

"Yeah, big trouble," I answered, pointing to the green mist spewing from the front of the truck. "The little bastard took a bite out of our radiator."

"That's just great, what are we going to do now?" Derek asked, shaking his head.

"Well the first thing you're going to do is take that serious squirt of yours and drain your main vein into the truck's radiator," I answered smiling, as I dug out the Cub Scout's mutilated upper body from the grill of the truck, and pulled the blood dampened uniform that was clogging our cooling system from the grill as well.

I then used the moist rag to insulate my hand from the hot radiator cap to prevent scalding myself as I loosened and removed it.

After the geyser of steam subsided enough to insure that Derek wouldn't be burnt by the super-heated gas, he unleashed his manhood in the direction of the radiator and relieved himself.

As Derek shook the dew from the lily, I prepared to make my contribution to our cause and unbuttoned the fly of my pants (no zippers on military fatigues).

The smell of warm piss hung in the muggy summer air as I too drained *my* main vein into the leaking radiator.

Then with the truck's radiator full, and *our* radiators empty, and both of our weezers tucked neatly back into our pants, I jumped down from the bumper, buttoned up my pants, and screwed the radiator cap back on tight.

Then I informed Derek of my plan.

"We're not going to make it too far in this vehicle, thanks to that newly formed quasi-paramilitary speed bump back there.

We're going to have to go into silent mode for awhile, at least until we get some reliable transportation."

"We need to stop shooting right? So no more gunplay unless absolutely necessary right?" Derek concurred.

"Roger that, we're running dangerously low on ammo anyway, and besides, my borrowed Glock is not suppressed. So if we need to do any shooting, *I'll* take care of it with my Beretta or M-4.

We need to get moving, the sound of that mammoth handgun of yours travels for miles, and since you just decapitated one of the slobbering beasts a few of minutes ago, unwanted company is already arriving," I warned, as I pointed to four zombies less than fifty yards away and coming in our direction. "I'm going to have to scrounge up some more bullets before I go into the Badlands."

Derek quickly moved to the passenger side of the truck and said. "Then let's move before all the piss leaks out."

Now responding to my traveling partners warning, I climbed into the cab of the mechanically unreliable vehicle and we drove off, leaving a trail of warm piss on the road behind us as the hot liquid spewed between the detached teeth of the deceased Cub Scout.

Although we had stopped the roadside target practice, partially because of fear of attracting zombies by the sound it was making and possibly not being able to escape if the truck were to break down *again*.

However, our main concern was that with all of the fun and excitement we were having while engaging in the sport of zombie disabling, we committed the cardinal sin of any apocalypse by using up more ammunition than was prudent.

Our only excuse, and it was a weak-tit excuse at that, was that with the surprisingly abundant amount of targets along the freeway, and with both Derek and myself shooting at the sinister savages, we had in what seemed like a very short period of time (time flies when you're having fun), through attrition, reduced our ammo supply to an unacceptably dangerous level.

We made one more stop along the way to pour the remainder of our water into the leaking radiator, and drained our weasels into it once more as well.

By the time we reached the outskirts of Indianapolis in the crippled truck, my once plentiful supply of 9mm ammunition had dwindled down to less than fifty rounds and my water supply was now non-existent.

Much to our surprise, by urinating and pouring the remaining portion of our precious water supply into the truck's radiator, we were able to make it most of the way to Indianapolis before the vehicle finally could take no more abuse, and with the radiator finally empty, its engine overheated and seized up.

We were on foot again.

Derek and I had been having such a good time breaking the bones of the undead along the side of the interstate, that neither one of us was paying much attention to the shrinking ammo supply. That was an amateurish mistake at best.

However, now that our ride was sitting in the alleged slow lane of North I-65 (I always contended that the speed limit was the same in every lane), ready to be towed to the nearest junk yard. We had no water and less than fifty rounds of pistol ammo between us, one magazine of M-4 ammo, and an old chainsaw that may or may not be operational; we were defiantly paying attention now.

Oh yes, we still had the coach gun with a few shells for it (thanks to Carla's generosity), we had a couple of empty firearms, a few edged weapons, a half of a fifth of drug-tainted whiskey, and of course my salty tit to tote with us too. None of which I was ready to abandon at that time.

However, without knowing what hellish circumstances might befall us during our hunt for another vehicle, to burden ourselves with heavy gear as we searched was not a cunning tactical maneuver.

We could always make an effort to backtrack and pick up the items that we left behind once we acquired a new set of wheels.

That's provided that we weren't running for our lives in the opposite direction, from one of the many dangers that could materialize at any moment in our brave new world.

"Just grab the shotgun and your cleaver; I'll bring my M-4, Beretta, and tomahawk, we'll leave everything else and come back for it later.

It looks like the nearest vehicles are down the road at least two miles, and we don't know if any of them are in running condition. So I'm not about to burden either one of us with the weight of this old chainsaw, hell I don't even know if it works.

If we're lucky and can commandeer some transportation in the next few miles, we'll come back for it and the rest of the stuff," I said, as I hoisted my rifle up and slid the sling onto my shoulder. "I will however be taking my tit with me, I don't want to leave any skin in the truck, there's always a chance that it might attract an eater that's not on a low sodium diet."

"Not a problem, I'll carry the shotgun, I'll carry the ammo for it too if that's all right with you?" Derek agreed.

"The guns are no good without the ammo, and the ammo is useless without the guns, so by all means, carry it all," I declared, as I stuffed Cassandra's rapidly drying out breast into one of the cargo pockets of my multicam camouflage pants.

"Are we sure that we don't want to bring that bottle of whiskey with us?" Derek asked, pointing at the bottle.

I laughed aloud at my hiking companion's offer; knowing that he had no idea what he was asking for.

"You don't want to drink any of this bilge water; I just keep it around for medicinal purposes; for cuts and scratches, that sort of thing. We'll find some of the good stuff in Indy, some good ole sipping whiskey," I told him, not wanting to reveal the secret hidden in my bottle of booze. "Anyway, before either of us partakes in any celebratory libation, we need to find ourselves a new vehicle, and I'm going to need a shit load of ammunition if I'm going to make it all the way into the Badlands."

I had known Derek for every bit of a couple of hours, and even though we were getting along just fine, I wasn't about to give away all of my secrets just yet, I wanted to keep an edge just in case.

"I've been meaning to ask you about that Jack, but I got so distracted by the target practice on those cool

288

moving road targets, what is it that you keep calling them... eaters? Anyway I got so caught up in all of the excitement shooting those eaters, that I just plain forgot to ask," Derek claimed.

"Ask about what?"

"About you going into the Indiana Badlands."

"What about it," I asked, as I scanned the neck of the woods we were in for a likely place to acquire more ammo.

"Well, I heard you tell those two dumbasses back in Louisville that you had business with that asshole baby (turd) called the Caucasian," Derek explained.

"So you've heard of him?" I asked.

"I've heard of him, I heard he's a real dick head," Derek answered grinning.

I pulled my tomahawk from my tactical vest and slammed its sharply honed curved blade down on the crown of an almost dormant zombie standing on the road with its back to me.

"*That was kind of weird,*" I thought. "*Maybe the eater was deaf, or sleeping standing up or something?*"

Upon pulling my small battle-ax from the skull of the unsuspecting zombie, which was now a twitching pile of road kill, I responded to Derek's statement.

"Come on dude, I thought we were friends, here you go sugar coating things again, no kidding, you can tell me what you really think of this Caucasian character that I've heard so much about."

We both laughed at my slightly amusing attempt at humor, in spite of the heavy burden that we both were bearing as we approached the first vehicle we would try to appropriate.

Just so you know; any burden is a *heavy burden* when you're walking through a zombie apocalypse. No matter how light it is.

"Couldn't see'um from back there, but look at all the vehicles in the medium and down in the ditch," Derek observed.

"There must have been an attack here, and from the looks of things it probably happened on day one of the outbreak," I contended, surveying the scene of abandon cars and trucks.

"Looks like we've got our pick of vehicles if we can get them started," Derek surmised, as he peered down into the shallow ditch.

In our search for a vehicle that could get us at least as far as the border of the Badlands, wherever that was, we began inspecting the abandoned cars that had been left on the road.

If we could make it into the heart of Indianapolis, there we could formulate a plan and decide if the supplies we would scavenge along the way, and our vehicle, were adequate to make the dangerous journey into the Indiana Badlands.

We of course, *meaning me*, as I had yet to ascertain whether Derek would be joining me in my quest to track down Beth and the Sarge in what I knew would surely be a very precarious undertaking.

We cacked a couple of the undead cannibals that had chosen to seek shelter in their cars during the onset of the zombie plague, of course, they weren't undead when they made that decision.

However, once their vehicles were at our disposal, the inside of said vehicles were not only covered with dried slime and rotting ooze from their occupant's lengthy incarceration within, but the sickening stench left behind by the encapsulated prisoners, along with the quantity of maggots squirming everywhere was a little too much to bear. Even for a couple of veteran *serial zombie killers* like Derek and I.

Besides, the massive amount of flies that the maggots had begot, left the whole interior speckled with fly dung, which rendered those vehicles even more unacceptable for our needs.

"We might as well not even bother wasting our time with the ones that have eaters in them, they're going to be useless to us," I concluded.

"Yeah, they're all going to be the same, nasty as hell and unusable," Derek agreed, as he ignored a ravenous female zombie in a small red sports car who had her face pressed up against the side window and was clawing at the glass in a feeble attempt to devour him.

The first thing on the agenda was to check the cars for keys.

With the newer computerize vehicles it was useless to even bother to check the battery if the keys weren't in the car, for without the key to stick into the ignition, the computer would not let the engine start anyway, even if the battery was fully charged.

Unless maybe you happened to be a mechanic or a professional car thief in the zombie free world of the past. Then you might know a trick or two to get the cars to run, but neither Derek nor I was either one, so we had to do things the old fashion way.

We had opened the hoods of the few older modes of transportation that we deemed useable, only to find that their batteries were completely dead.

Then Derek spotted it.

It was a completely restored 1951 Chevy Deluxe fastback, flat black with chrome fender skirts and a gray interior.

"Look at this Jack," he yelled.

"Shut up! I softly yelled back. "The eaters will hear you."

"Sorry," he whispered back, as I approached the vintage ride.

"It looks like someone just didn't have the heart to leave their pride and joy setting in their garage while they made a run for it; instead they decided to make it their get-a-way car." I said, admiring their choice in automobiles.

"Is there an eater inside?" I asked, expecting an affirmative answer.

"No, there're no eaters in it. This beauty is cleaner than a nun's cunt," Derek answered grinning ear to ear. "And the best part is that the key is in it too, and it looks like it's got a manual transmission, three-speed on the column."

"Which means if the battery is dead, we can push start it," I said, hoping that the battery still had some juice in it.

"Roger that," Derek agreed, lifting the heavy metal hood.

One trick that everyone learns rather quickly when they're thrust into a zombie apocalypse, is that a really quick way to check to see if a battery still is holding any amount of a charge, is to lay a piece of metal between the two posts on it and see if it sparks.

I bent the radio antenna on the old Chevy until it broke off in my hand (radio stations had stopped broadcasting over a year ago), and tossed the radio wave receiving wire across the battery posts.

To both of our amazements, sparks flew in every direction as the silver rod began to glow red-hot.

I quickly knocked the antenna from between the lead polls on the rapidly discharging black storage cell.

"We've got power, now let's see if we have enough to start this beast," I asserted, as I turned to implant my tomahawk in the skull of a walking disease carrier Derek had inadvertently called in by his earlier caterwauling.

I heard a thump, as the tomahawk split the forehead of the advancing brute, and as it began to drop, I shoved it to the side of the car so it would not impede our progress; as we would soon be attempting to flee the scene.

"Turn the key and see if it will start," I ordered.

Derek quickly turned the key that was already inserted in the ignition slot to the right.

"Nothing," he said, as he jiggled the key.

"There might be a button that you have to push, sometimes these older cars have a push button starter along with the key," I indicated. "Look around on the dash for some kind of a button."

I had no sooner finished my sentence, when I heard the engine begin to slowly grid: Derek had found the starter button.

"Pump the gas pedal," I suggested, slamming the hood closed.

The engine turned over slowly several times but didn't come to life. It slowly gridded and began to turn slower and slower.

"Enough!" I called out as I rushed to the driver's window. "The battery is too far gone; we'll have to try and push-start it."

"There's no way we'll be able to push-start this heavy beast," Derek, complained. "The grade of this hill isn't that much, just a few degrees, but it's still up hill."

"Get out of the car and let a real man take the wheel," I jested, knowing that Derek would retort in kind.

"I will, but where do purpose to find a real man around here?" he asked, with a smile, prompting me to answer.

"Shut up and get out, you're burning my daylight," I answered, reaching for the chrome plated door handle on the older car.

Derek relinquished his seat and exited the automobile, making a glib comment as he walked by me.

"You know Jack, you make an excellent doorman."

I returned his disingenuous observation with an insincere comment of my own.

"Shut up!"

With our bonding session complete, I jumped behind the steering wheel of the three-speed contraption.

With my foot on the brake, I made sure that the key was turned to the *on* position. Then I pushed the clutch pedal all the way to the floor and forced the transmission into its reverse gear.

I let off the brake, and the flat black steel behemoth instantly began to lumber backwards down the gentle slope.

Just before the 50's icon began to level out at the bottom of the grade, I popped the clutch and felt the vehicle shutter.

Quickly shoving the clutch pedal back down to the floor, I heard the powerful inline 6-cylinder engine begin to roar.

Black smoke poured out of the single exhaust pipe as I pushed repeatedly on the accelerator.

"What's the fuel situation look like?" Derek choked out, as he fanned away the dark exhaust fog that was drifting in front of his face.

"If the gauge works the tanks over half full," I answered smiling.

Cramming our new ride into 1st gear, I pulled the restored jalopy back up to the crest of the hill and onto the concrete road.

I maneuvered our new car around several of the vehicles that we had earlier rejected, or had rejected us, then parked and waited for Derek to join me.

Meanwhile, Derek dealt with two more zombies that at their own peril had chosen to menace him on his way to meet me, and had met their final doom at the business end of his meat cleaver.

After doling out the two well-deserved one-way tickets back to Satan's underworld, Derek again caught up to me and we were underway again.

Driving the old Chevy like I stole it (because I did), and with Derek sitting shotgun (Cassandra's hollowed out jug would have been riding bitch, but was still in my pocket at this time), we headed back as fast as possible to the place where we had abandoned our truck, so we could reclaim the weapons and supplies that we had left there.

We were lucky enough to find a new working vehicle only a couple of miles from where the truck had broken down, so it was a short and quick trip back to retrieve our stuff.

Upon our arriving back at the truck, I decided to leave the car running as we hurried to transfer the weapons, chainsaw, and what was left of our supplies into the trunk of the zooted out old Chevy.

"Let's not take any chances, we'll let the battery charge up as much as possible before we shut this bad boy off," I declared.

"Good idea, I'd rather waste a little gas than have to push this heavy son-of-a-bitch with a bunch of ravenous bastards chasing us," Derek stressed, as he put the last of our assorted junk in the trunk.

"As soon as I can, I need to find out if this saw works, there's no need to haul it all over hell's creation if it's busted," I proclaimed, slamming the trunk closed.

"Yeah, we'll check it later, more eaters are heading our way, let's get out of here before I decide to stick around and fuck'um up," Derek insisted, as he climbed back into the car.

I again jumped behind the glassy looking white plastic steering wheel of our reconditioned automobile before commenting.

"You really do have a rhetorical way with words don't you?" I asked sarcastically.

"Indeed I do, whatever in the hell that means," Derek answered smiling.

Without further hesitation, I slammed the clutch pedal to the floor and crammed the three speed manual transmission into first gear, and then in a coordinated fashion between pushing on the accelerator and slowly engaging the clutch, I let up slowly on the far left pedal.

The beefy steel-bodied 1950's Chevrolet began to rumble up North I-65 toward Indianapolis, and we were on our way to the Badlands once more.

BETH

Three days before Jack met Derek...

A woman's voice softly broke through the late night silence as Beth's bunk was gently rocked.

"Beth, wake up, it's time to go," Jolene whispered, "Are you ready? We've got to go now before they change the guards."

"Yes, I'm ready," Beth answered, sitting up and reaching for her .22 cal. rifle. "I just wish I could kill that bastard Ron before we go."

"Well you can't, not if you want to get out of here alive," Jolene pointed out. "So, come on let's get the hell out of here."

The guards at the compound changed shifts at exactly midnight every night, and the four that were due to come on duty that night had not made a deal with Jolene, and would surely stop the two girls from escaping from the Caucasian's fortress.

Jolene never told Beth what prompted her desire to leave the fortress, but she had been planning her escape from the compound for several months, and part of her escape plan was to bribe the guards on duty to look the other way while she and any companions that she might be able to recruit made their get-a-way.

There were four guards on each shift, and her plan was to leave before midnight so that she and her party would have all night to distance themselves from the camp, and anyone that might chose to come after them when they were discovered missing in the morning.

298

It was a very risky venture to try to leave the region controlled by the Caucasian. Even though he was not a stickler for details for some unknown reason, he was a sociopathic megalomaniac with delusions of grandeur, and he took great offense to anybody that tried to leave his self-proclaimed jurisdiction. Especially somebody that was not granted permission first, and very few were *ever* granted permission, first, last, or otherwise.

Nobody at the Caucasian's stronghold had much to bargain with; the nature of the socialistic structure pretty much brought everybody down to the same level. This equalization of the population ensured a black market type of mentality among certain individuals who were brave enough, or stupid enough to buck the system and risk the punishment that would be inflicted upon them if they were caught.

The result of such a system left most of the people with nothing that everyone else didn't have, and although the penalty for a person breaking the rules, or a guard that was found to be derelict in his or her duties was not set in stone, they could expect to be dealt with in a very harsh manner.

Fortunately, for Jolene and Beth the rotation of the guards had not changed for several weeks prior to their escape attempt, and all four guards that were scheduled to be on duty that evening were the men that she had bribed.

Jolene had used the only bribe that she had at her disposal that the male guards did not possess; in short, she had been sleeping with all four guards on a nightly basis for the previous three weeks before the escape attempt was to take place.

She had convinced the troop of paramilitary sentries that she would not rat them out if she and her group (Beth) were to be captured and brought back to the fortress, as long as she was the *only* female participating in the payment of the bribe.

This arrangement saved Beth and the other two women who eventually chickened out and turned down the offer to join the conspiracy to escape from having to become women of ill repute, and have to live with the fact that they had *whored* their way out of captivity; a fact that didn't seem to bother Jolene.

Beth had grown tired of being used as a water-filled punching bag at the Sarge's discretion, which seemed to be becoming more prevalent as each day passed.

Most of the so-called men in the place acted as if they were afraid of Ron, so nobody intervened to stop the all too frequent public poundings.

When she made the mistake of taking the issue to the Caucasian, thinking that as the leader, he would be inclined to protect *all* of his subjects and make the proper determination in her case, and then justice would be served. Or at the very least, the Sarge would be forced to stop beating on her.

He just laughed in her face and told the Sarge to try slapping her.

"It leaves less bruises," he said.

His advice also left Beth next in line for another public beating, which was administered moments after leaving the sight of the man in charge.

Beth knew that if she gutted the punk (the punk Sarge) within the compound, she would most likely be skinned alive (literally) and her dermis pelt would be fed

300

to the zombies that always ghosted the perimeter of the building while waiting for human scraps to be tossed their way by the Caucasian's henchmen. All the while, *skinless,* she would be forced to watch as they devour it.

If there was one thing that the Caucasian prided himself on, it was equality between women and men when it came to torturous punishment. It didn't matter whether you were a man or a woman, he would have you skinned equally.

This procedure was commonplace within the confines of the Caucasian's fortress, although it was usually reserved for those who had made assassination attempts on the leader (which for some reason seemed commonplace also), although it was not unheard of for this particular punishment to be arbitrarily doled out by some of the meaner guards for any infraction of the Caucasian's laws.

Thus, the zombies walking the circumference of the compound property were dubbed *Skin-Eaters*.

So, totally fed up with the continual pain from being beat on almost every day, being referred to as *Everlast* by wisecracking men that secretly wanted to fuck her, but were afraid the Sarge would have their skin peeled off of them and fed to the Skin-Eaters if they took any action to bring that fantasy to fruition, and having to endure constant jokes about her having to be told twice about everything (because of her perpetual two black eyes); Beth decided to take her chances with Jolene *outside the wire* so to speak.

Even though she knew that being caught would most likely mean certain death, she felt that sooner or later the Sarge was going to go into one of his intoxicated rages and beat her to death anyway. Therefore, she decided that she would be the one that would choose the method of her own demise, and it wouldn't be at the hand of the man that she had grown to despise.

With Jolene's plan now in motion, the two determined women made their way out of the communal sleeping area where the second-class citizens were housed.

The Sarge had Beth moved into the communal quarters after her countless rejections of his drunken sexual advances; a move that he considered as punishment for her, and she considered as a welcome relief from him.

However, every morning he would join her at breakfast, and begin her regiment of daily torment.

"The guard called Kenny said he would make sure that we made it out of here, as long as we got to his station before the changing of the guard," Jolene informed Beth.

"Then quit yapping and let's find Kenny," Beth whispered back, nudging her friend forward.

As the girls reached Kenny's post, they could hear the corporal of the relieving guards in the ready room giving last minute orders to his patrolmen.

"Hurry up you bitch's, are you trying to get us all caught?" Kenny scolded in a low voice, as the two females approached. "Well at least you two brought your guns with you, you're going to need them out there."

"Shut the fuck up and tell us which way to go, the other guards are right behind us," Beth scolded back.

302

"Go straight for that tall tree in the distance, that will take you into a residential neighborhood, and keep going from there and you'll be headed south into the countryside," Kenny directed them. "And watch out for zombies, they're kind of thick in that direction this time of night."

Beth and Jolene scurried out the door held open by the guard Kenny, who at the same time waved off the other guards that had been bribed (fucked), and ran as fast as they could toward the tall tree on the horizon that was barely visible in the dark.

As they ran, Beth fished out a small folding pocketknife with a four-inch blade from her pants pocket and unfurled it.

"We're heading into zombie country and we're too close to the compound to fire our guns," Beth warned. "Unless of course, we want to wake up every guard in the joint that is."

"All I have is my rifle," Jolene whined, looking concerned.

Once at the residential housing neighborhood, the girls stopped behind a row of bushes to rest for a moment and check to see if they had been seen running from the fortress by anyone that Jolene had not *bribed*.

"So let me get this straight," Beth asked panting, as she tried to catch her breath. "You planned this escape for months and forgot to bring a knife with you?"

"I guess I was just too busy paying out *your* bribes to the guards and it just slipped my mind," Jolene answered sarcastically as she smiled.

"Okay you got me, I owe you one," Beth confessed.

"One my ass, do the math, four guys, three weeks worth of bribes?" Jolene appealed fervently.

"You're right, it was your ass, at least a piece of your ass, but now it's both of our asses, so next time: bring a knife," Beth announced. "I don't see anyone following us; it looks like we made a clean break so far, but speaking of our asses, let's get them moving.

"Next time?" Jolene questioned curiously.

******

Beth was a seasoned fighter known to her peers at one point as a possible psychopathic killer wielding a .22 caliber M-4 clone. She was well versed in the killing of zombies, feral dogs, and rogue humans, and anything else that needed her services.

Jolene however; not so much. Before the planet went belly up and started coughing up dead bodies to feed on the living, she had been making her bread and butter as a fluffer in the porn industry while waiting for her big break.

After she got over the initial shock of the first days of the plague, she found that her talent from her past life offered her options against the roving man-eaters, by performing certain services to men in return for their protection.

She couldn't recall if she had ever put down a zombie or a dog, and she was positive that she had never killed a human being.

If the two of them were to meet in the square circle, the introduction of the fighters would go something like this.

Beth's introduction...

"Ladies and gentlemen! Fighting out of the red corner, standing 5 foot, two inches tall, hailing from parts unknown and weighing in at a mouth-watering 115 pounds, sporting natural blonde hair, blue eyes, and a 38-inch chest. Her record includes victories ranging from the rotting flesh of the zombies hordes, to the foaming mouths of roaming packs of feral dogs. She has several rogue humans to her credit, and at least one highbred hermaphrodite. Once know to her peers as "that cute little psychopath", she now makes her living as a freelance killer roaming across the purple mountains majesty and the fruited planes, fighting for the American way in the midst of the zombie apocalypse. Ladies and gentlemen... I give you Psycho Beth."

Jolene's introduction...

"Ladies and gentlemen! Fighting out of the Blue corner, at 5 foot, three inches tall, hailing from off camera on many of the porno movie sets that you once knew and loved, and weighing in at another mouth-watering 117 pounds. Sporting bleached blonde hair, brown eyes, and an impressively firm and perky 39-inch chest, her victories include, but are not limited to... four of the meanest perimeter guards in the Indiana Badlands, and numerous other weak-willed and sex starved males she's come into contact with throughout the plague ridden countryside. She once put an end to the life of a small mischievous rodent using nothing

more than a wooden mousetrap...and well... that's about it. Ladies and gentlemen... I give you... Jolene."

******

An hour before the sun broke the horizon in the east that morning, Beth and Jolene had force-marched nearly ten miles south of the Caucasian's fortress through the zombie-infested countryside.

At that same time, the alarm was being sounded at the compound and the search for the two escaped women had begun.

"Find Beth and that other bitch and bring them both back here," the Sarge barked. "You know how *he* gets when someone escapes... I mean leaves."

"Yes sir," the corporal of the guard of the graveyard shift replied, having no idea where to begin looking for the two women. "Sir, which way do you think they went?"

"How in the hell do I know? There is only four directions, north, east, south, and west, so send a patrol in each direction and get them back here," the Sarge raged, wiping the slobber from his mouth. "And do it now! Unless you want those skin-eaters outside to have your hide for lunch?"

The guard scrambled to rally his men for the search, and as he was ordered, he sent a small group of men to patrol in each direction.

"When I get that little bitch back here, I'll teach her to run away from me," the Sarge mumbled to himself, as he took his first swig of the day from his personal stash of warm beer.

306

******

While the Caucasian's compound was buzzing with the news of the latest citizens that were absent without leave, Beth and Jolene were busy with their own problems.

******

"Me and that asshole Ron traveled the last hundred miles to the compound on a motorcycle, we had to ditch our regular ride because the roads almost don't exist around here anymore. I don't know what happened in this whole area, but the place is filled with deep craters and burned out rubble from the houses and other buildings that look like they've been blasted apart.

I don't remember seeing all of this carnage on the way to the Caucasian's fortress, and certainly not all of these flies," Beth said, as she shooed away only a fraction of the massive amount of insects soaring around the area. "But we were traveling at night when we came through the Badlands, and most of the time I was busy fending off those ravenous bastards and trying not to fall off the back of the bike at the same time, so I guess I probably missed a lot of the scenic landscape the first time through."

"It sure does smell bad, but I think I'm getting used to stench, if that's possible," Jolene claimed.

Continuing to shoo away the flies that were circling around her, Beth said. "If the stink from all of these rotted body parts and the reek from those walking shit sacks isn't bad enough, these damn flies are just too much. And I don't care what you say, I've been out in this kind of shit for a long time, and I'm not even close to getting used to the smell."

"I can barely breathe without one or two of these little fuckers flying into my mouth," Jolene retched, as she coughed out a large hairy-backed fly with a metallic green and blue tint that had almost gagged her. Which was really saying a lot when you consider her former occupation; back then it took a *lot* more than a little fly to gag her?

"That guard Kenny said that the zombies were pretty thick out here, but I thought he meant just these walking zombies," Beth said with a grunt, as she drove her knife through the eye socket of an advancing female undead cannibal. "But holy shit, there are dead ones lying all over the place too, not to mention the quantity of severed limbs and chunks of decomposing meat."

"They seem to be faster than I remember; do you think they're faster than they used to be?" Jolene asked, just before tripping over the skeletal remains of two long dead soul-less reanimates.

"They are definitely faster than I remember them, which means that they are definitely more dangerous," Beth insisted, as she stuck the blade of her pocketknife into the middle of the forehead of another charging and angry freak of nature. "That's why I'm going to need some help holding them off. We're too far out to turn back now, and I'm not going to risk getting eaten fighting my way back through the same zombies that we spent all night avoiding. Besides, even if we did turn around and made it back alive, we'd just end up as the main course for the skin-eaters on the fringe of the compound grounds."

After pulling the blade from the head of the last zombie she had dispatched, Beth bent over and pulled the left femur bone from a semi-skeleton that had been separated into several parts by unknown forces, and had most of meat already rotted off it, or gnawed off it by hungry rodents in the neighborhood.

Handing the grisly 18-inch piece of whitish calcified bone to a cringing Jolene, Beth informed her partner.

"Here take this, you can use it as a club, there's too many of them around here, if we fire our guns they'll zero in on our position and a hundred of them will swarm down on us, we won't have a chance."

"Eeewwwuuu! It still has skin on it!" Jolene whimpered, hesitant to touch the macabre weapon.

"Yeah, shut up and take it, it's got some rotting muscle on it too," Beth insisted, shoving the human baton into Jolene's hand. "Club a couple of the dumbasses up side their heads hard enough to crack their brittle skulls and that shit will fall right off."

Taking the ghoulish weapon in hand, Jolene's actions were instantly dictated for her as two casually dressed male zombies accosted her simultaneously.

Jolene swung the heavy leg bone into the temple of the charging monster on her left, crushing its skull on the left side.

Without a pause, she then swung her calcium-fortified club in the opposite direction and planted the head of the femur (the round part of the bone that allows the leg to rotate within the pelvic bone) into the forehead of her next undead victim.

Just as Beth had predicted, chunks of rotting meat and skin separated from the bone and was hurled onto the head of the brain-dead monster upon impact, and was now draped over the zombie's punctured and bleeding face, leaving only strands of decomposing sinew and a section of the femoral artery dangling off the end of the bludgeoning thighbone.

Both of the former attackers fell to the ground in front of Jolene as she jerked the leg bone from the flesh-covered cranium.

"Talk about boning a couple of guys," Beth joked, trying to contain her laughter. "Let's get moving this area is too infested."

"Yeah, I think I've boned enough guys in the last few weeks," Jolene assured, easily containing *her* laughter as she coughed up another fly.

The girl's banter didn't last long, as more of the voracious undead appeared, blocking their path southward.

Although Jolene always felt that she wasn't really cut out for zombie killing, especially zombie killing on such a massive scale, her survival along with Beth's, mandated that she quickly acquire the skills necessary to carry out the extreme amount of extermination essential to completing their journey and finalizing their escape.

At daybreak, the girls found themselves standing beside a road sign stating that they were at the city limits of a small decimated Indiana town once called Lebanon.

Since they had began their trek south from the Caucasian's stronghold the night before, together they had claimed the lives (or deaths), of over a hundred

310

zombies that were roaming under the stars of the Badland's night sky.

Hungry, thirsty, and overall exhausted from their cross-country trek, and weary of all of the zombie killing, Beth formulated a plan and shared it with Jolene.

"I've got an idea, we need to get some rest and find some food and water, or we're going to do something stupid and get ourselves killed," she told Jolene.

"Well, I'm open for suggestions, let's hear your idea," Jolene admitted with a sigh.

"First we need to find a house that looks like we can use it for shelter for awhile, and if we're lucky, maybe the previous owners were stupid enough to buy bottled water before the epidemic hit, and still have some stored there," Beth dictated, pointing toward a group of destroyed houses. "Shit, look past those trees, one house is still standing. Once we clear that house, we'll secure it if that's possible, and then maybe we can get a few hours rest without having to worry about being eaten. Then we'll ferret around the joint and see what we can find, food, weapons, ammo, that sort of thing."

"Sounds good to me, and the sooner the better, but if we stop now, won't that give Ron and the Caucasian's guards a chance to catch up to us?" Jolene asked, with a concerned look.

"They don't know which direction we went, and even if they beat that information out of Kenny, between the burnt out houses and their basements, the craters, and the general rubble from all of the buildings that have fallen down, there're a thousand places to hide between here and the compound, they can't check all of them," Beth assured. "At least I don't *think* they can."

311

"Well that's reassuring," Jolene said sarcastically, as she followed Beth toward the one house standing within the cluster of demolished dwellings in the distance.

"Just in case those bastards did torture the shit out of that guard Kenny, and he did spill his guts before they fed him to the skin-eaters, I picked up a little trick in Texas that should serve to help us avoid them for a little while anyway," Beth bragged, as she quickened her pace toward the intact house she had spotted.

THE BADLANDS OF INDIANA

"Okay Jack, we're coming up on the city limits of Indianapolis, on the other side of the city is where the real Badlands start," Derek informed me, his traveling companion.

"If that's the case, I guess it's time that you decide if you're going to join me in my little jaunt through that scenic wonderland," I noted, looking Derek in the eye.

"Well, you know you've yet to tell me what your real reason for going into the Badlands is.

I know you told that fool Tony and his idiot friend Danny that you were going in looking for the Caucasian, but you never told them why.

They assumed that you were somehow connected to his group in some way, and you just let them think that. That's when they both about shit their pants," Derek declared.

"So you noticed that too?" I said smiling.

"I certainly did. So before I decide whether or not I want to risk my pathetic life by going deep into the Badlands in search of someone known to be a little on the crazy side of town, someone that is rumored to have a small army at his disposal, someone that has the ability to make a couple of hardcore Kentucky hillbillies about shit their pants at the mere mention of his name.

I think you can tell me the real reason that you are so hell bent on risking life and limb by trudging through the infamous Badlands of Indiana to search out this Caucasian character."

Having no intention of telling him, or anybody else for that matter, the real reason that I was willing to walk straight into a fiery inferno deep in the lower depths of the bowels of hell itself, stark raving naked if I had to, I chose to tell Derek a convincing half-truth, and let the chips fall where they may. He would find out the *real* truth soon enough when I found the Sarge.

"That's fair enough," I said, nodding my head as if I really believed the line of bullshit I was about to ask him to swallow whole.

Knowing what I was about to do, I *almost* felt sorry for my new found *friend*, as I looked into his trusting eyes.

"It's like this; I'm looking for an old Marine Corps buddy of mine, we served overseas in the sandbox, and then again fighting eaters down in Texas.

We were separated when a huge horde of eaters attacked us, and I've been looking for him every since.

I ran into a guy at a gun shop I was pilfering in Amarillo a few weeks ago, and he told me that he'd seen a man in Oklahoma that matched the description of my buddy, and he was traveling with a blonde girl named Beth.

When we were separated, my buddy was with a girl named Beth, so I figured it had to be my old sergeant.

I trailed them through Oklahoma and heard that the Sarge was headed for Indiana, and well... you know the rest," I told him as convincingly as I could.

Every good lie has a little of the truth attached to it, it adds cohesion if some of the facts are checked, and it makes it easier for the teller (liar) to remember what was said later on.

"This Sarge must be quite a guy for you to risk going into the Badlands looking for him," Derek stated.

"He saved my life almost as many times as I saved his," I answered, not mentioning that the next time that I would see him; I was planning to take one of those lives back. "So going into the Badlands for a person like the Sarge, well let's just say I owe him a lot, and I intend to pay my debt, every bit of it."

"What... are... you going to do if he has joined the Caucasian's band?" Derek asked hesitantly.

"This Caucasian can't be that bad, I know he seems to have everybody dropping dual deuces in their draws at the mention of his name, but he's not the reason that they call where he lives the Badlands! Is it?" I asked.

"No, the fact that the region got the name Indiana Badlands doesn't have anything to do with the Caucasian, although he certainly benefits from it having that moniker, because nowadays most people associate the name with him," Derek explained.

"If it's not the Caucasian's reputation, what is it then?" I asked him, genuinely curious.

"When the dead began to rise and the world, or at least this part of the world went nipples up, the population of Chicago, Detroit, and Fort Wayne panicked and scattered south into northern Indiana, people from Cincinnati, Louisville, Indianapolis, and the surrounding areas south of here, headed north hearing that there was a sanctuary somewhere near Chicago.

In a small town of about sixteen thousand, give or take a couple dozen zombies, is where five million frightened, panicked, disease ridden, and heavily armed people all merged. Slammed into each other is more like it," Derek continued.

315

"Anyway, between the brutality of the panicked live population, and the hunger of the undead that they left in their wake, mass-murder and unspeakable carnage on a grand scale took place throughout the northern half of Indiana."

What was left of the armed forces was assembled in mass on the borders of Ohio and Illinois to cordon off the whole region in an effort to try to contain the disease and keep the violence from spreading even further over an already steadily increasing area.

I'm telling you Jack, they had the top half of Indiana sealed up tighter than a nun's cunt, but it was no use.

The more the humans tried to defend themselves the more humans were killed without head trauma, and of course the result of such sloppy executions was just more of the dead coming to life and causing even more panic among the living. This continued until it was common knowledge that a bullet to the head or some other devastating impact to the brain was needed to stop the plague from advancing, and by then it was too late.

Seeing that the horrendous slaughter was widespread and seemingly impossible to prevent or contain, in a last ditch effort to stop the unprecedented bloodbath, the military launched what was to be their last coordinated mission before it was summarily disbanded due to desertions, deaths, and turncoats (soldiers turning into zombies).

They called in a massive air strike beginning at the circumference of the boundary of what would later be called the Badlands, and inward until they reached the epicenter of the massacre, that little town of sixteen thousand that's about 45 miles northwest of here."

"And let me guess. In that little town is where the Caucasian has made his headquarters, right?" I asked, already figuring that I knew the answer.

"Right, but it gets better," Derek continued. "This is the part that you're not going to believe, because it's unbelievable, I'm not sure that I believe it myself."

"Oh, I don't know, since this whole dead people coming to life thing came about, I've come to believe a lot of things that a couple of years ago I would have told you were completely impossible. You know like people trying to eat your brain while it's still in your head," I assured him, as I narrowly missed a mound of twitching zombie parts that someone had piled in the middle of the road. And by narrowly missing, I mean that I only ran over two of the snappers as we whizzed by at the break-neck speed (no pun intended) of 31 mph.

"Okay, let's see if you believe this shit that I'm about to tell you," Derek asked, almost boasting. "I almost told you this back at the roadblock, but I thought you'd think I was insane."

"*Okay*," I thought. "*You believed the shit that I just spoon fed you about the Sarge, and you lapped it up like a kitty drinking milk. So hit me with it, it can't be much more of a fantasy than what I told you, even though I did add some truth to my lie.*"

"Well, I already think you're insane," I said, sarcastically smiling. "So I'm ready, hit me with it, metaphorically speaking of course."

"Well first of all Jack, I would like to thank you for another emotional scar from that *insane* comment. But as I was saying, as the bombing raid was taking place, body parts of the living and of the undead, even the totally dead were being blown all over the place.

A few of the zombie's parts were beginning to twitch, snappers, as you call them were snapping, zombies were staggering all around lunging on folks, and people were running all over hell screaming and yelling, shooting and getting bit, and being eaten alive. You know the usual "Zombie Armageddon" type stuff.

It was early on in the zombie invasion so there weren't a lot of maggots and flies being tossed around like there would be if it happened today."

"Thank the *Eater Gods* for that," I interrupted.

"Yes, definitely thank someone for that," Derek agreed. "So amid the flying limbs and intestines zooming through the air spewing their soon to be fermented juices all over fuck, the people that were still alive and hadn't turned into the undead, began to see dinosaurs running amuck in the crowd, and tearing the zombies limb from limb."

"Bullshit!" I said loudly, believing every word. "Do you expect me to believe that horseshit?"

"I told you that you wouldn't believe it!" Derek exclaimed, almost proud that he had been right, or so he thought anyway.

"All right, finish your story of the mass optical delusion, and then I'll tell you about a giant bunny that hides eggs on one Sunday out of the year," I said, laughing in his face. "Oh, and I know another story about a fat-ass slob in a red suit that does home invasions while a herd of reindeer wait for him on the rooftops of the homes he's intruding into. One of the deer's has a red nose, probably from drinking too much."

"Very funny Jack, I'm laughing on the inside," Derek retorted sarcastically.

"All right, quit whining like the little girl that you are, and tell me what happened," I responded, also laughing on the inside.

"Well like I said before, people were starting to see dinosaurs killing off the zombies, and they weren't just any prehistoric beasts, they were the worst of the worst. I mean as far as *dinosaurs* go.

T-Rex's and velociraptors, no shit Jack, hundreds of them busting through the crowds of now even more panicked citizens, flinging pieces of zombies into the air and all over everybody."

"Okay, I believe you now," I said smiling. "But there's one thing that you haven't told me."

"What's that Jack?" Derek asked, still trying to convince me.

"Who told you this yarn about the end of the world and all of the dinosaurs anyway?" I asked sincerely, all the while knowing that Derek was telling me the truth.

"I saw it, I was there Jack!

You see, I was a corporal in the Army before *it* went to shit too.

We herded the civilian stragglers into what unbeknownst to us frontline soldiers at the time, was to become the kill zone. Even though we had strict orders to shoot anyone that resisted being funneled into that area, or that tried to run away.

We killed quite a few ourselves before the first planes came over and the bombs started falling. But like I said, we had our orders.

First the bombs started dropping, and then the body parts started falling out of the sky with the bombs as the bodies were blown apart, then when the bombs stopped dropping, that's when the dinosaurs came," Derek insisted, as his demeanor turned solemn. "However, the dino's just attacked the zombies, ripped them to pieces but not one of them even so much as touched any of the living people, at least not that I know of. Even after some of the soldiers and civilians shot at them and I think killed one or two of them."

"But you managed to get out alive?" I asked suspiciously. "How convenient for you."

"Yeah, I got out alive all right, but I wasn't the only one," Derek answered, as his voice lowered. "Almost everyone that was still alive, military and civilian alike figured it was time to get the fuck out of Dodge when the T-Rex's showed up, and I didn't see any reason to be the only one sticking around to see what would happen after the gigantic animals were finished ripping the zombies to shreds."

"Calm down dick-head," I said to Derek, as I laughed. "I had my own run in with the dinosaur population that was very similar to your account. As a matter of fact, that's how me and the Sarge got separated. T-Rex's and velociraptors came busting ass into the horde and chewing up the eaters, and we all started pissing down both legs and headed for the hills in every direction."

I figured I could kill two birds with one stone by telling Derek about my first experiences with the dinosaurs. I could convince him that I believed him, and

320

at the same time further add credence to my half-truth about the Sarge.

However, I would hold back the information about my second encounter with the vicious prehistoric beasts as not to betray my true intentions for hunting down my old *friend* the Sarge.

Derek looked at me, nodded his head, and after squinting his eyes slightly, he explained.

"The reason they call it the Badlands, is because the military devastated the whole region with its air campaign and left so much destruction, so much carnage, and so many dead bodies in its wake; and then the airplanes left, they just kind of evaporated, vanished, *poof*, they were gone.

Nobody stayed to clean up the mess, I certainly wasn't going to.

The dead were everywhere, the undead were everywhere, and the dinosaurs were everywhere.

The people that were still alive high-tailed it out of there pronto *thinking* that the dinosaurs were eyeballing them for their next rampage; and *knowing* that the zombies that hadn't been blown apart by the bombs or plucked off their feet and torn apart by the dinosaurs were eyeballing them for their next meal.

The bombing raid didn't come close to killing off all of the zombies that were wreaking havoc in the zone, and even though the velociraptors and T-Rex's mutilated multitudes of the undead, and did a pretty good job of deterring the flesh-eaters from their sole mission in life, which as you know is having us for breakfast, lunch, and dinner. They just disappeared as fast as they had appeared, they vanished without a trace just like the planes, and left tens of thousands of the undead still walking around unfettered searching for their next human dining experience."

I listened intently as Derek conveyed to me the reason that *that* part of Indiana was called the Badlands. Then I asked him how he acquired his vast knowledge of the zone.

"So, if you ran like a frightened school girl with the rest of the mob, how is it that you know what took place in the zone after you left?"

"I was born a few miles south of Indianapolis, and after I beat feet away from the killing fields and figured out that the Army and the other branches of the military had all but disbanded, I made my way south to where I grew up hoping to find my family.

Nobody that I ever knew was still there, but being familiar with the area, and the prevailing winds blowing the stench from the massacre due east most of the time, I decided to stick around, I figured that it was as good as any place else to ride out the apocalypse," Derek explained.

"I headed south myself," I interjected. "To a warmer climate."

Looking a little annoyed at my interruption, Derek continued.

"Yeah, right!

Anyway, some time back, me and this guy I partnered up with named Todd, decided that it might be a good idea to head up north and join the Caucasian. Of course, at the time he didn't have the reputation that he has now, at least not as bad as it is now, he was just the leader of another group of survivors taking in other survivors.

The spring rains kept the biting bastards at bay, they're scared shitless of water you know, but it turned the place into a mud pit.

So, Todd and I decided to pack our trash and fight our way through the city and up into the Badlands. We had no idea what we were getting ourselves into.

Stomping through the barren fields of mud, carrying five pounds of the sticky shit on each boot, made each mile seem like ten.

I'm telling you Jack, you haven't lived until you've slid down the side of a bomb crater and landed nard-sack deep into three feet of marinated churning body parts complete with bloated waterlogged heads chomping at your ass," Derek described graphically as he smiled. "I think I'm still carrying around some of *that* smell on me."

"Indeed you are. Your foul stench is gagging me as we speak," I joked, as I lightly punched him on the shoulder with my fist. "So are you going to hike your skirt up and go back into the Badlands with me, or am I going to have to make the trip alone?"

"What the fuck… I'm not going to live forever; and just sitting around waiting to die is just not my style," Derek answered still smiling. "Besides, I couldn't live with myself knowing that I let a little sissy like you hike into the fabled and dreaded *Badlands of Indiana* all by yourself."

"Okay then, wipe that shit-eating grin off your face and let's get to ransacking some of these houses, and find some supplies," I ordered, again laughing on the inside.

******

Jack and Derek began rummaging through houses in search of needed supplies and ammunition for the journey into the Badlands.

The undead population in the city of Indianapolis, was far less than in most of the cities of the same size that had been ravaged by the zombie plague (as all cities had been), due to the mass exodus north in the beginning by the panicked people searching for the none existent sanctuary that they sought.

That exodus also meant that there were fewer survivors inhabiting the town too. This equated to less rogue humans and hostile gangs roaming the streets taking pot shots at people, or trying to capture them for countless unsavory purposes that won't be mentioned here (remember your delicate stomach).

With the lack of the walking undead stalking humans, and the near total absence of the living within the city limits as well (it was a miracle that Derek met up with Todd), the search for supplies was easier than normal for Jack and Derek.

Even though during their quest, the men did cross paths with several zombies and a couple of inept humans that thought they were badasses, both hostile entities were divided equally and dispatched summarily by the boys in a classic zombie apocalypse fighting fashion.

Limbs hewn off, intestines hacked out of the torso, at least two skulls blown clean off their *stalks*, you know, the usual.

Somewhere off of Payne Road (no really), on the north side of Indy, in a quaint little house that they surveyed, Jack and Derek found a stash of ammo, guns, knives, and a plethora of hunting and camping gear.

******

"Jackpot Derek, we found the mother lode," I announced to my partner. "Look at all of this stuff, guns, ammo, flashlights, all sorts of shit, this guy had way more than he could carry, probably way more than he could haul away in his vehicle too. But it's clear that he took a bunch of his stuff with him."

"Well, in any case, it was nice of him to leave the excess here for us!" Derek exclaimed, sorting through the boxes of ammunition we'd found. "With all of this shit, he was most likely a prepped, or an avid hunter, and took with him what he felt was going to be necessary and adequate to be able to survive this hell."

I was less picky than Derek as far as the ammo was concerned.

My guns were mostly of the 9mm variety, my Beretta and Glock pistols were both of that caliber, as was my Sub 2000 folding carbine.

My assault rifle was chambered in the traditional 5.56mm NATO round, or again, for all of you slimy civilians, the .223 Remington cartridge.

Although there is a slight difference between the two shells (something about the headspace, it's technical, we wouldn't understand it), my M-4 can safely accommodate both bullets.

Therefore, unlike Derek who was busy digging through the quantity of ammo for .50 cal. rounds for his S&W revolver, I collected what I needed for my guns and began to ready myself for my search of other areas of the house for food and water.

However, before I left Derek prospecting for the ever-elusive hand cannon slugs he so greatly coveted, I suggested another avenue that he might consider exploring.

"That monstrously heavy gun you're toting around is pretty cool when it comes to relieving eaters of their brains and the skulls that they're attached to, but it only holds six rounds and sounds like an artillery piece when it's fired," I reminded him. "You might want to consider taking one or two of these 9mm pistols that the previous owner so magnanimously contributed to our cause with you into the Badlands, as a matter of fact, I insist on it."

Looking up at me while still fishing through the pile of diverse ammunition, Derek sarcastically whined.

"But I like my revolver!"

"Yeah, and I like my life, if you're going with me to meet the Caucasian, you're going to take more firepower with you than just that 500 Magnum cranium exploder of yours," I insisted once more.

"Oh shit, here they are, right in front of me. Hell, if they'd been a zombie they would have bit me," Derek said giggling, as he picked up a box containing 50 of the Magnum loads.

"Great, I'm getting a boner, now can we stop fucking around and get back to business?" I said, insisting one more time.

"Grab a light and the rest of the 9mm ammo, and pick out a couple of those spare pistols to use with it, and toss me one of those flashlights, we're going to need them. And God damn it make it quick," I said sternly, hoping my urgent tone would penetrate Derek's thick semi-loser skull, as I dropped two additional flashlight batteries into my pocket.

Derek quickly took my suggestions to heart and threw me a flashlight, put one into his own pocket, and then chose two of the abandoned 9mm pistols (another Glock 19 and a Springfield XDM), then grabbed the remaining 9mm parabellum ammunition and followed me out of the room.

Upon further perusal of the dwelling, we discovered several cans of tuna fish, and five 16 oz. bottles of supposedly spring water. Which was most likely water drawn from the hose out behind the factory that had been bottled to cater to the well to do *suckers* that purchased it?

In addition, we found a few miscellaneous items such as crackers and peppered beef jerky to take along with us.

Even though I was in a hurry to catch up to the Sarge, we decided it would be prudent to spend a couple of days in that house, resting up for the upcoming journey and getting our gear in order.

Besides getting the well deserved rest that Derek and I both needed, among other things those two days gave me a chance to finish drying Cassandra's womanhood, and stitch her *borrowed* shoelace around the edge of her severed tit to insure the opening of the titty-bag would close firmly when cinched up tight.

When I was finished, I ran my belt through the looped drawstrings (shoelace) and hung the bag at my waist on the left side so that it wouldn't interfere with drawing my gun from its holster.

In the early hours of the morning of the third day at the rest home, we were ready to resume our trek north.

"Let's go son, we're burning daylight, we wouldn't want to keep the Caucasian waiting," I jested, as I peeked out the front door to see if the coast was clear.

Geared up and on the move again, we sprinted outside and jumped into our restored 1951 *fastback* getaway car that had been so generously donated to us days earlier by an unknown benefactor.

Upon getting back to the interstate, we headed north again up I-65, and after driving slowly for about fifteen miles to avoid all of the usual pitfalls that we both had grown accustomed to, Derek informed me that things were about to change.

"Take this exit to highway 39, I-65 is blown all to hell about a hundred yards ahead," he warned.

I followed Derek's directions and eased onto the freeway exit that led to state highway 39. We turned right onto 39 to maintain our heading north, but after only a half-mile or so, the road ceased to exist.

"This is where we walk, unless you have a tank or a four wheeler hidden up your sleeve," Derek informed me as he opened the passenger door.

"How much farther to the Caucasian's stronghold?" I asked, noticing the extremely pock marked landscape.

"Fifteen or twenty long ass miles," Derek responded, pulling his meat clever from his belt.

"Fifteen or twenty long hard miles through this crater laden, eater infested frontier, wonderful," I retorted, as I stepped out of the car and planted my tomahawk deep into the face of the first of many walking corpses that I would cack along the way as I continued the search for my Marine Corps *buddy* the Sarge.

"Damn it Jack, you got the first kill in the Badlands," Derek spouted.

"Don't worry pal, from the looks of things there're plenty of kills to go around, maybe too many," I warned, pulling my weapon from the fallen zombie's skull and replanting it into another snarling and growling decomposing face that had quickly encroached into my personal space.

"Try and stay away from the craters, they have a tendency to trap the dumbasses in the deeper ones, and with rain water settled at the bottom of almost every one of them, the maniacs go crazy trying to claw their way out. Plus, almost all of them have snappers in them thanks to the dino's," Derek claimed, as he hacked the top two inches of a dwarf zombie's bluish-purple head off. "Look at this Jack; I just cut this midget down to size."

Stepping forward to avoid a maggot filled slaver that was dripping from a toothless goober's mouth that had tried to blindside me from behind.

"You're hilarious," I grunted, while disassembling the goober's lower spine by hooking it with the pointed beard of my combat ax and wrenching the vertebras apart.

As the brute bent at its knees and dropped to the ground, I ripped my hawk from its back and separated its skull, exposing the source of the white larvae in its drool.

With no time to respond with more tedious banter, Derek hurled his cleaver into the side of a brown-haired toddler's skull, which had attacked him at knee level.

With the force of a panicked golfer's nine-iron impacting the youngster's head, the heavy blade of the kitchen utensil carved its way through the soft immature cheek bone of the child and lodged three quarters of the way through the head just below the brain.

The young zombie continued to hiss and growl, intent on pleasuring itself by gnawing on the leg bone in front of it. The handle of the meat clever bumping against Derek's knee and obstructing its path, was the only thing standing between the miniature zombie and the meal it craved.

Derek now being besieged by several other ravenous corpses; pulled his model 500 double action revolver and squeezed the trigger.

Shooting from the hip, the mammoth wheel gun leveled off in the middle of the once adorable toddler's forehead, and I swear, the muzzle blast from the gun took the top of the kids head off just below the eyes before the bullet ever left the end of the barrel (impossible, I know).

Meanwhile I drew down on three of the undead that seemed not to give a shit that their little friend had just been partially decapitated right in front of them.

As Derek retrieved his butcher's tool from the remains of the little punk's skull, I broke my own code (everyone gets served before anyone gets seconds) and double tapped all three walking freak shows with tandem 9mm FMJ projectiles to each of their heads, dropping them like a bad habit just feet from where Derek was standing.

"Hey, this isn't working for me," I called out over the hood of the car. "Let's make a run for it, follow me, I've got an idea."

With the sound of Derek's stainless steel, .50 cal. *elephant gun* still ringing in my ears, and with curious new arrivals that it had summoned approaching us rapidly while seeking a mid-morning snack, we bolted away from our vintage automobile taking as much of our supplies (mostly ammunition) as we could carry and had time to collect, but leaving the chainsaw and other heavy items behind. Then we trotted north toward the Caucasian's fortress on the crater broken highway numbered 39.

Which under the circumstances I thought was rather fitting, considering that the original Star Trek television series had numbered each of their episodes, and the most relevant episode that dealt with the people we meet in everyday life, zombie apocalypse or not, was named Mirror, Mirror, and numbered 39.

I say it was the most relevant episode because it told the story of a mirror image universe where several crew members of the Enterprise including the Captain, were transported to a duplicate starship due to a transporter malfunction and switched with crewmembers of a barbarian race of people that were somewhat doppelgangers of themselves.

When Spock finally was able to rescue his Captain and the rest of the away team, and transport them back to their own dimension so to speak, Captain Kirk asked Spock how he was able to discern that the people from the alternate universe were imposters and escort them to the brig right from the transporter room.

Spock quickly explained.

"Captain, as civilized people it was easy for you to act barbaric, however, as barbarians, it was impossible for them to act civilized."

That statement rang true even before the Zombie Armageddon, when dealing with your average everyday dumbass that we all had to deal with, not only at work and at play, but everywhere else in-between was a constant staple in life.

However, now that the undead have brutalized our world, the barbarians are not nearly as docile as before, and their seemingly limitless barbaric tendencies have now been multiplied a hundred fold and turned us all into wearers of the dreaded Star Trek *Redshirts*, figuratively speaking of course.

TUNNEL RATS

The sound of an over aggressive mutant scratching at the back door of the house woke Beth up first, and realizing that they had over stayed their welcome in the abandoned house, she began to gather up her meager belongings in preparation for their impending departure from the premises.

"Jolene, wake up, we need to go," Beth said quietly, as she jostled her sleeping roommate. "Wake up, we gotta go!"

Jolene yawned and turned over.

"Just five more minutes," she implored, still half asleep.

"Five more minutes and we might be trapped in here, let's go, get up!" Beth responded gruffly, as she began to lose patience with her sleepy companion. "Now!"

"Oh all right, I'm getting up," Jolene insisted, as she slowly stretched and yawned again.

******

Beth wasn't about to get herself eaten alive because of some little bitch that was too lazy to move her dumb ass in the face of possible imminent danger.

However, not quite ready to abandon her partner and continue the journey through the Indiana Badlands alone, she prompted her traveling companion to move a little faster with a swift kick in the butt.

******

"Ouch!" Jolene squealed. "That hurt!"

"Not as much as having your throat chewed out by a group of maniacal dead cannibals," Beth proclaimed. "At least I don't think so."

Rubbing her butt with her left hand, Jolene propped herself up with her right arm and said. "Well if you're going to infuse logic into the situation."

"I am, now move your ass," Beth again ordered gruffly. "You hear that, their knocking on the back door, they heard the breakfast special is Jolene."

Jolene quickly picked up her gear and asked.

"Okay, what's this big trick you say you learned in Texas that you were yapping about yesterday?"

Beth moved quietly through the living room of the house, signaling Jolene to follow.

After stealthily checking the front yard for zombies and ascertaining that it was relatively safe to exit the structure, Beth motioned for Jolene to accompany her out the front door.

"Are you going to tell me or not?" Jolene fretted, as she caught up to Beth.

Stopping at a manhole cover in the middle of the street, Beth began to pry it up with her knife.

"Stick your fingers under it," she grunted, putting her weight on the knife handle.

"Okay, but don't drop it," Jolene cautioned, as she reluctantly slipped her fingers under the lip of the heavy cast iron sewer lid.

The two women struggled with the iron disk for a minute, and then managed to muscle it to the side.

"We're going into the sewer?" Jolene asked.

"Yes we are! Do you have a problem with that?" Beth responded sharply.

"I've never been in a sewer, what if there are zombies down there?"

"I guarantee you that there are zombies down here," Beth answered, as she climbed down into the hole. "But I also guarantee you that there are more of them up there where you are than down here where I am."

"If you say so?" Jolene faltered, as she slowly and reluctantly followed Beth down into the sewer.

As Jolene joined her in the dark muddy shaft, Beth pulled a flashlight from under her jacket, shined it down the sewer tunnel, and began to follow the light.

"In Texas, we used to go on supply runs using the sewers." She told Jolene.

"We would travel for miles under the streets. Keeping out of sight until we came to the area that we wanted to scavenge, and then we would just lift a manhole cover and climb up to the street. When we were done checking for supplies, back down into the sewer we'd go, and we'd make our way back to our shelter.

We had maps of the sewer systems and everything.

And we rarely encountered any zombies, but when we did we were ready for them because they were so loud, growling and stumbling around. The noise they made reverberated through the underground tunnels, echoing off the concrete walls, so we knew they were coming long before we saw them. That made them easier to put down."

"You mean like the echo coming down this tunnel?" Jolene asked, pointing ahead.

"Yes, that's the sound all right, we've got company," Beth warned, raising her knife and continuing down the dark tunnel. "I'll stick it or them with my knife, whatever you do, don't fire your gun down here, the noise will deafen us, I mean unless it's absolutely necessary."

Within moments, two of the merciless undead approached Beth and Jolene, and Beth quickly shined her light directly into the eyes of the lead zombie.

A zombie's eyes function the same as anybody else's eyes do, it's true that they look different; they're usually very bloodshot with a light green or blue glassy look covering the cornea.

However, if the crazed mutant is in a dark area for any length of time, it takes awhile for its eyes to adjust to any light that it's subjected to. Just like any other once human eyeball.

So when Beth aimed her light at the predatory corpse, it was temporarily blinded long enough for her to plunge her weapon into its twisted brain.

The second monster was handled in much the same way as the first, and the girls continued their trip through the darkness of the damp and dismal sewer.

The sewers in any town in the world, big or small, are just a hidden maze of tunnels that lie under the streets but don't necessarily follow the path of every street that's above them.

It was fortunate for Beth and Jolene that this anomaly in the underground systems exists, because they hadn't gone very far when Beth realized that the ease of travel that she had enjoyed through the sewers in Texas was not going to be the case in this Indiana town.

******

"I guarantee you that there are zombies down here, but there are more of them up there where you are than down here where I am. So get your ass down here before every eater in hell's half acre decides to follow us, unless you've got a better idea," I ordered, as I looked up at Derek through the sewer's open manhole.

"You make it sound like you've done this before," Derek stressed, as he climbed into the hole.

"The Sarge and I used this tactic down in Texas, and we were very successful," I informed Derek as he jumped off the last rung of the sewer's access ladder. "We traveled for miles under the streets without being seen by neither man nor beast."

I pulled my flashlight from my pocket and shined it down the long pitch-black tunnel in front of us.

"Let's move out," I suggested, as I again lifted my weapon and started to plant my tomahawk into the brain of one of the ungainly sub-human aberrations that had fallen down the manhole behind us as it tried to follow. "Fuck it, both of its legs are broken, it can't keep up with us, I'll just let it suffer."

"How humane of you Jack," Derek mused.

"Yes, it's another one of my many gifts," I informed Derek, as I walked away and left basking in the diagonal rays of sunlight that were draining into the sewer beneath the manhole; the slobbering zombie that had impaled its chest with its own right tibia bone and had two compound fractures in its left leg.

337

We made our way down the dark underground passage for only fifty yards or so when we encountered our first obstacle.

"This tunnel is blocked, how are we going to get through?" Derek asked, shinning his flashlight onto the rubble that was hindering our passage.

"We'll have to go through that off shoot tunnel over there," I explained, shinning my light at the smaller tunnel. "And hope it's not blocked too."

"The bombardment of the town has probably really fucked up the sewer system around here," Derek speculated.

"Around here hell, it's probably fucked up every sewer system in every city and town all over the Badlands," I replied, as I crawled into the four-foot opening of the smaller tunnel. "Keep your eyes peeled for manhole covers; we may need an escape hatch at any time."

Not only did the bombing raids destroy much of the sewer infrastructure in the Badlands. In doing so, they also gave the clumsy zombie population easier although accidental access to the tunnels under their feet, as many of the decomposing oafs inadvertently staggered across cracked sewer lines that collapsed under their weight. Or crevasses caused by the bombs breaking the large underground concrete tubes afforded the savage pagans openings by which they could haphazardly enter the subterranean roadways at will.

Now peppered with bomb craters and filled with an ever-growing number of the undead cannibalistic abominations, the sewers under the Badlands ceased to be the almost zombie-free haven that they once would have been.

After traveling for what seemed to be miles underground, and having to fight off several pairs and a few singles, and one fairly large group of the undead rotting tunnel rats, my burrowing friend and I had had about enough of the subterranean life.

When we came to a bombed out sewer pipe intersection that had been completely destroyed leaving us with only one option, which was to kill the posse of zombies that unknowingly blocked our escape route, and climb to the surface street above. We were almost relieved that we had no other choice.

"Do you hear that?" I asked. "It sounds like eaters are up ahead."

"I hear them and their flies, and I can smell them," Derek answered. "And I can see some light at the end of the tunnel too."

"That light is most likely coming from the hole that the eaters fell through," I guessed.

"So what now?" Derek asked, as he crowded up by me.

"We see how many there are, and if we can, I say we hack them to pieces and climb up out of this underground hell. Whether the tunnel is blocked on the other side of them or not."

"Sounds good to me," he agreed, as we weaseled our way forward to get a better look. "But isn't *Hell* always underground?"

"Hell has expanded, haven't you noticed? So shut up before they hear you." I ordered quietly.

Between us and a bomb crater leading to the surface, were five of the deadly menaces milling around and bumping into each other and generally doing what zombies do when they're not chasing people down to eat their brains, skin, internal organs, or other human delicacies.

"The sewers blocked, and the only way out of here is up the side of that crater," Derek noticed.

"Good, then we've got no choice but to climb out of this fucking place, and there're only five eaters standing in our way," I whispered. "We can kill two of them each before they even know we're here."

"I'll start with the one on the right, and then take out the one behind it," Derek planned. "You take out the two on the left, and we'll share the one in the middle. Okay?"

"Roger that," I whispered, as I gripped my tomahawk even tighter. "We go on three... one... two... three!

At the count of three, we rushed into the small group of oblivious cannibals, catching them by surprise as we had planned.

We hacked our way through our first two designated targets with a great deal of malice aforethought, which was becoming somewhat of a regular routine in the vast arena of the undead Armageddon.

Although our techniques for eliminating the horrible monsters was beginning to take on a sort of robotic essence, and to someone that for some odd and unknown reason hadn't been exposed to the rigors of the never ending zombie battlefields, it might seem; as Derek would probably say, as if we were *colder than a nun's cunt* and overly callous in our methods.

340

On the contrary: although our methods were coldblooded at times (most of the time), they were very efficient and more calculated than callous. Nevertheless, if you were to ask the zombie hordes, they might take exception to that remark.

Of course, like *they* always say.

Brutality is in the eye of the beholder.

However, nobody I ever knew was ready to die in the jaws of the undead, just to prove that they were a nice guy or gal.

So as the first four zombies bought their proverbial farms and fell onto the mud that covered the bottom of the gloomy sewer, Derek and I set our sights on the remaining menace that was now very aware of our presents.

The unnatural monstrosity lunged at Derek who was in the process of pulling the blade of his meat cleaver out of the middle of number three's now split brainpan.

It was close enough to him that he could smell the zombie's road kill breath over the odor of decaying flesh and defecation being emitted from it, and from the other zombies whose stench lingered in the stale air of the sewer.

It was rare for me to relinquish one of my weapons, especially in the middle of a fight.

However, when certain situations dictate that it is necessary for me to do so to save the life of a fellow human, I usually, although hesitantly, will grudgingly capitulate.

As the semi-warm breath being spewed from the attacking brain-eater's drooling lips advanced the droves of flies before it, the blade of my razor sharp tomahawk creased the rotting skin, bone, and brain of the obnoxious cadaver, ending its halitosis laced aggression forever.

"Nice throw Jack!" Derek exclaimed, congratulating me on my life saving ax toss.

"It's the Indian blood in me," I said, as I pulled the skull stuck warrior's ax from the head of the last downed corpse.

Then, holding my trusty tomahawk over my head, I let out the quietest *Indian War Whoop* that I could whisper, and then used it to swat at the orphaned flies still hovering over their former owners that lay at my feet.

"Time to leave Dodge, there's only one way out and that's up," I announced softly, as I wiped off the blood and maggots from my small battle ax on the shirt of the number five deceased.

Then I began to make my way up the loosely packed earthen ramp to the street above, with Derek close behind.

******

"This sewer is a dead end, the tunnel has collapsed and there's too many of them down in the system now, this is nothing like it was in Texas," Beth complained. "There are probably many more collapsed tunnels ahead, making it easier for the zombies to get to us, they're just falling into the sewers now."

Jolene took a quick appraisal of the situation.

342

"We'll have to take a detour and go down one of these side pipes of the bigger tunnel, maybe we can get through that way?"

"It's either that, or we go back up onto the street," Beth said. "I say we try the smaller tunnels first."

"I agree, at least as long as we can stand the smell," Jolene deduced.

The girls entered the smaller sewer on the right side, rejecting the one on the left after hearing buzzing sounds emanating from it.

They made their way through tunnel after tunnel, taking detour after detour every time they came to a blockage in the system from either the collapse of a sewer pipe, horde of undead homicidal maniacs, or the sound of swarming flies echoing through an open passage way.

The women traveled most of the morning through the crumbling system of concrete pipes that comprised the labyrinth of sewers under the town, dodging the crumbling structures and the zombies within, until they could no longer avoid either.

"We can't go any farther in these passages, they're getting way too crowded, and we're running out of alternative sewer lines to follow," Beth insisted, pointing to a group of dead cannibals frothing at the mouth near the exit of their tunnel. "Besides, I can't take the smell any longer, I need some fresh air."

"Me too!" Jolene whispered, so as not to alert the foaming undead ahead of them. "And my back hurts from walking bent over in these small sewer pipes."

"If we run by them quickly, they'll never be able to follow us up the side of that muddy crater," Beth surmised. "But we'll have to be fast, and whatever you do, don't fall down or you'll be doomed."

"I guess if they get too close, I'll hit them with the butt of my gun?" Jolene whispered again, raising her rifle.

"Shoot if you absolutely have to, most of the sound of the gunshot will be muffled by the dirt and will be directed straight up, so the zombies outside the sewer will have to be real close to be able to zero in on it," Beth asserted, as she too made ready to make a run for it. "I'll count to three and then we both run, okay?"

"Okay," Jolene agreed nervously, her knuckles turning white as she gripped her weapon.

"One... two... Three!" Beth unintentionally yelled, as she counted out the last number and began to run toward the slobbering mutants.

She passed through the innumerable flies that encompassed the horde, and made her way to the base of the bomb crater that comprised their escape route.

However, her impromptu shout at the end of her countdown had prematurely alerted the stagnant zombies of the girl's planned departure.

Although Beth had been successful in her bid for freedom from the underworld, and made it passed the mob of undead corpses, Jolene's attempt was quite different.

On the count of three, Jolene's nervousness had caused her to trip over her own feet as she began to follow Beth toward the undead and out of the sewer system.

"Shit!" She yelled, as she fell face-first into five inches of maggot-covered mud that caked the bottom of the sewer conduit.

Although the zombies had a hard enough time just walking, and the slimy nymph-coated muddy surface at the bottom of the concrete tunnels exacerbated their efforts, their proximity to Jolene made her situation dire.

As Jolene struggled to stand up in the slick muddy tube, wipe the fly larva from her face, and still maintain a hold on her rifle at the same time, the ravenous maniacal creatures were bearing down on her fast.

With the zombies between herself and Jolene, and Jolene's rifle now coated with mud and possibly out of commission for the time being, and fearing that she might accidently shoot Jolene if she fired her weapon at the undead, Beth felt the best thing to do at that moment was to scream and try to draw the monsters away from her friend.

A loud high-pitched piercing sound reverberated through the man-made underground infrastructure as Beth shrieked at the attacking horde trying to draw their attention away from Jolene.

Her first scream went almost entirely unnoticed by the marauding savages as their insatiable appetite for a fresh human deafened them to her vehement call.

The second harsh caterwaul made by Beth had a total different result, in more than just one way.

Upon hearing the howls of Beth's supplementary diversionary tactic, all but one of the unfed corpses turned toward her and began to lumber in her direction, their new-found swiftness and agility was hindered only by the lack of friction on the slick maggot-coated mud, the clinging clumps of said mud attached to their feet, and of course their *un*-natural ineptitude.

A shot rang out and echoed through the concrete passages as Jolene fired her weapon point-blank into the head of the lone zombie that had chosen to stay with her for lunch, and signaled, or so she thought, that her gun was still in working order.

Her bullet ripped through the right jawbone of the aggressor and lodged somewhere just to the left of its brain stem, knocking the walking corpse slightly sideways.

Jolene's off set projectile managed to slow the starving pagan beast down some, but failed to do its intended duty and stop the hungry malcontents attack.

As the wounded zombie shook off the effects of Jolene's misplaced headshot, along with several moist maggots from its lathery lips, it regained its momentary loss of equilibrium and continued its assault on the tasty female.

Jolene raised her rifle up and stuck the muzzle of the weapon onto the forehead of the charging cannibal, and pushed against its head as hard as she could with her gun, holding the monster at bay and at the same time, she pulled the trigger.

A deafening "*Click*" was the only sound that emanated from her rifle as the mechanism was fouled with mud and had failed to go into battery after the first shot, leaving the novice zombie hunter defenseless and struggling with her hunger-crazed attacker.

Boom! Boom!

That double tap was the only sound that Jolene heard as the lower spine of the zombie she was engaged in hand to hand mortal combat with exploded in two places, causing her attacker to lean to her left and quickly topple into the mud and slime at her feet.

Another two shots rang out, and the head of the mud-sopped cadaver at Jolene's feet split into several unequal pieces, all of which were now a few yards from its body.

Then the sound of gunfire filled the underground caverns, as zombie after zombie became estranged to chunks of their diseased brains.

Along with the ringing in their ears, the embattled women then heard my voice.

"Are you two ladies all right?" I asked, not knowing that the one with her back to me was Beth.

"I'm fine now," Jolene answered with a sigh, while scraping off a tightly packed throng of maggots and a clump of mud from her cheek. "You two got here just in time."

"I had it under control Jolene, stop trying to be so dramatic," Beth assured her, still with her back to Derek and me.

"How about you sweetheart, are you all right?" I asked Beth as she turned toward me. "You're lucky we were close enough to hear your screams."

"I'm fine too..., Jack..., is that you?"

"Beth?" I answered. "Holy shit in a doggie bag, it is you."

"I hate to break up this little reunion, but if we don't get the hell out of here now, we may never get out of here," Derek asserted.

"He's right, let's go, we can talk about old times later, after we get to someplace safer than this stinking hole," I said, more intent on milking Beth for information on the Sarge's whereabouts than chatting about old times.

Derek led the way back up the sloped crater wall and onto the street as the rest of us followed.

"All that gun play had to have aroused the curiosity of the eater's in the neighborhood," I claimed, climbing over the rim of the crater.

"Eater's, it's been awhile since I heard them called that," Beth recalled, with a smile on her dirty face.

Our gunshots echoing through the maze of sewers had dispersed the sound of our shots, and by doing so, dispersed the zigzagging population of famished ghouls that were menacing the town above, as they were drawn to the many different sewer openings and bomb craters in the area.

As we walked quickly up the street avoiding the pitfalls created by the myriad of bombs that were previously dropped in the region, and the ever-present undead that had not been as astute to do the same, Beth noticed that we were headed north.

"We don't want to go this way," she said. "There are people looking for us and we don't want them to find us."

"Who's looking for you?" I asked, hoping that she would give me the answer that I was looking for.

"Ron," Beth answered, "That bastard Ron."

"The Sarge?" I asked.

"Yes, that fucking bastard Sarge," Beth declared as she gritted her teeth.

"Are you two talking about the same guy?" Derek interjected. "The Sarge I've been hearing about oozes with the milk of human kindness, he's a credit to the human race, he's a..."

"He's an overbearing asshole-ish control freak with a beer in his hand," Beth interrupted. "And I want to be as far away from him as possible."

"You hear that Jack, your girl here thinks your buddy is a complete ass-wipe," Derek stated, laughing aloud. "Wait until she finds out that he's the reason we're here."

"Thank you Derek, I think she knows now." I said sarcastically.

"You're here looking for the Sarge?" Beth asked frowning. "Why?"

"You know, old war buddies and all," I lied.

"After that asshole drove off and left you and your family in the middle of that huge zombie horde?" Beth reminded. "Come to think of it, where is your family?"

"They didn't make it," I said sadly, as I drove my tomahawk into the frontal lobe of a tall longhaired male zombie dressed in khaki shorts and a shirt to match, as if he were a jungle guide in his past life.

"The horde got'um?" Beth asked, now frowning even more."

"No, we hid in the tank for a few days until we couldn't stand it any longer, and when we thought the coast was clear we climbed out," I answered, not wanting to go into all of the details.

Sensing that I was reluctant to discuss my family's demise, Beth abruptly changed the subject.

"Well do you know that we're going in the direction of the Caucasian's stronghold?" She asked.

"Yes, I heard that you and the Sarge joined his band of merry men," I answered, jerking my tomahawk out of Ramar's skull.

"That's right, we did, that's where I met Jolene," Beth said.

"I'm going to have to sharpen this thing, all this head cracking is dulling the edge," I said, trying to take my mind off my deceased family.

"We both had had enough of that place so we escaped during the night with the help of one of the guards," Beth explained. "But we figure they're looking for us as we speak."

"So are you trying to say that everyone there is a prisoner, held against their will?" Derek asked, looking rather hesitant to go any further north.

"Not everyone, some are guards, some are whores, some just like it there, like the Sarge," Beth told him. "I would have stayed, but Ron kept beating on me, and that got old pretty damn quick. I tried to find someone to leave with, and I was even going to kill that bastard before I left, but then I found out that hardly anybody is allowed to leave."

"Yeah the Caucasian likes to maintain a firm grip on most of the people there, although he does let some of them go out and search for people that run away," Jolene added.

"So you two ran away and now you think they're looking for you?" I asked, but didn't wait for an answer. "Which means that the Sarge may be outside the Caucasian's compound right now?"

"I'm sure of it!" Beth answered confidently. "And if I catch him out here I'm going to kill him."

350

"I'm sorry Beth, but I can't let you do that, I have plans of my own for the Sarge," I warned, watching Derek dispatch an older looking zombie with his meat cleaver. "Watch it; you're flinging maggots all over hell's creation."

"I figured as much, I didn't buy your Army reunion story for a minute," Beth said knowingly.

"Let's get one thing straight," I said smiling, as I flicked a maggot off of Jolene's shoulder. "It was a Marine Corps reunion story."

"Army, Marines, whatever, as long as that son-of-a-bitch dies," Beth stated adamantly, also smiling.

"Well, aren't we a happy group," Derek jested, as he split the skull of another creeping cannibal. "So what's our plan, if this Sarge character is out and about, and not at the Caucasian's house; there's no need to go there."

"I'm not going back there!" Beth insisted.

"Neither am I'm!" Jolene chimed in.

"Well I *am* going there!" I proclaimed. "The Sarge could be anywhere in the Badlands, and I can't search every nook and cranny in fucks creation looking for him. If he likes it so much at the Caucasian's place, sooner or later he'll go back there. And when he does, I'll be waiting for him.

If you girls act as our guides and take us there, when I've finished my business with the Sarge, we'll do our best to get both of you safely out of the Badlands."

"I really don't want to go back there Jack," Beth whined, grabbing my arm.

"They might kill me if I go back," Jolene insisted. "They'll torture me for sure, if only to force me to tell them who helped us escape."

351

"What was the guard's name that helped you?" I asked, thinking that it might come in handy later."

"His name was Kenny," Jolene said, as she figuratively spilled her guts. "But don't tell anybody."

"Well let me get this straight, you know, and you just told me, and you just told Derek, and Beth already knew, so at this point I don't believe that it's a top-secret-crypto piece of intelligence that we're discussing. However, I have no reason to mention his name to anyone, so yours and his secret is safe with me." I told her, not mentioning that I might use the information against him if I thought that I needed to.

As we walked north in the direction of the Caucasian's fortress and I tried to convince the women to join us, we came upon a gray haired zombie seated in a wheelchair.

The apocalyptic virus had the ability to change the physiology of the human body, making some things that were impossible when the person was alive, possible when the person contracted the disease and reanimated.

In this particular case, besides waking up from the dead, people that were crippled in life were able to walk in the afterlife. That is if they still had their legs.

However, this wheelchair bound zombie had not taken the initiative to try to stand up and walk, so it had inadvertently sequestered itself in the chair.

Being too stupid to propel the wheeled furniture by hand, the zombie sat in the middle of what was left of the street groping at any live pedestrians as they walked by, and live pedestrians in the Badland of Indiana were few and far between.

So as we approached the chair-bound fiend, we could see the gleam of excitement in his glazed over deadened glare.

Unfortunately, for the wheeled abomination, as Beth walked by, she took the liberty of sticking her pocketknife down through the top of its head as it reached for her.

"That eater wasn't even a threat, it was stuck in the wheelchair for some reason," I said. "You didn't even have to waste your time killing it."

"It's never a waste of time killing eaters," Beth replied, using my vernacular.

"That's one reason that I want you to come with me to the Caucasian's place, you're a good fighter, and you've got a good attitude too," I complimented. "You two girls don't even have to go in, just take us there and we'll find a safe place for you to wait while I go in and find the Sarge. Hell I might even let you take a swipe or two at him before I kill him."

"Well since you put it like that, I guess I can help you," Beth answered, with a gleam in her eye.

"I'm not going to run around here by myself, I wouldn't last a week," Jolene pouted, shaking out the last few dislocated maggots still clinging to her dirty dark-rooted bleached blonde hair. "So I guess I've got no choice, I have to go with you guys."

"Jolene, there's no need to lie, you're among friends," Beth teased. "Admit it, *last a week*, you wouldn't last an hour out here by yourself."

"You're right, an hour, a day, a week, it's all the same. If I don't go with you I'll be dead without a doubt, and probably sooner than later. So why don't we just

shut the fuck up and get the fuck moving, shall we?"
Jolene moaned, as she began to walk ahead of the group,
northward back toward the Caucasian's lair.

THE FORTRESS

About a mile from our destination, we found a two bedroom, two-bath ranch-style brick house complete with an attic and a basement and a small amount of food and water in the kitchen. It was one of the few houses in the Badlands that hadn't been totally demolished, and it was the perfect hiding place for Beth and Jolene to await our return.

"We're only about a mile away from the fortress," Beth informed us. "Go straight down this road and you'll see an old light brown brick high school with a huge domed gym, that's where you'll find the Sarge and the Caucasian."

"Okay, you two stay in the house and stay quiet, there's still a lot of eaters roaming around, we'll be back as soon as possible," I ordered, hoping the girls would heed my warning.

"You've got five days, not a minute longer, if you're not back by then you're most likely dead," Beth asserted, as Jolene nodded her head in agreement.

"Don't you worry your pretty little head, we'll be back, and in the mean time stay the hell out of the attic and the basement, you hear me?" I warned. "You don't want to get trapped in either."

Just before we opened the front door to leave, Beth pulled my head down and kissed me on the cheek.

"Be careful, where you're going is a dangerous place," she said with a look of concern in her eyes.

Jolene feeling the imaginary peer pressure leaned over and kissed Derek on the cheek as well.

I cracked the front door an inch and checked for any of the undead that might be ghosting the front yard.

With the lawn and neighborhood beyond, devoid of any standing, walking, crawling, or moving corpses that we could see, Derek and I ran out the front door and covered as much distance as we could to lead any people, dead or alive away from the house, just in case someone or something we hadn't seen, had seen us.

"Do you think we might want to wait a few hours and do this under the cover of darkness?" Derek asked, having second thoughts about going to the compound, and thinking of Jolene's goodbye kiss.

"If we go in the daytime instead of night, we'll be able to see everything that's going on outside with the so called guards and with the eaters that Beth says circles the place looking for free scrap's of humans to feed on," I explained. "Besides, if we show up during the day, we're just a couple of harmless and weary travelers with nothing to hide, looking for an old friend and a safe refuge to pitch our tent. And don't worry; Jolene will still be waiting for you when we get back."

"Who?" Derek asked, very unconvincingly.

"Who my ass, I saw the way you almost popped a woody when she kissed you on the cheek," I teased. "I can only imagine what would have happened if she had kissed you on the lips. I probably would have had to call for a wet cleanup on aisle five."

"Very funny, I almost forgot to laugh," Derek jeered. "You just make sure you don't get us both killed sometime during this little venture of yours. Because when we get back, I intend to do a little more than just kiss that cute little thing. If you know what I mean?"

"Well I hope you mean after you scrub her up, she still stinks of road kill," I laughed.

"I'm forgetting to laugh again," Derek said, grinning.

I paused not bothering to respond to my partner's jest.

"That's got to be it, it's just as Beth described it," I said, pointing to a beige brick building in the distance with a round domed roof. "Start making nice, it's show time."

The Caucasian's fortress was a high school before the worldwide zombie plague decimated everything.

Although the school's mascot had been some kind of rabid looking wiener dog with an attitude. Which seemed fitting, considering Center for Disease Control in Atlanta at one point had surmised that the disease of the dead could have possibly been caused by the overpopulation of feral canines. It looked like it used to be a nice educational institution prior to the planet being dismantled by the deadly virus.

The school was laid out on what were probably four or five acres, maybe more. It was self-contained having its own football field, baseball diamond, and of all things, tennis courts.

I would find out later that along with the schools swim team came an indoor swimming pool, and the basketball gym that sat beneath the dome was nothing short of world class.

That's most likely the reason that the Caucasian picked this particular facility to set up shop.

After all, the school was built close to the middle of the acreage that it sat on, giving at least a two-hundred yard no-man's land killing fields on every side.

The whole structure was constructed of brick, and had somehow managed to avoid being blown all to hell during the massive bombing raid that turned that part of Indiana into a pock marked wasteland.

If it weren't for the over abundant amount of undead carnivores inhabiting the surrounding land, I would have considered taking it away from the Caucasian.

We walked into the parking lot next to the gym and were within fifty yards of the building, when two men dressed in black uniforms with black hats and black tactical vests carrying black AR type rifles opened one of the doors and yelled.

"What's the password gentlemen?"

Not having a clue what the password was, and wondering why Beth had not mentioned anything about a password, I didn't answer, but I did the next best thing.

I pulled my tomahawk from my own tactical vest and carved the face off a rapidly approaching zombie that reminded me of my great-grandmother (on my father's side).

Then without a moment's hesitation, I spun around in a 360° circle to gain momentum, and chopped the left arm of grandma off at the elbow.

As the female zombie continued to lunge at me, *relatively* speaking of course, I hewed her right arm off at the shoulder after side stepping her unwanted advance.

Figuring that I had made my point, I twirled around once more and cleanly sliced the top three inches of gramma's head off.

"So much for harmless weary travelers, uh Jack?" Derek sighed.

"Well you know, the best laid plans of mice and men," I answered sarcastically, before yelling back to the two doormen.

"Doom, the name is Doom, Jack Doom, I'm looking for the Sarge, I was told he was here."

"We don't know any Sarge," one man answered. "Come closer and keep your hands where we can see them, and don't make any sudden moves."

"Don't make any sudden moves?" I thought. *"I wonder if he means like hacking pieces off an eaters skull?"*

"He also goes by the moniker Ron." I stated, now hoping that they wouldn't ask me his last name, because if my life depended on it I just couldn't remember it, and my life did depend on it.

"Oh, Ron, isn't he the guy that's always smacking around that cute little blonde girl?" One of the guards asked the other.

"Yeah, that's him, I think I heard him say he was a sergeant back before all hell broke loose," the other guard answered.

I bent down and wiped the maggots, and the usual slim off my weapon using grandmother's best *Sunday go to meeting* outfit as my rag, and then we moseyed toward the two sentries.

"What's your business with Ron?" The curious guard asked, now pointing his rifle at me.

"Exactly," I answered. "It's my business, not yours."

"Are you trying to get us killed?" Derek whispered, trying not to move his lips.

"Relax, everything is going to be all right," I answered, in a very calm voice.

"Nobody comes in here until they state their business, the boss is very particular about who he lets in," the guard announced.

"Okay, fair enough, you're just doing your job," I acknowledged, changing my harsh demeanor to a somewhat friendly one.

"The Sarge is an old friend of mine, we served together in the military, and we fought the dead together sometime back before we were separated. I heard in Oklahoma that he had joined your group, and me and my friend here decided that we might want to join you too."

"We did?" Derek whispered, still trying not to move his lips.

"Shut the fuck up idiot!" I whispered back, also trying not to move *my* lips.

"We'd be a valuable asset to your group. Both of us kill zombies real good." I told the guard.

"It will be up to the boss if you can stay or not, that's not our call," the guard spouted back.

"Well if you would be so kind as to inform the Sarge that his old friend Jack is here, I'm sure he'll put in a good word for us both."

"Ron is out looking for his bitch, we don't know when he'll be back," the guard said smiling. "He was pretty pissed when he left, said he was going to kill that little whore when he finds her."

"Holy shit," Derek whispered again, still trying not to move his lips. "These are serious ass holes."

Also still trying not to move my lips while maintaining a fake smile for the boys in black, I whispered back.

"I said, shut the fuck up, and let me handle this!"

For once Derek took my advice without retort, and stood silent as I conversed with the guards.

"In that case I'd... we'd... like to make an appointment to meet with your boss and pled our case," I said, still smiling. "I believe he goes by the name of *The Caucasian*, does he not?"

"Step inside, your attracting biters," the taller of the two guards ordered, with his gun still leveled at my chest. "And make it fast, we don't need every fly on the planet in here with us."

As usual Derek's mouth didn't stay closed for long, as he couldn't resist commenting on the sentinel's statement. "You're right; it won't be very long until these eaters are going to be thicker than pubic hairs on a nun's cunt! Hell, the flies already are!"

"Thank you for that astute observation buddy, we couldn't have figured it out without you!" I jested, while swatting several of the *really* dead grandmother's hostile newly orphaned flies off my face.

We wasted no time complying with the sentry's demand and entered the building quickly, waving our arms in a nonchalant fashion to shoo away a few of the more obstinate of the vengeful trailing insects before we did so.

"Put your weapons on the floor, all of your weapons, and then get up against the wall!"

Again, we complied with the guards demands.

We stretched out our arms and legs and leaned against the interior wall of the building.

Now with our weapons in a pile on the floor behind us, I was the one having second thoughts about whether coming into the Caucasian's den was such a good idea, and I wasn't even thinking about Beth's goodbye kiss.

The guard's search was as thorough as it could possibly be without having us peel our duds and giving us a full-bore multiple cavity search complete with a deep-seated anal probe.

Satisfied that we were of little threat without our weapons, we were escorted to a small room and informed that the Caucasian would be notified of our desire to meet with him.

Time passed slowly as we awaited the Caucasian's response to our request in the cramped room that still housed some physical education equipment for the school. When this bunch took over the gym they had turned the storage room into a minimum security holding cell, for lack of better term.

Finally, after many boring hours had passed the guards in black returned with the Caucasian's answer.

"The Caucasian will see you now," the sentry said. "But do yourselves a favor and don't fuck with him, or he'll have your nuts in a sling before sunrise, you already killed one of his roaming skin eaters."

"Oh, you mean the one you called the biter? You mean the Caucasian has them for pets or something?" I asked.

"Or something." The guard responded smiling.

"Well we wouldn't think of as you say, *fucking* with your boss." I replied, as I thought. *"I just know Derek is thinking homophobic thoughts about now."*

"It was grandma or me on the parking lot, I chose me," I mentioned in my defense of the wanton slaughter of the aged skin eater.

The guard ignored my comment as we were escorted up to an upper level of the gym to an area behind where the rollout bleachers were blocking the view of the gymnasium floor.

There we saw our first glimpse of the infamous Caucasian that supposedly ruled the Indiana Badlands with an iron fist.

THE CAUCASIAN

When we first laid eyes on the man that was known as the Caucasian. It all became very clear to us both why the leader of this feared cult in the heart of Indiana had such a name.

There before us in that abandoned school gym, sitting between two want-to-be paramilitary types that were armed with the dreaded *black rifles* complete with fixed bayonets, and sporting various other lethal weapons that were attached to their belts such as billy clubs and machetes, sat a giant.

The Caucasian was a full-fledged albino male, and I guesstimated he was every bit of seven feet tall and most likely even taller, although it was hard to calculate his exact height while he was sitting down.

The man's high and bulbous cheekbones seemed to magnify his already pale elongated face, giving it the illusion of being even larger.

Piercing pink tinted eyes with their pale crimson irises gave his stare an eerie and presumed evil intent, a premeditated persona that I figured the gigantic man was pleased to project.

His extremely long arthritic looking bony fingers adorned with their light pink fingernails were reminiscent of King Crab legs dangling at his sides.

Long snowy white locks capped with a bleached out and polished crown of a real human skull for a hat, hung straight down and allowed his huge ears to peek out from behind the strands of hair as if they were peering through a curtain.

He sat hunched up in his chair, which was several sizes too small for his freakishly large body, and his self imposed contortion made him look rather uncomfortable.

As I gazed upon the giant, a weird thought crossed my mind, and for the first few seconds of our encounter with the gangly freak, all I could think of was. *"Where in the fuck did this guy find a skull bigger than his own grossly protuberant head? One big enough that he could hollow it out and wear as a skullcap."*

Spreading his legs slightly, and staring at me through his elephant-man looking knees that were prominent as they peeked out from under his friar's robe type garb, he began to speak. The sound of his deep voice brought me back into the moment.

"Mr. Doom I presume?" the Caucasian asked, with an accent that I couldn't quite place.

"Yes," I answered, then adding to avoid any confusion. "That would be me."

"May I call you Mr. Doom?" he asked, not waiting for my answer.

"Mr. Doom, in my line of work, I have had the pleasure of coming into contact with many naive travelers that think that their journey through this here zombie apocalypse of ours is just another chance to gather around a roaring campfire and hold hands with the people that they meet along the way. A chance to roast marshmallows and sing a few choice choruses' of *I'd like to buy the world a Coke* in perfect harmony, and then hang together in peace and euphony forever after."

"I've ran across a few of those nimrods myself," I admitted to the giant."So what's so pleasurable about having to deal with those fools?"

"Well, they are much easier to get along with than people like yourself that seem to know the real intent of that thing that is called human nature," the Caucasian clarified.

"By the way, nice skullcap," I said sarcastically, to the abnormally tall cult leader.

"Thank you Mr. Doom, it was a gift from one of my followers. He inadvertently crossed paths with one of the outside beasts that seemed to have contracted a rather extreme case of macrocephaly," the huge albino explained to me, as if I knew what in the hell macrocephaly was. "After he had sliced the top of the biters skull off with his rigging ax, he realized that the big head disease (now I knew) had formed a rare and unique find, and that I had no such adornment in my collection. He surmised that this calcified cranial cap would be a suitable gift to present to his beloved master, so he cleaned and bleached the bony cap, and polished it to give it the brilliant sheen it now displays."

When the freakish dolt was finished bragging about his grotesque head cover, and making me wish that I had never mentioned it, I introduce Derek to him.

"Yeah, and this is Mr. Derek," I told him, not knowing Derek's last name.

"Hi!" Derek said cheerfully. "You can call me Mr. Derek."

Standing up, the Caucasian's disproportionately tall stature seemed dwarfed by the massive dome roof of the high school gym.

"Mr. Doom, Mr. Derek, come, I will show you how I get along with people unlike *yourselves*, provided that Mr. Derek is just like you Mr. Doom." the Caucasian said, as he led us through a side door and down a flight of stairs, leaving his two guards waiting in his chamber for our return. "They are just outside this door."

"What are they doing out there, having another sing along?" I asked snidely, winking at Derek.

The pale-skinned man bent down and swung open the door.

"No Mr. Doom, they are just hanging around out there," he said, making grotesque facial distortions as he spoke.

As the door opened wide, the stench was like a freight train smashing into my nose, even though it was a smell that I'd endured many times before, I was just starting to get used to the musty locker room odor in the former high school gym.

Outside the gym, inside a chain link fence enclosure, we could see by the light of the moon, hundreds of snapping heads hanging in small net bags on what looked like rows of make shift clotheslines made of heavy gauge wire.

Along with a slight breeze that was also sweeping their reeking stink into the building, the constant opening and closing of their chopping mouths propelled their motion as they bizarrely bit at the flies that hovered all around them.

Under each bag were varying sizes of maggot filled saliva pools giving off an eerie illusion of life, as the small larvae squirmed in the juices of the still propagating spit glands constantly secreting as the severed heads pumped their jaws.

"Every Saturday and Sunday night, we have what my followers refer to as fight nights; some of the heads that are hanging in front of you are from the fighters that lost their battles on fight nights.

However, most of the heads you see swinging in front of you are the weaklings of this world that thought they would... how did I put it before? Oh yes, they thought that they would buy me a Coke!

Well, except for the Coke part, they got their wish; they are hanging together in peace and euphony forever after."

Cupping his humungous right ear in his large right hand, the Caucasian leaned in the direction of the dangling decapitated heads and listened to the chomping, snapping, and crunching sounds made as the ravenous heads clapped their jaws together repeatedly, chipping their teeth and slapping their top and bottom lips against one another.

"Do you hear that Mr. Doom? That is the sound of euphony forever after that they were seeking."

Thinking that this psychopathic demigod was trying to scare the living shit out of me, my unemotional comment was meant to convince the maniacal freak show that his ploy to unnerve me was unsuccessful, even though it was working like a charm.

"Lovely smell you've discovered, you should bottle it, you'd make millions," I said, plastering a greasy smile on my face to help persuade the man that his appalling ploy hadn't worked.

My off the cuff semi-sarcastic remark brought a look of confusion to the man's face that seemed to bring out some feminine features that I had not previously noticed due to his misproportioned and malformed facial structure. His naturally bleached skin contrasted with his deep-set dark circled eyes and accentuated his high protruding cheekbones, which made him resemble some type of female kabuki dancer in drag.

I had to repress my thoughts as I noticed freakish subtleties in the man's bodily gestures and facial expressions; for fear of laughing in his face.

It reminded me of the good old days back at the buffoonery where I worked before the apocalypse struck.

Once I had determined that my boss Batshit Bobby was as crazy as his name implied, on numerous occasions as I was discussing business matters with him, I began to imagine him in a straight jacket with lipstick smeared all around his mouth, rocking from side to side in his chair in a futile effort to free himself from his insane asylum garment.

I stopped practicing that visualization exercise that was quickly becoming an enjoyable daily habit; when one day we were having a conversation about something that Batshit deemed very serious.

On that particular day I was busy picturing him with his arms crossed and strapped tightly into his favorite very long-sleeved tan jacket that buckled in the back; instead of listening to the gibberish that was as usual, spewing like a case of chronic diarrhea from his ever flapping pie hole. In my mind, I saw him yapping through the bright red lipstick that he had caked around his mouth as if a monkey had applied it for him, and tilting back and forth in his leather bound bosses chair.

That day I came very close to bursting out and laughing in *his* face.

After that episode, I decided that it would be a little more prudent of me, and a lot safer for my career, to abandon that simple pleasure and not take the chance of having to explain my odd reaction to my insane boss's serious demeanor.

With that memory instilled deep in my psyche, I decided that the current situation might become a lot worse if I were to burst out with a huge guffaw in the face of the feared and supposedly all-powerful Caucasian.

In any case, his thousand-yard stare at the conclusion of my comment about the stench that was searing our nose hairs to their roots, made me think that he was wrestling with the concept of my subtle humor.

Although he had the means at his disposal to terminate what I was sure he felt was our impudent and pathetic existence, he made no moves in that direction.

If he had tried to secure our demise at that time, I can assure you, both Derek and I had a completely different concept of how our relationship was going to proceed, and *his* demise would have been first on the agenda instead of ours.

Instead, he chose to continue to play his brand of chess with us.

"I like you Jack! May I call you Jack?" he asked, again not waiting for an answer. "That is why I have decided to kill you last."

I'm sorry, but I just couldn't help myself, the pasty anemic had left me with an opening that I couldn't pass up.

"Well that's mighty *white* of you Mr. Caucasian," I said to the freakish albino, trying my best not to crack a smile.

Derek however was not as successful at repressing his response to my colorful and timely, yet politically incorrect witticism that seemed to fly high over the Caucasian's head as he responded without as much as a blink of his red eyes.

"Please Jack, call me Caucasian."

Then as he noticed Derek smiling, he inquired.

"Why are you smiling Mr. Derek?"

Derek was caught completely off guard by the albino's question; he was still amused by my comment and answered the best way he could think of on the spur of the moment.

"Because I like you Mr. Caucasian," he said.

"Please, you may call me Caucasian too!"

"Caucasian it is then," Derek replied, hoping that the giant would settle for his pathetic off the top of his head explanation.

There was something very odd about this guy, his height, his color, his demeanor, his accent and speech pattern, everything about him was odd, something was not right.

But he had not shown any real aggression toward me or Derek, other than his constant willingness to try to scare the hell out of us, and sometimes doing just that.

He had promised to kill me last, I didn't know if that statement was just another one of his seemingly endless sick attempts to make me lose control of my bodily functions and piss down my leg, or if he really thought that he would kill everyone else before me. Whoever everyone else was?

I didn't know what to think, except that at this point he was standing in the way of me finding the Sarge, and as far as I knew, every second I spent dealing with the Caucasian, was a second that I wasn't looking for my old *friend*.

"Ok, Caucasian it is," I also agreed, walking back into the gym. "This isn't a social call you know, I looked you up for the sole purposes of getting some information from you and maybe joining your ranks."

"Jack Doom, I hope you have not come here to barter, many of those bags outside are filled with the heads of people that wanted to barter with me," Caucasian stated sternly. "I live by one simple rule, and that rule is. *What is mine is mine, and what is yours is mine.*"

"Let me tell you about people that think they can barter their way through life in... how did you put it, *"this here"* zombie apocalypse," I said, looking the freakishly tall mutant directly in his red eyes.

"Most of the barterer's that have approached me, have done so heavily laden with their wares, whether those wares were equipment, guns, food, or whatever.

Once I surmise that they are weighted down with their goods, I usually weigh them down a little more with lead. Then I take what I want, and leave the rest for the eaters to devour."

Back when I was a kid, projecting yourself as some kind of weakling sissy was the fastest way I knew to be fed a knuckle sandwich at the end of a bully's fist. It was also a good way to get yourself mugged if you found yourself in the wrong place at the wrong time as an adult.

However, in the middle of a biblical proportioned cataclysmic event such as a *Zombie Armageddon*, most

372

of the time projecting yourself as anything but being a stone cold badass, was like waving your own signed death warrant in the face of your assailant.

Of course there are always some exceptions to the rule, coming on like gangbusters at the Way Station would have gotten me nowhere, although trying to be reasonably polite got me nowhere either, and in the end I had to beat the living shit out of someone to get what I wanted, in the Armageddon times just like in the days before, you have to use *some* common sense once in a while, or somebody will have you for breakfast (maybe literally).

With that said, I continued to lie to the Caucasian (somewhat), boosting my reputation as a major league badass as I went.

The tall aberration smiled.

"Most impressive Jack Doom!"

"Yeah, I like to pump a couple of extra slugs into the pantywaists for good measure, just because I feel that they deserve it. You know how it is."

"Yes I do know how it is Jack Doom, and I understand why you would want to take precautions in these times of trouble," the white behemoth answered, as he lumbered back to his undersized chair. "Weakness, cowardice, and stupidity can sometimes be contagious. It is always better to be safe than sorry."

I found the albino's last comment about being safe mildly amusing.

Even though we had been thoroughly searched by his guards and stripped of our weapons prior to our introduction, he had allowed himself to be left with two total strangers that were fresh out of the Indiana

Badlands, as his guards did not join us during our tour of the hanging heads display. Instead, they stayed behind to guard his *empty* throne room.

Maybe he was so confident of his hand-to-hand fighting skills that our presents was of no concern to him, or he felt that his reputation was enough to cripple any assassination attempt that *we* might make.

Perhaps, he was armed to the teeth under the gray monk's robe that he wore, and was concealing his weapons from us, ready at any moment to reveal the hidden arsenal and slay us in turn.

Whatever the reason for seemingly going unguarded with us to view the swinging heads, now after our tour, we were back with his want-to-be military guys that were clinging to their boss like a pair of thirsty leaches, and I'm sure that the Caucasian felt even more secure in their soon to be inept presents.

Many *unknown* factors played into my decision to waylay the Caucasian and put him out of our misery and everyone else's for that matter, most of all was the *known* fact that he had threatened to kill me. Kill me first, kill me last, or kill me somewhere in the middle, the threat was still a threat, and it was all the same to me.

I hadn't found the Sarge as of yet, but experiences in the zombie wasteland had taught me that almost everything and everybody is either going to try to kill you, eat you, scratch you, bite you, or in some way, shape, or form, going to try to put an end to your existence the best way they know how. Therefore, when some joker decides he *or she* is going to telegraph the blow and warn you that they're coming for you, you had better take it seriously, or it just might be the last thing that you don't take seriously. So I decided to take the Caucasian's threat seriously and deal with him in a timely manner.

So sometime later, after both Derek and I had spun about as much bullshit yarn as we could make up under the emotional duress that we were suffering during our visit, the seven-foot lummox, seemingly enjoying our tall tales (no pun intended), smiled, and asked me.

"What is this information that you think I can provide for you Jack?"

"I'm looking for a friend of mine, he is traveling with a blonde haired girl, I heard that they might have joined your group," I answered, pretending that I was ignorant of the circumstances. "His name is Ron, but I always call him Sarge."

"My sentries told me that you were searching for Ron, and that you claimed to be his friend," the Caucasian admitted. "Ron and his blonde haired female did appear outside our front door some time ago, and they begged to be part of my family.

However, neither Ron nor his concubine is with us now.

It seems that his female decided to go on sabbatical, and she took another female with her.

Ron, or as you say you call him, Sarge, was so upset at her departure, that I allowed a few of my elite palace guards to accompany him outside the compound and help round them up."

Seeing a chance to not only leave the Caucasian's fortress unscathed, but to also have the opportunity of finding the Sarge with only a few of his *new* friends surrounding him, I said to our gargantuan host.

"If you or one of your guards could point us in the right direction, we'll not only help search for the blonde haired girl, but we'll return with the Sarge and join your group," I said, lying through my teeth. "Right Derek?"

"Oh, absolutely," Derek agreed, convincingly nodding his head.

"Fuck you Jack Doom," the Caucasian jeered, shaking his head and laughing. "If I let you go out into the Badlands looking for Ron you might get yourself killed or decide not to come back."

"Hey, I like that, do you mind if I use that, I'll have that printed on my business cards," I jeered back, also laughing. "Yeah, my cards will read, *Jack Doom, FUCK YOU!*"

Again, my droll sense of humor seemed to soar well above the large albino's head as his long colorless face exhibited a curiously unknowing look.

I couldn't figure out how the Caucasian kept all of the people at this fortress under his spell. I hadn't seen any outstanding leadership skills up to this point, and the man didn't seem to be what you might call the sharpest knife in the utensil drawer either.

Nevertheless, I had other things to worry about. I needed to convince the tall freak that he would definitely see Derek and me again, even if he did consent to allow us to depart into the vast Indiana Badlands in search of the Sarge's girlfriend.

"I'm not sure what all the fuss is about, I ran into a couple of good ole boys back in Oklahoma that told me that they had seen the Sarge as they were leaving your fortress," I divulged. "It sounds to me like you let them leave without raising a ruckus."

"That I did Jack Doom, but they were a special case.

You see they did not just leave this fortress, I sent them out beyond the safety of these walls to recruit people like yourself to join my flock," the Caucasian admitted. "They seem to be accomplishing their mission, if I do say so myself? Your presents here will attest to that."

"Sure," I said as I thought. "*Short of a few teeth, I guess they're doing a bang up job for you out there*."

"Well I am sure that you can see my point, after all of the hard work that my traveling minions have done.

To allow you to go back out into that world of the undead, would not only be cruel to you, but it would also be very counterproductive for them, do you not think?" the large albino stated, delivering his question with his usual odd way a speaking and his strange accent.

"My goal here is to find my friend and help him bring back his *concubine*, then join your band of soldiers, just like the Sarge did," I said, referring to Beth as the Sarge's concubine. "And if me and Derek don't come back, then that will just mean that we got killed somewhere out there in the wasteland, and it will save you the trouble of killing me last?

Besides, how can we be expected to maintain the fighting prowess that is the hallmark of your elite army, if you keep us sequestered here in the compound?"

"You are correct Jack Doom, when you enter into combat on fight night; I want you to be in prime condition and be able to give your best performance. It would be a pity if I had to hang your head on the wire outside, especially after only your first fight.

377

Do not feel that you and Mr. Derek are special people. Everyone except for the females that join us has to fight for the right to stay here, there are *no* exceptions. Your friend Ron fought many times and claimed victory each time, thus ascending rapidly through the ranks to become one of the leaders here at my sanctuary. Only the victors are allowed to bask in the safety and security of my supreme dominion, you see the fights are to the death, and that is the reason you did not see the Sarge's head hanging outside.

There was no way that I was going to climb into a ring and fight someone to the death just to satisfy this clown's insatiable lust for blood. But if letting him think that, would get me and Derek the hell out of there, then so be it.

So somehow, between my twisted logic and my yarn spinning, and convincing the Caucasian that it was a matter of keeping a sharp fighting edge on our skills, I had pleaded my case in a way that made sense to the off balanced albino and he shared this with me.

"Ron is one of my most favorite and trusted soldiers, because of that I will allow you both to help him in his quest to regain access to his blonde female and her runaway partner," the freak disclosed. "But if you are not killed and choose not to return with your friend and the two females, I will not hesitate to send Ron back out into the harshness that is the Badlands along with my best trackers, with orders to retrieve you both, and the result of that will not end well for either of you."

After he had told me that the Sarge was one of his favorites, I didn't have the heart to tell him that when I find my old friend, he would not be returning, with or without his *concubine*.

However, I figured that in this case the Caucasian was going to be a man of his word. And I had no intention of walking around the zombie filled Armageddon constantly looking over my shoulder (I mean anymore than I already had to walk around constantly looking over my shoulder), wondering when one of this tyrant's henchmen was going to stick a shiv in my back and bring back my severed head to hang on his bosses clothesline.

An even more nightmarish scenario could unfold if the giant albino freak offered a reward for my capture, *dead or alive*. Whether the reward would be money (which is worthless), sanctuary, food and water, guns and ammo, naked women, power, fame, or whatever; the result would surely be the end of my miserable life sooner or later, and most likely sooner.

Mainly because then I'd have every two-bit piece of shit that could pull a trigger out looking to cash in on my dead carcass, and I couldn't let that happen.

The Caucasian had to be dealt with, and I chose to deal with him immediately.

"Then we have a deal," I said, maneuvering closer to the freak show as if to shake his abnormally large hand. "My buddy and I will set out first thing in the morning to find the Sarge and his blonde concubine."

My true intentions were not to shake the hand of the alleged cult leader that had promised to kill me, but to get close enough to his guards to appropriate one of their weapons.

I stepped toward the imposing seated figure with my hand out as a gesture of good faith. My humble approach and kind demeanor caught the palace sentry on the Caucasian's right side off guard.

With my hand slightly cupped, I swung my out stretched arm up to the left side of the man's head and slammed my hand against his ear.

My concave palm pushed an over abundant amount of air into his ear canal and instantly broke the guard's eardrum.

The man screamed in pain while lifting both hands to his head and covering his ears as I grabbed his rifle and forcefully lifted it straight up.

A crunching sound was heard as the heavy metal weapon slammed into the man's chin and forced his jaw along with his lower row of teeth up into his upper row of teeth, fracturing several of his pearly whites and knocking him out cold.

As the palace incompetent dropped to the floor unconscious, I reached for his machete with my left hand and pulled it out of its scabbard on his way down, still maintaining a firm grip on his rifle with my right hand.

By now, Derek was aware that the shit was hitting hard against the fan, and it was about to be splattered all over the room, so he decided that it might be a shrewd move to join in the fray.

The second guard was also seeing that the situation was going sideways and pointed his rifle toward me.

However, the Caucasian had decided to create some distance between himself and the transpiring fight, by trying to move forward and out of the line of fire of his tussling sentry's gun, which put him directly in the line of fire of the guard on his left, and inadvertently shielded me from that guard's aim.

As I pulled on the black gun the unconscious guard had pulled to the floor as he fell, Derek had decided to tackle the sentry busy trying to get a shot off at me.

While the conscious guard franticly tried to maneuver himself and his rifle into a position to get a clean shot at me without shooting either the guard lying on the floor or his oversized boss, he failed to see Derek about to pummel him.

Unable to pull the downed guard's gun from him due to the sling being wrapped around his shoulders, I let go of the gun and turned my attention toward the Caucasian.

He now stood there almost paralyzed, watching in awe, as Derek beat the living snot out of the second so-called elite palace guard who was still more intent on getting a clean sight picture of me, than stopping Derek's fists from batter his now bloody face.

The grunts and groans that Derek made while he systematically walloped the shit out of the guard seemed to mesmerize the huge albino.

Maybe it was the speed in which the punches were being applied to the man's face, or the profuse bleeding that was the result of those punches.

Who knows?

But whatever the reason for the Caucasian's failure to take action in the midst of that palace coup would serve to be his downfall.

"Cauc!" I yelled, breaking the self-induced trance he had put himself in. "Over here!"

Before the tall pale man had a chance to turn around or even look in my direction, I swung the confiscated machete horizontally at my hip level, which just happened to be right at the kneecap level of the towering Caucasian.

The amateurish guard that was the first to fall, although totally out of his depth as a guard, was worthy when it came to sharpening edged weapons.

He had honed the blade of his machete to a razor sharp edge, and as I swiped the blade across the knees of my advisory, the flat cutting edge of the long steel blade hacked through the flesh, muscle, tendons, and cartilage in and around the sociopathic megalomaniac's left knee joint like it was made of warm butter, stopping only when it had cleanly sliced through the last remaining skin on the leg.

The giant albino let out a horrendous guttural scream as I jerked the blade from between the two leg halves, and he fell back toward his chair.

Fearing that other guards would hear their leader's howls, I jumped on the fallen giant and with all the power that I could muster, I swung the machete down vertically onto the top of his head.

The blow was so forceful that it shattered the brittle human skullcap that the man wore so proudly, and plowed the machete deep into the forward portion of his own skull, effectively performing a frontal lobotomy, and ending the tyrannical reign of the dreaded self-imposed ruler of the Indiana Badlands.

Meanwhile, Derek was still beating on the body of the guard that he had bludgeoned to death with his fists.

"Derek, enough is too much! I said. "That sucker is going to wake up and bite your face off."

"Right," he agreed, as he let loose one last powerful blow to the man's jaw.

"Just stick him in the brain and let's get out of here before more of this punk's guards show up," I warned, pulling the machete out of the Caucasian's head and planting it firmly in the first still unconscious sentry's skull.

No guards came rushing to their leader's aid: it seems that they were all too accustomed to hearing their master groan and howl as well as others screaming during what he referred to as his entertainment.

So as the albino freak show moaned and groaned in the agony of defeat, his minions ignored his yowling thinking that it was just another day in the life of their illustrious leader, and reveled in the fact that it wasn't they who were providing that days entertainment.

With the monster in charge taken care of, and no alarm being sounded, Derek and I hatched a quick off the cuff plan to make our escape from the dead Caucasian's compound.

First, we relieved the two dead guards of their dreaded black rifles, and Derek wiped the blood off his hands on the dead giant's robe.

Then we left the Caucasian's throne room as if nothing had happened, hoping that none of the guards in the outer area would check on the well being of their overbearing leader until we were well away from the enclosure.

The new blood splatter on our clothing matched the old blood splatter that we had brought in with us from outside, and no one noticed the few extra spots, so no one was the wiser.

The first sentry that we met in the hallway was gullible enough to fall for the line of bullshit that we spoon fed him. After all, he was dumb enough to believe that the Caucasian was some sort of demigod or some horseshit like that, so it wasn't too much of a surprise that he would believe that his boss would *loan* us the fine rifles we were carrying.

After we told him that we had been assigned to go outside and help the Sarge look for his concubine, he even led us to where they had stored our own weapons and allowed us to gear up.

We couldn't wait for the sun to rise the following morning to begin our trek back out into the Badlands, as we didn't know how long it would be until the bodies of the giant albino and his two guards would be discovered, and we certainly didn't want to be anywhere near the place when they were found.

"We need to leave now!" I told the guard at the door.

"You're going outside while it's still dark?" he asked. "That's kind of curious."

"Cauc wants us out there immediately to help Ron find his woman," I insisted, hoping that shortening the name of the leader would cause the guard to infer that there was some kind of favoritism going on. "But if you want to countermand Cauc's orders, that's fine with me. I don't mind going for a swim while we wait for sunrise, even though the water probably is somewhat of an emerald green in color."

384

The guard's face turned almost as white as the man he was so dedicated to, and he quickly responded.

"No, not at all! I just meant that there's a standing order that states that if anyone leaves the fort at night they have to go out in a group."

"That's fine, we're leaving now, who's going with us?" I asked, walking toward the front door.

At this point Derek threw in a nice touch by seemingly taking charge of the situation.

"You two, come with us!" he ordered, pointing at two men sitting at a table playing cards near the door. "Here, take these guns your boss gave us and let's go; you can shirk your duties later."

Falling hook, line, and sinker for our ruse, and fearing that we might tell their boss that they were goofing off while on duty, the two men quickly joined us, and departed the premises immediately, carrying the two black rifles we had taken from the guards we had just killed.

My only regret upon leaving the fortress in the middle of the Indiana Badlands was that I didn't get the chance to take advantage of what could have been the Caucasian's gracious yet unexpected hospitality before the day's perilous trek, by utilizing the schools swimming pool that I previously mentioned, even though the water probably was somewhat of an emerald green in color.

As the sun broke the crest of the horizon the next morning, Derek and I began what I hoped would be the last leg of my long journey to apprehend my former Marine Corps buddy.

The Caucasian had slipped in a ringer just before we were to depart his compound and forced us to take two of his men with us by decreeing a standing order of *groups only* outside the safety of the fortress at night.

Normally I would have dispatched both men as soon as we were out of sight of the compound.

However, shortly after leaving the building, the men reveled to us that their main job was tracking down what they called *misguided* people that had seen fit to leave the safety and security of the compound.

Although one of the men had given us the general direction that the Sarge had gone when he had left the building, I felt that it certainly couldn't hurt to have a couple of experienced *manhunters* guiding our little venture.

I would deal with them later, once they had led me to my prey.

We headed out in a direction that was a few degrees off the course that would take us directly back to Beth and Jolene's hideout.

I hoped that the Sarge's trail wouldn't lead us too near the girl's hideout. They were only a mile or so away from the compound, and if the Sarge and his men were that close, it most likely meant that they were closing in on the girls. If that were the case, having the two girls with us would double our force, but it might still complicate matters slightly in one way or another.

The population of the undead hadn't diminished any in the few hours that we had taken our uneasy refuge in the defunct high school facilities.

The four of us weren't even off the parking lot before we were accosted by three of the decomposing decadents that we saw bounding toward us from some distance away.

After disposing of the terrible trifecta with our edged weapons, we cleaned them off on the soiled clothes of the downed zombies as usual, before continuing on our quest.

That's when one of our escorts made the comment.

"I think they're a little faster than they used to be. Those three were on us faster than Mr. Chain Blue Lightning *his* self."

"I don't remember them being that fast either," the other man remarked.

"It started a few days ago; it seemed to happen all at once. They were pretty slow, some were almost dawdling, and then all of the sudden they began to come at you like a herd of rabid warthogs in heat," I informed the two trackers. "You guys should get out more, you know, see the world."

"No thanks," said one tracker.

"I'm with him," Derek chimed in, smiling as usual.

The Sarge's trail led us into a residential neighborhood that had a multitude of fenced backyards, and was heavily treed.

Following the Sarge and his men was easy in those surroundings as pieces of wooden fences and the carcasses of freshly butchered zombies littered the landscape where they had been.

As we closed the gap between them and us, the trail of fresh twitching cadavers we followed were more active as their nerve endings had not yet deteriorated under the relentless feeding of the larvae they hosted.

Hoping to obtain some valuable intelligence and begin formulating a plan for dealing with the group that we were quickly gaining on, I pointed out the obvious trail of rotting corpses in our path and asked our guides.

"They're leaving a lot of carnage in their wake, how many people does the Sarge have with him that they could do so much damage?"

"I don't know for sure how many people Ron took with him, but I know that he wanted to catch up to those women as fast as possible, so he would have been traveling light. My guess is five or six people, seven at the most," the lead tracker answered. "We should catch up to them soon, we just have to follow their trail, they have to check every house, and any other place they think the girls could be hiding and that takes time.

Judging from the foot prints and the freshness of all of these carcasses, Ron and his men most likely left the compound and made a wide circle five or six miles out to keep those two bitches from getting to far away, they are thinking that they hid somewhere close to the fortress after they escaped, I mean left, and now Ron and the boys are working their way back to the center of the circle hoping that they have trapped the whores somewhere inside the perimeter."

"Those fucking devious conniving sluts, how dare they not run far," I stated, as if I were just one of the guys.

"Yeah, what he said… bitches" Derek recapitulated.

One advantage to following a group of *seasoned* zombie killers was that they had a tendency to clear a wide swath of zombie free real estate in front of you, creating a zombie-free zone.

However, one disadvantage, at least in our case, is we were trailing a group of *seasoned* zombie killers that are being led by a *seasoned* combat veteran (not to mention winner of numerous battle to the death fighting contests at the Caucasian's compound), and when we catch up to them we are going to have to deal with all of them in one way or another.

In a zombie-infested world, there's really no such thing as a zombie-free zone, sooner or later the undead will find their way into that zone. This is especially true in the Indiana Badlands where the zombie count had increased exponentially over your normal everyday bloodthirsty monster arena.

"We're getting closer; these twitchers are shivering so much, it's all the flies can do just to land on them," the lead tracker noticed.

"I see that," I said, shooing some of the distressed flies away from my face.

I had barely uttered those words when our lead tracker stepped through a gap in one of the broken fences and was immediately preyed upon by two obese female zombies with the usual murderous rage in their eyes.

The two hungry man-eaters had ambled along the fence line sometime after the Sarge and his bunch had passed, and were inches away from the hole in the fence when the man stepped through the narrow opening. They were on him so fast that he stood no chance of surviving their brutal attack.

He was drug to the side so quickly that by the time any of the three of us could see passed the fence, which was obstructing us from getting a clear shot at either of the two monstrosities, his frantic screams had stopped, and the starving rotund ones had already chewed off most of his face and scalp. Their hunger pangs were apparently just as strong in the afterlife as they were in their pre-zombie existence. The only difference was that their metabolism was much slower now than before, so even as starving zombies roaming through a zombie apocalypse, they continued to have a weight problem. On the other hand, maybe they were just *big boned* or had a *gland* problem? Just saying!

Because of our alleged close proximity to the troop we were trailing, at least we were according to the latest update from our tracker whose face was now missing, without asking permission from our remaining chaperone, I decided to send the two bloated behemoth carnivores back to the fat farm with a little less weight attached to their heads.

In short, I blew their fucking brains out of their skulls with my Glock, at the same time hoping to send a signal to the Sarge that other people were in the area, and lead him away from Beth and Jolene if he were somewhere near them.

"Are you trying to get us killed?" The surviving tracker reeled. "The dead will hear us!"

"Your dead buddy said we were close to catching up to the Sarge, if he was right then the Sarge also heard those two shots," I replied, pulling the trigger on my Glock one more time to end the faceless guides torment permanently.

"Sorry, my mistake, three shots," I said, correcting myself.

The remaining tracker must have had some kind of relationship with his fallen companion, because he didn't take too kindly to my nonchalant attitude about putting my third bullet into the base of his partner's skull.

In fact, he was so upset by my final termination of his friend, that he made the mistake of pointing his rifle at me while I still had my pistol in my hand.

His spontaneous attempt to intimidate me, or kill me, was the last ill-advised thing that the man would ever do.

I didn't wait around to see which choice he was going to make with him pointing his loaded weapon at me.

As fast as my reflexes could make my muscles react to the threat, I aimed the four-inch barrel of my Austrian made handgun at the *dead* center of the man's torso and repeatedly pressed the trigger of the weapon to the rear. As I squeezed the trigger five times as fast as I could, five bullets sped the short distance down range just as fast, and *buried* themselves into the man's body.

The first two shots were so quick that the second bullet fired entered the man's body through the same hole that the first bullet had made, shattering his *xiphoid process,* and dropping him faster than I had dropped the Latin class that I'd mistakenly signed up for in 9th grade.

The following three projectiles walked themselves up the man's body as he collapsed to the ground, the fifth one tearing through his Adam's apple and ripping out the back of his neck.

"You put two full metal jackets right into his solar plexus," Derek said gleefully, as he watched our dead former guide begin squirming on the ground. "Right through the same hole!"

"They were hollow points, but I get your drift."

Actually taking the time to aim my pistol, I pulled the trigger one more time.

"One more for good measure," I said nonchalantly, as I ventilated the tracker's head by putting one final slug into his brain.

As predicted by the misguided companion that had pointed his gun at me, some rogue zombies were now narrowing the swath of zombie-free turf that the Sarge and his compadres had graciously, however, unknowingly left for us.

Amid the moans, groans, slurps, growls, and slobbering sounds made by the undead as they approached us and were each hacked to pieces one at a time, a single gunshot was heard in the distance.

"Did you hear that?" Derek asked, tugging on the handle of the heavy blade of his chef's utensil as he tried to wrench it out of the cranium of a gray-haired zombiefied Catholic Priest who was dressed in full regalia and who had fallen prey to the Devil's handy work.

"No doubt that's the Sarge's bunch thinking the gunshots were from one of the Caucasian's clan," I answered speculating.

"Well they're half right, well they *were* half right, before our other half bought the farm," Derek attested with a smile, then grunting, he forcefully jerked his cleaver from deep within the Father's diseased brain, before wiping the gore off his blade on the hem of the embellished hypocrite's black frock.

"It sounded like it came from that way," I said, pointing in the direction of the shot with my left hand as my right hand firmly gripped the handle of my tomahawk and twisted it out of the head of an accosting zombie it had just split.

We walked another hundred yards dodging the bomb craters and the clumps of twitching ex-humanity, not to mention the massive amount of harassing flies that they sponsored.

I raised my gun over my head, and as I was about to let loose another round to signal to whoever it was that was ahead of us, and hopefully get the same response in return, a man's gruff voice warned.

"Don't do that again!"

Then the tone of the voice abruptly changed.

"Jack! Is that you Jack? Well I'll shit a brick house. It is you."

Peeking out from the rubble through a rather large hole in the only standing wall of a once very expensive mansion which had been obliterated, was a red haired man with a familiar face.

Putting on my best *I'm so glad to see you* face, which wasn't all that difficult to do considering that I'd been searching for this elusive man for quite some time, I answered enthusiastically.

"Sarge, buddy, is that you?"

Considering that I had no intention of going back to the Caucasian's fortress, and now that I had found the Sarge, I had no intention of letting him go back either, so I saw no need to even mention the tall freak or his compound. After all, the weaklings that the albino's standing order had saddled us with sure weren't going to rat us out.

"What in the living hell are you doing here in the heart of the Indiana Badlands?" I asked, hoping that Derek would go along with my ploy.

Fortunately, for us, Derek had no desire to return to the compound either, so he kept quiet and watched as I lied my way through the reunion with the Sarge.

"Holy shit Jack, I could ask you the same question, I mean after all this isn't exactly a vacation paradise you know," he answered.

"I took a wrong turn somewhere, and ended up here in... what did you call this place? The Indiana Wastelands?

"The Badlands," the Sarge said, correcting my intentional misstatement.

"Yeah, well anyway, I met this guy here a couple of days ago, his name is Derek. He thought his family had headed up this way, and when we met, somehow he talked me into helping him try and find them, and then he was going to lead me out of this hellish countryside," I said pathetically. "We didn't have any luck finding them, all we found was a whole lot of eaters, so we decided to give up the chase and head back south, he's got a couple of friends waiting for him not too far from here. We were on our way to meet up with them and then get the hell out here."

I had no trouble at all showing my grief when the Sarge asked me about my family.

"Where's Gin and your boys, I hope you didn't bring them into this hellhole of a place?" Sarge asked.

The jovial attitude was quickly replaced by one of what I felt was false sorrow when I replied to his question.

394

"They didn't make it Sarge, after we got separated."

"*Abandoned is more like it!*" I thought.

"We went north out of Texas and thought we were doing pretty good, you know, surviving.

Then one day outside a little town in Oklahoma, eaters took them away from me," I told him, lying out my ass. "I really don't want to talk about it."

I really did want to talk about it, but I wanted to talk about it in private, just before I killed the man who was acting so sad.

"What about Beth, is she okay?" I asked, as I silently counted the men at the Sarge's side.

"Beth is fine, well I hope she is fine, that's the reason we're out here in the middle of this shit, we're looking for her, she's lost," my old Marine Corp friend told me, lying out *his* ass.

"Looks like you're traveling light, is this all of your search party?" I asked, with the intention of gathering vital intelligence as to the force of the enemy Derek and I were destined to confront.

"Looks like we're not traveling as light as you Jack," he answered. "I guess that accounts for all that shooting we heard, got surrounded by the dead did you?"

"That's the name of the game Sarge," I said. "We pulled through, but I can't say as much for those eaters back there though."

The Sarge smiled as he drove a Marine Corps Bowie knife through the forehead of a nimble brute that tried to grab one of his men from behind.

"I hate cowards," he announced, as he tweaked the top of the sneaky cannibal's brain sideways and squished it against the inside of its skull by twisting his knife counter clockwise.

"*How ironic, my old buddy the Sarge says he hates cowards,*" I thought. "*I wonder what he says about people that run off and leave their friends to be devoured by a giant horde of eaters?*"

"Yeah, I hate them too," I admitted, kicking the chicken-shit dead zombie in the face as it lay lifelessly twitching at our feet.

"Come and join us Jack, when we find Beth I'm sure she'll be glad to see you," the Sarge surmised.

"*I bet she will be,*" I thought. "*More than you could possibly know.*"

"And I found another sweet setup, almost as good as the YMCA," Sarge bragged. "The only difference is that I'm not the boss, at least not yet."

Again I thought. "*Well, at least that's one saving grace that the Indiana Badlands has. He's not the boss.*"

"I'll help you find Beth," I answered, nodding my head and acting concerned. "How about you Derek, are you going to return the favor and help me try to find one of my friends?"

"Sure, tit for tat," he answered grinning, looking down at my *leather* titty bag that was tied to my belt.

"Well let's get moving then," the Sarge insisted, swatting at some dive-bombing flies that were trying to find a new home. "This place is starting to get a little rotten don't you think?"

Derek and I, the Sarge, and his five henchmen trudged through the tall-uncut grass and weeds of the neighborhood that was once filled with well-manicured palatial manors, in search of the girls that we had hidden away only a few hundred yards from our current location.

I gradually began to walk slower than the main body of the group, and used subtle hand signals to stealthy and silently urge Derek to do the same.

When the gap between us and the other men was large enough that I felt it was safe to tell Derek the plan that I had conjured up without them hearing me, I whispered to him.

"Ask the Sarge how long he thinks it will take to find Beth, because you're anxious to get back to the two girls you just met. He'll put two and two together pretty fast and then you can lead us all to Beth.

He never mentioned Jolene to us, so as far as he knows you just know where two females are that you met just before you accidently ran into me."

"Won't that be like selling out the girls?" Derek whispered back.

"They both have weapons, and they both know how to fight, well at least Beth does." I replied. "If we're lucky they'll see us coming and ambush these guys. If not, the element of surprise will still be on our side, and it will be only six of them against the four of us once the girls hear the commotion outside and join in the fight."

"That doesn't seem fair, there'll be six of them," Derek said, not smiling this time.

"You're right, it doesn't seem quite fair, maybe we should wait until they get a couple more guys?" I said sincerely, while carving the nose off a tumor-ridden corpse in serious need of a good dermatologist.

"Quit playing around back there Jack and get up here, we've got work to do," Sarge called out to me.

I quickly preformed my own version of trepanation on *tumor* with the pointed end of my tomahawk; introducing its cranial juices to the outside world and aerating its brain at the same time, and then Derek and I trotted back up to the pack of concubine hunters where I explained our rear guard actions.

"Just watching our six Sarge," I told him. "We can't be too careful with all of the eaters roaming around the Badlands, with their newly found balance and dexterity you know."

"Well just stay close, we got separated once, I don't want that to happen again," my old *friend* claimed.

"*No fucking chance of that happening*," I thought. "*Not a chance in fucking hell.*"

Seeing an opening, Derek made his move.

"Hey Sarge, speaking of getting separated, how long do you think we're going to be out here looking for your friend Becka?"

"*Nice touch using the wrong name!*" I thought, as I watched Derek work his magic.

"Why, you got someplace you gotta be?" Sarge asked gruffly, as his men looked at Derek and sneered.

"As a matter of fact I do.

I met two of the sweetest smelling poontangs a feller could ever want to run into in the midst of a cataclysmic apocalypse," Derek boasted. "It's true they're both a little grimy, but as soon as I get back there and find a pond that's not completely polluted, I'm going to scrub them up and then we're going to party, if you know what I mean? Jack and I were on our way to join up with them when we ran into you."

The look on the Sarge's face was everything that I had hoped for; I could almost see the light bulb hovering over his head as the gears inside turned.

"What do these girlfriends of yours look like?" the Sarge asked nonchalantly, although he was about ready to pee his pants with excitement like a cow pissing on a flat rock.

"Both of them have a pretty healthy chest on them, one is short and blonde, and the other one is a little taller, and she is really blonde," Derek explained, not revealing too much information. "I really didn't see too far past their tits. I told them to say put while I looked for my family, then I ran into Jack and... Well you know the rest."

"Well I wouldn't want to keep you from anything," Sarge insisted, as his men looked knowingly at each other and smiled. "Maybe we'll just escort you to where you left them, that way you won't miss out on anything. And who knows, maybe they've seen Beth.

The Sarge thought that he was being clever and that Derek was being duped into showing him where Beth and Jolene were hiding.

Thinking that I would convince the Sarge that I was helping him out with his ruse, when I was really posing as more of a double agent, I added.

"That sounds good to me; I'd like to meet these ladies you've been whining about since I met you."

"Which way?" Sarge asked, looking at Derek as if the matter had been settled.

Derek pointed to a cluster of treetops that we could see; over what was left of the roofs of several dilapidated houses to the southeast.

"This way, passed those trees," he answered. "Not too far from here."

As our small troop began to walk in the direction that Derek had pointed to, I knew that I would have to make my move soon.

Again, I began to walk slightly slower than the rest of the men, and quickly found myself at the back of the pack again.

The only way my plan was going to be brought to fruition, was through a surprise attack.

I would have to ambush the five total strangers in front of me, and I would have to do it before any of them realized what was going on, especially the Sarge.

In the past, a plan to back shoot a group of strangers that had not tried to harm me in any way would have outraged me.

Unfortunately, for the men that were blazing the trail in front of me, as I said before, sometimes sacrifices must be made during these times of trouble, and if a small party of alleged Caucasian loyalist needed to be sacrificed in the name of my families revenge, then who is Jack Doom to argue with fate.

I mean after all, if I was to allow all of them to mosey on back to the fortress and find their leader D.O.A. (Dead On Arrival), they just might decide to hold his murder against me, form a posse, and track me down.

If that happened, I would be forced to defend myself, and I would hope that the outcome would be the same.

So I was just saving everyone a lot of time and trouble by purchasing them a first class ticket straight to hell's 35th level, on the express elevator so to speak.

As we came nearer to the house where Beth and Jolene were holdup, the neighboring area began to look familiar, and I knew time was running out. My quest to slaughter the men before me had to begin soon.

"We're almost there, it's just past this house and across the street," Derek informed the Sarge.

Derek had taken a slight detour on the way to the girl's house, a detour that forced us to cross a street just before getting to the home, giving the women inside a chance to see us coming.

Although it was a good improvised plan that Derek had initiated, as it turned out, our approach to the house didn't matter.

I had decided to make my move in the middle of the street, thereby leaving no place for my targets to find cover. I was prepared to fire as many weapons and make as much noise as necessary to accomplish my grisly task, and we would all worry later about the horde of undead that it was sure to attract.

However, as usual, the best laid plans of mice and men have a tendency to go south rather quickly, especially during a Biblical cataclysm like a zombie apocalypse, and again my plan was not the exception to the rule.

As bad and widespread as the reputation of the Indiana Badlands was, with all of its adopted monsters, like hordes of ferocious zombies, packs of vicious feral dogs, and an assortment of other vile creatures that were ready to snuff your lights out at any given moment, all of which were roaming through the countryside and most of its cities.

Most people had a tendency to envision the undead as the main threat.

However, the Badlands seemed to have a special allure to some of the nastier survivors that *plagued* the country. In fact, the mysterious lure of the region was so strong that it seemed supernatural, almost magical in its power of seduction.

As a result of this mystical power of persuasion, the Badlands of Indiana was teeming with unsavory types, and not all of them were canines, undead, or your occasional raptor.

Case in point; after meeting Beth and Jolene in the sewers, we were all so busy reminiscing, killing zombies, and making plans to find the Sarge and see to it that he received his just deserts, that we were totally oblivious to the small group of male humans that were stalking us.

They had staked out the safe-house where we had left the girls, and when they saw Derek and I leave for the Caucasian's compound, they decided that that would be a good time to do a home invasion scenario with the intent of getting a little "*strange*" on the side.

However, what they hadn't counted on, was trying to invade a house that had a heavily armed and combat tested petite blonde psychopath that was posing as a den mother for a sociopath in training.

Well, needless to say; although I still will. Beth and Jolene were having none of the scheming male's advances, which actually was very surprising considering Jolene's sorted past.

402

Anyway, the girls opened up on the gang of thugs with a barrage of small arms fire, dusting them off before they could say *zombie apocalypse*, and littering the lawn around the house with the hooligan's twitching dead bodies; then watched as the uncivilized heathens waited to join the legion of the undead, making sure that there weren't more of the pagan band lurking in the neighborhood's shawdows.

The noise from the short but lethal firefight had summoned every walking corpse within a three-block area of the house, and they were now patrolling the circumference of the building and the surrounding property. And even though Beth had drilled a hole in the heads of a couple of those uninvited neighbors with her small-bore M-4 clone, the majority of the curious and ruthless renegade trespassers just plain refused to leave.

As we approached, we saw a large crowd of ravenous cadavers milling around the house and surrounding area, and then Derek whispered to our pack of zombie killing/concubine hunting misfits.

"Eaters are all over the place! There must be fifty or sixty of them."

"You say your girlfriends are in that house. Then I don't care if there are five or six hundred of them, we'll kill them all. Unless of course, you want to just walk away and leave your new found friends there to be eaten alive?" The Sarge replied, knowing that he wasn't going to allow that option to take place.

"Sarge, I say we kill them all and let Beelzebub sort them out when they get to hell," I stated categorically, trying to push my agenda forward.

"Indeed!" the Sarge retorted, not suspecting what was about to happen to him and his men.

Shoving Derek toward the house, and following him out into the open, the Sarge insisted.

"They're your friends, you lead the way!"

With Derek hesitantly leading the way, and the Sarge close behind him almost drooling in anticipation of getting his dick-skinners on Beth one more time, his five men trailing in close approximation to each other, and me bringing up the rear, we left the minimal concealment of the rubble in the crater pockmarked posh neighborhood and marched into the open area of the street, guns blazing.

While the Sarge was preoccupied with the horde, I found the zombie cleansing to be the perfect opportunity to do a little more than just thin the herd of the walking dead bodies.

Although I was doing my fair share of harvesting the vile creatures in the neighborhood, most of which were now aware that what they were hoping would be their next meal of guts and brains was migrating toward them. My main concern at the time, however misguided it might have been, was alleviating the human threat before me.

With their mouths watering at the thought of devouring the succulent yet well-armed morsels marching toward them, the ravenous man-eating beasts quickened their pace and stumbled toward us from all directions.

With our group preoccupied with the charging horde, I took the liberty to give a lethal dose of high-speed lead poisoning to two of the Sarge's men, by systematically administering them an epidural with my suppressed M-4 assault rifle.

I weighted down two more of the Caucasian's followers with lead and watched as they dropped to street level under the poundage of my bullets.

In the noise and confusion of the battle, no one in our group but me noticed the four men fall to the asphalt, as the attacking zombies dropping all around us was the perfect distraction.

The bodies of the men quickly began to be devoured by several of the undead which penetrated the weak point in our perimeter left by the Sarge's fallen comrades, and who I let feast upon their remains.

Zombies ripping, tearing, and biting at their flesh, would mutilate their bodies enough to hide the gunshot wounds if I was unable to secure my real prey immediately following the fight.

And their hunger for the brains of the fallen combatants left no need for me to waste a bullet to stop their post-death animation, as their brains would soon be devoured as well.

Beth and Jolene still vigilant after the failed home invasion, watched our approach to their hideout, and the seeing the red-headed ex-marine and ruckus outside, left no doubt in their minds that I had found my elusive prey and was in the process of securing his captivity. With the melee outside in full force, Beth and Jolene began to pick off the revived dead from a bedroom window.

Now with only four of us fighting the zombies in the street, and our gunfire attracting even more dead bodies to the area, I began to have second thoughts about my decision to ventilate four of the Sarge's soldiers before the zombie menace was extinguished; especially considering that because I had dropped the four punks in front of me and allowed the dead to feast on them, I found my path to the safety of the house blocked by the dining cadavers.

Besides the influx of more ravenous cannibals staggering into the fray, I was also concerned that Beth might take it upon herself to exact her own revenge on the Sarge from that window she was shooting from, and cheat me out of the pleasure of killing him myself.

However, before Beth could shoot the Sarge, or the ever-growing population of the horde of zombies could over run our position.

"We're fucked!" Derek announced loudly, as he saw the first of twelve dogs out of the corner of his eye.

I had been lucky since Armageddon had raised its ugly head, and this was only the third time since the beginning of our world's undoing that I had had to deal with the *Canine Corps*.

Derek on the other hand, had not been so fortunate. Surviving in and around the Indiana Badlands, he had been on the shit end of the fetching stick many times before, and was well versed in the dangers of a feral dog pack.

He raised his revolver and took aim at the lead dog as he called out.

"God damned dogs!"

As he sounded the alarm, the lead dog charged, which signaled four of the other curs to follow.

Three more came from beside the girl's safe house and darted directly under Beth's position at the window and four others dashed toward us from across an adjacent street.

Although I didn't say so at the time, my thoughts were the same as Derek's as I raised my rifle.

We were now not only surrounded by a mass quantity of ravenous dead bodies walking in our direction bent on serving us up as a four course meal, we were also being attacked by a pack of vicious and ruthless mutts that would no doubt be relentless in their pursuit as well.

And if it wasn't bad enough that the undead had seemed to find their second wind, and were now at least twice as fast and agile as they had been in the past, now we had to contend with a pack of callous curs who's speed and agility far eclipsed the unfed man-eating beasts I call *Eaters*.

Just as panic was about to set in among the four of us, and as we each took aim at our respective charging canines, an odd thing happened.

With my chosen dog perfectly aligned in my gun sights, and my finger applying three pounds of pressure against my M-4's four-pound trigger, my target suddenly changed course and leaped onto one of the stampeding zombies.

Without regard for the hundreds of flies whizzing by the slobbering monstrosity, or the multitude of maggots swimming in its drool, and giving no thought whatsoever about the terminal case of ringworm that covered the bluish skin of its victim, my former target began to dismantle the slowly rotting two legged carnivore piece by piece.

Our gunfire ceased as we stood in awe of the carnage that was taking place before us.

We were no longer the chosen prey of either the mongrels or of the zombies. They had both stopped pursuing us and focused their complete attention on each other.

"Let's make a break for it!" Derek yelled, as he trotted toward the house.

The Sarge followed him toward the house and without looking back shouted to me.

"Come on Jack, move it!"

With only one man left on the Sarge's team, I think his name was Steve, the four of us ran to the safety of the house.

Well three of us did anyway.

Unfortunately for the Sarge's last remaining squad member, after I tripped Steve and pushed him on top of two zombies that were being ripped to shreds by three of the feral dogs. In the heat of battle, neither the dogs nor the zombies could discern the difference between Steve and the enemy that they were fighting.

Sadly, Steve didn't make it.

The back door of the girl's hideout opened and Beth called out to us.

"Get your dumb asses in here!"

As one might think, none of us wasted any time complying with the cute little blonde's demand.

We entered the home in single file, in the order that we had escaped the deadly fracas, except for Steve, as I said, sadly, he didn't make it.

Once inside the sanctuary, the Sarge wasted no time trying to tell Beth twice (give her two black eyes).

"You fucking bitch, I'll teach you to run out on me!" he screamed, as he raised his left hand across his body to apply a conventional backhanded pimp slap.

Just as he had wasted no time beginning Beth's public flogging that he *thought* she deserved, and obviously felt that I would not have an issue with. I too wasted no time in preparing him to accept the punishment that I *knew* he deserved.

As the Sarge's arm began to move forward towards Beth's face, I laid the barrel of my M-4 against the left side of his skull with the proper amount of force to render him unconscious.

"Thank you Jack," Beth said softly.

"No, thank you Beth," I replied.

"Thank me for what?" she inquired.

"Thank you for not shooting this son-of-a-bitch when you had the chance!"

"Believe me, it did cross my mind, but I knew you wanted to take the first whack at him," Beth confessed. "I even took out one of the dead that was about to pounce on him."

"When you two are done flirting, you might want to tie your buddy up before he comes to," Derek suggested, with his usual smile. "When he wakes up he's going to be really pissed!"

During all of my planning and all of the tracking that had to be done to find the Sarge, all I could think about during that time, was killing the son-of-a-bitch.

However, after thinking about all of the people, zombies, and canines that had to die for me to successfully complete my self-ordained mission. I had come to have a change of heart concerning my former Marine Corps buddy.

In light of all the death and destruction, and all of the carnage that preceded the capture of my old friend, I decide not to kill him after all.

My thought process went something like this.

With all of the heartache and anguish he had cause me, and all of the agony and suffering that I had caused people during my search for him. All of the pain and torture that would have never happened if the Sarge hadn't driven that school bus away from the armory that day, leaving me and my family to stand alone and almost defenseless against an unseen sniper, and in the middle of a colossal attacking zombie horde.

I wouldn't have had to commandeer Jason's truck, and he would still be alive. I wouldn't have been anywhere near the Wolf River, and Cassandra's "Bull Lesbian" sister Carla would still be alive.

I wouldn't have had any reason to be traveling through Arkansas, so Eric and Matt might still be alive, and Tim would still have his hair. Not to mention the leather bag hanging from my belt is a constant reminder that if it weren't for the Sarge's cowardice, Cassandra wouldn't be walking around right now one tit lighter.

So with all of that said, I reiterate, I decided not to kill the Sarge at this time.

Because... Killing is to damn good for that cowardly shit-bum motherfucking piece of excrement!

I could have killed him before he regained consciousness, but then it would have been over.

I could have waited until he woke up, so he could see me put a bullet into his pea-brain, but then, unlike

Cassandra, he would never get a chance to learn his lesson.

No, killing him would serve no purpose, his punishment would need to be far greater than mere dying, after all, dying is part of life nowadays.

People die, zombies die, feral dogs die, even my family died. Dying is too much of a natural thing to do in the unnatural world we live in, so I decided to deny him that particular option.

"Turn the dining room table over, and tie this bastard spread eagle to its legs," I demanded. "But stripe him buck naked first."

"That will be a job for you two girls!" Derek insisted. "Touching naked men isn't my thing."

"I don't mind," Jolene announced. "I've had some experience doing that kind of thing."

"I'll help you strip this punk," Beth said. "Remember Jack, you said you'd leave something for me."

Derek smashed a couple of lamps and ripped their cords out, while I tore the telephone off the wall and removed its cord too.

The heavy oak table made an excellent rack to stretch out a human body.

As I tied the final electric cord around the Sarge's ankle, he began to wake up.

"What in the fucking hell is this Jack?" he asked. "Untie me right now, this isn't funny."

"Fuck you Ron!" Beth shouted, as she kicked the sprawled out naked man in the ribs.

"You fucking whore, I'll kill you for that!" the Sarge shouted back.

Standing over the bound up man, I stared at him for a moment before informing him of his fate.

"Calm down ass wipe, you're not going to kill anybody, at least not for awhile," I told him.

"What's this all about Jack?" he asked, with a confused look on his face. "I thought we were friends?"

"You thought wrong, our friendship ended about the same time I was sucking exhaust fumes out of the tailpipe of the school bus you drove off in," I answered, gritting my teeth. "And inhaling poison gas from the exhaust pipe of a forty-foot school bus happened to be the least of my worries that day; considering that at the time my family and I were surrounded by about ten thousand angry and very hungry eaters."

"I didn't have a choice Jack," Sarge insisted. "We were surrounded too, we had to leave right then or we would have never made it out of there, tell him Beth, we couldn't wait any longer."

"Funny, we waited, because we didn't have any other choice, and we made it out of there alive," I maintained, feeling a tsunami of rage surging through my body.

"We'll never know now, will we?" Beth stated. "You were so busy whining like a little baby, and bitch slapping me at the same time that it's a miracle that we did get away."

Beth leaned into another kick to the Sarge's ribs.

"Ouch! You little bitch, I dare you to do that again," the Sarge said, immediately regretting his challenge, as Beth again drop kicked the man in the ribs.

"Easy Beth, remember, I'm supposed to save some for you, not the other way around," I reminded.

"Okay then, you better get started before I lose my temper and waste this dick-head," Beth warned.

"All right honey, just one more thing," I assured. "I want to ask this piece of shit punk something first, and then we'll get to work."

"Well, please make it quick, I've waited a long time to get even with this motherfucker," Beth professed in a not to lady-like manner.

"Sarge do you remember what I used to say when we were stationed in Afghanistan," I asked solemnly.

"No," the sergeant answered gruffly, still grimacing from Beth's last kick.

"I told you on more than one occasion, that pain is the *Great Teacher*. Today I'm going to be assisting the Great Teacher with your lesson.

"Enough of this banter!" Beth insisted, as she forcefully drove the toe of her shoe into the Sarge's rib cage one more time.

"Okay, you talked me into it darling, if you would be so kind as to fetch me that bottle of hooch out of my pack, we'll get this party started."

SERGEANT

"Well, well, the conundrum begins," I said, as Beth handed me the whiskey bottle.

"Which conundrum is that?" she asked.

"Where to start," I answered, unscrewing the bottle cap. "That's the dilemma we face."

"I know… Sarge you better have a drink before they get started, I think you're going to need it," Derek added, thinking that I requested the booze for us, not realizing that the bottle of whiskey that I had in my hand was no ordinary alcoholic beverage.

"Excellent suggestion, I'd take his advice if I were you Sarge," I stressed, holding the bottle up to the ex-marines mouth.

"I don't need any of your rotgut!" the Sarge spewed defiantly.

"Well, if you change your mind, you just let Beth know, okay?" I told him, as I pulled the tainted drink away from his mouth and handed the bottle of liquor to Beth.

"Fuck him, let him suffer," Beth said, screwing the cap back onto the bottle. "Just like he let me suffer. Fuck him!"

I grabbed the bottle out of Beth's hand and removed the cap.

"I changed my mind, he's going to take a drink, he just doesn't know it yet," I said, as I again pushed the bottle toward the Sarge's mouth.

The Sarge's attempt to avoid the contaminated liquid was futile as I stuffed the neck of the whiskey bottle into my old friend's mouth and crammed it halfway down his chicken-shit throat.

"You do what I say, and I say you take a drink!"

The sergeant choked and gagged, and spit up about half of the whiskey that I poured down his gullet, but swallowed enough to render him unconscious moments later.

"Shit Jack, what is that stuff?" Derek asked, pointing to the whiskey bottle.

"Just a little Mickey juice I picked up down in Arkansas," I answered. "Three hillbillies I met had no more use for it, and I thought it might come in handy sometime so I took it with me when I parted company with them. I told you before it's for medicinal purposes."

"What were you thinking Jack?" Beth fumed. "Now we're going to have to wait for him to wake up again before we can continue."

"I don't think so darling," I said, as I patted her on her butt. "He's going to feel one hell of a lot of pain when he wakes up; watch this."

I pulled out my tomahawk and drenched it with some of the tainted booze to kill off any zombie germs that might be lingering on the blade, and then I began to peel the skin off the bottom of the Sarge's right foot from where his toes attached clear down to the back of his heel.

"I think a quarter inch of flesh should do the trick," I claimed.

"You think?" Derek asked. "A quarter inch of skin is all that's on the bottom of his feet, you've exposed the bones."

"Opps! I'll be more careful on his left foot," I promised, as I placed my hatchet at the base of his toes.

"I can't watch this," Jolene proclaimed, turning her back on the sergeant.

"I can!" Beth asserted with a smile, as she knelt down beside me. "What's next after this foot?"

"Well we don't want to mutilate him to the point where he gets gnawed on by eaters as soon as he goes out in the open," I answered. "What fun would that be? Pour a little of that whiskey over his wounds, we wouldn't want him to get an infection."

Beth slopped some alcohol onto the Sarge's feet then recapped the bottle.

"That should do it," she affirmed.

"Keep that bottle handy, we've only begun to teach this ass hole a lesson," I said, moving up to the Sarge's head.

"He's not only going to be hobbling around through the apocalypse, he's going to be scaring the fucking shit out of everyone he meets along the way," I explained. "When I get done with him, not even Jolene will want to fuck him."

"I turned my head, I didn't cover my ears," Jolene began to rant.

"Okay, my mistake, I'm sorry," I said, interrupting her before she got up to speed. "You probably will still want to fuck him."

Derek burst out laughing, as did Beth and I, Jolene couldn't remain angry and began to laugh as well. After all, she knew better than anybody did about her whoring ways, and she knew that I was probably right.

"Let me borrow that little pig sticker you carry, but sterilize it with the whiskey first," I said, grabbing the Sarge's red hair and pulling it back to expose his hairline.

Beth did as I asked and unfolded her pocketknife, doused it with whiskey and handed it to me.

I pulled the razor edge of the small knife along the Sarge's hairline on his forehead, making a deep incision all the way down to the bone as I went. When the blade reached the opposite side of the man's head from where I had started the cut, I tugged on the clump of hair that was clasped in my hand, and peeled back his scalp away from his skull as if I were skinning a wild animal that I had hunted down and killed.

As Beth watched me scalp the man that had beaten her so many times in the past, a stern look gradually melted over her face.

"You should have done that to him while he was awake!" She asserted.

"He would never hold still enough for me to make such a precise cut if he were awake," I replied, snipping the remaining skin that held the scalp to the head. "Besides, he'll feel plenty of pain when the drug wears off."

"Remind me never to cross you Jack, I've become accustom to my hair," Derek broke in running his fingers through his thick bristly locks. "And let's face it, your barbering skills leave a little to be desired."

Jolene unable to resist the temptation finally turned around and looked at the Sarge.

"Holy fuck, shit," she gasped. "You've really fucked him up."

"He's not done yet, are you Jack," Beth assured her calmly.

"Not even close," I answered. "Jolene, sweetie, instead of standing there turning green, see if you can find some more booze, I don't want to use all of this drugged whiskey sterilizing shit."

"Watch your mouth Jack, don't pat me on the butt, and then call her sweetie," Beth warned, replacing her stern look with one of false cheerfulness.

I took Beth's warning to heart, not wanting to piss her off. After all, not counting the mutilated carcass of the Sarge, which was tied to the legs of the dining room table, there were two girls and two boys in the house, and it was beginning to look as if Beth had chosen the partner she wanted to spend the rest of Armageddon with.

Remembering what Derek had told the Sarge about scrubbing up the girls, before doing some serious partying, I revisited for the umpteenth time, the vision of what I imagined Beth's naked body to look like (it was difficult not to with that little blonde's cute butt wiggling in front of me constantly), and spending the rest of the Zombie Apocalypse with her began to look quite appealing to me.

I decided to make my first and probably my last attempt at playing matchmaker for the group, so I suggested.

"Derek, why don't you go help her find some more whiskey, or vodka, or something. I don't know how long this *anal opening* is going to stay asleep, and I would like to be finished with his makeover before he wakes up."

"Roger that boss," Derek giddily replied, as he and Jolene trotted into the next room in search of more alcohol.

I figured Derek wouldn't mind being paired with Jolene, she was an attractive woman with a more than adequate set of mammary glands hanging on her chest, plus she had a track record of sharing her assets. What's not to like?

It wasn't long before the two of them returned to the dining area.

"We found some, there's more in the other room, but these two had the most alcohol percentage in them," Derek said, handing me a bottle of 151 proof rum.

"You keep it," I said. "Sterilize that meat cleaver of yours and let me borrow it for a minute."

Jolene began to hang on Derek's shoulders as he soaked his cleaver with the rum.

As far as we knew, the house we were in, along with the immediate vicinity was still surrounded by feral dogs and feral zombies going at each other's throats; this at hand menace along with the constant threat of imminent death around every other corner of our cataclysmic hell made our desire for companionship very strong.

The lack of human touch the apocalypse had deprived us all of (except for Jolene of course), had begun to take its toll on everyone, so even a small amount of touchy feely grabbing, patting, and cuddling with the opposite sex was a welcome and much needed reminder that we were still human. And no amount of zombies, feral canines, rogue humans, or anything else traipsing around the neighborhood or the wasteland beyond, was going to stifle that primal need.

"Here Jack, it's more sterile than a nun's cunt," Derek announced proudly, as he handed me his favorite butchers utensil still dripping with rum.

"Okay, I've got to ask. What is it with you and nun's cunts?" I inquired, giggling, as Jolene blushed.

"Oh, my mother was a nun!" Derek answered not skipping a beat.

"Eeeewwwuu!" Beth and Jolene sang out in unison.

"Okay, well I guess that explains it then," I said, smiling and shaking my head in disbelief.

The Sarge was tied spread eagle to the legs of the heavy wooden table, bound at his wrists and ankles, each of his limbs lashed tightly to their respective post.

"Beth honey, could you please hold this fuck's index finger up against the wood like this?" I asked politely, wrenching the Sarge's hand backwards and pressing the tip of his finger to the table leg."I don't think he's going to have any use for this trigger finger anytime soon."

Beth took the Sarge's finger, pressed it hard against the hefty wooden leg of the table, and held it firmly on the wooden pillar his wrist was tied to.

One good well placed swipe of Derek's meat cleaver, and the index finger on the Sarge's right hand was lopped off just past the second knuckle and dropped to the floor.

"Jolene, pull one of the boot laces from this asshole's boots, we'll use it for a tourniquet," Beth ordered, tossing her one of the Sarge's boots. "We don't want the punk to bleed out."

"You better take both of them off, I'm going to chop off his other index finger too," I insisted. "You can't be too careful in these times of trouble ya know, and safety is always our number one concern, we wouldn't want this *asshole baby* to have any accidental firearm discharges because he couldn't keep his finger off the trigger… now would we?"

"Derek, see if you can find something to start a fire with, matches or butane lighter would be good," I said, while pinching off the blood flow from the bleeding nub that was left by the finger extraction. "And check the windows; somehow these god damn flies are getting in here."

"What do you need matches for?" Jolene asked, pulling the second lace from the boot.

"To cauterize the wounds, just like I did to that bitch that tried to kill me down by the Wolf River in Tennessee," I answered without the slightest sense of guilt. "I'm still keeping *a breast* of the situation for her."

Beth and I tied off the bleeding stub that replaced the Sarge's trigger finger, and waited for Derek to return.

It wasn't long before Derek returned with what he'd found.

"Somebody left the bedroom window open," Derek accused, knowingly looking at Beth.

"Sorry, I was concentrating more on trying to save your sorry ass than worrying about a couple of insects getting in here," Beth teased, crinkling up her nose.

"I found this propane torch out in the garage, will it do?" Derek asked, waving the torch from side to side.

"Perfect, if you brought the flint mechanism to light it?" I answered, reaching for the torch.

"Of course I did, my mama didn't raise no fool," Derek stated proudly.

"That would be your mother the nun, right?" Jolene laughed.

Derek started to respond with some of his homemade horseshit, but when he saw all of us grinning and waiting to hear his concocted answer, he just handed the flint to me and said nothing.

I lit the torch and adjusted the flame to full. Then I held the yellow portion of the fire at the end of the blue flame to the Sarge's newly formed stump and charred it until the blood turned black.

"Loosen the tourniquet slightly, and let's move on to this bastard's left hand," I ordered, setting down the torch and retrieving the meat cleaver once more.

Beth and I repeated the amputation process on the Sarge's other hand, and cauterized that wound too.

"It's about my turn isn't it?" Beth inquired, smiling. "You promised that you'd leave some of him for me."

"Okay, as long as you don't kill him," I insisted. "What do you have in mind?"

Beth picked up the propane torch and began to heat up the blade of her pocketknife.

"This will not only sterilize it, but it should cauterize each side of the cut as I go."

The operation so far had taken the better part of an hour, and we started to hear moans coming from the Sarge.

"This turd is waking up, I'd better get started," Beth uttered, as she climbed between the Sarge's legs.

"Holy shit in a sack, what are you going to do?" Derek screeched out.

"This fucker never tried to fuck me after I made it clear to him that I didn't want a sexual relationship with

422

him. He never raped me or anything like that, he just beat the shit out of me constantly and stuck me in the communal housing unit," Beth admitted. "Nevertheless, I saw him sexually abuse a lot of other bitches along the way, some of which his actions took by surprise, others deserved what they got, some thought they needed it, and some even begged for it.

Don't get me wrong, I don't really give a shit about any of them, but he enjoyed their company whether they liked his crude advances or not, and I'm going to make damn sure that he never gets to enjoy the pleasure of a woman's company ever again! Even if he can find some whore that can stand to get naked with the freak!"

We all looked at Jolene.

Not finding our timely stares amusing, she stated.

"Fuck all of you!"

With her knife blade now glowing red hot, Beth proceeded to make a cut along the bottom of the Sarge's scrotum.

"She's cutting his nard sack!" Derek bellowed, at the same time grabbing his own nut satchel, as the scent of singed bag hair filled the room.

Beth continued to slice the underside of the testicle hammock, cauterizing the open cut as she went, until both of the Sarge's balls were peeking out the slit.

"That should do it," Beth said, as she laid her knife on the floor and reached for the left nut.

"Do you think that you might be going a little overboard?" I asked, cringing at the sight of the exposed nards.

"No more overboard than you hacking off some woman's tit and tying it on your belt," she answered.

423

"The only difference that I can see is that I'm not going to castrate him and wear his nut pouch as a fashionable accessory like you're doing with that boob. Though, I probably should."

"Oh, you noticed my titty bag?" I asked proudly, lifting Cassandra's leather tit for all to see.

"I wondered what that was," Jolene admitted, as she grimaced at the thought of a severed breast and crossed her arms over her own. "Now I get it, you're going to keep *a breast* of the situation for her."

"Indeed he is!" Derek laughed, until he saw what Beth did next.

As the redheaded ex-Marine slowly began to regain consciousness and feel the pain of our revenge, Beth wormed her thumb and index finger into the gap in his scrotum and carefully slid out one of his testicles.

"First one, and then the other," she said, as she gently pinched the remaining gonad between her fingers.

"I think I'm going to puke!" Derek announced softly, as his face turned almost as pale as the Caucasians.

"Grow a spine," Beth ordered, as she began to reheat her knife. "And quit squeezing your nuts or I'll make *you* take a couple of swigs of the drug laced hooch." Implying that his balls would be next to be aired out.

While the Sarge's groans increased in regularity and volume as he continued to come to, my new girlfriend applied the red-hot blade of her knife to his rocky mountain oyster sack once more, this time to close the incision around the stems of his dangling nards to prevent them from being sucked back inside the bag.

"All done!" Beth exclaimed proudly, as she stood up and wiped some of the seared skin from the crinkled nard sling off her knife and onto the Sarge's bare thigh.

By now, the Sarge had awoken enough to begin screaming in agony. The pain was so overwhelming that he would slide back into an unconscious state for some time, then regain consciousness and begin screaming again, and then he would repeat the process repeatedly. All accomplished without the assistance of any spiked grog, or pharmaceuticals of any kind.

"If he keeps this shit up, he's going to lather up any eaters that are close to the house, and we'll never get out of here," Beth warned.

"I noticed you called them *Eaters*, I have taught you well Sweetie," I jested, even though I was concerned with Beth's warning.

"If you say so," Beth responded. "I say we shut this guy up before he gets us all killed."

"I agree," I conceded.

"Me too," Jolene chimed in.

"Me too," Derek repeated, his face back to its normal color again, and his own prairie oyster pouch now hanging free in his skivvies.

I ripped a piece off the dining room tablecloth, wadded it up and stuffed it into the Sarge's temporarily unconscious and quiet mouth.

Then I walked into the living room and looking out the front window.

"His child like howling brought us to the attention of several eaters outside," I informed the group. "It looks like the dogs are gone, but there're a lot of eaters out in the yard munching on the carrion."

"What are we going to do?" Jolene asked, again draping herself over Derek's shoulders.

"Well I don't know what you and Derek are going to do, but if we can keep this piece of shit that's tied to that table quiet for awhile, me and Jack are going to get properly reacquainted," Beth answered, pulling me toward the bedroom she had been sniping from when Derek and I had arrived back at the house with the Sarge.

The flies that were inadvertently allowed inside the bedroom after Beth had left the window partially open were still there when she shoved me onto the bed. I would have preferred to peel my duds while standing, but I did the best I could in the prone position while lying on the bed watching her peel hers.

I soon found out that no professional bronco rider still alive in the country or for that matter that ever lived, had anything on Beth.

Right out of the chute, Beth impressed me with her ability to maintain a steady rolling motion while she balanced with one hand in the air and shooed away some of the menacing flies that were attracted to the smell of fish with her other hand.

As I lay on the bed beneath her fulfilling my manly obligation, I felt that with her expertise in the saddle, she was more than capable of extending her 8-second ride indefinitely.

I'm not sure what Derek and Jolene were doing while Beth was busy performing at her own personal rodeo, but when we emerged from the coral, *my* manly duties had been performed to Beth's complete satisfaction, as well as my own.

"It's about time you two got back out here, *Red* here has been awake for awhile now, and he finally shut the hell up," Jolene said, still hanging on Derek.

"I think the coast is clear, most of the undead have moved on to greener pastures," Derek added, as he casually groped at Jolene's boobs.

"Get a room you two," I joked. "I'm going to talk to my old buddy Sarge."

The Sarge was in shock from the righteous carving that had been done on him, and we hadn't even let him see himself in a mirror yet.

A stream of urine flowed onto the floor as his tortured and confused brain tried to discern which muscles to tense and which ones to relax.

"I am not as warm and fuzzy as I was in Iraq and Afghanistan Sarge," I told him while pulling the torn tablecloth out of his mouth. "I might have been able to forgive you if you'd just run out on me, but you left my family to suffer at the hands... well the mouths of hundreds of eaters, and there is no forgiving that. You might as well have put a gun to their heads and pulled the trigger yourself."

"Beth left with me, she left them too," the Sarge mumbled, as he pleaded with me.

"Well Beth wasn't driving, you were, she was just a passenger in your getaway bus," I explained, turning and winking at Beth.

The Sarge strained to lift his head and look down between his legs to see the cause of the immense pain emanating from that area of his body. And after seeing his air dried and wrinkled man eggs hanging outside of their natural habitat, his girlish voice squealed.

427

"What the fuck did you do to me?" he yelled as loud as he could, given his circumstances.

"Well like they used to say in the ancient Near East harems, *tough tunics said the eunuchs*," I answered, smiling. "And if you keep shouting, I'll cram this rag back in your mouth."

"I'll kill you for this," the tied down former military man promised with a groan.

"Calm down Sarge, technically you're not a eunuch, your balls are still intact, they have just been relocated slightly," I assured him. "And besides, I didn't do that to you, my girlfriend Beth did."

Beth leaned down and looked the Sarge directly in the eye.

"That's right, I did that to you, tough shit for you," she said, glaring at him.

Even though it was difficult for Ron to see through the intense pain he was suffering, he managed to muster enough strength, and saliva, to attempt to spit in Beth's face.

As the sputum left his mouth, I raised my right hand and blocked the spittle's path.

"Nice stop Jack," Derek blurted out.

"Yes, a very nice stop," Beth agreed, kissing me on the cheek. "And that makes me think, if he can see me well enough to spit in my face, I think he's carrying around one too many eyeballs."

"No don't let her do that Jack, please don't let her do that," the Sarge begged, as he began to weep, knowing that his cowardly pleas for mercy were falling on deaf ears.

"You've got to learn to eat the pain like candy Sarge," I consoled him, as I wiped his goober off my hand onto *his* face. "I thought I taught you that in Iraq?"

The Sarge screamed in pain and once more passed out as Beth plunged the first two inches of her small pocketknife's blade into the his *dominant eye's* socket and severed some of the muscles holding the eye in place, allowing her to pluck the eyeball out of its concave haven and let it dangle limp on his cheek.

"No need to tear it all of the way out, it's damaged enough that he'll never see out of it again," Beth assured, as she cleaned the juices off the blade with one of the Sarge's socks.

"If you two are done playing around, do you think we might want to get the hell out of here before those feral dogs get a wild hair up their ass and decide to return to the scene of the crime?" Derek asked, picking up his gear.

I turned to Beth and whispered in her ear.

"He's right; we had better get going before the dogs come back, anyway if we keep cutting and piercing him, we're going to end up killing him, and I really don't want to do that, the Sarge deserves better than that don't you think?"

Beth agreed and we all picked up our stuff and prepared to leave the house.

"You guys go first, I'm going to release this shit-hook back into the wild," I ordered, as I pulled my tomahawk from my tactical vest and chopped the cords in two that were binding the ex-sergeant's feet to the table.

With another swift blow of my blade to the cord holding his left wrist tightly to the table leg, the cord snapped and let his arm drop to the floor.

I was not completely satisfied with the results of the mildly heinous acts that Beth and I had perpetrated on the Sarge (he hadn't suffered enough), and even knowing that with the injuries that he had sustained, it would take nothing short of a full blown miracle for this man to ever have the means or the ability to catch up to me and Beth, and if by some strange quirk of fate, he was somehow able to follow us into the zombie wastelands without being eaten; his mutilated body would *probably* only pose a minimal threat to us.

In fact, he reminded me of a flyer that I once saw attached to a telephone pole which referred to a lost dog. It went something like this.

Lost one brown and white male dog, he is missing his left ear, which was chewed off in a fight with a vicious bigger dog. He had to have his right hind leg amputated due to being hit by a speeding automobile he was chasing for fun. Sometime ago my dog developed a dreadful infestation of flees which he has been unable to shake, and an incurable case of mange which the vet says is terminal. He is friendly and won't bite because his previous owner knocked out all of his teeth with a crowbar. He answers to the name "Lucky".

So, with that poster, and *Murphy's Law* fresh in my mind, I decided on my own to take the Sarge a little further into the realm of horrific possibilities and monumental pain and suffering; even though I had warned Beth that we should stop before we killed the punk. Hey, call me greedy and selfish.

As I lifted my tomahawk to cut the last cord, and the sergeant began to stir once more.

I quickly changed the direction that I was going to swing my small ax, and instead of clipping the last tie that bound the man to the table, I sliced off one half inch of the end of his nose. You know, *cut off his nose to spite his face*.

While I was at it, I decided to carve off both of the Sarge's ears too, you know, give him that complete *Frankenstein* look that biker chicks dig.

Only one cord held him to that dining room table, and even with his index fingers missing, I assured him that he would have no trouble loosening his bond and freeing himself.

"I've got to go now Sarge! See ya, wouldn't want to be ya," I told him, thinking that he most likely didn't hear a word that I said over his girlish screaming.

Satisfied that my work there was done, and my vendetta against the Sarge was now complete, I stuffed both severed ears and the tip of my old friend's nose into my titty bag figuring that later on I would use them to make a pair of ear rings and a necklace for Beth.

Anxious to catch up to the group before they had too much of a lead on me, I left the house quickly, only to find that Beth and the others had waited for me just outside the door near a pile of twitching rejects that couldn't cut the mustard in the Indiana Badlands.

"Where to now Jack?" Derek asked, shrugging his shoulders the best he could with Jolene hanging on them.

"Well, the Caucasian's men are north and I doubt that they will be too happy to see us if we show up back at the fortress." I answered. "Anyway, who in the hell

431

wants to stay in the Indiana Badlands, I certainly don't. I'm going to head back down south and see if our Chevy is still where we left it. I'm falling behind on my weekly quota of felony hit and runs you know."

"You mean *we're* going to head back down south don't you?" Beth asked, smiling and raising her eyebrows.

Hoping that Beth would ask that exact question, I responded with a smile, a wink, and a stealthy creeping grope on her luscious callipygian buttocks; before answering.

"Indeed I do honey, indeed I do."

You see back then I used to call her honey, of course that was before she found out that it was *bee shit*. Since then I have chosen my words a little more wisely.

We scurried out of the neighborhood as fast as we could, fearing that the pack of feral dogs might still be in the area, only hesitating momentarily on occasion, to alleviate any cannibalistic threats that tried to encumber our trek south.

Approximately 10 hours after we left the Sarge wishing that he'd never met me *or* Beth, the hue and saturation of the daylight began to change rapidly.

"What's happening?" Beth asked. "Everything is getting brighter and turning white!"

"I see that!" I answered.

Derek yelled. "What the fuck!"

Then we all heard Jolene scream.

CAPTAIN XARR TO THE RESCUE

"Captain Xarr, all of the successful conscripts have been taken aboard the ship, and the pre-extinction bipedal carnivorous creatures have been released to destroy the remaining control groups left on the planet as per your orders," Lieutenant Commander Zeem reported.

"Lieutenant Commander Zeem, what determination have you made to cope with the remaining test subject groups that our research on this planet have found to be unsuitable for use in the Anunnaki military cause that has brought us to this world?" Captain Xarr asked.

"Captain Xarr, I have ordered that the genetic differentiation chips which were inserted into the pre-extinction bipedal carnivorous beasts prior to their initial release and properly readjusted after Lieutenant Commander Jol's debacle to insure the proper result for our mission, to again be readjusted to reflect our needs concerning the remaining test subject groups that are unable to meet our minimum requirements." Lieutenant Commander Zeem explained.

"Elaborate Lieutenant Commander Zeem," Captain Xarr ordered.

With the fate of Private Jol, formally *Lieutenant Commander* Jol fresh in his mind the replacement officer answered his captain.

"Captain Xarr!" Lieutenant Commander Zeem shouted, as he snapped to attention for effect. "The latest adjustments made to the genetic differentiation chips will ensure through attrition, that the remaining test subject groups will no longer be able to travel unencumbered on the planet's surface or in their man-

433

made subterranean caverns. All test subject groups or individual test subjects still existing on any one of the seven continents of this planet, or any other land mass will be looked at as a main food source for the planet's prehistoric beasts we have released, and be devoured by them on sight."

"Excellent Lieutenant Commander Zeem!" the Captain barked, indicating his approval. "You may not need to join Private Jol in the indoctrinating persecution chamber in Bay 5 after all."

"Yes Captain Xarr, I mean, No Captain Xarr," Lieutenant Commander Zeem replied, as he again felt his over exerted sphincter muscle strain as it put a strangle hold on his overly exercised alimentary canal.

"Now bring me the sole survivor of the test subject group 32452013, the one that the earthers call Jack Doom," the commander ordered. "And see to it that no harm comes to the rest of his newly formed group, or any of the other test subject groups that were brought up from the planet's surface."

"Yes, Captain Xarr!" Lieutenant Commander shouted, before leaving the bridge to execute his Captain's orders.

******

The next thing that I remember, I found myself, along with Beth, Jolene, and Derek, sealed in a small metal room, and with what could only be described as oversized metal furnishings that were somehow seamlessly affixed to our encapsulating metallic space.

"What the fuck just happened Jack?" Derek asked.

434

"I have no idea what the fuck just happened," I answered, as I surveyed the enclosure for a door.

Beth looked around the room and at each one of us and remarked. "I don't know what the fuck happened either, but I know I don't fucking like it."

"I'm scared," Jolene admitted, as she clung to Derek.

"Where are all my weapons?" I asked, making a cursory search of myself. "And the rest of my stuff (meaning Cassandra's titty bag and the Sarge's ears and nose)?"

"All my shit's gone too," Derek said, patting himself down.

"All of our stuff's gone, except our clothes," Beth announced, looking around the room.

"I don't see a door or window in this place, how in the hell did we get in here?" Derek wondered, holding Jolene tightly.

"The question isn't how did we get in here, the question is how are we going to get out of here," I said, now running my hands along the surface of the walls. "There are no seams anywhere, not on the walls, or the floor and ceiling, not even in the corners."

Still hugging Derek tightly Jolene recalled her last memory.

"We were just walking along and then we were here," she said.

"Yeah, the last thing that I remember seeing was that cool '51 Chevy sitting right where we parked it, and then everything faded out to a bright blinding white, and then this place," Derek added, with a look of concern on his face. "What the fuck?"

"Whatever is going on, it looks like we're stuck here until someone lets us out," I surmised, still probing for some kind of an opening, and thinking that the confines of the metallic structure reminded me of that burnt out tank, without the dead bodies and smell.

"Well somebody better let us out soon, I'm starting to get claustrophobic," Derek acknowledged, with a hint of panic on his face.

"Me too," Beth said, with the same look on her face.

I didn't say anything, but I was beginning to feel the same way, and with Jolene scared of her own shadow most of the time, I figured that she was more panic stricken than any of us.

Several hours passed and we were all about at the end of our ropes, the hard cold and oversized metal furniture was beginning to get very uncomfortable no matter how we tried to adjust ourselves on it.

We guessed that the shiny metal monolith that was standing at a slightly awkward height in the middle of the room and emitting a very low bass tone vibration was a toilet. That was the only thing we could think of that such an odd-looking contraption with a hole in the top could be used for, but nobody was to the point that they were ready to test the theory, at least not yet, especially the girls. However, we all knew that it was only a matter of time before someone in the room was going to have to be the first to make the choice of either testing the metallic megalith, or dropping a series of deuces in their drawers.

Fortunately for me, as fate would have it, I wasn't chosen to be the first one to be put on display in front of my peers. That honor went to Jolene who had consumed a whole bottle of water just before we found ourselves trapped. However, she too was fortunate, that she did not have to drop the kids off at the pool; she only had to adjust the pH balance of the water after several long minutes of doing her version of an Indian rain dance in front of us. That is if there was any water in that strange mechanism at the center of our new metal world.

After Jolene had thoroughly tested the humming monolith and found that it was not only a toilet, but it was a self-flushing toilet at that, nobody in the room was too surprised that Derek had decided that if the toilet in the middle of the room was up to Jolene's apocalyptic standards, it was definitely up to his own standards, and quickly dropped trou and conducted his own extensive tests on the metal mechanism while stating categorically.

"I hope this thing has an industrial fart fan attached to it!"

Moments after Derek had finished his session on the oversized commode, one of the walls of the room seemed to melt away forming a doorway, and an odd-looking, what I believed to be a male, stepped through the opening and addressed me.

His outfit was not one that was familiar to me; however it slightly resembled a uniform that would have been worn by a Nazi officer during World War II.

"Jack Doom?" the uniformed *person* asked in a monotone voice.

Thinking that we were finally about to get some answers to where we were and why we were there, I answered back in a monotone voice.

"I'm Jack Doom, who are you?"

"I am Lieutenant Commander Zeem. I have been ordered to bring you to Captain Xarr," the Lieutenant Commander answered, again in a monotone voice.

"This guy's military," I said, looking back at Derek. "Maybe now we'll get some answers?"

"It's about time!" Beth sighed. "Tell them to let us out of this tin can, or at least give us private quarters. I'm not sure, but I don't think Jolene is too juicy about the prospect of taking a full-fledged dump in front of you boys, I know I'm not."

"Well first of all, if you see a boy around here, especially me, you'll need to get down on your knees and blow him up to a man." I said jovially, trying to lighten the dreary mood of our group, and hoping that sometime in the future Beth might heed my advice and choose to inflate me into the man of her dreams.

"There will be no use of explosives without the express order of Captain Xarr." Lieutenant Commander Zeem informed us sternly; seemingly unable to discern the difference between a joke and a serious comment, or deduce that some words in our language have more than one meaning and that they can be used in different contexts.

Meanwhile, Jolene sat silently at Derek's side staring at the foreign features of the military man in front of her, while Derek subtly giggled at my remark, all the while hoping that Jolene would also heed my advice and make a man out of him too.

Beth was busy wondering what in the fuck was wrong with this strange looking guy with the hokey accent, and at the same time giving me the buffalo eye for my off the cuff comment.

438

Myself, I stood there wondering why I even bother to submit my own brand of levity in an effort to try and cheer up my forlorn female friends, who never seem to have any sense of humor.

"If I only had my little titty bag, I could make Beth that necklace; that would cheer her up," I thought.

"You will follow me now," Lieutenant Commander Zeem ordered, as he turned and walked away, leaving two other odd-looking *people* also in uniform standing on either side of the doorway to escort me.

I was anxious to get out of that metal room even if it was only for a short time, so I didn't hesitate to follow the Lieutenant Commander down a long hallway and into an elevator with the two others at my side.

However, as I walked along, I wondered who in the hell are these guys. I had done my time in the Marine Corps and been many places around the world, but I didn't recognize their uniforms or insignias.

"They might be CIA or NSA," I thought. After all, with all the high tech shit I was seeing they couldn't be just regular military. But no one in those two organizations wore uniforms, except for their low level security personnel. At least not dress uniforms like these guys were sporting.

Maybe they were some foreign group of fighters like the Israeli Mossad, but then they didn't wear uniforms either, at least not that I knew of.

I didn't have any of the answers I was looking for, and when I did finally get to the truth, I truly wished that I hadn't.

So, once in the elevator I asked the Lieutenant Commander.

"What's going on here? Who are you people? Why did you bring us here? When are you going to let us...?"

Lieutenant Commander Zeem interrupted in an irritated tone.

"Captain Xarr will answer all of your questions, please remain silent until you are asked to reply to any inquiries that the Captain may have."

Right off the bat, this clown's arrogant attitude didn't sit well with me. I'd been through too much shit, I'd seen too much shit, and I'd done too much shit, to take a bunch of crap from some want-to-be soldier in a pristine uniform that looked and spoke like he'd never even seen a zombie, let alone got his hands dirty killing one.

I thought. *"If we were out on the street, I'd plant my tomahawk in this guy's foot just to teach him a lesson in etiquette."*

However, we weren't out on the street, and I didn't have my tomahawk or anything else. Although it's true I could have leaped on this turd and snapped his neck like a twig in a blink of an eye, but his two goons that were flanking me would most likely subdue me before I could get away, and then who knows what kind of world of shit I would have landed myself in. Besides, even if I did get away after croaking the Lieutenant Commander, where would I go then, I didn't even know where we had been taken, and I wasn't about to leave Beth for any reason.

Therefore, I stood there between the two escorts, kept my mouth shut, and waited to see this Captain Xarr character the Lieutenant Commander kept yapping about.

The elevator doors opened and we stepped into some sort of futuristic looking control room.

The room was configured in a circle with panels of colored lights, monitors, gauges, knobs, and joysticks, and every panel had a person sitting in front of it operating that particular station.

Centered in the middle of the room was a command chair on a swivel, with buttons and switches encased in both arms.

Sitting in the command chair was a very confident looking man in a different colored uniform than the rest of the people in the control room. He was busy attending to his duties and giving orders to the other *soldiers*.

"Captain Xarr, Lieutenant Commander Zeem reporting as ordered."

"Excellent Lieutenant Commander Zeem, I see you brought the test subject as ordered," the Captain remarked.

"Yes Captain Xarr, as you ordered."

"Mr. Doom I presume. May I call you Mr. Doom?" Captain Xarr asked, not waiting for my answer. "Mister Doom, I wanted to meet with you personally and answer any questions that you might have that may concern you."

Deja vu hit me like a ton of bricks, but I just couldn't put my finger on it.

"What's going on here? Who are you people? Why did you bring us here? When are you going to let us go?" I asked, staring at the Captain.

"I like you! May I call you Jack?" the Captain asked, again not waiting for an answer. "That is why I have decided that I am glad that you did not get killed down there."

"Killed down where, what do you mean killed down there?" I asked, now completely confused.

Then it came to me. The Caucasian used those exact words when we first met. But this guy wasn't nearly as big as the pale giant I had killed. However, his accent was similar to the freakishly tall mutant.

"Lieutenant Commander Zeem!"

"Yes Captain Xarr!" the Lieutenant Commander quickly answered.

"Has Jack been informed of his whereabouts?" Captain Xarr asked as if he were my best friend.

"No Captain Xarr, none of the test subject groups have any knowledge of who we are, why they are here, or where they are now," Lieutenant Commander Zeem answered. "And this test subject is no exception. All of the test subjects have been sequestered in their respective holding compartments until now; this one is the only earther that has been allowed to leave the containment area."

"Captain Xarr, it wasn't very long ago that someone said that very thing to me," I told the Captain. "He also spoke in much the same way you people do."

"Yes Jack, I know all about the one you speak of," Captain Xarr acknowledged. "He and ones like him are the primary reason that you are here."

"And exactly where is here?" I asked, staring at the Captain with a stern look on my face.

"Why... here on the bridge of an Annanaki intergalactic spaceship, it is your new home, at least until we return to Annunak for your final training," the

Captain informed me. "You see, the one you knew as the Caucasian is just one of many gynandromorph's whose binary genitalia was medically altered through a dangerous, yet quite efficient marinating process whereby their loins were soaked in an electrically charged chemical for an extended period of time. A process similar to the way your people electroplate jewelry. The result of this chemically induced biologic transmodification genital surgery was the shrinking of the sex organs down to a point that they not only no longer functioned, but also for all intent and purposes were almost non-existent to the naked eye. At least not in the state that they would normally be recognized.

This converted each gynandromorph that underwent the process and survived it, into what was the equivalent of what was called a *eunuch* during your planet's ancient history.

The difference being, instead of being cut off, the chemically treated sex organs of those gynandromorphs chosen, shrank due to the change in their DNA composition after a prolonged dipping in the proper chemical compound bath. A residual and unavoidable side effect of the DNA restructuring, caused the rest of the creature's physical body to expanded geometrically and lose all pigmentation in the skin and hair, rendering them albino giants, even as compared to my own tall pale-skinned Annunaki race."

"Are you telling me that the freak show I killed in the Indiana Badlands that called himself the Caucasian, was a bloated gynandromorphic eunuch from some other planet?" I asked, jokingly, not believing a word of the Captain's bullshit story.

443

"Jack Doom, that is precisely what I am telling you," Captain Xarr answered, with a blank look on his alien face. "However, I would not have described the transformation of the chemically treated gynandromorph in such colorful terms, yet your vernacular enhanced chronicle is nonetheless accurate."

"So what was the Caucasian, or gynandromorph, or eunuch, or whatever the hell he or it was, doing here on earth?" I asked, trying to take in and process everything that was happening around me, but still in disbelief.

"The albino gynandromorphs are part of the reason that the superior Annunaki race is currently at war with the gynandromorphic race," the alien Captain explained. "Many hundreds of thousands of Kronal sections ago, several top Annunaki scientists traveled deep into one of the forbidden zones of the Cyan Prime cluster without authorization from the Supreme Being of Annunak, and carried out what the inhabitants there called unspeakable experiments on captured civilians."

"Let me guess, the experiments were done on the gynandromorph population in that so called forbidden zone," I said. "And just what in the hell is a Kronal section?"

"You are correct Jack Doom, our scientists experimented on gynandromorphy citizens," Captain Xarr replied. "And one of your earth months is the closest time measurement that I can relate to you that resembles the Kronal sections that we on Annunak use to gauge certain aspects of time."

"That's all fine and dandy Captain, and I'm getting ready to pop a woody, but you didn't answer my question.

444

What was the albino gynandromorph as you call it, doing down on *my* planet?

As a matter of fact, while you're in the mood to answer questions, what in hell's creation are all of you so-called *aliens* doing here anyway?" I asked, as my mood began to deteriorate, and I began to shout, still not believing the answers that Captain Xarr was telling me.

Seeing that his Captain was being accosted by a mere earther, and ready to take advantage of another opening to make some major league brownie points, Lieutenant Commander Zeem broke in.

"Do not raise your voice to Captain Xarr or I will escort you to Bay 5 personally!"

I had no idea what he meant by *Bay 5*, but I was pretty sure I didn't want to find out anytime soon, whether they were from another planet or not.

So I decided to profusely apologize to everyone or everything (depending on how you look at it), on the bridge of the ship, especially Captain Xarr. I would play along with their ruse whatever it was, and hope that the Captain would see fit to reunite me with Beth and the others.

"It is all right Lieutenant Commander Zeem, I am sure that our guest meant no disrespect toward me or any of the crew, he is just confused about who is in charge here," Captain Xarr said, very condescendingly. "His attitude is exactly the reason that he was one of the earthers chosen."

"I'm sorry Captain Xarr, I didn't mean any disrespect to you or your crew, and I have the greatest admiration for all of you. Like you said, I am a guest on your ship, and I would never intentionally do anything that would upset you or any of your crew," I told the leader, as I tried to think of a way to slit the young Lieutenant Commander's throat and not get myself killed in the process.

Up to now, nobody in this control room, or on the spaceship's bridge, or wherever I was, had paid much attention to me, they were staying busy at their stations and doing their jobs.

However, as I uttered my insincere apology to the Captain and crew, their sudden curiosity of my presents caught my attention, and I noticed the depictions on some of their monitors, most of which were images of earth from a great height, miles above the planet in fact, pictures of earth from an orbital altitude.

I also became aware that the labels by all of the switches and knobs were written in some kind of weird looking hieroglyphics that resembled nothing that I had ever seen.

"*Holy fuckcycles!*" I thought. "*Is everything this guy's been telling me true?*"

The more I thought about it as the crew stared at me, the more the Captain's explanation made sense.

"*A virus that brought the dead back to life to eat the living?*

The illusive shadows during the day and the flashes of unseen light at night?

Dinosaurs rampaging through the countryside?

That beam of light coming from the clouds that disintegrated the building by the armory where the sniper had his nest?

The weird lighting change and missing time that preceded our arrival on the spaceship.

446

The wall in what the Lieutenant Commander had called the holding compartment melting into a doorway?"

With all of that happening, and from what the ship's Captain had told me, it was obvious that people from earth didn't cause the bizarre events of the past couple of years.

"Okay, let's just say that I believe everything that you've told me so far. What possible reason could you have to invade my planet and cause so much death, carnage, and destruction?" I asked, this time sincerely. "And what in the fuck do you want with me?"

"As I have informed Lieutenant Commander Zeem, and his predecessor I might add, my family lineage has a long history that connects them and me to your planet.

Those pre-extinction bipedal carnivorous creatures that we deployed to saved you from the overwhelming amount of control subjects that were attacking, before you and the rest of test subject group 32452013 retired into the large metal, mobile, projectile hurling mechanism...

"You mean that bunch of vile dinosaurs that killed my family?" I fumed, interrupting the Captain as he explained.

"Yes, I see that you remember them," the Captain answered straight faced and non-caring.

"I remember them all right," I steamed, trying to control my rage.

"That was a slight miscalculation on the part of one of my officers," Captain Xarr admitted, still with an unconcerned look on his face.

"Oh, that's all right," I said, sarcastically. "You wouldn't mind introducing me to that officer would you; you know the one that made that *slight miscalculation*?"

"Not in the least, as a matter of fact I need to check on his progress down in Bay 5," Captain Xarr answered, almost giddily. "Lieutenant Commander Zeem, you will accompany Jack and me down to Bay 5."

"Yes, Captain Xarr," the Lieutenant Commander shouted as he flailed an Annunaki salute toward his commander.

Without having to be ordered, the two guards also accompanied us, flanking me as we made our way down to Bay 5.

Along the way, Captain Xarr told me of his ancestors and how they, coupled with what he called the archaic Annunaki technology of the times, caused the global demise of the dinosaurs, but only after they had retrieved several choice specimens of both male and female to as he put it *farm* their species.

He proudly mentioned the Great Pyramids and the Sphinx, and told me how and why they were built, and how the humans had defiled them and the good name of his ancient relatives.

As we stepped out of the ship's conveyor onto Bay 5 and walked down a drab hallway, he finished his rendition of how he and his crew had released a genetically altered protein molecule into the atmosphere. That protein molecule targeted certain human blood types and attacked their antibodies, thus causing people with said blood types to contract the zombie virus (*zombie virus*, my words not his) and rise from the dead with a voracious appetite for living or dead flesh, provided the dead flesh hadn't been dead too long.

As we neared the end of the hallway, the Captain began to tell me about the mysterious *Bay 5* that his junior officer had earlier threatened to escort me to personally.

"Rylo Kesbvoff of the Science Academy on Tarsa II is the top persecuting officer assigned on this mission; he is in charge of all disciplinary actions designated to take place during this expedition."

"Is he the officer that made that *slight* mistake?" I asked politely, plastering a fake smile on my face.

Lieutenant Commander Zeem who had been silent until now spoke up quickly and apparently a little too excitedly for his own good.

"Oh no Jack Doom, Rylo Kesbvoff would never make a mistake like that!"

"Really, just what kind of mistake would I make?" Rylo Kesbvoff asked, seeming appearing out of nowhere.

Even in the middle of the dire straits that I knew we were in, I noticed the priceless look on the young Lieutenant Commander's face.

His eyes bulged out even farther than normal as his slack jaw dropped almost to the deck (that's the floor in naval jargon).

I could almost see the crotch of his uniform pants pucker under the strain, as his anus sucked in the garment under the tension of his overly stressed sphincter becoming taut.

"Am I hearing a false accusation lodged against me Lieutenant Commander Zeem?" the persecuting officer

449

asked, with a gleam in his eye, as he remembered the Captain's promise that he would be the Lieutenant Commander's teacher if he were to continue to bend the rules.

"No sir, Rylo Kesbvoff, not at all," Lieutenant Commander Zeem answered squeamishly, his eyes and sphincter both bulging out as he remembered the greenish-yellow light that flooded down on Private Jol and the metallic recliner. "I just meant that Private Jol was the perpetrator at fault."

"Oh, well that's too bad, because I would love to see what you look like in a greenish-yellow glow," Rylo Kesbvoff scoffed with a smirk.

"Enough of the childish banter, Jack wants to see Private Jol in all of his glory," Captain Xarr ordered gruffly. "By the way Jack, how's my English? Am I pronouncing all of the words correctly?"

"*What the fuck?*" I thought. "*Who am I, the schoolmarm?*"

"Yeah Captain, you get an A+ in English," I told him, as I watched his chest puff out almost as far as his Lieutenants sphincter. "Now can I please take a look at this Private Jol clown of yours?"

"Certainly Jack, but you've got to teach me how to speak in that colorful vernacular you are so fond of using," the Captain insisted. "I have become quite proficient in the proper English language used by the inhabitants of your land, but I am a little confused when it comes to employing the North American continents slang. That particular jargon of your dialect changes too fast for our foreign language library to keep up with."

"Sure *Cap*," I said, thinking that I might be pushing my luck. "Here's your first lesson. Open the fucking door and let's see the asshole that got my family killed."

Captain Xarr wasn't sure whether to smile and thank me for the lesson in American profane slang, or to have me put under the greenish-yellow light that I was about to see shinning on Private Jol, or what was left of him anyway.

After a slight hesitation trying to decide my fate, the Captain gave the order to open the door in front of us.

"Open the chamber door!" He stated loudly.

"Yes Captain Xarr," the guard on my right side responded as he pressed the dark blue octagonal button on the seamless wall.

The door of the chamber quickly and quietly melted away just as the door to the holding cell that still housed Beth and the rest of my party had, and revealed a room bathed in a pale greenish-yellow light.

In the middle of the room was a blood drenched metallic chair hanging from the ceiling that reminded me of some electric chairs I had seen in photographs of nineteen thirties era prisons, only glossy and without any wood attached, and a little more high-tech. Okay, a lot more high-tech.

"This is one of Bay 5's indoctrinating persecution chambers; it is where officers and crew members alike are sent for punishment and rehabilitation," the Captain bragged proudly.

"Yes, officers like you Lieutent Zeem!" Rylo reminded the squeamish subordinate officer.

As we entered the chamber, I caught a slight smile break the horizontal plain of the seated subject's mouth, as he heard the veiled threat from Rylo Kesbvoff.

We walked toward the suspended chair that was dripping with an off color red blood which oozed onto the floor of the chamber, to take a closer look at its disfigured occupant who had since stopped his attempt to smile.

Suddenly, one of the sentries that were assigned to guard me yelled and dropped to the deck. The other guard quickly closed the small gap between us and gave me a steely glare, as if to tell me to remain where I was.

"Sorry Captain Xarr," the fallen guard apologized. "It is these toes that are scattered all over the deck; they are like cobalt orbs that have been soaked in Trilax lubricant."

"I told you to get those toes off the deck before somebody fell," the Captain barked at Rylo. "Did I not make my order clear enough for you to comprehend?"

"Of course you did Captain Xarr, I picked up the toes the moment you and Lieutenant Commander Zeem left the chamber," the persecuting officer in charge insisted, as he noticed a smirk creep onto Lieutenant Commander Zeem's face.

Pulling a metallic container off one of the shelves behind him, he opened it and displayed the severed toes in question, all of which were neatly packed into the metal jar like Vienna sausages in a can.

"These are Private Jol's toes," he explained, squinting his eyes and frowning at the Lieutenant Commander. "The guard slipped on the Private's finger tips, I would have had them cleaned off the deck if I had known that company was coming."

The guard picked himself up from the puddle of blood he had landed in, and tried to act as if nothing had happened, pissed that his clean uniform was now smudged with Private Jol's disgusting ooze.

"You are a very lucky Annunaki, Rylo Kesbvoff.

If Mr. Doom had fallen and been injured to the point that he would not be able to carry out his mission for the Annunaki cause because of your lack of discretion, old friend or not, I would have had no choice but to make a very painful example out of you." Captain Xarr, threatened sternly.

"Yes Captain Xarr, it will never happen again," Rylo promised, as he caught another smirk from Lieutenant Commander Zeem out of the corner of his eye.

"What mission?" I asked, not liking what I was hearing.

"I will explain everything to you in due time, but first I want to introduce you to Private Jol as you so colorfully requested."

The Captain nodded to the guards giving them permission to allow me to advance toward him and Private Jol unencumbered.

"This pathetic, how do you American Earther's say it, let me think, oh yes, this *piece of shit*, is the former second in command of my starship. That duty now is the responsibility of Lieutenant Commander Zeem over there," the Captain informed me, pointing in the Lieutenant Commander's direction.

"This is the guy that killed my family?"

453

"You are the lone surviving member of test subject group 32452013 because of then Lieutenant Commander Jol's failures to carry out his duties adequately."

"Uooouueeww!" moaned Private Jol, trying to deny the false accusation.

"He can't speak clearly Captain Xarr, I have already extracted his tongue from his mouth," Rylo explained. "I used a new procedure that I developed myself. Very painful I might add."

"It is good to hear that you continue to educate yourself in your chosen craft," Captain Xarr replied. "Now hand this earther one of your tools, he would like to apply some suffering to Private Jol, wouldn't you Jack?"

Surrounded by what I now knew were beings from another world, I felt that I had no choice but to accept the Captain's offer and torture his former officer. Knowing nothing about my captures, turning down his request might mean taking the Privates place, whether they thought that I had some kind of a mission or not.

However, don't get me wrong, if this son-of-a-bitch was the one responsible for the deaths of Gin and my boys (I mean besides the Sarge), I would be more than happy to take my *pound of flesh* out of him; or maybe a couple of pounds out of him.

"I cannot let you kill Private Jol," the Captain warned. "Pathetic or not, he is still an Annunaki and we do not allow other species to wantonly take the lives of our kind if it can in any way be avoided. This is especially true when it comes to a vastly inferior and primitive species such as yours. However, because Private Jol has not yet reached the end of his persecution session, I *can* allow you to inflict an exorbitant amount of pain onto him."

Rylo Kesbvoff then carefully handed me an item that resembled a piece of twisted white plastic with spikes sticking out of a cube that was situated at what I believed to be the top of the instrument.

The tool weighed somewhere around three pounds and had sharp edges everywhere except what seemed to be its handle.

With the alien tool in my right hand, I turned back to the entity in the metal chair and raised the implement over my head. A hard and swift vertical swipe down onto the knee of Private Jol with the spiked cube, forced him to fill the room with another scream.

"That tool is supposed to be used on the upper torso of his body," Rylo called out. "With a swift jabbing motion!"

"If that is the case, then why does he yell so loudly when I do this?" I asked, as I plunged the plastic torture mechanism into the side of the alien's face.

"Aaaaoouuww!" screeched the *man* in the chair while I dragged the imbedded spikes across his cheek, leaving a trail of blood and deep scratches in his skin.

Glancing around the chamber at the unemotional members of the spaceship's crew as I repeatedly beat their private with the tool that they had provided me. I couldn't help but to think if they would do this to one of their own for a miscalculation, what would they be capable of doing to us humans for some minor arbitrary blunder that we might commit?

The shrieking coming from Private Jol's mutilated oral orifice was beginning to give me a headache. The

Captain had made it abundantly clear to me that I was not to kill the Private under any circumstances, so I decided to see if I could put an end to my turn as the torture chamber master, and see if I could get back to Beth.

I swung the spiked plastic mallet down once more, this time onto what was left of Private Jol's right hand.

"I guess that should do it, since you won't let me kill this ass monkey," I told the Captain smiling, as if I were satisfied with the results of my alien beat down. "Now can I see Beth? All of this fucker's caterwauling is starting to get on my last nerve. And besides, it looks like your man Rylo has everything under control around here."

With Rylo smiling and nodding his head in agreement of my comment, and after ordering Lieutenant Commander Zeem to remain behind and assist him with the fingertip cleanup, and any other mess that needed his attention, I was marched back down the hallway and into the waiting elevator.

Several minutes later I watched the wall of the holding compartment melt away again, and saw Beth sitting in the far corner smiling at me.

"May we come in?" Captain Xarr inquired, as if he needed permission to enter the room. "It is now time to inform you of the Annunaki mission that brought us to your planet."

I watched as the smile on Beth's face faded and was replaced with a look of confusion. That same look was all too noticeable on Derek's and Jolene's faces as well.

"Who the hell are these guys… and what in the fuck is he talking about? Brought them to our planet?" Derek spewed, pissed and confused.

"Yeah, what does he mean Jack?" Beth asked, not knowing whether to be scared or pissed off too.

"Captain Xarr," I said. "Maybe this will go a little smoother if you allow me to preface your little announcement.

"That is an excellent idea Jack Doom," the Captain answered, with a hand motion signaling me to proceed.

"This is Captain Xarr," I began. "He is in charge..."

"In charge of what?" Derek interrupted.

"Shut the fuck up and listen," I said, clenching my teeth and glaring at him. "Everything he is about to tell you is true, everything. Some of which I will be hearing for the first time with you.

You're not going to like what he has to say, I know I didn't, but that's just tough shit for us.

I don't think that we are the only people that they brought aboard, but I believe that I am the only one that got the grand tour, and you wouldn't believe the shit that I've seen.

We're here, we're trapped here, and from what I've seen so far, there is absolutely no way to escape. So unless we all can do a God damned good impression of *Kuda Bux*, *Houdini*, *Flood the Magnificent*, or some other icon of deception, evasion, and escape, we are *doomed*.

I've been told that for now this is my new home and my guess is that it is your new home too.

I don't have any idea what they have in store for us, but I don't think that we have any choice in the matter, so listen to what Captain Xarr has to say, it's going to shock the shit out of you, but all you can do is just grin and bear it."

I walked over to where Beth was sitting, sat down beside her, and put my arm around her.

"It's all yours Captain Xarr."

The Captain stood in the doorway with the two sentries by his side, and with his usual blank expression draped over his face as he barked an order.

"Bridge!"

"Yes Captain Xarr," a voice from the ship's bridge answered, blaring through an invisible intercom system.

"You will immediately put me on fleet wide communication, including the test subject group's holding areas."

"Aye-aye Captain Xarr!"

The Captain then began to explain.

"All of you have been unwitting participants in a military exercise. The purpose of which was to weed out the weaklings of your species, and devolve the remainder of the survivors into formidable soldiers who will be used to help bring victory to the Annunaki Confederation and glory to the Supreme Being of the Annunaki race in the ongoing interplanetary Gynandromorph wars."

"What in the hell is the Annuaki race?" Jolene spouted.

"Shut your fucking pie hole and listen like you were told to do," Captain Xarr retorted back. "How is that for the proper vernacular use Jack?"

"I have taught you well Captain, and I am extremely impressed with how quickly you've mastered the

458

introduction of profanity into your sentence structure. If I didn't know better, I'd swear that I was 9 years old again, and back at home having Christmas dinner with my idiot father," I jested sarcastically, trying to make the best of our horrible situation, and at the same time show Beth that I wasn't scared shitless. Even though I was about to shoot a double deuce down both pant legs, and that was while I was sitting down.

My sarcasm again soared high over the alien Captain's head as he proudly replied to my comment.

"I have been studying in my spare time; I just needed some guidance in the subtle idiosyncrasies from an expert like yourself," the Captain gloated. "I am glad that my hard work is reaping positive results."

Jolene quickly shut her fucking pie hole as the Captain had recommended, and allowed him to continue.

"Jack was correct when he told you that you are not the only test subject group that was brought on board this vessel. Although you were initially chosen because of your association with Mr. Doom, it quickly became clear that you too were of the fighting caliber of earthers that we had come here to collect; except for Ms. Loud Mouth there; that concubine was brought aboard for the sole purpose of pleasing the one called Derek."

Beth squeezed my hand and snickered when Captain Xarr referred to Jolene as a concubine, but stopped smiling when he suggested that Jolene could also service me if I so desired.

You could almost cut the tension with a knife when the ship's Captain made his next statement.

"Your planet has been turned back over to the pre-extinction bipedal carnivorous creatures that we released to exterminate the control subjects that you call zombies," Captain Xarr continued. "We will allow them to over populate the planet to insure that all of the control subjects will be eradicated. You might even say that I have rescued all of you from your miserable existence on your home world and from the fate of those who were not chosen to join you in your honorable quest to serve the glorious cause of the Annunaki Confederation and the Supreme Being of our planet.

You see, the earthers that were not able to regress into the primal brutal primitives that they had evolved from many eons ago, and thus failed to meet the needs of the Annunaki military machine, they too will be extracted from the planet as well. However, the means by which they will depart will be through the grisly jaws of the wild beasts that we have unleashed upon your world.

Of course, all of that will take place shortly after a select few of the rejected earthers that we will abduct at the request of our science department, have been administered the usual authorized anal probes and various other medical prodding and poking and are returned to the planet.

It will be my recommendation to the Supreme Being that an order be given that no Annunaki ships will return to this planet for at least five thousand Kronal sections.

That will give the pre-extinction bipedal carnivorous creatures along with other prehistoric carnivores that we have set free to populate your world, in cooperation with an atmospheric re-molecular transgression stabilizer unit, an ample amount of time to cleanse the planet of every trace of the control subjects, their altered DNA, the genetically altered protein molecules, and the unfortunate earthers that are not being transported to Annunak."

With the Captain's explanation finished he again barked an order to the bridge via the unseen intercom.

"Bridge!"

"Yes Captain Xarr," the voice on the bridge once more answered.

"Immediately conclude the fleet wide communications."

"Aye-aye Captain Xarr!"

Captain Xarr paused and looked at us as if waiting to answer our questions.

He seemed to have taken a liking to me for some reason, so I figured that if I opened my fucking pie hole I might not be told to shut it, so I asked the officer in charge.

"What happens then Captain?"

"After the control subjects and the earthers that did not make the final cut have been properly exterminated, and the planet has been deemed duly cleansed by an authorized sanitation team.

Then what usually happens on planets like this one is that after the recommended hiatus of the Annunaki people. For a short period of time, one or two hundred of your planets solar orbits, possibly less depending on how soon and how many Annunaki are killed by the brutish wildlife, it will be used as a hunting preserve for the elite of the Annunaki race.

Then once it has been determined that hunting the pre-extinction bipedal carnivorous creatures is too dangerous for the civilian population to continue their

461

endeavors, military personnel like myself will enter the hunting arena. I have already reserved a prime five thousand square zordon (acre) area for my primitive animal hunt.

At that time the planet will be used exclusively by the military for hunting, training and anything else deemed necessary to further the Annunaki military establishment until the attrition rate of our soldiers becomes prohibited.

Then the animals will be put down in a massive planet-wide extinction event identical to past events that the Annunaki scientists have triggered.

After that, when your world is found to again be fit for human consumption, seeding ships will arrive with several primitive human species that will be positioned in tribal units in various areas around the planet.

Sometime later, teams of Annunaki scientists will arrive on this world, pick out certain tribes, and genetically engineer their DNA.

The genetic engineering will increase the intelligence quotient of the chosen species as well as a few other factors, and new patriarchs of what you call the human race will be created. Then in a few hundred thousand of your planets solar orbits, future generations of my family will return to this planet and do further experiments on the evolved inhabitants."

"Excuse me Captain, but you talk as if your race has some experience in this type of matter?" I asked, still being the only one brave enough, or foolish enough to speak.

"Indeed, Jack Doom!" the Captain answered, hesitating for a moment as we all watched the wall melt away once more, and Lieutenant Commander Zeem enter the room. "The Annunaki race has a very long history in the arena of interstellar space exploration, and we are quite familiar with tens of thousands of life forms that are spread throughout many galaxies in the universe."

"How is that possible?" Beth spoke up.

"The answer to your question is very simple," Captain Xarr answered, in a calm monotone voice. "You see during our extended monitoring of your planet and its inhabitants, we observed repeatedly that the people's short-sided thinking tends to always lead them to the same conclusion."

"What conclusion might that be?" Beth asked, clutching my arm.

"The conclusion that time is on a linear path and cannot be rerouted, and must maintain its course in only one direction which is into the future," the Captain explained. "Furthermore, although the idea has been put forth by some of your forward thinking scientist in the past, most of your people cannot seem to grasp the concept that any other race of intelligent beings could possibly have existed thousands of your earth years before theirs, let alone millions of those years, not that I am referring to your race as intelligent by any means."

"Are you saying that your Annunaki people have been flying around the universe for millions of years?" I asked, not really sure whether to believe his answer or not.

"How else would he have dinosaurs on board this ship?" Beth asked me, clutching my arm even harder.

"There are no, as you call them dinosaurs on this ship, they are on the transport ships that accompany this starship," the Captain explained.

"That's not what I mean. Where did you get the dinosaurs in the first place?" Beth asked a little annoyed.

We collect the pre-extinction bipedal carnivorous creatures in a variety of ways. Of course they are only referred to as pre-extinction creatures on planets that have at sometime in the past either been seeded with the creatures or they have naturally evolved on those planet, and then been made extinct by us to make room for other entities of our choosing," Captain Xarr explained.

"I think Beth is getting juicy over your answer, but she didn't ask you..."

Beth interrupted.

"You didn't answer my question! Where did you get the dinosaurs?" she asked again, this time maybe a little too loud.

Lieutenant Commander Zeem stepped forward and began to speak, but was stopped in his tracks by his Captain.

"Lieutenant Commander Zeem, Jack Doom's concubine named Beth is afraid, and she too does not realize just who is in charge!" the Captain informed his subordinate officer.

"Captain Xarr, I could take her to Bay 5 and let Rylo Kesbvoff show her who is in charge," Lieutenant Commander Zeem, quickly countered.

"I just came back from Bay 5, and trust me, you don't want to go there," I whispered in Beth's ear.

"Lieutenant Commander Zeem, my orders were quite clear on this subject. None of the test subject groups on this ship, or any of the other earther transporting vessels are to be harmed in any way," Captain Xarr bellowed, as once more, the Lieutenant Commander's eyeballs bulged and his sphincter muscle tightened as a prelude to an involuntary under uniform feces release. "You would do well to recall your predecessor in Bay 5, and how he managed to arrive at that juncture in his life."

"Yes Captain Xarr," Lieutenant Commander Zeem reassured, fearfully jumping to attention while feeling his pinched rectum twisting.

The alien Captain turned his attention back to Beth and began to answer her question.

"In regards to your question, Beth, may I call you Beth?" Captain Xarr asked, again not waiting for an answer from a mere earther.

"There are many planets that support a host of ferocious lizard-like beasts scattered throughout the realm of the Annunaki Confederation.

Several of these reptilian planets are within the visual range of Annunak *our* home planet, and can be seen as a heliocentric parallax brings them into view of the naked eye.

We use such planets as natural storage stations for the creatures, and pick the proper beasts needed for certain experiments and missions from those planets when the expense of using a time portal mechanism is prohibitive.

That is why the fossilized remains that your paleontologists had found were so diversified; the animals that produced them were from several different planetary systems.

One of those planets is where the bipedal carnivorous creatures needed to reseed your planet in the future will be harvested from if the need arises; as were the bipedal carnivorous creatures you call dinosaurs that are currently down on the surface of your planet."

Flabbergasted by the explanation the extraterrestrial Captain was giving us, Derek asked the alien officer.

"So you're interdimensional beings?"

"No, we are just like you, and a billion other species that inhabit this universe. We just use interdimensional space to travel when great distances are involved, or time is an issue in some manner. As it was when my ancestors exterminated the bipedal carnivorous creatures along with all of the other over sized lizards that originally inhabited your home planet, that is, your home planet after your species' DNA was altered to fit our future needs."

"Holy fuck Jack, I think we're screwed!" Derek moaned.

"Ya think?" I answered, feeling the blood flow in my arm being cut off by Beth's white-knuckle grip.

"I see that you are upset. Do not worry, other more comfortable accommodations are being prepared for you as we speak," Captain Xarr maintained. "Your journey back to the Annunaki home world for your training will be very relaxing.

Again, I begged forgiveness as I dared to ask another question.

"Excuse me Captain Xarr, but that's the second time that you have mentioned our training. Training for what exactly?"

"I had expected my second in command Lieutenant Commander Zeem to explain that to you, or should I refer to him as the soon to be Private Zeem who resides down in Bay 5," Captain Xarr criticized, glaring at his Lieutenant Commander. "However, it seems he has chosen a slightly more perilous path."

You could've heard a pin drop after the Captain's discourse, but as usual, there was no pin available. So all we heard were the sounds of Lieutenant Commander Zeem's intestines gurgling as their quickly liquefying contents made their way south.

After a moment of being entertained by Lieutenant Commander Zeem's internal slurping serenade, and failing miserably at holding back a smile, the Captain continued.

"The trials and tribulations that you have endured during the past several of your earth months, were part of an Annunaki experiment and recruitment process. That process was designed to weed out so to speak; the weak and useless of the planet's human population and at the same time toughen up and devolve the survivors, making them ready for the horrendous conditions of planetary combat that awaits them in their near future.

"Planetary combat?" Beth asked, as tears started to well up in her eyes.

"Indeed! Planetary combat," Captain Xarr answered. "You four, as well as many others have been selected for a great honor. You will be part of an elite combat unit that will spearhead an attack on the gynandromorph's home world.

You will be part of the glorious Annunaki victory over the gynandromorphs that will end the ongoing galactic war with them.

"Gynandromorphs? What the fuck is a gynandromorph?" Jolene spouted, forgetting or just ignoring the Captain's earlier scolding.

"Yeah, what in the fuck is a gynandromorph anyway," Derek chimed in.

"Gynandromorphs inhabit a group of planets in what your astronomers used to call the Sirius binary star system, and since the unfortunate scientific experiments that I previously mentioned, have been our dreaded enemies for thousands of your earth years, as we have been theirs," the Captain informed us. "At 2.6 parsecs from your planet, Sirius is the brightest star of the constellation you call Canis Major and can be found by following the belt of Orion southeast.

Gynandromorphs are a disgusting race of beings, which continually put their own pleasure before their duty, their integrity, and their honor, they will do anything to further their own desires and goals, no matter how loathsome those goals and desires might be.

They also slough their outer covering every three *earth* years like one of your snakes sheds its skin; it is a nasty and foul habit."

"What kind of training will we be getting?" I asked.

"Why are you at war with the gynandromorphs?" Beth asked.

"Why are you doing this to us?" Jolene wept.

"What the fuck *is* a gynandromorph?" Derek asked again in vain.

468

"Your mission for the Annunaki Confederation is classified top secret crypto, and I am not at liberty to disclose anything more about it or about the gynandromorph threat." Captain Xarr insisted. "All pertinent information concerning the gynandromorph race and your primary mission will be divulged to you during your training period sometime before the operation takes place.

However, I *am* at liberty to inform you that most of the test subject group members that have been taken aboard this ship, and ships comprising the rest of the fleet, will be immediately subjected to the first phase of our science department's latest cloning procedure in conjunction with the most modern scientific biologic transmodification techniques. The advanced cloning process will be initiated in an effort to expedite what has been named as the *Earther's Expeditionary Force* once we have returned to our home base and to the training and staging *arena* located on the dark side of my beloved planet Annunak."

"Holy shit stain!" I thought to myself. *"The last time I heard the term biologic transmodification, Captain Xarr was talking about shirking somebody's dick and balls."*

If that procedure was going to be performed on me, I was pretty sure that Beth would not be pleased. So for Beth's sake, I vowed not to let that happen to me; Derek maybe, but not me.

However, upon seeing that our only option at this point was to bend over and kiss our asses' goodbye, I nervously joked.

"So it's a secret, if you told me, you'd have to kill me? Right?"

"That is correct Jack Doom," Captain Xarr told me without emotion. "I would have to have you and everyone else in this room killed, including my subordinate officer Lieutenant Commander Zeem along with my crew members that now guard you. I of course would be the only exception."

If there was any doubt before that we were dealing with some serious assholes, every bit of that doubt had just been erased from my mind, as one could actually hear the three sphincters of the soldiers surrounding Captain Xarr being twisted out of proportion. The low pitched moaning squall resembling that of three industrial size rubber bands being stretched to their limits, told me that his men were taking the Captain's unemotional admission very seriously as their posteriors prepared for unauthorized anal expulsions.

I knew that this type of attitude was prevalent in the culture of ancient Egypt, when a Pharaoh died; their body was carted out into the desert and buried in a secret place. Then the people who knew where the corpse was hidden were summarily slain, then the people that killed them were also put to death to make sure that if they had been told where the body was buried, that they too would not be able to tell anyone its location, and the secret would be safe.

"I have other duties to attend to Jack Doom, we will be leaving this solar system momentarily to begin our journey back to Annunak," Captain Xarr announced. "You and the rest of your newly acquired test subject group will be escorted to your new quarters, there you will undergo DNA testing, blood and tissue samples will be extracted, by force if necessary, and there you will all remain until we arrive at our final destination.

And if you cause no trouble, I might personally escort you to deck 69 to meet with an old acquaintance of yours that will be making the journey back to Annunak with us.

However, if any one of you chooses to cause me or any of my crew grief in any way, your despair at this moment will not compare to the journey back to my home world, which will be anything *but* pleasant. However, that choice will be yours and yours alone to make.

Just remember, escape is impossible and your destiny is sealed. As is the destiny of all of the hundreds of test subject groups that have survived this *experiment* and met the Annunaki criterion for this mission."

"Excuse me Captain, but are you trying to say that we are not the only humans on this ship?" I asked.

"No Jack Doom, I am not *trying* to say that, I am saying that. There are many Annunaki ships in what your scientists used to call *low earth orbit* around your puny planet. We have recruited scores of humans like you, which fit the specifications required to complete this portion of our mission. They like yourselves are aboard our ships, and like you, they will undergo DNA testing, blood and tissue samples will be taken, and if they meet all of the special qualifications necessary to serve the Annunaki Confederation's cause, and the Supreme Being, they, like you and your group, will be transported to my planet for further training."

"So we're not alone?" I responded, despondent with the Captain's answer.

"Jack Doom, I thought that I had made myself clear with my previous statements. Possibly you are so distraught and disoriented that you didn't comprehend the meaning of my comments. Let me try one more time to insert the reality of the situation into your thick inferior loser skull."

"Again, most impressive vernacular Captain," I said, trying to win back a few perceived *lost* brownie points.

"Thank you Jack Doom, *you* were my inspiration," the Starship Captain stated with pride.

"You and your group of test subjects are far from alone Jack Doom. In fact, there is several thousand of your kind on board my fleet as we speak. So you are of but a few that falls into an elite category of humans that should do very well as a soldier in the military branch of the Annunaki Confederation as long as you pass the DNA, blood, and tissue sample tests."

After the Captain's explanation, we were all forlorn and speechless, and if I wasn't distraught before, I certainly was now.

My only thought after Captain Xarr elaborated on the subject of other humans, was very simply.

"*Fuck!*"

With the mention of deck 69, Lieutenant Commander Zeem's memory was jarred and he informed his Captain of the state of one of the non-Annunaki aliens that was being held prisoner on that deck.

"Captain Xarr," Lieutenant Commander Zeem broke in.

"Yes Lieutenant Commander Zeem," Captain Xarr answered, annoyed at the Lieutenants brash interruption, even though he had finished his commentary.

"The unsavory gynandromorph on deck 69, the one that calls itself Patty, is complaining about neck pain, and would like to be transferred to sick bay for the duration of our flight back to Annunak," Lieutenant Commander Zeem informed. "It is the gynandromorph that put our mission at risk by its despicable behavior down on the planet during phase one of the pre-mission reconnaissance actions by seeking and retrieving forbidden sexual stimulation with the employer of the progenitor of test subject group 32452013!"

"I am aware of the gynandromorph in question, however, I still don't understand why the upper echelon thinks that these treasonous creatures that have forsaken their own planet will be of any service to the Supreme Being of Annunak, their thought process is beyond me. Oh well, far be it from me to second guess my superiors, if they want those traitorous wretches to fight for the cause that's their determination. But personally I don't trust the treacherous animals. And as for that unruly gynandromorph on deck 69, a little bit of neck pain is the least of its worries," Captain Xarr replied. "The *penalties* for its crimes against the Annunaki Confederation will be much more severe than the minor pain in the neck that it is feeling right now."

"Yes, Captain Xarr," Lieutenant Commander Zeem agreed.

"Inform the gynandromorph that its request for a leisurely sick bay voyage back to Annunak has been denied," the Captain barked. "After all, it brought on this alleged muscle and vertebrae neck pain, with over exertion during its dishonorable behavior throughout phase-one of our assignment. Would you not agree Lieutenant Commander Zeem?"

"Yes, Captain Xarr," Lieutenant Commander Zeem replied.

"Continue to do your duty Lieutenant Commander Zeem, and keep me informed of the health status of that insubordinate gynandromorph."

"Aye-aye Captain Xarr," Lieutenant Commander Zeem responded, snapping to attention.

"After all, we would not want anything to happen that might deprive Patty the gynandromorph of any of the physical trauma that *will* take place once we return to Confederation space, now would we Lieutenant Commander?" Captain Xarr maintained.

"Absolutely not Captain Xarr," the Lieutenant Commander barked, still at attention.

"Excellent, Lieutenant Commander Zeem! Now, if all of the parameters of this phase of our mission have been complied with, and the planetary safe guards are duly in place, set a course back to our beloved Annunaki home world.

"Aye-aye Captain Xarr!" Lieutenant Commander Zeem belched his compliance.

"Inform the beast transport ships that they are cleared to release the remainder of the carnivores to complete the sterilization stage of this mission as soon as the science ship has concluded its final *probes*. And relay the message to the rest of the fleet of our intentions to depart.

Then take us out of orbit, order the helmsman to engage the interdimensional parsec drive, and get us the hell away from this God forsaken solar system."

"Aye-aye Captain Xarr!"

"And make sure that the inertia compensators are set *all the way* to infinity this time, because if that female pilot slams me against the bulkhead one more time; I will be forced to personally continue and possibly prolong her lesson in transdimensional navigation and phalanx preservation, and I will definitely see to it that her remaining breast is hanging alongside her other gazunga in glorious coexistence beside my newly acquired titty bag that the earther Jack Doom graciously donated to me; just before I have her *and* her supervisor escorted to Bay 5 to meet with Rylo Kesbvoff of the Science Academy on Tarsa II for additional counseling! Is that clear Lieutenant Commander?"

"Yes, Captain Xarr!" Lieutenant Commander Zeem barked loudly as his sphincter muscle once again furiously strangled his already chafed anal opening; because he was well aware that *he* was the female pilots immediate supervisor and that in the event that the Captain's *deja vu* vision of the near future came to fruition, at least one of his own very personal, private, and prized appendages that was now *attached* and dangling freely slightly below his waist, would most likely be disconnected and then conjoined with the pilot's detached feminine *chestical* (or in this case *chesticals*, after the fact) shortly after the unfortunate event that would cause Captain Xarr to have to peel himself off of one of the starship's interior walls yet again.

475

"All right Lieutenant Commander Zeem, carry on!"
"Aye-aye Captain Xarr!"

THE END?

TITLES BY WILL LEMEN

ZOMBIES "Chronicles of the Dead" (The Prequel)
https://www.amazon.com/dp/B00IHJCOKA/

UFO
https://www.amazon.com/dp/B00GBFIKB4/

The Magic Clock
https://www.amazon.com/dp/B00FARX2RQ/

Chris and Friends
https://www.amazon.com/dp/B00F2M5WOU/

Don't forget to visit Will's author page!
@
http://www.amazon.com/Will-Lemen/e/B00O17RZ3S/